Tanith Lee, born in London, began writing at the age of nine, and was first published in her early twenties. Since then she has produced numerous novels of a fantastical nature and several radio plays, and has twice won the World Fantasy Award for her short stories. Also published by Headline are her novels *Heart-Beast*, *Elephantasm* and *Eva Fairdeath*, and her story collection *Nightshades*.

She lives in East Sussex with her husband, the writer John Kaiine, and a black-and-white cat.

'Restores one's faith in fiction as the expression of imagination and original thought' – *Guardian*

'One of the most powerful and intelligent writers to work in fantasy' – *Publishers Weekly*

'Bizarre imagination and elegantly decadent atmosphere' – *Daily Mail*

'Unlike most fantasists who wish they could write magnificently, Tanith Lee can actually do it' – Orson Scott Card

A Heroine of the World

Tanith Lee

First published in Great Britain in 1994
by HEADLINE BOOK PUBLISHING

First published in paperback in 1995
by HEADLINE BOOK PUBLISHING

A HEADLINE FEATURE paperback

10 9 8 7 6 5 4 3 2 1

ISBN 0-7472-4748-X

Typeset by
Letterpart Limited, Reigate, Surrey

Printed and bound in Great Britain by
Cox & Wyman Ltd, Reading, Berks

HEADLINE BOOK PUBLISHING
A division of Hodder Headline PLC
338 Euston Road
London NW1 3BH

A Heroine
of the World

BOOK ONE

Part One

THE BLACK HOUSE

Part One

THE BLACK HOUSE

Chapter One

1

My aunt's house stood at the corner of Hapsid Forum. It was thought unusual, and so it probably was, with its midnight walls, thick scarlet columns and shutters picked out in red. From the garden a gigantic pine thrust its way high over the roof, the branches becoming visible the moment one drove into East Avenue. And, 'There is your aunt's pine tree,' my mother would say briskly.

'There is your aunt's pine tree.'

'Yes, mama.'

'The gales have not been kind to it,' remarked my mother, with slight malice.

I turned myself in the carriage to see what had happened to the pine.

'Don't wriggle so, child. Did we bring you up to be a stoat?'

'I'd like that. Being a stoat.'

'No, you would not. What's worse, you would be shedding your winter coat all over my carriage. That is, if I hadn't already lost patience with you and had you made into a muff.'

But my mother, despite this interchange, was preoccupied. My father, a major of the White Lions, had been recalled to the mysterious and valiant war at some hour during the night. I had dimly heard the flurry in my sleep, but he did not come to say good-bye to me. This was a grievance. Also, I suspected that I was to be fobbed off for the day on my aunt, of whom I was not entirely certain. My mother I knew and

5

loved, but she was only mine when she was not being my father's, and the same might be said of him with her. My aunt, though my father's sister, was no one's. She belonged only to herself.

Our carriage turned the corner of the Avenue, was walked across the edge of the Forum, and drew up under a pair of black iron gates.

'Pansy,' said my mother to her maid, 'get down and ring the bell. Must I tell you everything?'

Pansy, a girl of sixteen, only three years older than I, and looking, I thought, more frightened than was necessary, obeyed. The bell rang, the porter came and unlocked the gate.

The pine, bursting over the rooftop, seemed the same as ever as we went up the steps. The red shutters were wide on the polished windows. Vines crept over the pillars out of their lacquered urns.

'Dia,' said my mother, as we waited in the Red Salon, 'it's all been a great rush, and I suppose that I should have explained to you earlier. Darling, your father has to go back to Fort Hightower, as you know, and I – I'm to join him.'

It was unimaginably worse than I had feared. My mouth dropped open.

'Sweetheart, victory is sure, very soon. I'll be home again with you – oh, long before winter.'

Before I properly realised why I should, I began to cry.

My mother held out her arms and I fled into them.

'Don't go! Don't go!'

'I must, I must. There now, is this the proper way for a sensible little stoat to behave?'

At that crucial, personal moment, my Aunt Elaieva entered the room.

Like guilty lovers my mother and I sprang apart. I wondered later if my mother and father had ever had to do so in front of her; there was a sense of repetition in it. But my mother had the wit to keep hold of my hand as, messed with tears, I turned.

I had not met Aunt Elaieva for several months, which

interim seemed years to me. She appeared always a stranger. Unlike the fairness of my mother's side, she was, like my father, olive-skinned and dark. Black hair smoothed itself back from her forehead, below which brows and eyes had been marked with such ebony decision. Her clothing was neither in the fashion nor out of it. Really, you could not say where it was exactly. But if her style was ambivalent, also it was bold: a viridian sash, a pair of silver earrings. My mother was like some busy flower before her, a hyacinth or sweetpea.

'Elaieva,' she said, in the brisk tone that invested all their dealings, even at the remove of a pine tree, 'you'll have heard, he was recalled last night.'

'The wide-open gape of war,' said Elaieva, in a beautiful, cold, unremembered voice.

'Well, there it is. And here, I'm afraid, are the child and I.'

'I received your message. You wish me to take your daughter off your hands.'

'To take her rather under your wing,' amended my mother, most civilly. 'My husband has some claim on me. I believe you'll have been told the strategy—'

'A singularly stupid one,' said Aunt Elaieva. She did not look angry, but she had interrupted.

'Dear sister,' said my mother, with every ounce of falseness she could summon, 'I have only this one morning to arrange it. I'm to have an escort and must be ready to leave—'

'Dry your eyes,' Elaieva said to me, interrupting again. 'It's useless to cry. She's going.'

I turned back and stared at my mother in anguish. To be informed of my defeat by the enemy was more than I could bear. But my mother only bent her hyacinth head to me and retracted me into her embrace. 'Sweetest, your things are to come round before midday. Our rooms will be shut up and you are on no account to go there and bother the servants. Pansy is coming with me—' Oh, lucky hateful Pansy, might the earth swallow her— 'And you, my dear, must be splendid and make your aunt, who is so kind as to take you in, not regret for a single second that she has done so. Now, have you listened? Do you understand?'

I sobbed that I did. My tears had stained her silk bodice dark as blood. As she left me, I felt bereft beyond words, or thoughts. I seemed to have lost my mind. But I choked down my weeping before my dreadful aunt, not to please her, but because she was an alien.

She allowed me, as if to try to break me nevertheless, a last view of my mother and Pansy being driven away from me across the Forum. My heart strained and cracked within me, but I cannot say it was a premonition. I had no idea at that time I would never see my mother again.

2

During the next two weeks I settled sullenly into the new temporary life. I had only one flash of respite, when I decided, as my birthday fell in early autumn, and as it was unthinkable my mother should miss it, she was sure to have returned by then. Even so, ultimately, this only made things worse, for autumn was an age away. We had never seriously been parted before. Indeed, I was born in a village in the hills on a long-ago campaign when she had, against advice, gone visiting my father, then a mere lieutenant. Afterwards she had had to leave him and bring me home to cheap lodgings in the City. We were poor in those days.

My aunt was very far from poverty. Her black house was filled by efficient and nearly invisible servants, some of whom, when seen, alarmed me, for they acted as if scarcely human, more like ensorcelled dolls. It was these beings who tidied my bed, brought my breakfast, and water for my bath. The midday meal was served for me alone in a small pleasant purposeless chamber on the first floor. This had become for me a sort of playroom, where I might do very much as I wanted. I was also allowed the garden, but to roam the house was discouraged. For my aunt's bedroom, library, study and chapel, they were forbidden and in fact kept locked against the world. I saw my aunt rarely during the day, but at night we would normally eat together in the Sphynx Salon. Elaieva did not bother to keep me to a child's hours of dining, or retiring, which until then I had had fairly rigidly observed on my behalf. At home my supper was presented to me at the fifth hour of the evening, and Pansy would have packed me into my bed by the time the old cracked bell of the Pantheon gave tongue for ten. But in Elaieva's house we took dinner between seven and eight at night, reclining on the scrolled couches of the Sphynx Salon in the classical way my family seldom troubled with. After dinner Elaieva might offer a scatter of sentences to me. My education had been rather random. I was taught to read and thereafter what I learned was largely dependent on what books I chose to put in front of my eyes. Those tutors I had had never properly succeeded in convincing me of the true reality of anything beyond my home life. This had been so happy and comforting, and just strict enough, and just eccentric enough to content me to the exclusion of most other matters. My aunt detected my shortcomings. I could not follow her most ordinary flights. For example, she spoke of the East and at once I saw – and vocalised – golden domes rising from a magician's mist and princesses riding upon flying carpets. She raised her brows, and the conversation closed. I seemed to bore her. And even the treat of falling asleep on the carpet of the first floor room, my head on a game of Temples, at midnight, did not make up for the loss of love and happiness.

There had been, in the apartment below that of my parents, another girl, of fourteen, with whom I had sometimes played, and gone walking in the public gardens. One morning, finding my aunt in a corridor, I suggested I should go to call on this other girl. To add weight, I virtuously murmured she and I might put flowers before the shrine of Vulmartis, at the Pantheon.

'No,' said Elaieva, her black eyes already moving by me and the rest of her about to.

'But Litty and I have often done it. My mother always lets me go. Litty will take her maid—'

'I mean,' said my aunt, 'that your friend's family have left the city.'

I was amazed, outraged. Had my and Litty's mother taken

her away to the fortress in my stead? Something of this dashed from me.

'Not everyone rushes into the cannon's mouth,' said my aunt. 'The people you refer to have escaped in another direction.'

I could not fathom this. My aunt did not say another word.

That afternoon, sitting under the pine tree in the spring sunshine, I heard male voices very near. Two pairs of army boots came around a lilac hedge with two beautiful uniformed officers in them. I was overcome, and my face caught fire, not being used to sudden meetings alone with exotic unknown young men. Even so, I recognised the insignia instantly. They were captains, and their regiment was the Eagles.

They seemed very much at home in Aunt Elaieva's garden, and had been chatting about gambling, not that I really knew what gambling was. Now they stood above me and exclaimed.

'It's a child.'

'*Origos!* Can it be *hers*?'

'Don't be a fool,' said the shorter of the two. He looked vexed, but then laughed. He had a mane of light-coloured hair and unnerving odd-shaped humorous eyes. 'Madam,' he said to me gravely, 'it is a delight to find you so prettily here on the grass. Pray tell us to whom you belong.'

Old training not to speak to strangers set in. I held my tongue and gazed at the flowers I had been plaiting.

My aunt spoke from over the hedge. She had come up soundlessly as was her wont. 'This is my brother's daughter, gentlemen. Her name is Aradia.'

I glanced up proudly at my proper title, and so saw the light-haired young man going as red in the face for my aunt as I had done for him. But he carried it better, seeming amused to blush, and bowing to her soldier-fashion as she moved around the hedge. She gave both men her cold slim hand to kiss. It was not that I had thought her elderly especially, she was only on the timeless plateau of the adult. But it had certainly never occurred to me that, like one of our flighty maids, my aunt received admirers.

She allowed them to walk with her across the lawn to the sundial, and the pond where the marble swan with a woman's head sat stilly in the water.

Curious, nostalgic for the elements of my father's army, I trailed after.

'Finished by the winter?' the second, taller, young man was saying. 'High summer should see it out. Half their troops are sick with dysentery. The other half are rebelling and clamouring to go home. I tell you, Elaieva, for us it's just a little holiday. And, as you see, eternal leaves.'

'Your brother, of course, the major, is distinguishing himself in all directions,' said Fair-Hair, laughing again.

Elaieva seemed not to notice. But I wanted more.

'What is he doing?' I inquired.

Fair-Hair turned round and looked at me intently.

'Why, madam, riding at the head of the charge, making gallant sorties, taking prisoners. And at night, in full dress uniform, he dances with your lovely mother between banquet tables groaning with game and cakes.'

This only bewildered me, but since he had been good enough to offer it, I tried to seem enlightened.

'They go to bed,' added the tall captain, not to be left out, 'at four in the morning, and rise at six to bombard the enemy positions.'

'And may we stay to dine with you?' asked the other, gazing at my aunt.

Her assent was indifferent. Yet he sat down at her feet, and they all began to talk of the entire universe I did not know, in forms I could not follow. Presently I left them, having crowned the swan-woman with my flowers.

I went to playdream under the pine. Where my remorseful mother was soon hurrying home and finding me pale and sad, and my father was leading a charge, flying through the air on a horse with wings.

Fair-Hair's name was Thenser, as I found out that evening.

He and his companion lounged elegantly on the scrolled

couches and red and yellow wine was served in glass kraters. Otherwise nothing seemed any different. We ate from the Sphynx service, to match the salon, as always, only more of it. There were, as usual, no flowers on the table, and Thenser's companion – whose name I heard but forgot – offered to have some sent to my aunt from the hothouses.

'You're very kind, but I prefer not,' she said.

'Isn't there anything,' said Thenser playfully, 'a man can be allowed to give you?'

She sent him one icy stare, and he flushed again.

Greedily intent on my dinner, I did wonder why he should want to visit when she was so unfriendly, or why she let him when she disliked him so much.

After dinner, they played cards, and I joined them for one or two sets of expurgated Red-and-White, but I was not clever at cards, nor very interested. Forgotten Name became rather irritated with me, so I declined another game, though Thenser tried to call me back. My aunt then said that I would probably prefer to go downstairs and draw or read, and this had the effect of propelling me away altogether.

About midnight, still wide awake with my crayons in the first floor room, I thought I heard them leaving, and stole out to catch a last glimpse of Thenser and the army.

Only the lamp in the foyer was burning before the house-god, but by its glow I saw Forgotten Name, sworded, cloaked and helmed, vanishing through the black door, which one of the servants shut behind him. As the servant withdrew, the door of the Sphynx Salon opened wide above and yellow light fanned down the stair.

'There is no point at all,' I heard Aunt Elaieva say, 'in your remaining to tell me that.'

'Perhaps. You knew already,' said Thenser. His voice was soft and blurred.

'You should leave now,' Elaieva replied.

I could not see them, but abruptly both their shadows appeared in lieu of them, thrown on the damask wall. He was the same height in his boots as she was in her high-heeled slippers, and this did not fit with my notions: The hero should always be some inches taller than the heroine.

No one had told him, presumably, he was disqualified from the role.

His shadow leaned precipitously towards hers, his shadow had got hold of hers, so that they blended and were monstrously one. Save for a very slight flickering, this shadow-beast did not thereafter move for some while.

Then, as quickly as it had joined, it fell away, became again her shadow, and his. And now his shadow was violently agitated, all of it shuddered, gesticulated. Hers did not alter.

'Now will you let me stay?' he said breathlessly.

'No,' she said.

At that, his shadow again converged on hers, but now there was an explosion of movement, the monster unable to reform and wildly opening into diamonds and squares, ovals and oblongs of light, before breaking apart.

'No, is what I said.'

'Then I'm never to trouble you again.' He had got his breath back. His voice was leaden.

'It might save you some annoyance.'

'And you. Since apparently I do annoy you, Elaieva.'

There was a silence. (Fascinated, I had naturally realised I should not be watching, and was ready to dart into cover.)

'In fact,' he said, 'my leave's cancelled. I'm to go out again tomorrow. These things are minimised, you understand, in case the citizens grow uneasy. But I think you know our danger.'

'Of course,' she said, 'but if you mean I should invite you into my bed because tomorrow you may die, or the day after the enemy may be at the City gate – you'd be very foolish, Thenser.'

'Yes, I'm a fool, a fool for you. But I don't expect that. Either you'll have me or you won't.'

'Give me up,' she said with a brittle lightness I had never heard in her voice before.

'If you tell me to.'

'I do tell you.'

'Then, I give you up,' he said. His voice was suddenly

theatrical, eloquent, full of the relish of pain. 'And I can die and be damned now. Good night, priestess.'

Behind my door, astonished, I heard him run like a cat down the stair and out of the house.

3

There was a letter from my mother: *Dia, dearest stoat*, it began. It made me cry and I slept with it under my pillow, carrying it about with me by day. At least twice an hour I reread it. But the letter told me very little. Only that she was with my father. That (she said) she missed me. That my father sent me kisses. She described snow on a far-off mountain, and a spring-savage river that clashed through a green gorge. For it seemed they went to picnic there, as the business of the fort was so easy. She mentioned dinners and dances, too, as Captain Thenser had done. My mother appeared to find fort life dull, and some of the other ladies laughable. By night, Hightower was seven cones of lamplit, torch-girt stone grinning down at the pathetic foe, who slummocked in rainy bivouacs beneath the slopes, unable to get up, and, poor things, refused permission by their commanders to get down.

Our war was with the North, as it had often been. The lands of the Saz-Kronians, one more meaningless name in my hapless, unheeded history and geography lessons.

In turn, I wrote to my mother. I included complaints, and did mention that two captains of the Eagles had called on Aunt Elaieva, but nothing about shadows or dramatic demands and refusals on the stair. I did not even inquire as to why my aunt should be called 'priestess.' My father had mentioned she once meant to be a nun. I censored what I said, as I am fairly sure my mother, in the interests of fort security, had also been obliged to do. My urge, however, was not the City's safety, or even tact. The stair-scene had disturbed me.

The spring weather broke unseasonably. It snowed. Only for

half a day, but sufficient to kill the flowers in the garden.

After the thaw, I was taken for my occasional healthful drive in Elaieva's carriage, accompanied by a woman servant, chosen presumably because she was dumb.

The City, it seemed to me, was in a peculiar mood. Many of the shops were shut on the broad Avenues circling Hapsid Forum, and on Wintoclas Street. More than anything I saw, I *felt* a kind of echo. People promenaded in the gardens, bells rang, and carts and private chariots rumbled over the roads. Yet there was something which had gone away – or another thing, which in the absence of the first, was drifting down like a second snow.

I said nothing about this intuition to my aunt. We sat at dinner that night in customary silence. Since the pair of captains, she had had no guests. It was now the third week, and I was heartily tired of the place and my prospects. I spent hours on end staring from the window of the first floor 'playroom,' which, like the bedroom above, faced over the garden wall into the street behind the house. Very little went on there. Only once I saw a couple of fine carriages, driven very fast, bolt between the hedges, and wondered where they were off to and, some days later, if they had ever come back.

4

'And I told madam, there isn't a joint of beef, sheep, or venison to be got in the whole City. As for flour and sugar – well, it's a crime. These hoarders. No sooner is there any sort of rumour than everything's bought up.'

'Yes, but it's more than a rumour. My sister is making arrangements already to go to our grandmother in the provinces. I suppose I shall have to see it out. Madam would dismiss me if I asked her.'

'They say ten days, don't they,' cut in the boastful baritone of the under-steward.

'Vulmartis merciful. Is it true?'

'That's what they're saying, over at the City Hall. There are placards up all along the Avenues. The terms the Sazos

15

want, and his Majesty's answer. Well, our wise King is off on his island; that's safe enough.'

'Ten days before *they* get here.'

'It can't be so.'

'Even if it's twenty days, thirty days, get here they will,' said the under-steward. The maids hung there on his utterance, as I did up above them in the window. The notes of their voices, so infrequently did any of them chatter about the black house, had startled me to attention. The subject of their dialogue I could not make out. Only tremors of fear and gloomy resignation.

'But the forts are all in the way,' said the younger of the maids. 'The Gunnery, and Hightower, and Oncharin—'

'Oncharin went down yesterday. Mined and blown to bits. The others are pounding away and calling for reinforcements. Which they won't get.'

As if I swung in space, I strained now from my cliff. A wonder I never fell on them, but they caught the roar of my heart anyway.

'Hush, don't let that child hear, or madam'll be wild.'

The child, though, had heard enough. She dropped back and looked around her like a lunatic at a waste of coloured drawings and games and books, which were meaningless.

Someone must be asked, but none of the servants would be any use. They had failed at all other moments – inquiries on a noise of muffled drums, feet and wheels, crossing the Forum in the dead of last night, for example, had elicited only, 'Did you hear that? Well. Drink your honey-water.'

Now that unseen reverberation took on horrible importance.

Panic arrived. Panic awful but only an order of awful panic I had already once or twice experienced – losing my mother on the street at the age of five, my first attendance at a Vulmartia – childish, limitable—

I rushed out of the room and up through the house to the top floor, my aunt's locked sanctum. With my fists I beat on the carved door, where wreathed naiads gazed impervious and hurt my knuckles.

There was no answer. Perhaps she was not there. In confusion I raised my voice and out came a scream, further upsetting me, for it was more barbaric than I could have dreamed.

'Aunt! Aunt! Let me in – let me in!'

Still, no response.

Then I went mad, hammering and howling.

Not one servant, though surely I rocked the house with my cries, approached. I had climbed beyond their jurisdiction. Only Elaieva the priestess could help me now.

Suddenly, a key turned in a lock. The carved door opened, and there she stood. She looked down on me from her pale face, miles away, as if from a turret of olive ivory.

'What is the matter with you?'

I blurted what the matter was.

'Yes,' she said. I smothered my moans to hear what she would say next. She said: 'Your mother has been foolish.' (Thenser had been foolish, too; they were all fools, it seemed, to my aunt.) 'She should have warned you. Naturally, she did not.'

'What is it?' I wailed. And, going completely to pieces, 'I want mama—'

After that she put her hand on my shoulder. Though slight, she was strong. She brought me into the sitting room of her suite. Shutting the door, she pushed me slowly down into a chair. Admitted to one of the forbidden chambers, I saw nothing of it.

'Listen to me, Aradia. This vaunting City has engaged itself in a war it will never win. The fortresses are falling and very shortly the City itself, unless prepared to surrender instantly, will be besieged. Do you understand?'

I did, in the manner of understanding a nightmare, in sleep. Sieges and surrenders were more of the stuff of unlearned history.

'Mama—' I said.

'Hightower will probably have the sense to give in. I regret your father will be taken prisoner. Your mother, conceivably, you may get back.'

This was so bleak, so appalling, spoken in her cool and expressionless way, that I gaped at her in silence.

'You can do nothing,' said Elaieva. 'I can do nothing. We're powerless. You must accept that.'

This was the bare meek teaching of the inner sects of Vulmartis. I beheld my aunt, a virgin nun of a virgin goddess. For me, acceptance was no comfort.

'I don't believe you,' I said.

She shrugged. She gave a little smile, which might well have been ironical. To me, it seemed cruel and inhuman.

Leaving her hated chair, the unseen holy room, I ran out and away through her house. In the mirror outside the Red Salon I caught a glimpse of myself. Colourless white skin, hair my father called 'sunshine,' but which was only a light soft brown, and wide eyes my mother called 'grey-as-glass.' My young girl's body had already formed into full curves. All totally unlike the woman I fled from. Even my father, though he had her sable tone, was not like her in the least.

Somehow I was outside on the front steps. Then, in the large expanse of Hapsid Forum.

My mother had forbidden me to return to our rooms on Pantheon Mile. But my mother was in Hightower, dancing with my father the prisoner, and I might not get her back— No. That was impossible.

Already there was a stitch in my side, brought on mostly by distress.

The Forum, with the stately houses and the law courts making its tall stone and stucco border, was deserted. Only the statue of a king balanced on its pedestal, and a few sparrows whirred about the horse trough.

For a second, I had an image of the City wholly vacant. In nightmares, such a thing could happen.

But there were flickers of motion in an upper window. And I heard the murmur of the City's life, and flew across the corner of the Forum and down the tree-lined pavement of East Avenue.

Spring was bright in those trees, the brief snow had not quenched its flame. Surely, while the City growled and the treetops blossomed, there could not be such entities as siege, or loss.

Having ignored history because I was running, I collided with it, in Pantheon Square.

An enormous crowd, a reassurance at first after the whiff of desertion, was packed across the space.

I suppose I had run straight by the purple placards in the Avenues, but here men were waving them in their hands. There was a lot of shouting. Huge male bodies in rough clothes, and the clink of bottles passing, and the glitter of sunlight on bottles tilting to lips, this was what I became aware of. And a frightening electricity was in the air.

A blowsy woman in front of me, finding me pressing against her by accident, said, 'You won't get a good view here, girlie.'

A wall of flesh impeded me indeed, and I could not see over it. Only the highest white columns and the three gilded domes of the Pantheon were visible above the crowd, burning on the clear sky.

Another ghastly shout went up, stinking of bad teeth and wine, sweat and rage.

I struggled from the tangle of living things, and as I went, saw some well-dressed women standing on the roof of a carriage, a promontory in the surge. Warrior plumes blazed in their curled hair. The wine they were drinking sparkled. They laughed, and one called out, 'Death to the damned bloody Sazos!'

Never had I heard a woman swear, save for the silly little oaths of Pansy who, pricking her finger, would squeal, '*Oh, pickle!*'

Getting into a side street I hurried down it. Most of the shops were boarded up. A bakery, where I had now and then gone to be bought pastries, yawned on a glum queue. Some more men slouched in a doorway. They grimaced at me, making me oddly ashamed.

When I emerged on the Mile, I could still catch the row of the crowd in the Square, but again, here, a curious quiet had come down. Pantheon Mile had never been quiet. By day, processions filled it, soldiers marching from Origos Field, with trumpets and burnished brass, and the war god with red hair borne on a golden staff; these I had watched avidly from our lodgings, and Pansy with me. Otherwise, the milk carts clattered to and fro, or hawkers with fish and ribbons. By night singers and poets from the taverns passed, and once there had been a duel, two men with swords under our very windows, until the City Guard came to separate them.

Now Pantheon Mile shone in the sun of noon, empty it seemed to me as a desert in a story.

The street door of the Briary, the building where we lodged, was open. On a chair in the foyer sat, not the comfortable elderly housekeeper I had known, but a sharp-chinned skivvy in a dirty apron.

'What do *you* want?' said she to me.

'I—' lost for an explanation, trained to be polite, I stammered, 'Madam, where is—'

'If you're looking for the old biddy, she's off. But you,' she squinted at me, 'aren't you the young major's daughter?'

At recognition I felt some relief.

'Yes. We live on the upper floor.'

'Do you? No. The rooms are shut up. Why aren't you with your mother?'

Pushed again into unreality, I was about to tell her where my mother was. Something restrained me.

The woman looked me up and down, and said, 'I dare say you'll be all right. Living with some relation, are you? It'll be hard on the rest of us. They're recruiting now, in the Square. My man's gone, and my boy. Either go, or get taken. One silver penny a day, but they'll spend it on drink.'

She had begun to talk the same incomprehensible language as the others.

The building did not even smell as it had. It had been clean and busy, but now there was the tang of cats' urine, and a withered cabbage leaf lay on the stair.

'Come back,' she said as I went out. Perhaps she meant to be kind. But I was in the nightmare, truly meshed. There was

20

nowhere to run to, nowhere to stay still.

I wandered into a slender street that led to the Peacock Gardens. Here Litty and I had thrown a ball and chased each other last summer. How quiet now, no one on the pruned walks. Not a parasol, none of the tame monkeys which had so delighted us, ambling on leather leads. By the gate was the chapel to Vulmartis the Forgiving. Always the door had been barred, but now it stood wide.

No one was inside. The floor was dusty, and the altar was bald – all the precious metal utensils had been taken away. A window with faint blue glass rayed down on a statue in a classical gown, and an Eastern headdress dyed indigo which contained a little golden crown. Her alabaster face was sweet and smiling, and into her hands someone had put a spray of white lilac from the park.

I knelt at her small feet, which had gold hearts painted on them, and asked her to assist me. Did it lessen my case that I was incoherent? I tried to make all plain to her. That if I had not always gone to worship, it was a fault of my ignorance. That if my thoughts had wandered at a service, I had been stupid. That always I attended the festivals of the Vulmartia. That I would bring her an offering soon – oh, soon. But she must rescue my mother and my father and let them come back to me. Please, Lady, please, please.

Her sweet face was compassionate. And yet I knew she did not hear me. Like a moth I dashed myself helplessly against her gleaming stone.

Exhausted, when the light had turned more grey in the window, I got up again and left.

I had nowhere else to shelter me other than the house of my aunt.

So, to that place I went. The City also was confused and did not molest me.

No one queried where I had been to. No one had noticed my absence. Like Vulmartis, no one was concerned.

★   ★   ★

And that evening, a new army, the City Militia, smote on the gate.

Coming out on the landing I watched, not surprised or frightened, still lulled dull in the nightmare.

The uniform of the Militia was makeshift. Not glowing helmets and plumes, epaulets and insignia, swords and boots like mirror. This was a rudimentary sash like a sling of blood across the chest, and for the corporal a tuft of red and mauve in his cap.

Aunt Elaieva descended to them. They looked at her and decided she must be treated with respect.

'You know how it is, madam. Every able-bodied man not serving outside. For the defence of the City.'

She said, 'You must do what you must.'

He gave her a letter then. Something official, with the City seal.

And as they herded up the pot-boys and the under-steward, protesting (vainly) his immunity on account of a gammy leg, the corporal went on to my aunt, 'They're burning the woods, starting out on the north perimeters. And the wheat fields. Can't have the bas— the enemy getting that. And emplacements and barricades. You wouldn't know the north boulevards now, madam. All the paving's up.'

He was cheerful, enjoying a silver penny's worth of bravura, maybe.

5

The shock was like thunder, and waking up, I knew it was not thunder at all. I had heard cannon before, fired in salute for the King only a year ago, on Origos Field. I was nearer to the guns then, had been taken to watch (and been disappointed, for all I could make out of royalty were the froths of lace and stab of diamonds from their vehicles). Cannon to me were a festival noise, like hymns at the Pantheon.

There was a vague upheaval in the house, however, and out in the Forum, when I had gone across and entered, unallowed, a room on that side, I saw people standing, or leaning from windows and balconies, pointing northward. When the flat rumble came again, there was some applause.

The Sazo enemy had arrived, it seemed, and were sitting down around our walls, which had been banked with earth and paving stones, and decorated with the City guns. These guns now spoke their greeting.

For days, wagons had been coming in from the northern provinces. They brought provisions, but also extra mouths to feed on them. Sometimes, wagons and homeless vagabonds went through the Forum. A flock of sheep were driven over, and later a stray goat was pursued by excited lawyers from the law courts. These events I saw from this same room across from my bedchamber. I went into it freely, without Elaieva's permission. I never spoke to her now, and after the evening of the Militia recruitment, refusing to go up to dinner in the Sphynx Salon, I was served that meal also in my 'playroom.' In this room I ate not much, and 'played' less. I slept a lot, and would not get up, and stole about when I had like a ghost, listening at doors for scraps of tidings I barely grasped.

There was a sort of idea in me that a plot had been laid to keep my mother from me, to terrify and make me doubt her. I would not have it. Neither would *I* treat with my enemy.

The siege, as I saw and heard it start to happen, turned me cold and sick with dread. Yet in my heart's core my mother and father continued to dance and dine, picnicking above the gorge, hunting under the snow-tipped mountain. While I held them so, they were secure. I had charge of them and must not fail.

The cannon did not go on very long the first two or three days. They always finished at sunset, not to disrupt our theatres or rest.

On the fourth day, in the middle of the afternoon – I had just risen – one of Elaieva's youngest maids ran through the garden screaming, in hysteria. She carried a paper. Other women servants crowded round her. They were white. One said, 'Some traitor. It's a lie.' One shrugged. 'You can hardly expect the beasts not to do it.'

They took the hysterical one away to give her a cordial

23

before *madam* should hear the racket, and forgot the paper.

In an agony of fear I crept upon it.

Citizens you are warned, it said, *that if a surrender is not effected, the enemy will commence bombardment at midnight tonight. Give over this madness and save your lives!*

They had been greeted, they would reply. I had heard tell that men had been out putting planking and blankets around certain monuments. They had removed the window glass from the Pantheon and other high buildings. Such snippets had made no sense, until now.

It was unbelievable.

It occurred. Long before midnight, at seven in the evening, after the booming of our own guns had ceased.

First the familiar thunderclaps resumed, and then, a novel thing, a roar, a passage like tearing cloth – then a thud, and the uncanny trembling of a glass on the table.

I went to my bed and pulled the covers up above me. Now and then, at a concussion, the bed would quiver all over like a neurotic dog.

The Forum was far in from all the City walls, which, by now, the Kronians had apparently entirely encompassed. But there was a direct hit upon Maiden Hill, and there the sky burst itself along a red seam, visible through a gap in the drapes of my window.

In my heart's core, my parents danced on, beautiful as two puppets. They were safe but no longer real.

Near midnight one of the servant girls came in.

'Oh, you poor little mite,' she said. 'Don't knot yourself up like that, it'll stop soon.'

She sat with me and tried to comfort me, but every time the cannon clapped and the sound came like tearing cloth, she tensed tighter than a fist. At the crash she jumped with the bed. In the intervals she attempted to pray and encouraged me to join her. In the end she cried. I did not pray or cry.

We fell asleep, both of us, when that night's bombardment shut down, and a huge ringing silence, deafening and awesome, stunned our ears.

★ ★ ★

The City changed. Being part of the nightmare, it began to look and smell and sound as it should. There was always smoke, fine as pollen, more often thickening to flour. Seen from the top windows it lay on parts of the City and they vanished. Now and then smoke covered all. There were forges working in the streets, recasting metal cups and bells into knives and shot; part of the smoke was that. Buildings which had been hit sent up an incessant fume. It would go on for hours or days, after which other places had been struck. Fires broke out in abandoned houses. The cannon shells fell continuously in the suburbs, where no one remained except thieves, they said, in cellars, and stray dogs hiding from the butcher's men. For I heard, too, dogmeat was now being sold, and a high price asked for it. The best restaurants served horse and sparrow. I had long ago, at the first hint, stopped eating any meat, though in my aunt's circumstance I think it was still mutton or poultry on the pretty plates. The rich, or any who had ranking army connections, had not yet begun to feel much pinching. But in the slums they were catching the rats. 'And there are plenty of those,' said the servant who spoke of it. 'Besides, what difference, little girl, between this poor bit of a poor cleavered little sheep, and a dead cat? You should go to the abattoir, missy, and see what happens.' The servants had started to take on colour and actuality. They were not magic dolls after all. Some had run off, forgetting fears of dismissal and lost wages. The ones who stayed behaved oddly, strutting about, or slovenly, although with Elaieva in person they kept up quite a lot of servility and obedience. She did not test its limits, either from wisdom or indifference. When she was not there – generally she was behind the door of naiads – these chameleons resumed the shades of the nightmare.

The City smell was burning and tinder, the shrill odour of gunpowder. In the earliest morning, the dew would glisten oddly on the grass of my aunt's garden. Summer was pressing nearer and nearer with the enemy. Summer woke the flowers, but the flowers were charred-looking and dusty. The dew was like mercury. If it rained, the rain had a stink of cinders, as though it came from the vent of a dirty chimney. I was afraid for the sparrows in the garden. Was this their sanctuary from the slingshot of the hungry streets? Did not one of the maids, trained by her brother, try to bring them down with stones in a handkerchief? Or was that another falsehood bandied about?

Long long ago, in the other world, we had had a gentle cat. The cat had grown old and died peacefully when I was eleven. How I mourned. I was glad now. They would have taken our cat otherwise. They would have cooked her in a pie.

The City noises were shouts and rumbles. Or hoofs clattered madly across Hapsid Forum. I saw some companies of soldiers from the Eagle and Black Bull regiments go galloping through one afternoon. Later, all the horses were supposed to have been put down for food, and all I saw was a band of Militia on foot, with their red sashes in tatters, drinking.

There were numbers of casualties, from off the City walls, and the suburbs where shells had crashed. The Pantheon had been turned into a great hospital. Private houses were required to accept the wounded. The pine tree in my aunt's garden might have to be lopped for wood, for the City was also running out of oil and coals.

On some nights, when there was no bombardment, the City made its loudest noise, that of total silence. The theatres had been shut weeks back.

Two months of the siege were gone.

6

That morning, they had brought me water for my bath, which often now they did not. One of the maids, perhaps, I thought, she who had sat with me through the first shelling, had put a withered apple by my bed. I ate the apple, though mostly my appetite had left me. The impoverished fruit gave out a scent of former things, winey and comfortable, the windfalls in the orchard of a village where, as a small child, my mother would whisk me for a few weeks in late summer. There had been creamy milk, too, and honey. I thought of this and my stomach sluggishly growled. But my mind kept slight affiliation with my body. It was concerned with two jewel-bright puppets, who danced.

The water had turned cool by the time I washed myself in it. I took my tempo from a bell, tolling somewhere in the City from one of the fanes, to mark death most likely.

I was in the playroom sitting on the rug, when I heard a dull commotion at the front door. Then I made out men's voices, boot heels, even the click of spurs. The army, perhaps even some of the true army who were still in the City to oversee its defence. They had come for pine tree felling, or another task of the nightmare.

Something made me want to look at them, their uniform; a memory. I went out, and coming up the stair was an officer, an Eagle major, with a face that was familiar, like a painting from another house.

He stopped when he saw me, and swore.

'Aradia?'

I nodded. That was who I was.

He came off the stair and along the corridor. When he was close, I backed into the playroom as far as the window. Recently its glass was never attended to, it was grimy. Nevertheless, light described him. The beautiful uniform was spoiled, stained, its braid ripped; his boots were clogged with mud. His mass of fine hair, dyed with oil and smoke, was smeared back off his sallow face. Rare he still was, but ten years older. His cheek had been cut, healed to a purple scab, and his left hand was bound with a filthy bandage. The eyes of him were all I remembered, differently set and shaped, blazing and darkly pale.

'Do you know who I am?' He paused and tapped the insignia of rank. 'War makes for swift promotion. Who knows, tomorrow?' He laughed. I knew the laugh also, false. Then he checked himself. 'I'm more sorry than I can say. We've been on the walls two months.' A look of disgust, put

27

aside, at the two months, and the walls, and something else. His eyes looked so incandescently pale from the shadows all around them. My eyes, in mirrors, had a look like this, now. How interesting to see it, in another.

My hearing had become painfully acute, and I heard Elaieva's carved door softly open above. They must have told her. He heard, too. He said, 'Excuse me,' and walked out, and went up the stair.

Not sure why, I followed, as I had followed him before. Thenser. The name came back, unneeded, pointless. Far up the vault of the stair, I heard them talking together, she and he, as I overheard them talk that evening of the dinner. But their words, their voices were not the same. Or, his voice was not.

'It's official, my being here, Elaieva. No other reason. Is there anything you lack? I warn you, there's not much food left, but some nice wine for our friends.'

She said she lacked nothing.

He said, 'Very well. That's good.' And then, 'What will you do about the little girl?'

Either she did not reply, or expressed herself by gesture.

'When did you tell her?' he said.

'I have not,' she said, 'told her anything.'

So clearly I heard her, like a silver tingling on the air. Cold, cold, the waters of their speech sluiced upon me.

'You – haven't told her? But the state she's in.'

'I have told her nothing.'

He broke out swearing again. The oaths were terrible, blasphemous, violent, but did not jolt me. He said, 'You frigid bitch, you let her rot here and you never told her, no pity, no help. You never give any quarter. What runs in you, the piss of the ice? You bitch.' Then I heard the soft shutting of her carved door.

He returned down the stairs. Halfway between her door and my landing, he stopped, leaning heavily against the banister. I heard him breathing, as if he had run for miles and still had some way to go.

But when he got to me at last, he was collected. He moved

toward me, firm but slow. 'Let's go back into that room of yours a moment, shall we?'

We went back into the room. He sat me on a chair by the grimed window, and sat down beside me. He said, as if he wanted reassurance, 'Will you give me your hand, Aradia?' Presently, I did. In my brain a tiny brilliant formless coloured whirling went round and round. It absorbed me, and everything else was quite vague. His hand felt warm, I suppose my own was very cold.

'They sent us to the City,' he said, after a moment. 'The defence. My battalion and three others. They reckoned Hightower was invincible. Of course. They let the officers' wives go there because it was so safe, and to show the Kronians how safe it was. Brazen mockery. The dances and the dalliance. And, by then, you couldn't have risked the women on the roads. We had an exciting time enough of it, getting through. Snipers and ambushes— No, forgive me, Aradia. I have to say it out. The news is bad. Your father, Aradia. He died bravely. Quickly. A sword charge. He was one of the first to go down. Your mother – I wasn't there. But when the arsenal blew up, that was when. Sudden. They say you don't— She wouldn't have felt it. Nothing, Aradia.'

We sat still, and he held my hand.

Very gradually, the whirling jewel in my brain went farther and farther off. A huge hurt swelled through me, like an organ note, a droning in my ears. The tears came through my eyes, tearing at them to get out, sharp and scalding. The tears fell on our hands.

'Yes, Aradia,' he said. 'Cry, cry.'

And drawing our two chairs together, he held me as my mother had been used to hold me, to the uniform which reeked of gunpowder and smoke and blood, for men had died against him where I only wept. I barely noticed him. He could not console me. I had known all along. The greatest untruth of all was a fact.

When I had cried myself into a stupor, he picked me up and carried me into my bedroom, where he put me on the bed and pulled the untidied sheet and quilt to cover me. I heard him calling harshly for one of the women of the house; he sounded angry in a detached and uninvolved manner. I fell asleep, and dreamed my mother, in one of her most attractive gowns, was hiding with me in a muddy hole in the earth. The butcher's men were hunting us. I sobbed in terror and anguish. But sleeping or waking there was no pretence even of a barrier, finally, between the devils of life and dream.

Chapter Two

1

Two slim shadows stood over me, rustling and whispering, and the window behind them was a topaz of smoky siege sunset.

'Little girl, little Ara,' one kept saying.

'Don't be scared,' said the other. 'Look, we've brought you something.'

It was a dish of sugar sweets, rather stale and sticky. I took one and ate it because they urged and urged me. They were very pleased when I ate the sweet. 'Have another, Puss. Go on. We saved them, for the victory. Only, that doesn't seem too likely.' They giggled intensely. The sweet, dusty, and with a saccharine strength almost poisonous, lined my mouth and throat. I took another, to please them again. Which worked.

They sat on my bed, and one began to comb my hair. They had a bottle of wine, too, from Elaieva's cellar, which they passed between them and from which they gave me a few sips. It was a sour vintage, not like the fragrant quarter glasses I had sometimes had . . . once.

But Once was gone. Gone for ever. And this was why they had come, the two young maids from the understairs, having heard of my plight, how *madam* hadn't told me, or cared for me. The dashing officer had made such a palaver about it the other day, before he strode out. The two girls, about seventeen, but in most other ways very much older than I, whose own former time had been a world of blacking and

31

polishing, breaking their spines on wet tiles and high-corniced cobwebs, emerged now into the country of chaos afraid but refreshed. Their need to have also about them sympathy and milk-of-kindness they assuaged with me. They would adopt me. Poor little kidlet, they would look out for me. I was to be theirs, for I had no one else.

I was numb, but later, partly frightened. In the red-phased booming of a night's bombardment, when they curled beside me to comfort me, I was less reassured by it than oppressed. I had never been crowded like this. But as the days and nights, so formless and inexplicable, continued, custom was established.

The darker girl was known as Loy. She had the features of a heartless wild bird, bright eyes of yellowish green. Mouse, the younger milder plainer girl, was the more sly, and spiteful – for I saw her pull the wings off moths.

In the daytime, Loy and Mouse went to perform perfunctory duties which could not be escaped. A morning and afternoon did not pass, however, without either or both sneaking in to visit me. Frequently they brought me treats – sweets or bruised fruit, once an egg, hardboiled, its shell painted with a funny face that made me laugh. My laughter caused them smug rejoicing. They had known they could cheer me. They referred to it for days after. Loy said the egg had come from an old shoemaker on Wintoclas Street who secreted hens, unbeknownst to the army or City Hall, in his closet. By flirting, Loy got two eggs, one for me, the other shared between herself and Mouse. Beyond the flirt, the shoemaker apparently received nothing. 'I'm an honest girl,' said Loy. 'But I tell you,' she added, 'there's a time coming on, it could be clever to turn old Vulmartis round to face the wall.' On a night after this, when the guns were silent and we could not sleep, they told me things about carnality and the sexual act. My mother had never lied to me, but she had sometimes been reticent. From her I had had enough to give this monstrous gospel weight. I believed, loathed, and put aside. In doing so, I felt again sensations – normalcy was returning into me, and balance of a kind, for I had had to alter in order to survive. Without knowing what I did, I made Loy and Mouse my guides, and partially my models. That was their triumph. When I laughed now, I laughed with Loy's fierce gutter laugh. I stared sideways from my eyes like Mouse. Alone, sometimes I constructed jokes to make them chuckle. I combed their hair. They tried on my dresses.

What disarray the black house must be in. I had not seen my aunt for weeks. Her meals, when there were meals to be had, went up behind the carven door.

'Mad, *she* is,' said Loy. 'She always was. The kitchen stewardess says madam sits there glaring at the paper on the wall. Never hardly touches her dinner – but that leaves more for us. Have you ever eaten a sparrow? Not so bad.'

But that I would not do.

There came a dusk when the guns had started early. The girls crept into my room.

'Let's dress up,' said Mouse.

'Let's go out,' said Loy.

Mouse and I were astonished by her boldness.

'We won't go far. Just up West Avenue, and round to Wintoclas Street. You hear all the news there. Don't you care,' she added to me, 'what's happening to that handsome lover of yours, that officer from the Eagles?' Forgetting, I did not know what she meant. 'If we went to Maiden Hill, you can see out to the walls, and over to where some of the enemy are, muck on them.'

Mouse squeaked with horror at the fancy.

'What cowards,' said Loy. 'Fine ladies go there all the time, in their carriages, with spy lenses.'

'There aren't any horses left, how can there be carriages?' said Mouse slyly.

'Oh,' airy Loy declaimed, stripping to her shift for my blue skirt and bodice, her favourites, 'their gentlemen admirers draw the carriages, running in the shafts.'

She had been out before, if only by day – how else the eggs? She recounted adventures she had had, an elegant sergeant of the Militia who offered her a diamond pin and – more interesting – a Vulmartia cake for the unobserved spring festival, if she would only let him peep inside her corset. But Loy refused the fellow and ran, for she was 'honest.'

They dressed me, too, and, for added garment, rouged my cheeks like their own, and kohled my lashes. 'Why, a proper little beauty, our little Ara!'

We had a drop more wine from the cellar, then out we went, sailing from a side door and across the garden where all the trees, still untoppled, were kohled black on the rouged, fluttering sky.

'Something's on fire, over Pantheon way.'

Brraam went the guns of the Sazos, and we jeered.

The air tore, but the crack of impact was miles off.

Most of the street lamps were out, for the oil was long since spent. In private houses here and there a wan light showed itself, shamefaced. The Avenues seemed all of them empty, but the girls swung along westward, I swung like the clapper of a bell between them.

I had not been out of Elaieva's house since the siege began. Years and centuries had slunk by. The mouthful of wine or the smell of cheap scent about us buoyed me up. The past fell from me and was kicked away behind our tip-tapping heels – for Mouse had shared a pair of her shoes with me.

The night woke up in Wintoclas Street. A duet of bonfires was blazing, and the new army Militia lurked or lurched there, with bottles, and something was roasting with a wonderful smell. Citizens had come by to idle and perhaps plead for a scrap of meat. A mob, but not to be afraid of. Though, 'Watch out, girls,' said Loy, the army-wise.

We swung forward, more cautiously, to the rim of the first firelight.

'Who goes?' demanded a rough male voice.

Loy and Mouse giggled. Their eyes were wary.

'Well, if it isn't three nymphs of paradise,' said the Militia soldier, emerging from his doorway. He was girded with a knife and a baton. His sash was mostly gone, and through the murk the bandage on his head glowed like phosphorus. 'I've died and gone to the afterlife.'

Loy said, 'I hope you took plenty of Sazo pigs with you.'

'What else are we roasting on the fire? You can eat them, you know, they're not human, Sazos.'

I was appalled, Loy and Mouse giggled some more. Was it a jest?

'Best be careful,' said Loy, challenging the soldier with her lawless eyes. 'I heard, those Sazo pigs could be in the City by Yellow Rose Eve.'

'Not so. *We're* here to defend you.'

Loy let the soldier draw us nearer to the flames. When asked, she said Mouse and I were her sisters, we came from Mitlis Lane.

The meat was donkey. I would not, could not, but the soldier gave Loy and Mouse some spirit in a flask and Loy gave it to me. I ate the strip of meat after that. It had a savoury taste.

The soldier talked a lot about the siege. He had been on the walls. Men fell all about you. A ball of black death had passed right over him, clipped his forehead. Sometimes he heard people talk to him now, who were not there, but he knew that was his wound and not anything uncanny. He wished to walk Loy back to Mitlis Lane. But no sooner were we on one of the Avenues than we broke from him and fled. He tried to run, too, laughing, not yet thinking of cheats. But he was drunk and a cannon shell had kissed his brow. After a few bounds, he splashed into a hedge.

Wined and dined and nothing paid, we got home to the house. Freedom seemed limitless.

Later in the night, when the cannon were still, I woke and recalled I had eaten donkey, and went to the closet and was sick. I did not admit my fault to the girls.

Loy slept in my blue clothes, on her back, noiseless. Mouse had coiled shut against the pillows, and sometimes let out a tiny innocent snore.

The wine bottle was near the window, half full. I had another swig.

In the mirror of the vanity table where Loy had rouged me,

I saw my painted face, my hair unwashed but tonged into corkscrews of curls.

I went out quietly, and climbed the stairs of the black house.

When I came to the carved door guarded with naiads, I knocked.

Not for a moment did I truly think she would answer. She did not. Inside her siege ramparts my aunt sat glaring on wallpaper, not a candle burning. I told her softly I hated her, and called her names under my breath I had only recently learned. *Bitch*, he had said.

Then I went down the house again, and restored myself between my slumbering sisters.

Yellow Rose Eve, Midsummer, was only days away. There had been supper tables dressed with the saffron flowers, and roses, too, in hair and sash and bodice, and music, and staying up late, to see the year turn.

I hoped the guns would begin again soon. I found it difficult to sleep now without them. They obliged me.

2

A colossal nothingness crushed the City. Morning light harsh and blistering seemed squeezed out beneath the lid of it. Like scum, the smoke settled in slow low eddies over Hapsid Forum. Above the head of the stone monarch high on his pedestal the vault of the sky was pure blue, like the sky of another planet.

Half an hour later, Mouse came leaping into my bedroom.

'Ara! It's all over – finished. It is! Bat-Face – you know that groom – he came in and told me so, straight off the emplacements.'

She was used to my dim witted lethargy.

'You see,' she said, 'the old aristocrats, the captains and clevers, they couldn't keep those Sazos out. Terrifying men,' she said, 'like great old black Northern bears.' She flashed her teeth, dainty and white at the front, mostly pulled at the back, and trotted out again.

Before noon, riders were cascading through the streets, on horses somehow uneaten. A group reined in across the Forum.

'*Surrender! It's surrender!*'

Not one window or door opened. The horses looked worn and thin, maybe not worth roasting. A couple of the men tacked up placards by the statue, and pushed a paper onto a nearby railing. They rode away.

Loy went out soon after and collected the paper. It was green, and the letters were printed in a patchy black. *This day, tenth of the Rose Month, Midsummer, by the decree of his Majesty, the Sovereign* . . .

Unable to bear, any longer, the groans of his suffering capital, the King had advised the City Senate to lay down arms and sue for an honourable peace with the enemy.

There was raucous amusement from the underlings of my aunt's house. On his royal island of gardens and mistresses, the King had decided we had had enough. No oil left, no bread, scarcely a rat left in the cellars. And, more to the point, a dearth of cannon balls, powder, and fighting men with more than one leg or arm or eye apiece. Not a provision had been sent us. Not a battalion. Seventy days.

But my mother and my father had died for it. To surrender was to make believe this had not happened.

Loy perched before the vanity mirror in my blouse of white muslin which she had cut away and threaded with ribbon, so it would sit off her shoulders and the rounded dip of her bosom. She had placed a yellow rose for the season, its stem shorn of barbs, between her breasts.

'Oh, yes, fuss and rant and rave. But they've conquered us, those pigs. What else will they want to do but come in at the gates, by Origos Field, down Pantheon Mile to the Pantheon? If we're beaten, and the City's theirs, what do people reckon the Sazos'll do? Lie down and lick the walls and go away? Not likely. The commanders, the Bear General pig, he says he's charmed by us, wants to rest the summer here with his poor tired troops.'

'*She's* no patriot,' said Mouse, brilliant-eyed. 'Wanting to go and ogle the Sazos as they ride in.'

Loy gave a flounce. 'I'm a patriot but not a silly.'

Mouse had put on my blue skirt and a red bodice of her own. There were silver earrings in her ears. I thought they were my aunt's, but did not dare ask how and if and when Mouse had stolen them.

They did not bother to dress me for this outing. In my dirty rumpled cotton and uncombed hair, face white as pipe-clay, they danced me with them.

The sun had westered and an unheard bass roar pounded through air and paving, bone and brain. A storm was approaching or a tremor of the earth. It was nearly ten o'clock. The sky, so cleansed and empty, was pale raspberry red and deep hollow bronze over the western Avenues towards Wintoclas Street, yet rosy blue along the eastern walk where we were going. The trees at least had not shaken off their cloy. Their foliage was a sepia hue, and most had been hacked for fuel.

No one was forbidden to watch the torchlit entry of Saz-Kronian legions into the City. Some patriots had sworn to die rather than do so. Otherwise, the citizens were curious. Now at last they would see the monstrous beasts which had encompassed them. Food had already been sent in, a gift of the conquerors, which had not added to their unpopularity. Battered and tattered, the remnants of Militia and City Guard were positioned all along the way, embalmed in part-healed scars and surgeons' wrappings, propped on crutches, gaunt and ashen. Not so much to keep order, perhaps, as to point the difference between ourselves and those who came to claim us.

Cunning Loy had got a position for herself and incidentally for us on the balcony of a tavern. All drinking shops were shut tonight by order of the Senate, but it scarcely mattered, the quantity of flagons and bottles that were going round. A brace of families squashed in with us, and more on the roof where the slates rattled ominously. The scenario was repeated

38

on all sides, and mostly windows were full. On the Mile below a throng piled against the buildings. The broad road had been left well clear.

Some lights were already lit, the hoarded tallow squandered against replenishing tomorrows. On the whole, the mood was not tragic, nor dire. Those in real dismay had stayed at home. In spots there was even a festive element, though it was to be frowned on and soon quietened itself. Some, like Loy, were pert.

The weird vibration that seemed to invest the stones of the City went on, but now I began to think it was the percussion of the enemy chariots, for they were coming. Their trumpets pealed out, and there was the clash of arms. I had heard similar noise so often, fanfares from Origos Field in some mute dawn, uncountable booted feet tramping in unison.

The darkening sunset their perfect backdrop, the Saz-Kronians flooded down Pantheon Mile.

One of the engines of the siege was first, presumably strategically advanced, a concrete emblem of their might, what they had done and could do yet. It was a terrible magnificent thing, ornamental, made like a huge dragon of glimmering iron and riveted steel, with tremendous jaws from which the shot would erupt in a dragon's fire-breath. Its eyes were living brass, and scales ran down it to the wheels, blinking and burning in the torches of its escort. The dragon rumbled and rolled by, and some twenty drummers measured out their pace behind it. They wore the black uniform of the North, with the pelts of black bears across their shoulders, and the snarling, silver-fanged heads surmounting and negating their own. Behind the drums, on a carriage draped with gold, reared their bear deity, the Kronians' war god. He was fearful, overall bigger than a man, great with claws, girdled with gold, and with battle trophies hung on him and his cart. In his mindless mask, blood-eyes flamed and seemed to look from side to side. After him, rode the men with the battle standards and sigils of raven, bear and wolf, raw tongues of colour and dripping gilt. Two trumpeters with barbaric helmets into which the tines of stags had been fixed, and breastplates of silver, passed, uttering the scream of their war horns as if to split one's ears.

'There, *there*,' muttered Loy, digging me with her elbow.

It was the Commander. He was a black-browed and bearded man, like most of the others. They had altogether that look of bears themselves, shaggy and massive, pitiless, unthinking. Yet his eyes were pastel, almost too pallid for his bearded burned storm-cloud of face. In him, the Kronians' ugliness and their pride were focused, as in the bear deity on its cart. He, too, rode a war chariot. The nourished horses, shining like rubbed coal, hauled him forward. In his hand, a drawn sword. Whatever had been said or promised, whatever the insolence or relief of the crowd, the sword demonstrated what he had meant to accomplish, and that it was achieved.

After this sinister figure, rank on rank, infantry and cavalry, the legions of the Saz-Kronians, with their flags and drums, marched along the Mile. And in their midst, now and then, a gun mounted on wheels, or a pack of wolf-dogs such as they keep for hunting, stepping forward on tight leash, or some other decorative interruption intrinsic to them, the playfulness of the iron fist.

Surely it took hours for them to go by. I was drained as if I had been leisurely bleeding as I stood there. Nor was I the only one with that look to me. Loy's face had lost its impudence. Her lip curled only as if it withered. She spat under our feet. But the enemy was gone by then, she would not have wanted it to see.

What she had been thinking of I incoherently guessed. But evidently she felt herself thwarted. Men made of metal and dark forests. Impassive cold iron on which her liltings slithered and slipped.

Night had closed down in the wake of the Conqueror. Night too silent. We walked unmolested, under hinted windows and seared trees.

The black house with the scarlet columns was unusual, and the smitch of war had not much faded it. The pine towered, unlopped, a signpost. It had been seen.

They were rooming their important men all about the City. The old royal palace at The Lilacs was to be the General's residence, and the headquarters of his military staff. For lesser stars, the best mansions. We had let them in, and must go on in that vein.

Every night their patrols policed the streets; they were omnipresent but disciplined. The soldiers of the North did not fraternise with the City. Even had they desired it, their language was not ours, and mostly they had not taken much trouble to unravel linguistics. Let the invaded set that to rights. They knew the words for *Halt* and *Come* and *Go*, the word for *No*, which anyway was sufficiently like their own we might divine it. I heard their dusk commands struck like blades across the Forum. Loy, sent out now for groceries, and gossiping with that wonder, a milk cart, at the side door, returned to regale us. Like naughty children, Saz-Kronia meant to keep us in for the summer, and we should be whipped. 'And they're hanging our soldiers – the proper army. Or throwing them in cellars to rot.' This from Loy with enthused rage. Of the Kronians, not one had whistled after her, or wished to undo her frock.

Then, as the gate now stood open, thunder on the house door.

'What will madam say?'

My hair washed, and screwed up in bits of cloth to curl, in my dirty dress, without stockings, eating a shard of bread, I came onto the landing, half hiding, to see if *she* must come down in answer to this summons.

But instead, the bears were called up into her sanctum.

'White as death she was,' said the salon steward, who had been given back to us from the walls unmaimed, though the under-steward had lost an eye, and himself vanished. 'She said, "Gentlemen, I've been expecting you."'

My Aunt Elaieva no longer existed. The tales they told of her were conceivably facts, yet if so, she dwelled on some other plane, visible through gauze, untouchable as a ghost.

Shortly the Kronians came down. They took the steward aside and spoke, as if to a thinking plank, of arrangements.

'Madam has to get out of her apartment,' said the steward. He doddered since his service on the wall. He did not even seem affronted, though he tried vocal interjections of affront. 'She is permitted to have rooms on the lower floor. In all my days—'

But who was coming here, to oust madam and knock the establishment on its end? The questioners were avid. Fresh food had gone to their heads. To us, said their hands and mouths and the pupils of their eyes, this carry-on might be a chance. Look what we have come through to reach the oasis.

The steward was uninformed. Some officer of the Kronian horde, that was all he knew.

'Young, or not so young?' said Loy, whose position in the house had already so much altered.

The steward would not answer. He bustled (shuffling) away.

One of the maids with whom I had no intimacy picked at my sleeve.

'Madam says you're to go up.'

What could I say? Madam had ceased to exist. And here was I, hair in curlers and eyebrows plucked like the eyebrows of Mouse, a red stain on my lips, unbathed and in disgraceful garments. I had longed for her to observe me in this mode, that night I ate donkey. Or had thought I did.

I was frightened now. I wanted not to have to go to her. I began to shake from head to foot, clutching my snack of bread, nauseous, eyes blurring.

The servant girl had hurried off. Before I knew what I was at, I started to climb the stair.

All so bizarre, the house swathed in its forlorn and unloved neglect. The rugs with marks on them, and the walls. Dust between the banisters. I saw as if for the first time. But her door, oddest of all, was standing wide.

The last occasion, I had not seen her sitting room, and I did not see it now.

Elaieva was seated at her desk, on which papers were neatly spread, and coins, and some little boxes, and a large single casket of tooled green leather, shut. She wore a morning gown, her hair was loose as I had never beheld it, very long and thick but fine as my own, though black as pitch.

Her face was delicately sunken. She looked much too youthful. Like a girl a year or so my senior, who had been sleepless all her life.

Black eyes. They rose and rested on me, and saw nothing. But she said:

'Aradia.'

And I remembered that had been my name, though I was Ara now, and Puss, and Little Dunce.

'This key,' she said. She extended it towards me. 'It belongs to this casket.'

No, she could not see me, or who I was today. She put the key into Ara's hand.

'The house was to have been your father's, and in due course, yours. Therefore, it is yours, Aradia.'

I had snatched the key away. I held on to the bread in my other hand. What she said meant nothing. Did I hate her enough? I must force myself. She was all that was left to me, and she was worlds away in a tower of ice. Ice bitch. Bitch.

'I apologise, Aradia,' she said, 'that I couldn't love you. That was not in me. Go down now. Look after the key. You will need it, later.'

I might spit at her, at her feet or in her face. Not possible. When I had been with her, I had been my mother's daughter.

My mouth, frozen by Elaieva's winter, fumbled around foul words I could not sound.

All at once I sprang away and sped from the room.

I fell on the stairs, rolled and dropped the key, and recovered it. In the unplaying-room, finding I could no longer eat my bread, I thrust the key into it, as if to stab it to the heart.

Aunt Elaieva committed suicide during the afternoon. She had had some draught prepared, some alchemist or surgeon of the City might have made it up for her. She had put a white flower from her garden before the little Vulmartis in her private chapel, but then blown out the watch-light in the lamp. Returning to her bed, she lay on it, swallowed the drug, and died.

The outer door was unlocked, though closed, and in the evening the maid went in with the dinner Elaieva had, supposedly on purpose, ordered. Screams and shrieks issued from the apartment and the whole house went galloping to see. All but I, for – slotting home the ultimate chip of the jigsaw – I knew immediately. Thus I crouched rooted to the rug, undecided, to my amazement, whether to shed tears or curse her. But then Mouse slithered into my room, and forestalled everything.

'Yes,' I said. 'That woman is dead. Now this house is mine.'

Mouse gave a squawk. She appeared very scared.

She said to Loy afterwards, when we had the green box open on my bed and were eating cream and sugar from a bowl, 'She gave me a proper turn, little fiend. She spoke just like – *her* – like madam.'

3

Flag-Colonel Keer Gurz entered the house the next morning. He dealt with Elaieva's death. A rider went for orders and came back with them, and they were carried out by two Kronian subalterns and two Kronian soldiers with spades. Gurz had the household assemble and addressed us in our tongue with curt familiarity. The demise of our mistress was regrettable, but it was not politic to make a funeral show. The graveyards were also, at present, overbusy with our war dead. At some future date the lady might be disinterred and placed in a more pious area. For now, we should not hasten tidings of her unfortunate and hysterical act.

They set her, in a military wooden case, in the earth of her garden, and covered up the spot, even going so far as to disguise it with a pile of logs. No one was invited to attend the burying or to steal there afterwards with flowers and prayers.

Once the spadework had been seen to, Flag-Colonel Gurz

again collected us, and told us that the house had fallen into a
rank state he would not tolerate. It must be seen to instantly.

He was not young. He spoke our language peculiarly and
his accent was so glutinous, it made it seem he talked always
through a mouthful of food. His frame was big and thick in
its black uniform, lacking any honour pinned or stitched to
it. His weather-baked face laired in a forest of beard which,
with his clipped hair, was typical of most of the Sazos, unlike
the classical style of the City men, clean-shaven, and with
hair often worn long.

The house gushed into a frenzy of labour. All the slipshod
ways were given up in three minutes. Stairways, corridors,
and chambers were full of maids, scrubbing, brushing, and
thwacking. Dust rose like winds from the disturbed drapes
and carpets.

He assumed his residence in Elaieva's suite as intended.
The soldiers bore up his army chests and a portable shrine.
At this Loy had managed to peer. The shrine contained
replicas of the bear and the wolf-jackal gods of the North.
'Horrible, hideous things,' affirmed the steward who had also
seen them carried in glory in madam's bedroom.

Not once did it occur to me, though the documents in the
casket proclaimed my rights, to go to Flag-Colonel Gurz and
tell him I was now the owner of the house. Nor did anyone
advise that I should.

During the afternoon, one of the Sazo soldiers strolling the
passages and catching sight of me on my bed, took me for a
truant maid and wordlessly bellowed, waving his arms.
Quick to learn for once, I hastily jumped down and began to
plump the pillows. Satisfied, he left me.

By the evening, all but two soldiers, seemingly attached as
bodyguard to him, and his own servant, a wizened ratty-
looking individual, had left Colonel Gurz in possession of his
new home. Dinner was served to him in the sitting room of
the suite, but nevertheless on the Sphynx Salon service. The
very best food, for now the Kronian army victualled the
kitchen, and a krater of red wine. He demolished all,
including every drop in the wine jar. The steward was heard

to comment that if this Sazo hog was to get through a full krater every night, madam's cellar would soon be void. The servants, of course, had already made inroads upon the drink, and now no longer dared to.

Loy decided that we should be safe enough, she, Mouse, and I, continuing to sleep in my bed. The door should be shut by dark and day, however, and a chair propped under the knob for good measure.

Something had prevented my telling the girls of how the Sazo had thought me a maid. I had meant to, surely it would have made them howl with mirth – or rather, not howl, for we were careful, too, of the noise we made, lest the hog-bear hear and come down to investigate.

'Pooh, what an old guts he is,' lamented Loy. 'When I remember our own officers, with their beautiful hair and narrow middles.'

Mouse chided her for wantonness, and they sparred, but their verve was gone. We were prisoners now in a way the siege had never made them, at least.

4

'Open this door, or I will smash your timbers.'

I had heard his thumping footfalls on the stair, but thought they would go by as on other days. There was no reason for him to investigate this passage. When he came clumping along it, I held my breath. Why should he try my door? He tried it. The knob wriggled and the propped chair tottered.

'Open, I say.'

And why should he imagine anyone was in the room? Could it not have been locked and left—

'*Open*, Urtka-damns.'

The unwieldy oath unnerved me very much.

I had been careless at the window, probably thinking myself unseen behind the lace. But Kronian patrols went up and down between the hedges. Some pig had noticed movement and alerted *him*.

He had never knocked. Now he struck the door a blow to

fell it, I thought it would collapse instantly. When it did not, I ran across and threw the chair aside.

'Ahrh!' growled Gurz.

He turned the knob and the door opened.

It was the first time I had viewed the enemy so close. He seemed to fill the doorway and all the space beyond. His face bloated, bending itself to me in surprise. I was mesmerised by its coarseness, the craters and pocks of pores, the rampant life of the cloud-beard. His eyes were small and pastel, bluish, like the General's. Hair grew from his nostrils in wires. He smelled of tobacco, which they said he habitually smoked; he smelled intensely male.

'What is this?' he said. His voice had changed. It was no longer threatening but ludicrously sprightly. 'Made the little nest for yourself you have, eh, cat-eyes?'

I blurted, 'This is my room.'

'Yes, I see it is. Madam in garden and you in here. Queen it.'

He, too, took me for an opportunist housemaid. I felt a moment of unnatural rage, but that was no use. Frightened and repulsed, I leaned from him but would not affront him by backing away.

His small eyes wrinkled up, with friendly encouraging laughter.

'Well, why not,' he said, nodding. 'Yes. Big bad officer in the upstairs. Little maiden snuggled in guest room.' He stood straight up again, and left me standing on the floor. 'Tonight,' he said, 'you serve dinner.'

I stared at him.

'Yes, that is you,' he said. 'But clean up yourself first.'

I blushed with shame. This vile thing thought me grubby.

'Wash all over. Hair. Nails. Find a dress. Look on this bed.' He pointed at the blue clothes Loy had discarded there. 'Put on that and bring me my food.' He seemed to take note of my fear at last. 'I will not harm you.' He frowned, angry at my immutable fright. 'These stories they tell of us. Damn their lies. But you do what I say, and shall keep your nest.'

He left me, and went on downstairs, to wherever he had

originally been going. I heard the house door shut on him and his two saluting bodyguard.

I considered flight. But there was nowhere to run. The house itself could not conceal me.

Some amorphous vestige, myself at five arrayed in a party frock for a visit of officers and their wives . . .

My shame stayed terrible, that he had been able to think me dirty. I drew off cold water from the closet, not wanting to assert myself with the servants for hot. I bathed, every inch, also soaping my ears, face, hair, and paring and trimming my nails.

Then, as if for one of the obscure outings with the girls, I rouged my cheeks and lips, darkened my eyes, put on the blue skirt and bodice that smelled now of Loy's perfume.

This was how one dressed, for men. I had been educated.

I knew what was his dinner hour, by now. He timed it exactly, by the bell of the curfew the Kronians had imposed, ringing from all the spires and belfries of the City at sunset.

The windows flushed, and I was ready on the landing, waiting for the procession of dishes and the evening's krater to come up. I would simply take some item and go with them.

I was not so much afraid finally as acutely uncomfortable. A physical sensation continually went through and through me for which there was no name. It made me want to crawl under the bedclothes, knot myself together, and cover up my head.

The bells were ringing.

Loy appeared before me, with four dishes on a brass tray. A kitchen lad was just behind her bearing the glass decanter, ruby with wine.

Both halted. Both were amazed.

'He wants me to help do it,' I said to Loy.

'Come on, Puss-Dunce, move yourself or I'll be late. That old Colonel's a stickler for his meals.'

'No, Loy. He caught me in the room. He said I have to take up his food. Is that all there is? What shall I carry?'

'You?' said Loy. Her expression was extraordinary. I could not decipher it at all. But suddenly she thrust the whole tray at me, so abrupt and awkward I almost could not receive it. I staggered and saved myself and the tray, and she was gone down the stair. The boy grinned, but he followed me without other comment.

One of the bodyguard was at the carved door, mortar-faced between the naiads. He flung them back and I went into my aunt's apartment. My third visit.

I saw it, now. The rat servant was groping about, lighting the branches of squat yellow post-siege candles. The doors of bedchamber and study and library stood wide on sunset shadows. The bathing chamber I had been told of, and never shown, was closed, and the chapel, too. But through the bedroom door, there winked a swarthy glint that might have been the eyes of the Bear and the Wolf, keeping watch over their own.

A table was laid in the sitting room, and he sat at the table. The Kronians did not much favour the reclining pose for eating. He was not, however, wearing his uniform but a robe of silk, somewhat in the classical style. On him, incongruous.

A book lay among the plates and napkins, and he was writing in it, scowling, using a pencil-lead in a holder of silver filigree that must have been Elaieva's. As I came towards him, he looked up, and the scowl lifted like a black-winged bird. He smiled, huge teeth bared in beard.

'Arhh, the little cat-eyes. Here she is in her pretty dress for me.'

He sent the rat servant and the boy away at once, and saw to the wine himself. I put the dishes on the table. Not sure what to do next, he had to direct me. I spooned out soup for him. He consumed it. Then the meats, the fried cabbage with raisins, the creamed vegetables and gravy, I somehow got on to his plate.

I was expected to remain. I stood there. He ate, golluping up the food like a starved ox, copiously replenishing his goblet from the krater. The ruby sank with speed; the dinner disappeared into his body.

When he was assuaged, again he looked up. Again, smiling, he greeted me.

49

'And is there food enough, now, in your kitchen?' he said
to me.

I said I thought there was. My voice was a frond.

'And do you feed? Come, that chair here, and sit, sit.' He
began to fill a bread plate for me, helping me now, smother-
ing the haughty porcelain sphynx in sauce.

He poured a quarter glass of wine for me.

A wild throb of pain-memory choked my heart.

'Drink that, yes, it will do good. White face under that
paint. You city girls. Now, I was born,' he said, proudly, 'out
in country lands. There our Kronian girls have strawberry
cheeks.'

As I pecked at tiny slivers of cabbage and lamb, he ate a
wedge of orange cheese, and began an attempt to tell me of
his 'country lands.' But in this, his grip on my language let
him down. He could not get the words, and grumbled with
laughter and annoyance, his eyes glittering. It came to me, he
was galvanised by a gigantic, inappropriate *fun*. He wanted to
enjoy himself, in this comfortable room, among the plush
chairs, the satin wallpaper, the candlelight and food. He
wanted me to aid and abet his happiness by becoming happy,
too. And Loy had said, 'Always make a man think you're
having such a lovely time.' I smiled in return on my enemy,
until my jaws ached at the strain.

Presently he reached for his pipe rack and selected a pipe of
polished malt-brown wood. He packed it with tobacco.
Smoke cloud and beard cloud hung about his smiling face.

I had drunk my wine. I felt that I could not bear much
more. Like a spring coiled up too tightly, coiling tighter yet.
Let him release me soon.

He told me something about being a boy in the forests, a
house, an estate, a wolf hunt – and he named the god, but I
could not grasp such a name – and he lapsed now endlessly
into his Northern tongue.

Eventually, he lost the joy. He became sad. He uttered
long sonorous gutturals of untranslated recrimination and
dirge. His eyes turned to me for sympathy. He sighed.
Perhaps he recalled, I was not a strawberry-cheeked Kronian

girl, but one of the trampled and conquered.

'Well,' he said, in my language, 'so, little maiden. You are tired out. I will send you down to your nest now. No one shall know. Our secret we share. Go.'

The relief nearly washed me away. Reborn, I rose, I danced across the room.

'But your name,' he said, 'how you are called?'

'Ara.'

He repeated this, making it sound only like that growl of his, *Aarhh*.

Getting my name, he chained me. But then, he had not got my name, only a piece of it.

The bodyguard was at the door. I might have been invisible to him.

Did my feet touch the stairs?

I shut the door of my bedroom. No chair, for I had been discovered, and soon anyway Loy and Mouse would come to bed and could not be shut out.

I wished I could shut them out.

Aloneness was my treasure.

I knotted myself tighter and tighter in the bed, and the contrary spring slackened. It had not been so very awful. And now, I could sleep.

Loy woke me. She was wrenching my hair, shaking me.

'You – you – you—'

I rolled on to my back, and her hard thin hand clapped against my cheek. I caught at her, already hissing back at her, trying to make her stop, half-asleep, unsure yet she was in earnest, mindlessly recollecting not to make a noise.

'Bitch – you – bitch—'

'Loy – no. Loy – what is it? Loy—'

Mouse was on my other side. She pinched my arm like a crab's pincers. I cried out before I could help it.

This checked them. They started up from me.

'You little cheat,' said Mouse, with lapid righteousness.

The sentence hung like a crystal on the dark. I stared at it.

'What have I done?'

51

'What has she done?' (Loy.) 'What*ever* has she done, her ladyship.'

'Underhand trick,' said Mouse.

I lay before them, they kneeled above me.

At last, Loy said, 'It was me that was planning on him, that old bellybag. What have I ever had? Saved myself. Do myself some good. But no, you have to make up to him. *You*.'

My mind blinked, and everything was remembered.

'But it was – he came to the door and found me.'

'Took care he should, didn't you. I saw you, eyeing him, that first day. I couldn't believe it of you, you so wellbred and your daddy a Lion major. What would your daddy say to *this?*'

'Her blessed mother would turn round in her grave,' said Mouse.

Something happened inside me, my lungs or stomach or heart. I whirled up flailing and screaming.

A broken kaleidoscope of motion. Their hot breath acid from pastries, their sharp hands biting at me. Their frantic shushings, and heaving me off the bed, and Loy's voice like a thorn in my ear, '*Out* with you, then. I don't want you by me. I'm honest. I don't want to catch his Northern pox off you.'

And they cast me from my bedroom. I lay in the passage and they shut my door, and wedged my chair against it to keep me out.

I got up. I had on only my petticoats, in which I had gone to bed. But all was not confusion, yet. For I would go down to the playroom.

And to the playroom I went. A lamp burned there, and one of the bodyguard sat playing a game of Temples.

He did not see me. I took precautions.

Well, now I must find some unlit empty room, and wait there, for morning.

No, that was no particular remedy. For many of the rooms had now been locked, or were bare, the Kronians having carted off the furniture to other places. Besides which, another world had just ended. The world of Loy and Mouse. Even were I able to reclaim the territory of the bedroom, which was its landscape, it could not any longer be a valid world. For when I had sought them that time, the rooms of my parents had surely disintegrated with them, as I had done – what I had been.

In limbo, I waited in the foyer of the house, to which point I had got down, unknowing.

The house-god still presided in his niche by the black door, a stuttering candle for the night at his feet. My mother had always travelled with the protective goddess of her childhood, installed otherwise in our lodging, a genius of spring, whose niche we had garlanded with harebells and asphodel, or ivy to appease her in the cold. The spirit of Elaieva's house was a robed man with a staff.

The stairs sagged and sounded behind me. One of the Colonel's guards had heard me wandering, and come to see what I did. It might mean trouble for me.

I could say I had been sent to trim the god's candle.

What did trouble matter, any way?

'Now what is this?' he said, as before.

Gurz loomed over me again, soft-footed, for him, in his house shoes and robe. He had come all the way downstairs after me.

'I have heard screams. Cries,' he said. 'You lost that nest. Shall I turn them out, the wicked ones who steal from you?'

The sombre glim underlit his face, as the god's face was underlit. Both were robed, but the god was slender, and light spangled in the Kronian's beard.

'Well, then,' he said, 'instead you shall come to sleep with me.' His eyes anxiously examined my face. 'I shall not harm you,' he said. 'But it is the will of Wiparvet. Did you know? It is he brings the man to the woman. But nothing is as gentle as the wolf with his own.'

Like the house falling, he reached for me and possessed himself of me. The tobacco smell, the wine, the pressure of maleness.

He bore me up the stairs. I was boneless. I could not understand. The bodyguard – gone from the carved door, perhaps he had been sent on an errand. Had Gurz, in his fantasy of fate, been waiting for me to come back?

All the building had seemed floating by, its ceilings and mouldings tangled in the vast beard of night. Beyond the naiad door, a deeper dark. At the table, the smoking, blown-out candle-branch, insomniac books and papers. And through the arch of a second door. Arm's length from me I saw the black mask of the wolf-jackal, stippled with its gold, and lamplight breathing like a soul in its eyes.

He put me into the bed. He covered me with the sheet. He arranged my hair upon the pillow.

He lay beside me, sighing, hot as a furnace. He did not touch me again.

The eyes of the wolf god flickered and closed.

Chapter Three

1

For two burning months, the last of summer, I belonged to him in the black house. I was a virgin until the night after the autumn Vulmartia, the night of my fourteenth birthday.

Flag-Colonel Keer Gurz was not among the most important of the City's resident Kronians. A complex, tenuous kinship united him with the family of their General. Gurz's rank was largely honorary; his role administrative, or scholastic. He had charted the march, described the route, numbered the guns, the casualties. Sometimes he had been called upon to sign warrants of death or reprieve for minor prisoners.

His tasks had taken him nowhere near Fort Hightower. He had simply entered, from the dispatches of others, its statistics in his log, the charges and breachments, the explosion of the arsenal, the capitulation. The whole episode had not occupied more than half a page. I found out such things long after. Would I have sensed the taint on him otherwise, if he had been present, if he had sparked the powder even, that brought down all the high towers? How could I have done? What did I know? They were separate things, the death of love, the wilderness of life outside the door.

The full name of the Kronian General was Hetton Tus Dlant, but they called him by a nickname, Urtka-Tus – which Gurz explained to me meant something like the Bear's Boy: He was the god's favourite.

Gurz wished me to learn his language. He wanted to be

able to speak to me in Kronian, to have my understanding. Such sympathy he had seen, in my 'tender glance,' for so he termed it, he knew I had already taken pity on him. So the enemy addressed me.

He had himself compiled a primer on our two languages, with a grammar and vocabulary, for the use of the Sazo troops. He gave to me a copy of this little volume, and scrawled his name across a blank page, dedicating it to me. He was pleased with the book. Of his own errors in his employment of our tongue he was either unaware or discounted them. Probably those soldiers who diligently conned his primer repeated them faithfully all over the City.

I had somehow kept the habit of former random lessons. I studied indolently on the hot afternoons, when my drawing crayons grew too adhesive. I was able to get like a parrot, by rote, many phrases and a great many words, knowing what they were intended to mean, though scarcely comprehending the syntax. My accent was good, for it had for me, on their lips, such extreme, almost comic, stresses, I found them easy to copy.

He was often away, days and nights together, summoned to incessant military conferences at The Lilacs, or perhaps only thinking he must attend. From fragments I grasped of asides to his servant, it seemed he would spend three or four hours at a stretch kicking his heels in anterooms, or wandering the overgrown palace gardens, fascinated by unusual butterflies, and mutated plants broken from the orangery.

The servant, Melm, left me strictly to myself. His method of dealing with me was to pretend I was not there. He was so adroit that alone in his vicinity, I seemed to myself to disappear. When, later on, I directed an order or request at him in Kronian, he did as he was bid, yet with such a prim rat's face of aversion, such unseeing rat's eyes, I normally preferred to attend to my own wants, or go without.

The custom of oversleeping stayed with me in the suite. Seldom did I rise before noon. A twitch of bell-rope, and in was brought the bath water, always scrupulous and hot. They were none of them, when I glimpsed them, girls I had known. Most I think were new to the house. And Loy and Mouse I never saw – which initially I had been afraid I must.

A breakfast-luncheon was also served me each day, as well as the nightly repast, but I took small interest in either. My appetite had not recovered, though I acquired instead a ravening lust for sweet or fruit drinks, presses of citrus or berries, or pears with cream and cloves.

I filled what there was of my days much as I had before, with the making of coloured pictures, or in playing Temples or card games I invented. In addition I would study Gurz's language, or read portions of the books in my aunt's library. I was childish, pampered. But it sat ill on me now. Again and again a sort of fit would come over me, restless, inexplicable, a kind of fear, although I could not have said of what, for all the ogres had drawn off. Loy was restrained from me or had been dismissed. The pig-bear took care of me (even brought me presents, new crayons, a ribbon, a bracelet), and attempted on me none of those insane, nearly unbelievable antics the girls had described in their sexual anecdotes.

He slept in the bed with me, when he did come home. He never, at those times, laid a hand on me. My nun-aunt's couch was oddly wide. He rolled about his side of it like a column in his laundered nightshirt, and would cheerily leave me sleeping there when he went away. However, when both of us coincided on the vertical plane, and in our clothes, he would kiss my cheeks, smooth my hair. Sometimes he took me on his knees, but never for long. 'So young she is,' he said. 'I know she is only a baby.' Contacts with him I had come, internally as well as demonstrably, to accept. They reminded me of nothing reassuring or liked, but merely unthreateningly *were*, like the less comfortable chairs, or the stormy heat itself.

In the cool of the evening, when he was in the house and had no work, he would have me dress in my best clothes (rescued from below), and out we would go for a drive in an open carriage, sometimes alighting, strolling the boulevards or entering the parks.

Since the imposition of the Kronians' curfew, the City after sunfall had become a mystic place. At first, every few minutes we were halted and his pass examined. Later, perhaps our trips became common, trite, and rarely were we challenged.

Only Kronian soldiers were on the streets that I saw. Though every so often a phantasmal, human-sized animal would scuttle through an alley or shrubbery. Gurz, if he noticed, was tolerant. 'Some lover,' he said once, 'not to be parted from his lady.' Sentimentally he beamed, telling our driver to hurry or slow the horses, to distract the man. For all Gurz knew, the curfew-breaker might have been a rebel plotting murder. Himself a childish man, the Flag-Colonel.

By night, as I had never seen them save at some festival, then broadly lit by coloured lanterns, the parks were hung with dark velure, with only the bright stars strung between the trees, and sometimes the mirroring of a summer moon in a basin or a lake.

He wished I might view the gardens of the Lilac Palace. Had I never been there? Such insects, such roses—

We walked frequently an hour at a time, along the gravel avenues under the chestnuts and acacias, where statues flashed like ghosts of salt. In the day, children and monkeys might still cavort here, but I was never privy to it.

The enigmatic sorcery of night on a starlit expanse not paving or wall, *whole* darknesses, the special fragrance of the trees, this enchanted me. I longed for him to be silent, and for a great part of the time he was. We moved innocently together. I might have been his little niece.

After our genteel perambulations we would return in the carriage to my dead aunt's suite, and climb into her bed, one at each side. I was inured to him. I paid him less attention than a large dog. Then again he would, six nights out of seven, work late at the table in the sitting room, rustling his papers, scratching in his books, pipe-puffing.

On its perch, the bear god, Urtka of the legions, brooded, a dish of dried herbs before him, a droplet of wine in his cup. It was the Wolf, Wiparvet, who stared. Some tendency of the lamplight from the outer room would keep him wakeful, watching. I no longer feared him. But I believed in him, if only as one credits another country far away.

'My decision,' Colonel Gurz said, returning suddenly at midday to the house. 'You shall see this Lilac Palace. Here is your city. The princes have fled it. Come. Put on all of your best, now.'

He thought me a skivvy of a scullery, destined to have nothing until the bold conquerors swept down to bring me justice. Now I should roam, under the sun, the pleasaunce of a king.

We rode at a medium pace westward, for more than an hour. Doubtless I had been shown the palace behind its walls, as a tiny child. Or had I only been told of it?

A wood ran across the slopes above, older than the City. In lilac time, the hanging escarpments garlanded the roofs and turrets below with fondants of pink, mauve and tawny blue. But lilac time was past.

Our carriage, for this excursion, had been closed, and stifling. I had not been able to see much of the state of the daylight streets, yet they struck me as busy, even bustling, as full of noise and venture as ever. Sometimes we had to pause to avoid colliding with other traffic. When a column of Sazo soldiery went stalking by the window, the crowds on the pavement did not appear much disturbed.

But the area about the palace had been cleared, whole thoroughfares and buildings appropriated by Kronian military.

More soldiers were drilling on the open forum before the palace walls, and the great guns sat on their wheels as if only waiting.

Ruddy, black and azure, the Saz-Kronian totem banner, a raven that flapped its wings if any wind blew, hung motionless on a stout round tower. No need to fly, perhaps. It had come far enough, that Northern crow, for now.

He communed with me crisply, slowly, in his own language, as we drove in at the gates of wrought-iron all

59

clustered with hyacinths and poppies of gold.

'We will keep to the paths of the garden. There is much to show you. I have begun to write a modest volume on it. Never have I seen anywhere that is quite the same. You will be able to help me.' It was a prepared speech, for others as well as myself, the justification for bringing me with him.

The carriage stopped in a yard. Horses had been lodged in the dilapidated stables, and a Sazo groom was repairing harness, seated on the mounting block. He eyed me, but looked away at a rotation of my protector's head.

We went out through an archway, along a covered passage fingered thick by ivy and creepers, emerging on a high terrace.

The vista was beautiful, almost overwhelming. I had been cooped up so long in the black house, and set at liberty only in the unpigmented rooms of the darkness.

To my right, the palace piled up, slaty stones and crenellated towers, roofs like scales of a tarnished lizard. Windows reflected the sun fiercely, and a weathervane, a golden peacock, blazed. Smoke pulsed from some kitchen chimney. Yet rooks had nested against the antique eaves. There was a soft deficit to the palace, disuse, indifference, and when in the woods above a jay chattered, it pointed the vast distances of silence between.

But the gardens, erupting from restriction, had become a wondrous jungle, like something from a story book, where lost princesses slept for centuries, or princes cursed to the shape of beasts brooded and skulked.

Green lawns of tasselled grass, green torrents of trees into which roses had sinuously ascended, breaking out like fire to all the shades of pink and amber fruit. There, a doll's temple done in white marble and poured with a sauce of hibiscus. Farther off, downhill, everything merging to a turquoise abstraction, from which the pagodas of pines came up with pigeons sewing in and out. Where the palace had relinquished its voice, the murmur of the arteries of its life, the wild garden thrummed and clamoured. The songs of birds wind-chimed through it, the purr of bees and dragonflies.

'You see the bush,' he said, in my own language, to be sure. 'That is from the lands of the Equator.' In Kronian, gusty with admiration, he added, 'A rogue seedling from their hothouses. But the foreigner has taken root. It thrives.'

The huge tubular leaves, black-green, were full of juice or oil, gleaming, drinking the sun. But what of winter, what did it do for itself then? It had survived, so presumably had evolved some system. I went to touch the leaves, and as I did, a Kronian officer appeared on the terrace from another door in the wall.

They spoke rapidly together, and I could only catch a word or two. But it seemed that General Dlant had heard of Gurz's presence and now called him into headquarters.

Gurz regarded me worriedly.

'I must go in. You will be the sensible girl? You may walk, but keep to paths we have cleared. If any speak, reference them to me. You see the pretty summer house? There I will meet you.'

The other man waited impatiently behind him. Gurz turned and said something harsh, jocular, in Kronian. He was blushing in his beard. They went in at the wall.

Oh, the happiness, the bliss. This paradise, and to be alone in it.

Vulmartis the Maiden had been my friend. She gave me this unexpected blessing.

Such sweetness, like the tipsiness of certain wines I had, at that hour, never known, bubbled through my blood. I came alive.

I got down the steps, at first walking, then in a kind of dance.

Butterflies exploded from the wild lawns, petals showered me from a low and perfumed branch.

My heart had enlarged, it seemed about to crack my ribs, stifle me, and this did not matter.

It was very strange, as if sadness itself had been the prison, and it had taken only the unlocking of its door to release me, back into the true, real world.

★   ★   ★

A miniature army was processing through the grass, its dainty flower-standards waving whenever the breeze blew. But there was not much breeze that afternoon, and the elf army spent a lot of time at a standstill.

I had gone below the summerhouse, an exquisite ruin, and found a marble nymph who once let a fountain jet from her left breast, but not now. The path was unclear beyond, but I continued, and lost myself where trees had woven together in a panelled corridor of boiling green. Savage grapes had fruited here – employing the trunks of the trees for stocks – like milky blue-green jade, sour to my taste, but the bees were intent on them.

The corridor ran on, while from the undergrowth occasionally a tilted slab, left from a path, made my excuse. This magical passage might lead out to anything, any miracle. At one place, it had a window, and gazing, I saw the hills of the garden descending to a hallucinatory city, lapped in haze. Otherwise, the avenue seemed to have no end.

When a brutish sound clocked through the trees, I was startled, but the birds, after a second of doubt, resumed their conversations. The noise was that of an axe, blunting home on sentient wood. I had heard woodcutters before, and often during the siege. To hear them now was unwelcome, not necessarily a threat. The blow came again and, regularity established, again and again.

I took another step, and an olivine toad bolted through the grass.

As if at an omen, I hesitated. Did the miraculous corridor terminate only in Saz-Kronian soldiers felling trees?

On and on, the tiresome *thunk-thunk* of the brutal axe. In another moment I was not sure of its direction. It might even be behind me, back along the route I had come.

Cautiously, I moved forward. The rough track was curving slightly, and ahead a vault of shadow had suddenly opened. Another window, or maybe door in the passage.

I reached it presently, that gap in the green sunlight. An oak guarded the breach, its mighty talons sunk deep into wet shade and emerald mosses. I held the sinews of its stem, and peered around it, into the abyss of a glade.

Thirty feet below, the axe was at its work. Helpless, unable to run away, a dying cherry quivered at each strike. Kindling for the kitchen and autumn hearths of the General and his staff? Cherry burned with a pleasing smell. Two Sazos sat or leaned on the stump of a previous victim. One smoked his pipe. A pair of the black dogs lay watchful at his feet. The man axing the King's tree was stripped to shirt and breeches. The three other men who stood across from him in the glade's underwater dimness, were similarly dressed. That was their uniform, the filthy torn shirts, the faded breeches. Before, it had been the uniform of my father's army. No insignias remained, only the reflections of four single stripes along the left outer leg. These breeches no longer held a colour, but the shirts had gone from pristine white to a variety of tones and patterns. Their boots were broken, but only one man was barefoot. They also had axes, or were equipped with knives. They were ready to cut up the tree when it was down. The Kronians, who were not down, but filled the City, the earth, need have no fear of cutting.

The third of the waiting prisoners stirred, shifting his weight. He sighed, or yawned, but for a moment lifted his head. There was a brown bird fluting on a branch. He seemed to stare at it. The man was Thenser.

He looked almost exactly as when I had seen him last. His eyes bruised into a mask of hollows. But he was thinner. His hair, matted, almost black, had grown longer, and his face was stubbled with several days' growth of beard. Apparently, he had at some juncture been able to shave. His fellows were fully bearded by now, like their gaolers.

He went on watching the little bird until it flew away.

Then the tree cracked and cried and fell over, and the wood was full of the effervescence of butterflies. Orders were barked in Kronian. Their dogs rose lazy yet snarling. All the prisoners began to toil at dismembering the cherry boughs and portioning its trunk, like grave snatchers on a corpse, and he was one of them.

In my green dress, clinging to the oak, he had not seen me. None of them saw me.

And I had been turned to stone.

I could not leave the spot until the tree was all in sections, and they loaded it on a sled, or on their shoulders, and carried it away. When the glade was quite empty, I came to myself. I let go of the oak stem. I wandered back along the corridor, now drooping with long liquid shadows. Turning my heels on pebbles, catching my wrists on thorns. I did not look to see. Blackbirds and nightingales chimed and rang and I never listened to them, not any more.

Gurz found me in the summerhouse, obedient. He was late. The sun was dropping towards its set, the sky rosaniline and sublime, and everywhere the scent of flowers and the shirr of nesting birds.

He said something to the effect that he and I, too, must go to our nest.

His big face was congested with some trouble, but I barely took it in. He asked me, noticing some extra silence on me, if I had been afraid, alone. I shook my head. He chafed my hands, and we walked back to the terrace and the stableyard, where the carriage was ready.

He talked to me all the way through the City to Elaieva's house, trying to make up for the desertion. I never heard a syllable.

2

Of course, I had not known what was the cause of our war with the Emperor of Saz-Kronia. Perhaps it had once or twice been discussed, between my father and his colleagues and friends, at a lunch or supper table in the Briary lodgings, but I had seldom had a part in these military meals. And I had never asked a pertinent question. In those days, what had a war meant?

Colonel Gurz, the scholar-soldier, with his volumes of march records and notations of flora and fauna of the Lilac

Palace gardens, was also prepared to keep serious matters from me.

I think it was not he did not trust me. After all, what was I? Some ignorant kitchen drab. But though he liked female company, and to speak long to it of piety or nature, or the forests of home . . . war was the business of the warmongers, the men. In fact, I believe he did not himself care for it, save as the means to travel and thus to nostalgia for all he had left behind.

As for the rumours of the City, I had less contact with it that summer than I had ever done. None of the servants gossiped with me any more. Melm the Rat continued not to see me. Anything I spied on from the windows of the house had seemed normal, the resumption of day to day living.

Several mornings after my visit to the King's garden, an outcry in Hapsid Forum awakened me from my hot and restless sleep.

I went unwillingly to a window. I thought that some faction from the lawyers' offices, which the Kronians had mostly shut, had come again to batter on the doors of the court.

About thirty Sazo soldiers were straggled across the Forum, most of them roaring and calling, in their own tongue. Two had climbed into the dry horse trough. They seemed to be fighting. Another man was attempting to climb the king's statue, carrying trailed from one shoulder a gilded Kronian bear banner.

Abruptly, a contingent of Sazo cavalry came clattering up West Avenue and burst into the Forum. They galloped straight at their own men, scattering them. Some of the horsemen yelled. Their swords were drawn, brandished but held aloft. Only one soldier was knocked over that I could see. He rolled frantically aside from the hoofs, under Elaieva's railings.

When the charge pulled up, the unmounted soldiers were marooned in patches, disgruntled, no longer making a noise. But the climbing man had gone on, up as high now as the stone king's knee.

The cavalry captain shouted an order at him, to get down. The climbing Sazo paid no attention.

At that, the captain gestured one of his riders forward. This fellow had a flint-shot which he proceeded slowly to load from a pouch at his waist. The horses stood stock-still, even when the captain bellowed again after the soldier on the statue. That time, he glanced down. Two or three of the foot-soldiers in turn shouted up at him, urging him to descend.

He seemed undecided. In that half minute the officer lost his patience. He rapped out in Kronian: '*Bring him off.*' I understood the words.

The flint-shotter wound back the spring, pointing the funnel up into the morning.

The climbing soldier made a mad flamboyant cast with his flag, trying to get it over the statue's head. It failed him, and the flint-shot clacked. The soldier screamed, and one of his legs was bright crimson from knee to ankle, and then he dropped directly down into the Forum, the banner going with him. They landed at the statue's base and did not move.

Presently the soldiers had taken him up, cleared him away, and all the Kronians were gone, leaving a few horse droppings to be collected, and the astonishing brilliance of fresh blood, which soon dried to black along the king's pedestal.

I sat on the bed to think about what I had witnessed. I was not concerned as to its meaning, not even properly shocked by injury and perhaps death, for though I had never seen them so close, I had heard so much of them. Nevertheless, a deadly unquiet settled on me. It adhered itself to the depression that had dogged me from the beautiful garden. They were facets of a whole. Other fragments must be added before the shape of the monster grew visible.

The leaves of the Avenue trees had had an autumn look all summer long, but now they began to fall.

People came out to collect them off the streets, and I saw the house servants gathering them between our hedges. It would be for fuel or compost, portending, like the anxious

66

foraging of birds, a difficult winter for the invaded City.

Gurz had been often away even by night, a treat marred only by his inevitable returns.

'I have told you something of the Homeland,' he said to me in Kronian one afternoon, when we lunched together in the sitting room. 'Should you like to see my country, Aara?'

I gazed. Then said politely that it would be very interesting. It was as if he had offered to show me the surface of the moon: Out of the realms of the possible, and I did not wish anyway to go.

Nothing else was said on this subject until seven that evening, when he was again summoned, by two mounted officers, to attend General Dlant.

'You see, Aara,' he paused, with his gloves and cloak, in the dusky room which, as only I would be there, Melm would not bother to illuminate, 'you see, little girl, your King has done a very foolish and unprincipled thing.'

I suppose I looked surprised. I had been brought up on the royalist courtesy of the commissioned army.

'Yes, Aara. He surrendered your city to us, and with it, all cessation of a capital implies. Now he has made a pact elsewhere, with our enemies.'

Bemused, I lowered my eyes. Saz-Kronia was the enemy. Were there then others?

'It is conceivable,' he said, 'the Emperor may relinquish the city.'

But surely this was fine news for me – if it had conveyed anything.

'I can't leave you,' he said all at once, his face darkening, 'to what will come after. No.' Then, shaking his head, falsely as well as ponderously skittish, he added, 'You will say nothing of what I have said? Put it out of your mind. I will care for you.'

When he was gone, I lit candles and a lamp, and sat down to crayon the picture of a castle borne high upon a cliff of trees. But it was too like other scenes, palaces, forts. I dawdled, doodling, nibbling the colours, arranging the sticks in squares and stars on the paper, going to the windows to stare at the curfewed night.

But I did not want to go to the moon. It was unthinkable; therefore the thought of what he had said did not loiter. Out of my mind indeed it was put.

In sleep, far down, it was the siege again, a deep rumbling moved, and screaming skittered batlike through the rafters of night. Fire lit the mirror. Thenser was running with me down an endless alley. The smell of cinders and gunpowder replaced the air. Nightingales sang in bloody, smouldering trees.

A door slammed in the house beneath, and I woke and something was alight across the City. The cries and pummelling of feet had died away.

Without warning, I was terrified. I got out of bed, crowding into a robe, rushing to the sitting room.

Melm was there, smoking one of his master's pipes calmly. He did, this once, glance at me. In my language he said, 'Go back to your bed. Nothing. A small riot beside your Pantheon.'

The pipe smoke had indecently entered my dream. The slam of the door – someone had brought something, for a large leather box was on the table. Sometimes Gurz received papers in such a container.

There was no one who would help, so I returned to the bedroom, closing the door. I lit the candles, and the two gods of the Kronians, bear and wolf, reared up and opened their eyes.

Taking the krater, I poured a trickle of wine into the cup of Urtka, as Gurz had taught me. To the Wolf I might not offer. He was the creature of the domestic Kronian tradition, home and culture, marriage, birth, honour, and the intimate rites of burial. He would perhaps protect me since I was the belonging of Gurz.

How quiet the City had become. As if it had been slain.

I lay on my back and watched the bear and the wolf. As I did so, I remembered that today would be the festival of

Vulmartis, the autumn Vulmartia. They would crown her with poppies and cornflowers, and lay wheatsheaves, rye, grapes and apples at her slender feet. In the villages they carried her icon in procession, but at the Pantheon, her image was static, worth, they said, ten bags of gold. Gold leaf was thick on her, and costly jewels were in her eyes, green sapphires from the Orient. Her silk robe was embroidered with pearls, chrysoprase, amethyst . . . Had Thenser been running towards the Pantheon? Surely, yes. It was an alley that threaded along behind the Mile. Why should that be? But in her hands, chrysanthemums were placed, the flowers of victory and death—

The black polished eyes of the Wolf-god were telling me to sleep, for night was his time, when he quartered all the woods of the world, coming like a spectre on the feeding deer, who did not run away but lay down before him as if sleeping, for his will. Those who heard his song would perish, but to find his long footprint, in the dew or winter snow, that was lucky. Lupins grew from the print, the grey-blue wolf flowers.

Lupin grey, the window at last. Vulmartis Morning.

I huddled into my robe again and crept to the bedroom window. There was a chill today, at first light. Outside, uncertain flickerings in the trees of birds or vanishing spirits. Smoke – or mist – in one low pool, across the half-drawn roofs. Soon, the sun.

I crept the other way, to the bedroom door, thirsty for a pitcher of barley drink partly full on a sideboard of the outer room. Would Melm-Rat still be sitting there, like a warden for the box of documents? He was not. Only the shadows had sat down about the table where Elaieva had allocated her possessions, her hair all loose. I had recollected her age. She was twenty-six, when she killed herself. Tomorrow – I would be fourteen.

Having got and gulped my drink, I stood irresolute. Somehow, because I had slept so well and to excess, I was to be denied the gift of sleep. I should never sleep again.

I drew the curtains of the windows, and the lupin light

shone like ice on the lock of the leather box.

To these locks Gurz kept two keys, one always on his person, the other in a drawer of Elaieva's desk. I went to the drawer, and tried it. There was no reason for my action, only something to do in lieu of sleep. The drawer did not give. But this lock also had two keys. My protector was unaware of the fact, let alone that in the green casket my aunt had rendered me, the second key reposed.

The casket was stored with my things, in a cupboard of the bedroom. He never pried. It was some toy I had stolen, along with the dresses I and the two maids, Loy and Mouse, sported.

When I had the official leather box opened, I found that, as usual, it was full of papers, mostly in covers and tied by strings. Above, a sheet of vellum, capped with the Kronian arms and the raven, and marked in ink: *From Pantheon Sector*. In a tight, unpleasant hand, the letter read in my pedantic translation: 'To Colonel Gurz, in haste. According to the general policy, you will commit by code and thereafter destroy. Beneath are names of those who, under present conditions, are deemed dangerous if living. Again, as is usual, other men will take responsibility for a similar task. Your signature is requested before noon, day following. You will note, some names have subsequently been erased, after deliberation on their potential as servants of the Emperor's plan. Conditions here do not leave space for the nicety of drawing up this list again, and you will neither query erasions nor hesitate to sign on this account.'

There was below an indecipherable scrawl and a seal punched into black wax.

I lifted the order and there lay the death list, on dull red paper, traced by official signs, but dirty, and with a blot of ink upon it.

I did not count the number of the names, but noted three were scored through rapidly, until illegible, and a single letter, perhaps an initial, scratched next to them.

Fifth along the column, Thenser's full name, written neatly, and not scratched out.

I raised my head, like a beast that scents the dawn, the blade of light, too near.

My heart was cantering inside me. I was deafened by the surge of blood in my ears. If he were on the stair, I should not hear him through it. But how could that prevent me?

As with Pantheon Sector, meting out justice in the throes of riot, there was no space for niceties. Had I, with my faulty expertise, misread the word *some*, was it maybe an exact number, penned in a new way unknown to me – would the ink of the desk not match the ink of the list – should I be able to copy, my hand sweating, the initial of the scorer?

When I tore the pen across and across, the paper ripped. I was appalled, but – rather than disqualify – this frenzy set my deletion more at one with the rest.

Not once did I think of the other men I might have saved, or that I left to die. I could not rescue them all. They were not real to me. Vulmartis on her Morning bound my eyes.

When it was done, the box shut up again, all evidence removed, I staggered exhausted back into the bedroom, I curled myself together, whimpering softly, covering my head against the sword of the sunrise.

And in a trance I waited, and when he returned in the yellow, shut-lidded day, I feigned unconsciousness, and heard the huge breathings and grunts of his own, but did not sleep.

Long before noon, he was out of bed again, breakfasted, undid the box, received the matter within, looked heavy, signed without any check a dull red paper. An envoy on a horse collected it and sped away.

In the bath chamber I knelt and vomited. I had a fever.

'No, no, you must not be ill, my chick. Not now.' He was very concerned. He had a doctor in. It was only a female ailment, some colic. A medicine of chalk. I should be well tomorrow.

The bells rang for the Vulmartia, I thought, but perhaps only in my skull.

3

Fear came to me, riding a bottomless inner silence. I dozed
and did not sleep and ideas circled in my brain, but under all,
the enormous vat of nothingness, and I, a tiny speck, floating
at the brim. It had been really most simple, what I had done.
Vulmartis had given it me to do. But I had brushed against
Fate, Death and Truth, giants towering in a child's stumbling dark.

That I was, overnight, a different age, that in some form
assisted me to bear it. But it was not enough. What sequential
deed could now put right the jarring of the inner machinery,
my heart, my soul?

Must I confess to him? Yes, an awful wave coming over me
at the notion seemed to affirm that this certainly would
relieve me. As to a priest, I could give up my burden. But to
confess to Keer Gurz was to negate the act itself. And if I
somehow yearned for that, I would not embrace it.

The chapel of Elaieva's suite was accessible to me. He did
not ever forbid me respect for my own gods, and had told me
that with the peasant women of the Homeland, *Vulmardra*
was revered in small ways, a pastoral deity.

She poised above her altar, very white and hygienic. (A
maid came to attend the shrine, the lamp was lit again,
Elaieva's withered flower had been swept off.)

I knelt, as I had knelt for illness. I prayed, but thought of
how she had failed me, before. But I must not insult the
goddess. The goddess had utilised me as her instrument – oh,
take away the onus, the debt. And I have no offering, please
forgive—

Daylight wept a petal-pool of stained glass from the
rose-eye oriel haloing her head. I stared at it, and knew. I had
an offering. That should be my relief. No need, this done, to
search for absolution. Not a word need ever be said.

That evening, the Colonel returned in the twilight, when they
were lighting the street lamps, and the candles in the houses
round the Forum. Certainly I knew that he approached, for

Melm, forearmed, wound himself through the suite, with taper and flame.

I sat ready, at the table, bathed and groomed, my face painted in the Loy way, and wearing my blouse Loy had cut and fretted with a ribbon.

When Gurz leaned to kiss me, his fingers touched my bare shoulders and he started. I did not speak, it was too soon. I had to relearn him as my companion, for I had come to know him in that manner very well.

Dinner was brought. He ate and drank. I picked about as was my habit, 'Like a little hen,' he would say. Then, the quarter glass of wine was passed to me, which tended to signify an occasion. Tonight I needed it, and was grateful.

The large face, the beard that comprised two thirds of it, confronted me across the candles and the wine. He began to talk to me in my own tongue, which had not really happened for days.

'I do this hoping to be sure you comprehend. I have told you – the king of this country has reneged upon the vows made my Emperor. We cannot hold the city, for—' here he mentioned lines of communication, provisioning, and fighting and enemy tactics – all a strange stew composed from his unwieldy clasp of my language, and my own mute inattention. For, whatever this was, I was far beyond it, now. 'And so, we are to go North, at least, I will inform you, to the border. The General has said, "This city has become a gallows, but we will not hang ourselves on it. Let them do so, with their own ropes." This saying I have noted down in my book.' He was grieved at my country, my king, my city. We had behaved wickedly. And I, too, did you but know.

'So now, in two days, we begin to leave. There are some other ladies going. There will be for us a carriage. You may take what is necessary. This journey is quite a lengthy business. But you need not be afraid. I kept you safe, have I not?' He smiled. He was hearty and full of woe. 'Nothing shall make me desert you here. It will be – not a healthy time. Besides, she is my little friend, my Aara. How can I be parted?'

'Yes, I'm yours,' I said, in Kronian. His face altered, as if a tide of harmony had suddenly smoothed over all its strain, washed it to a kind of peace and youth.

'My sweetling,' he said.

'But,' I said, and I was confounded a moment, knowing no proper decorous phrase, only the coarse euphemisms of Loy, but then the line of an old silly song came to me, and I was sure it would do, it was even translatable. I murmured, 'But make me one with you.'

His eyes flashed wide. His face flushed and blushed.

He said, 'No, no, what are you meaning?' in Kronian. He had had women, he was many years older than I. Yet I, the naive virgin, must lead him. I said, in Kronian, 'As if it were the marriage night.'

In his eyes were tears. Terrified now, this was lost on me. He took me between his hands, against the black beard, and held me close. 'Aara,' he said. 'I wanted that you would come to me. I shall be gentle. I know, you are very young. I won't harm you, my pretty, tender girl.'

I relaxed somewhat, and leaned against him. At least, now he would see to everything.

A being of honour, he was true to his promises. He was considerate to the limit of possibility, and though the congress could not, for me, be without pain and a great deal of discomfort, surprise, embarrassment, and frank disbelief, yet it was managed, I survived. My unknowledge and my flesh were rent, but otherwise I remained intact.

Afterwards, he tended me, the tiger soothing the hind. He assured me he had not, and would not, chance my pregnancy, for I was only a child still myself.

He was happy. He recited to me love poems of the Homeland I could not follow, nor did I try.

The sacrifice had been awarded the goddess. I felt how the burden had gone from me, and in the arms of my lover, remembered the lesson of sleep.

Part Two

THE RETREAT

Chapter One

1

Urtka-Tus, the Bear's Boy, led his troops out of the City loudly, as he had brought them in. The drums thudded and the trumpets pealed. Every regiment leaving that day marched behind its standard and battle honours. Many of the trees were leafless, and the first White Wind, as the villagers call the Northern winds that bring the frost and finally the snow, was puffing along the avenues and boulevards. The domes of the Pantheon sparkled on a silver sky.

After every battalion rattled its mile or so of provision wagons, and carts full of loot taken from the city, or 'given' by citizens. Women rode in some of these vehicles, who had given *themselves* to the Kronians. I heard it said that they were spat at, from windows and door-cracks. But there was also a handful of another sort of female – ladies – shut in the carriages of officers. Like these, I. Keer Gurz's equipage, its blinds down, well-appointed and drawn by two stylish geldings, had also been packed with baggage, which lay about my feet and over the seat opposite. Gurz was obliged to ride ahead, with the staff officers. For some reason it was important to depart in a show of strength. Five thousand men, under the command of a Quintark, were temporarily deposited in the City, to settle the last of Kronian affairs; if needful to offer rearguard action to rebels, or forerunners of the King's troops.

The mathematics of this were made known to me, perhaps even at the time, but I assembled them in proper order months, years, after. My ability with the Kronian language improved with every hour I journeyed, for now it was almost the only thing I heard around me. My cognisance of the terms of adult war and adult method remained fairly vague. I left it all to them, the universe they seemed to know so well. I was only adrift there.

For several days the exodus, or my part in it, was uneventful. The first two days, and the intervening night, we travelled without a halt, save for purposes of relief, and briefly to rest the horses. The pace was steady but not relentless, the road itself excellent. For some while we kept to the ancient Great North Walk, built for a king's armies three centuries previously and always in repair; the Kronians found it highly satisfactory. My spells in the country had taught me not to be shy or in difficulties at natural functions performed in the wilds. The travelling commode with which the carriage was supplied I ignored. (And the first evening, when an unseeing Melm came to attend to it at one of the longer halts, how glad I was that, possibly because I was invisible, such baseness did not involve me.) My knack for sleeping regained, this was also fortuitous. I drowsed in the rocking cradle, oblivious for hours. Though once through the out-skirts of the City, Gurz had ridden back, enormous on a horse, to inform me I might raise the blinds, I saw nothing very novel at the start – flat fields of burned grain, bare bushes, dry vineyards. Only the night upon the open land reminded me of our excursions to City parks. Dawn, how-ever, soaking through the dark with one limpid dazzling star (Vespal), above a rumpled coverlet of woods, recalled the village holidays again, and caused me to dream of my mother. I woke crying, but the hurt was soon gone. It did not have much purchase on me now.

The worst of the carriage was its stuffiness, although after the blind-raising I was able to ventilate the windows a fraction on their hinges.

The second night, already some six hundred miles from the City, the forward contingent, which included much of the cavalry, the carriages and the wagons of Tus Dlant's staff, made camp on a broad upland of which I had taken some notice in the sunset, where it rose dramatic on a vermilion sky.

The first camp was picturesque. This was even remarked on. I beheld two or three of the celebrated officers' ladies strolling with their escorts about the bosky terraces, even a telescopic lens being set up to criticise constellations, or distant mounts of interest in the country around: It was clear, a moon-blazoned night.

Melm, veteran of the march, set a fire, oversaw the care of his master's horses, and when Gurz appeared, waited on him, and incidentally on my nonexistent self, laying a snowy cloth upon an unfolded folding table, serving us on the usual sphinx service which had somehow come with us.

Gurz was animated at being with me. He drank to my health in the (normal) krater of wine. He had missed me, he said, and been anxious, but I was brave, his valiant little chick. When a tent had been erected, we went into it, and he possessed me with accustomed caution followed by upheaval. The heat of his body, his heaviness scalding on me, oppressed me atrociously, but the pain was much less. I foresaw I should soon be able to endure the union perfectly well. To my immense pleasure he was obliged to go back to Dlant's tent, and regretted he would not return again, probably, that night. We should set off at sunrise.

Later, comfortably solitary, I woke, and found that the absence of carriage motion did not lend itself to my rest. Crawling to the entrance of the tent, I gazed out.

The full moon, veiled now by our smoke, was setting. The hundreds of fires that bloomed across the upland, and away and away into the recesses of the dark, were altogether one huge dying hearth, some of which was going out, some gone, and some still a lively scarlet. The nocturne was not silent either, since battalions of foot-soldiers were continually marching in through all the hours of darkness, and making their own camps or bivouacs. The sentries prowled. I watched one high up on a rocky promontory, a long while leaning on a lance or on the sky, his outline gilded by the moon.

This, then, was the formula of the beginning of our retreat from the City. It prophesied intriguing things in an aspic of boredom. And it seems I had not yet learned the falsity of beginnings.

On the ninth day, which was a feast of the Bear-god, Hetton Tus Dlant gave a dinner for his staff and high-ranking officers.

Keer Gurz told me of it, and flightily inquired if I would go with him as his 'lady.' The other ladies, it seemed, would be present. I was nearly shocked to be asked, for I had learned by heart my current status. As if he read these humble thoughts, Gurz went on that I took such a pride in myself now, he had come to realise I had been one of the personal upstairs maids at the black house, not the gutter-dross of the kitchens. The siege had brought me low, but his protection had restored me. He had observed this with gladness. My demeanour at table was quite acceptable, I was modest and dulcet. He would ask only that I put up my hair – did I know how to do it? – also, if any remark were made on my youth, I should avow that I was sixteen, small for my age. He knew, he said, I could not be much above fifteen. (I think actually he was aware I was a good deal less, and may even have reckoned me younger than I was.) In his own home province, girls of twelve were considered nubile, but the cities judged differently. To vaunt a mistress under sixteen would be frowned on.

I said I would answer to sixteen, and that I would put up my hair. I had seen my mother do so endlessly, and Loy, for that matter, some of whose pins and combs had come to me, muddled with my own brushes and curling rags.

Rather than nervous, I was curious, quite hungry for the happenings of the evening.

Having taken such huge and barbarous strides, I had no criterion left, no balance in which to weigh any occasion. Besides, I was coming to a bizarre affinity with the aura of this army. I had known the being of armies all my life; and the word 'enemy' had no more pith than a lemon rind, for I had had to swallow the acid fruit entire.

Just as I never mused on Thenser's name on a dull reddish paper, how I had barred it through and through, so I did not think that I was fourteen or sixteen, or that I could not put up my hair, or sit across a table in a pavilion lit by flambeaux from a man who had given orders to destroy the forts of Oncharin and Hightower.

Half a dozen tents had been opened into each other to form the dining room. Melm might have laid the spotless draperies of white, while behind the leader's chair, of carved ebony, brought all the way from the North and now going all the way back, the raven standard stood crossed with the banner of the bear. Urtka himself was at the farther end, the same tall image I had witnessed borne in the triumph, but off his chariot now on a golden plinth. There were jewels in his claws, which were themselves each some five inches long. A golden bowl smouldered incense in front of him. He wore a garland of autumn crocus. Soldiers of the Fifth Spears, arriving at camp ahead of the rest, had found the flowers for him, and earned a double issue of the wine ration tonight awarded the troops.

Gurz and I were seated far down on the south side of the long table. There was not a hint of reclining, but servants brought more garlands, for the human guests only of coloured paper.

I began to count those present. There were forty-three men, aside from the General, the servers, and the aides waiting by his chair, and eleven women, scattered like lush flowers themselves in fervid dresses among the black uniforms. From their garments solely one could tell they had had, or had been brought to, riches. Their style showed they could claim breeding, were aristocrats every one. All of these women were attractive, and two were beautiful, the nearer a flaxen blonde in a flamingo gown. In thrall to their refinement, I wondered what they were doing here, seemingly willingly, with these bearlike men.

81

Not a single circumstance of theirs could be like my own.

I felt one minute an infant, fastened in my prim girlish silk to the throat and wrists, my single jewel a gold and coral bangle, Gurz's gift. At another, I forgot myself, all eyes. And then, too, the oddest sensation would be coming over me, another of those moods of mine, and I seemed eldritch, decades ahead of the women here, on some road they would never tread.

No politics were mentioned at the lengthy meal. The pastel-eyed leader, the Bear's Boy, led us in the toasts to the god, and in reminiscences of the Homeland. It became a larger, gaudier version of my suppers in the City with Gurz. At intervals, the men flirted gallantly with the ladies, and toasts, too, were drunk to them – to us. Talk was conducted completely in Kronian.

For the dinner, it was opulent. Things appeared on the plates I had never seen in all my days, though had sometimes heard of. I ate pieces of these uneasily. There were, too, many sorts of drink, including a black beer and a straw-pale brandy, these latter served only to the men. The party became slightly uproarious, but I had not joined in the drinking, either. Gurz on my right constantly covered my glass from the servers, though once or twice he gave me a sip from his own. The god-toasts I drank in water. He joked about his cosseting of my sixteen years to his neighbour, a grizzled Tritark who drunkenly nodded.

Only the lure of the blonde's half-holy loveliness staved off ennui. Of course, for all her exquisite airs, and though younger, she was like my mother – like the mother therefore of my earliest and most secure season.

I did not let her catch me staring. The eyes of such a quantity of men were on her, in any case.

Her cheeks had soon flushed, a blonde's high colour, from the wines and the hot tent. From her escort's attentions, too, conceivably. You could not miss he supposed her a prize. From his insignia I had told he was another Tritark, a commander of three thousand. Despite his rank, he was one of the youngest men in the pavilion, even I could see, for I had Gurz now to compare him with, not much more than thirty-one perhaps – my father's age – but otherwise, unlike my father. Was he handsome, this Sazo? How the blonde lady hung on him, denuding for him his fruit, putting it into his ripe pink mouth. His beard was trimmed close to the jaw and the moustaches archly combed. His short hair covered his skull like that burnt black stubble fossilised on the razed fields . . . brown eyes – which were staring back at me, humorous, and menacing—

Turning the shade of his lady's dress, I averted my glance. What I read in that abrupt meeting, his vanity, his sheer *righteousness* of self, I did not interpret, but a feeling of aversion, and of fear, went through me.

Then surreptitiously I looked to discover if Gurz had seen, and he had not. Not even that the other man was still waiting there, across the table on the north side, the better side, like a hunter at the mouth of a trap. A horrid realisation: Presumably throughout the evening he had partly intercepted my glances at his woman, imagining I gazed at *him*. Now, I wanted to run away.

Not long after this had happened, General Dlant rose from his place and went down the table to the Bear-god, into whose cup he poured a concoction of wine and brandy mixed. Then, on his feet before the bear, he proposed a toast to the Emperor. Every man and woman at the table rose in turn and drank it. The City women drank. The blonde. I drank it. It meant nothing, I was only concerned to avoid the eyes of hunters.

Following this toast, the women began to go out. They were not escorted, for they had their servants attending outside the pavilion. On a cue, ushered forth by Gurz, Melm appeared. Although I had drunk little, the fumes of the tent and the late hour, the chill hillside, the fear and unsureness, made my head swim. I was thankful for Melm with his lantern, even if he could not see me.

We started across the frosty grass, and the pavilion folded back its light into itself, and the men were mured up with it. I

could breathe more easily, and just then I heard the blonde
give her high springing laugh.

'Look, there she trips, old Gurz's darling. Not more than
thirteen. A babe.'

Below, the night noises of the restless fluctuating camp
came and went, but here, in the pool of quiet, her voice sped
like a bird.

And then I heard another woman saying crisply, 'She's a
pot-girl from that black house. You recall, the woman
Elaieva. The one who went mad when her brother died, and
cut her veins in the bath, in the classical mode.'

2

Although the cold is born, they say, in the North, as we drove
up through my unknown country, we had come among a
landscape hardly touched by the war. The fields, not burnt,
had only been harvested. Many trees, unpoisoned by smoke
and cinders, untapped by axes, still bore light clouds of
foliage, the colour of olives and a fox's fur.

From the chest containing my clothes, my crayons, and
other necessaries, I removed my books, or those of my aunt's
library I had confiscated. I read, I slept. Then I would sit
hypnotised by pictures in the carriage windows. Round-
shouldered hills went by, flat blades of water, and woodland
where browsing deer, on their castle walls of rock, regarded
our migration warily. Flights of geese crossed the sky going
the other way, southward, to the King. Sometimes there were
villages or settlements – unpeopled – once an ornate but
neglected temple in the middle of pasture where sheep were
grazing. The Kronian army appropriated the sheep.

I would try to draw these images. The tumble of the
carriage was against me.

Where the going was slow, I would be offered the choice of
a promenade, and take it. My limbs, cramped by sitting or
lying down, sizzled with woken blood. I was not chaperoned
on these treks, save by the attention of the coachman, but the
tide of the army, two discorporate legions advancing at

varying speeds in a weird and plastic unity, flowed all about. Now and then I would see one of the officers' ladies, in gorgeous bottle green or magenta skirts, chancing exercise as I did, or riding boldly upon a mare. Dropping back in my walk, I saw other women, too, seated in carts or stepping through the ruts of the wagons, handkerchiefs of hair blowing about their heads; ladles, knives, saucepans, and strings of onions through their belts. Quantities would have a baby on their backs. One, I recall, which wore a fleecy cap against the coming cold, appeared older than the mother, a girl of fifteen, doubtless not having to pretend otherwise.

The marching soldiers seemed a cheery rough lot, familiar in essence. Cavalry detachments on sable horses galloped up and down, kicking high clods of the frost-hardened soil, for which they were sometimes whistled. Certain aspects of discipline had relaxed.

On better ground, the carriage would again outdistance the main mass of the soldiery. The cavalry captains who passed my windows occasionally grinned at me, but more often than not did not spare a glance.

The window was very dark. Could I have slept out the afternoon? No, cavalry was riding parallel with the carriage, the sweep of black cloaks, the helms of polished iron wreathed in gold and coxcombed with storm plumes, it was these which had come between me and the daylight.

One of the men grimaced at me through the window. On his shoulder was the badge of office: A Tritark. He leaned and rapped with his gauntleted fist on the glass. It was already partly open, and I heard him say, 'What do you think of this shrimp, this fat fellow's toy, daring to put up her wanton eyes to me?'

The men laughed. I cringed. Yet seeing my terror and shame was not apparently enough. He made some other remark I could not properly understand, it had to do with my lack of allurements.

Another of them said, like the woman on the night of the Bear Feast, 'Some potscrubber. Good enough for that old

Gurz fool. At least, she has breasts. I thought he liked them still in napkins.'

The Tritark said, 'She's a slut. She couldn't keep her hot little eyes from me. Look at her. Wax skin, rat's tails. Urtka's foreskin.' (Though I had heard the oath before, I did not yet know its meaning.) 'She deserves something for her bloody cheek.'

I was in hell, and there was no rescue. But this seemed to be, at last, sufficient. They spurred their horses and swirled away.

Fright sat on with me the rest of the afternoon. But nothing else occurred. The coachman, seldom much conscious of me, would not have challenged the riders, who outranked him. In fact, he might not have heard their words.

When my protector arrived to dine with me on the unfolded table, placed in the tent now, for the nights were no longer friendly, I wondered if I should speak to him. But I could not see how to manage it. I must juggle with the adult code again, whose rules I did not really follow. To tell Gurz anything seemed to implicate me in flirting with the Tritark, or wishing to. Visualising a report of his comments on my person caused me an icy sweat. Was I so ugly? I had never before dwelled on the problem, believing I would come to sophistication and prettiness when older, by some form of inevitable sorcery. My mother had been lovely—

Gurz was melancholy that night. I did not listen to his ramblings. When he took me to bed, I was almost impatient with the struggle and death throes of his pleasure— Whatever was it that happened to him? He must be mad. Did all men, as Loy had seemed to imply, make idiots of themselves in this fashion, gasping and biting at the pillows?

He slept. I lay awake, and bit my lips in fretting at tomorrow.

The blonde woman's Tritark did not come back for two days, during which I concluded it had been his whim, now forgotten.

However, because I had heard cavalry some minutes before and revised my opinion, I had had the inspiration to let down the blinds. Once the riders passed, a red-hot noose unsqueezed from my throat. Then, he was there.

He thumped the carriage door.

'Who's in this carriage?' he cried. 'Some filthy spy?'

My impulse now was to hide among the baggage.

His voice came in another tone, fawning and treacly.

'Oh, won't she let me see her, the dear little dolly? Not see her matchless beauty?'

Then he must have kicked the door from his seat on the horse; the animal protested, and he curbed it, cursing while the carriage shook.

I was nearly sick with horror. But he rode by. I heard that and hoped, and next I heard the coachman's voice, the Tritark's challenge, and the vehicle slowed and stopped. He had made us halt.

His boots now on the hard cold earth. His hard cold hand on the door. It was wrenched open.

'Hah!' he said. 'Well, what's this?' The coachman stood sulky and powerless at his back. 'All this bloody baggage, all books and brass trays and cushions. Trust Gurz, that fat buttock-brain. And look here, some white pig he's brought, some ragdoll with its stuffing out.' He reached in and put his hand on my left breast. His touch was not Gurz's touch. It was like the words.

Insane with panic, I struck him in the face with my clenched fist. He sprang back, and hit his head on the door frame.

The coachman had walked off, he was smoking a pipe under a tree. Wagons were going by. No one paid heed.

'I never looked at you!' I heard myself, amazed. 'I didn't. Leave me alone!'

But I had caught him just under the right eye, hurt him, for the eye was watering. His grin fixed rigid in a snarl. He lowered and inserted his head back into the carriage, carefully, and now I shrank away.

'You have no manners, nasty girl. Maybe I'll teach you some.'

The panic boiled up again, the smell of him, the iron and horse smell, the man-smell, the pomade with which he rinsed his close-cropped beard and hair – or just the smell of his particular brand of aliveness. The brass tray on which I had rested my drawing got under my hand. I lifted it and brought it down across his head. Contacting his helmet, it caused a terrific and farcical noise. It must have made his ears ring. He quickly backed out again and a gush of sweet white hate went through me. Holding to the door, I leaned after him and smote him again, now in the middle, sharp, with the tray's corner; I felt the impact up my arm. He staggered, knocked into his horse which, battle-trained, only sidled, but he swore at it, swore at me, and, drunk now, I struck him a third time, across a galaxy of medals on his chest, which doubtless conducted and enhanced the blow, for he shouted.

A straggle of foot was going by, they were turning to view us with restrained glee.

He was aware of that, and himself swung round at them and I crashed the tray against his side. The figure he cut, an officer of high rank, standing to be whacked by a very young girl from a conquered city – I did not consider this, nor the value he might put on it.

Suddenly he came round again and had the tray out of my hands. Pushed, I was falling backward into the luggage, and I heard a group of the Sazo soldiers giving off a sort of growling sound, but whether in gratification or disapproval I could not be sure. He took no risk. Straightening, he said, 'I shall make you sorry. Trust me.' Then he went into a catalogue of my loathsomeness too exotic for a novice's vocabulary. It still left me trembling. Finally, he delivered these words: 'By the by, tell old fatty Gurz, if you'd like him run through.' And, to my blank incredulity, he added, more plainly, 'I mean, you foreign vermin, if you think Gurz can stop me dealing with you as you deserve, I'll settle you with one hand and him with the other.'

When he went, cantering away on his horse, the coachman

cast me a glance full of contempt. I could dream of no help from him, but he had already shown that.

The carriage started off. Oh, why had I attacked the beast? Now it could not be propitiated – I sensed blindly and too late that I had only incited, *invited*.

3

This Tritark's name was Drahris. His family connections were not to the General, but circumstantially to the Emperor himself. He was young for his command, and not popular, but men were mindful of his position. Even Dlant would not wish to fall out with him. In war, Drahris was incorrigibly reckless, his bravery was renowned, but three battalions had already been sacrificed to his fire-eating. Himself, he would ride headlong, against the walls of mounted men, against the mouths of active cannon. Charmed, he never received a serious wound. His prowess with women was also legendary. But, though socially chivalrous, he was reputed to treat his mistresses roughly. They would wear their bruises unabashed or coyly conceal them. In the Kronian capital he had fought sixteen duels, and won them all, killing the other men – husbands, brothers, or fathers. He had once titled himself a liberator of enchained womanhood. He said he had sometimes duelled only to get a lady free from some dullard spouse. (I associated this with his threat that, if Gurz intervened, he would be 'run through.')

His blonde lady, a princess of my country, and said to be once a pet of the King's, could not stand to see her lover leave. She had pleaded with him, offering him the comforts of her carriage, her magnificent bed – which travelled with her on a wagon – and her cook, trained in the fabulous Oriental dishes of which many Kronians had grown fond on an earlier campaign.

This then, the Tritark Drahris.

Perhaps, if I had been older, wiser in the ways of these mysterious adult lands, I might have fathomed his designs, handled him or put him to use – at least, evaded him. Of course, I could not for a second suppose he was desirous of me. Why should he be – that beautiful blonde lily hanging upon him. To him I was repulsive, he had told me so, and Gurz he despised.

After the extraordinary encounter with the brass tray, I held myself in miserable alertness for any ghastly thing. That night, Gurz's talk irked me nearly to screaming, and Melm, who for once cast on me a sudden look of aversion, unleashed hysterical outcry. In floods of tears I exclaimed that Melm hated me, that I had borne his evil glares and unkindness too long. I wept for the City. Everything was mixed, I did not know what I said. Gurz comforted me ludicrously and ineffectually, saying he would chide Melm, that Melm must care for me. Melm stood by, gazing on space or infinity. Naturally, at Gurz's feeble remonstrance, loving to Melm, asking his tolerance of my weakness, Melm would rate me yet more lowly, and perhaps turn spiteful. They were all against me.

In the lamp-dark, the outer fires of the camp staining with red our tent, I refused my lover his rights. But I had an excuse which, with lumbering tact, he accepted. It was true enough. I was now demoralised by the onset of my monthly female time, whose advent I had been dreading. Unlike the ordinary functions, this would pose difficulties, for I had no maid, no woman to assist or advise. I could only do what I could, involving much waste, and pray that we should arrive at some civilised settlement where I might lay in fresh stores for myself.

Vulmartis, setting this chore upon women, had always seemed to me to have played them an awkward trick. An old wives' tale had it that the goddess took blood from women in this way as an offering, in lieu of the blood men shed for Origos on the field of war.

Next morning we were up with the larks, which had neither the distress of menstruation nor sadists to contend with, and careered about the opal sky in a threnody of autumnal lament. The year was dying. In forty days or less we should be at the border, not a moment too soon.

4

We were to go picnicking. An accent of fine mornings, sunny afternoons, and wooded valleys with hunting to be had – in four days the retreat altered to an excursion. The gods of the Kronians were obviously with them. The north of my country was not populous, and by getting off the Great North Walk and on to lesser tracks inside a week, they had avoided our towns, and only passed through the intermittent villages of the region – many of which had been voided (and stripped) in anticipation. There seemed nothing to it all. I did not marvel at the picnic, and yet a curious chord was sounded within me, something ominous I could not name.

Four days, too, I had not been plagued by Drahris in person. But I had heard a lot of gossip about him, learned his name and fame, from the coachman with the grooms, stray soldiers, or the camp followers as we went by their cookfires in the dusk. His momentary proximity had roused up the chat. Sometimes, one would nudge another, indicating me, or Gurz's carriage.

I was too distressed to determine on a course. The respite – he was away to the west with his men, foraging and hunting, I gathered – scarcely consoled me. I almost wondered if he had tipped those about me to mention him in my hearing. Where his interest could only perplex me, his disgusting malice seemed now inevitable. I did not begin to guess what he would want of me, what torture or penance would be exacted. Probably he would beat me. In hopeless terror, I had reasoned that I must refuse to leave the carriage and must remain in sight of others. Though I had no one who could or might come to my help, I had already seen he reined himself before witnesses.

In a way, I do not know how I lived with that first real personal fear. But anything prolonged, even terror, becomes habitual, losing, if not its edge, the power to startle or stun.

For the picnic, Gurz had me placed in a small chariot behind two piebald mares. My driver was a plump subaltern attached as aide to Gurz. I had seen him once or twice at the black house (he had attended the burial of my aunt in her garden). Cheery enough, pleased to find me on his side, he was gallant and told me long, complicated jests, at which I dutifully laughed, when he did, though generally I had fallen by the wayside of his language minutes before the kernel was cracked.

The legions trudged behind and below and sometimes in part ahead of us, as we rattled away aslant the march. Up ahead, Gurz on his horse, studying a twig or a bug on a bough, while the horse ate mast from the lower tree. Much farther on, the ladies had come out in force and were riding pell-mell through the bare avenues on horseback with their officers, a flash of mantles and laughter. But the blonde princess had gone hunting with the Tritark's detail. My subaltern sighed and said he was sorry we should not see them, since how lovely she was, that princess.

The woods became peaceful, softer and brighter at these words. I had not been sure. Now the sun woke and peeled the stems to yellow; wild roses, blighted by frosts a moment before and hung out like crushed paper, showed me they were still alight. The leafless beeches, the fletched cones of evergreens, belled with birds. Then I thought of a young man in a soiled shirt, staring up at a bird in a glade – and it came to me that the awful little chord which had sounded within me had not been due to apprehension of the Tritark. What was it then? Thenser – no, not Thenser. I could not even recall his face. *He* had never existed.

It was a dream I had had, long since in the City . . .

Gurz rode back to show me a branch where blossom had begun, gone mad at the sunshine, to bloom all out of season. He had broken the branch in any event. This was its reward for blooming. As a cherry tree was cut down for the perfume of its logs.

Through the lower defile of the woods, about half a mile away, the Kronian army trundled on. Men in ranks, or not, the standards lying stacked in carts, some scrambling at a ditch and a mule down, being urged with caresses and kicks, a war-chariot piled with flour sacks, slack-bellied. Odd indicative vignettes.

I held the dying blossoms and laughed at another of the subaltern's incomprehensible japes.

Soon we reached the picnic ground.

Hetton Tus Dlant was not among us. A few officers of the staff were present, and a batch of colonels climbing trees like schoolboys to toss pine nuts to the outheld skirts of their paramours or the helmets of respectful majors. There were women here who had not attended the Bear dinner. For a second, seeing some of them were quite youthful, and of my own class as it had been, I ached at the possibility of friendship. But they were preoccupied with their masters, and I – I had a reputation already, a maid who had bettered herself, a little tart. Besides I was the youngest there, and Gurz one of the oldest. This had never properly been borne in on me before. He was the pedant of the party. They tolerated him. He had never fought a single engagement.

Servants spread cloths, and set out our feast. It was not comparable to the dinner, rather spare in fact, though this was no annoyance to me. Knowing my preference Gurz brought me a goblet of red currant juice, but it was not sweet enough. The subaltern, smiling behind Gurz's back (even he), offered to lace it for me with straw brandy. I refused.

In the distance the rumble of the legions continued, like a river in a gorge.

The other noise had no prelude.

There was an abrupt dull thud, muffled, almost meaningless, but the earth seemed to quiver under me. Every bird in every tree ceased its music.

After the noise, silence. Then one of the aristocratic ladies screamed, faint and thin, and there was the punctuation of her glass dropped and smashing on a stone.

The men were leaping up, buckling on cast swords. Fruit went rolling over the rugs, the tree roots. All was in motion, and the horses neighing. Gurz rose before me. 'I have said this would be,' he announced. 'Their king, this Alliance of

93

Charvro—' Cannon had sounded. The muddled ranks would be and were in turmoil, all the lackadaisical disorder rushing for positions, the outriders sprinting to describe the pitfall, the ambush, some part of the forward march already embroiled – and Gurz would give me a history lesson. But no, he was thinking better of it. 'You will stay here,' he said, 'all the ladies will be safer here.' He moved off, to dispense his advice. But everyone was getting to horse, or into the little chariots. My subaltern ran after Gurz, bleating that he must return to his battalion—

I stayed where I was, seated on a rug, listening to the shouting of the soldiers, the raw notes of a trumpet, then another. I was waiting for the next blast of cannon. It came. My stomach pitched. I had grown so used to them, in the months when the Kronians shelled the City. But— These guns were the guns of the King's allies, perhaps even of my father's army, his regiment, the White Lions— Finding myself on my feet I did not know what to do. Gurz was on his horse, he rode over to me. 'Sweetling, stay here. The servants will remain, you'll be safe. The General will wish my presence.' As if bounding off to take on single-handed all the enemy at once, he plunged away.

The guns again, one, *two – three*. I could smell pitch and smoke, saltpeter. Were they nearer, or was the land simply sliding down into the mouth of war? I wanted to see. This time, I truly did.

The servants were pressed together under a conifer tree, as if to shelter from a shower of rain. Unhindered I walked away through the wood, in the direction of the forward lines, keeping to the sloping height that ran from the picnic ground.

As I went, the day changed. It intensified to a fleshy thickness, of the light, and of the atmosphere. There was a steady roaring, like winds. All the birds had flown. Once some deer arrowed past, shot out of the smoky coverts ahead. Then a thunder of cavalry came crashing down from the higher woods, breaking the sapling trees like a black gale, their standard a streamer of blood and fire. The hair stiffened on my scalp. I stood aghast one instant, then I was running after.

A fissured tower on a hill, that was where they had placed their cannon to command the exit from the valleys. There was a flag flying there now, far away and smudged in vapours, but a pale flag I had never seen. The hillside beneath was awash with the battle, and the scoop of the valley, like a turbulent sea. The smoulder-cloud lay heavy, save when it split to the flame-splash of Kronian guns, jammed into the throat of the track where the valley narrowed, or an exploding shell. (Some trees were burning across in the wood, a straight column of sparks and smoke.) Things roiled and surfaced in the sea of cannon-cloud. The banners tore it, a wagon was subsiding like a sinking ship.

Quite near to me, three Sazo soldiers broke from the depths. The man in the middle, held up by the others, was bleeding, his face grey, and he laughed stupidly, or he was sobbing. As they blundered by, one of the outer soldiers bawled at me meaningless phrases in an alien tongue. Then I remembered that I could speak some Kronian. He had been telling me *Down, lie down*. I did so, crawling on my belly, my chin scraping the bearded chin of the world.

The guns on the hill spoke again. Their firework was more clear, for they were higher in the morass. In fascination, I watched a ball, a tail of aimless black, go over half the sky and descend as if weightless into the valley. Where it broke – a surf of light, curious shades of blue and orange.

I saw the charge which took the hill. It looked like nothing of much importance, a stream of men and horses, the white-black mirror-blink of steel, and then like ants overrunning an anthill, a medley, a bewilderment. One last Kronian shell burst on the escarpment below. Then the flag toppled from the tower. It occurred to me to wonder what I did there, the savage excitement that had hurled me forward, and deserted me, finding a scene so unlike any tales I had been told of war.

The last men were hacking, slaughtering and dying in the

valley smoke. They would, my companions, take no prisoners. The Charvro Alliance, of which my country had become a part, had offered irritation, but nothing more, a flea-nip in the flank of their power.

The tower had been part of a convent or other religious building. As the upper air cleared, I made out an archway, a pillared cloister, and one of the guns speechless there, the long headless neck still breathing its last plume.

Riders arose from the smoke. Their faces were powdered with black, and some had blood on them, and all had blood on their swords and lances. I could hear screaming now, hoarse and strong, away in the smog. The horses rolled their red eyes, steam came from their mouths like the cannon plume. A stink came from them all, the foul stench of battle.

In his helmet of iron and gold, his blackness crossed with silver and blood, face black, hands black with blood, red sword, a man riding leisurely across the wood had angled towards me.

The vistas closed again. The sun smothered in an eclipse of smoke. The cavalry troop was gone.

Tied to his stirrup was that which I did not believe. Even when I accepted its reality, it made no impression, it was too frightful for that. Somewhere in his reckless charges he had decapitated a man. The long hair had proved handy, in attaching the bauble. I had heard the Kronians did such things. Who had said so? Was it Loy? Some other girl—

'Wiparvet,' he said, 'brings the man to the woman. I might have known you'd be here, lapping the blood.'

I got up. I felt no fear. Like the severed head, I did not believe in this.

I began to walk without haste back through the wood, the way I thought I had come. He walked his horse which was snorting, stinking, like the others, rolling its scarlet eyes, beside me.

Drahris spoke gently to me. He told me what he would do to me. Astounded, I heard it all. Even Loy had never whispered of anything this obscene or improbable. He said, too, he would beat me, the only act I had conjectured. He

96

said my ugliness would grow lovely as he laboured on me, the welts and bruises. He would let me fight him.

All at once, I ran away. There almost seemed no reason to, for what he had promised was not possible.

The horse trotted behind me, blowing, burning so I sensed its heat like a scorching breath.

A path slithered down between the trees, twisting, and I jumped on to it, through swathes of smoke. Something felt as if it snapped then between the man and myself, a net ripped or a leash giving way. I sprawled forward, and came against the side of a cart. There were soldiers crouching there, bloody and foul and rowdy, and a woman was doling out to them beer from a broached barrel.

'Here, girl, do you want a drink? Celebrate the victory?'

But I pushed through them and they let me, amused to accede to an unarmed woman after they had sliced Charves.

So I thrust on, through warriors and beer barrels and overturned carts, across an area where they were taking wounded men, who screamed and howled blasphemy, and through a knot of women arguing over a dead donkey. But all the time, the tendrils of the snapped leash, ripped net, were dispersing. At last, I saw some carriages drawn up together, and Gurz's vehicle was one of them, even to the coachman, who stood cleaning his flint-shot on a length of his coat. There was blood on him also. Everything was powdered with red and black. Everything stank.

I was extremely thirsty. I would have drunk the currant juice now. I asked the coachman for water and he laughed in my face.

Sitting in the carriage, I wondered what would become of me.

But when, hours later, Gurz appeared, furious with my disobedience and jeopardy, ranting, eyes bloodshot, a lunatic like all the rest of us, I could not tell him of any of what I had seen, or of the pursuer and his vows.

Chapter Two

1

Winter, born in the north in an antique song, wakes from brooding unconsciousness among the spires of the mountains. In his armour of ice, his cloak of weather, he rides a thin stallion across the skies. Rain lances down, then sleet and snow. He covers in stone the head of the shivering earth.

After the battle in the valley, things were changed. From that point, despite their losses, the slightness in military terms of the offensive they had offered, the Emperor's foes began to harry us. They snapped like wild dogs at the hem and heels, the wheels and fringes of the Kronian retreat. It was unwise to fall too far behind the main body of troops. Small squads, loitering to toast a scrawny chicken at a fire or water their horses at some pond, were set on and decimated, only the lucky ones getting away to spread their news. Where the country assisted, the overhanging places or thicker woods, there came the clack and spat of flint-shot, and tall men were flung down. There was one town ahead, in our path, the name of which, Zoli, had become familiar. The Kronians had sacked it on the route south, and left a garrison in the wreck, fifteen hundred men, to cow the border district. Now rumour began to hint that this garrison had in its turn been ousted. The Charves were all at once brisk. They cluttered the town of Zoli, planning to shut the border and take the conqueror in his own snare. This would mean a fight, larger and more conclusive than any skirmish in a valley. The Kronian response was grim high spiritedness, the intense return of discipline, avid refurbishing of arms, drills, mock charges, parades and inspections, and a ceaseless mewing of bugles in the twilights of the camps.

But the winter was an enemy of another calibre, no pitched battle would settle the score with him. The scintillant days were put into their chest. The nights set to iron. White Winds came and did not ebb, sleet began to sheer across the land.

The General, his staff, quantities of officers, were every sunset now off the beaten track into abandoned villages or farmhouses, to sleep between bricks and tiles. Where there was no room of any kind for them, no shed or hut, the wretched soldiers clung about the sundered walls of sheep pens, sties, latrines. Lacking even that, carts were turned over, to provide a barricade against the driving screeching wind. The fires burned in low waves, a bitter yellow.

The stripped villages had also taken another toll. The supplies of food were now greatly reduced. The same men under the carts were already making do on a fistful of biscuit and raisins a day, whatever meat their company could hunt for itself, whatever part-rotten cabbages or black fruit were to be gleaned from the fields and orchards. Gurz and his peers fared better, it is true.

A week following the valley engagement, snow fell.

That morning at first light, from the door of the cottage, a single chamber I had shared with Gurz, I beheld the sugar-icing world, spoiled only by a few dull scraps of flame, the black bears of stamping men, the black stalks of a pine forest on the slope above. On the cottage roof some soldiers were seated, having climbed up in the night to warm themselves at our hesitant chimney, but they, too, had been snowed over, with helms and humpbacks of white. Somewhere the Kronian wolf-dogs were howling, but not a bugle sounded. The wind had sunk. The silence was a different one from any I had heard. It took all sounds, and made them nothing. The cold was so dreadful that it had stopped me breathing.

I had gone on with my gnawing fear of the pursuer, unable to speak. The drills and forays and harryings had kept him from me. The sheltering hovels and the winds had somehow formed up between us. Still I had known him there, behind the flimsy partition of weather, action and time. And the snows seemed to make straight his way to me. I could not have explained.

As I drew back, Gurz wrapped me in a fur cloak he had given me some nights before. Being too big increased its value.

We breakfasted meagrely, served by a mauve-handed, blue-nosed Melm.

Depression weighed upon us, as on all the world about. Only the dogs now and then still howled, horses and men were inaudible. Perhaps in each the snow unlocked, with cruel fingers of steel, some private, uncommunicable terror, more than the mere ordinary surmise that death would march away in step with all of us, from this spot.

At the start there was resistance, anger almost. One felt it in the very shape of men, as they forced their way forward, heads down against a fleering wind, or as they dug each other from snowdrifts, or sat by night about the fires, no longer solemnly dicing or drinking or polishing buckles. Presently, there was only endurance. The snow came at us, the winds, and under the wing of darkness, the heartless ice. Men were found dead before their hearths. Sentries were ensorcelled to stone, toppling like a chopped tree at the comrade's touch. You saw them carried to the fires, the living eyes in faces that had died. Then the soul went from the eyes, too. Soon I would see dead men lying by the sides of the road, and sometimes on it. The snow was deep and hard, and the frozen way bumpy. Who made comparison between the obstacles, a mound of snow, fallen bough, corpse. And out on these white wastes, in the folded forest which now accompanied the route, the stragglers, the groups of ten or twelve men, met with the warmer death of Charvish blades.

The carriage slowed. The horses hauled. A mile an hour or less. And the cold washed through as if the carriage were made of glass. One would get out to walk, desperate, but the pain of the cold, like razors or white fire, soon drove me back again. And the sight of the land, bloodless, endless, and the pines and hemlocks loaded like packbeasts with the snow, and the snow-sky, thick as alabaster – that drove me back also.

The cold ate into the lungs. To breathe was hurtful, and always you heard the coughing and cawing of men and beasts, yet such noises, with the unwieldy churn of wheels, some far-away twang of breaking branch or sword on buckler, all such the silence of the snow had mouthed.

I caught myself thinking time and again it would stop.

Coming in from the freezing street, running up the stairs to my mother, who would rekindle my hands in hers, the prancing fire, the mulled herbal tea with sugar, putting my numbed feet under the patient cat to warm them. But here, such states as the cold, or the fear, were eternal.

2

'There's nothing. You may take yourself off.'

It was Melm who was speaking, irate and decisive, at the entrance to Gurz's tent, which had been set up tonight in the lee of a ruined wall. For a second shock burned through me. I had an idea illimitable horror, a fiend – Drahris – approached, and that Melm possessed some ability to send him away. But it could not be Drahris, oh no, not to be spoken to like that.

And through the muffle of the snow-mouth, accordingly I heard a timid female voice, 'This is Jilza.'

'So,' said Melm.

'But – it's Jilza.'

Melm said nothing. His omission was the answer. Then, another woman's voice, contralto in tone: 'I've things to tell her, his mistress.'

Melm said, 'Go along with you.'

There was a noise, like a shaken bridle, bells or coins.

'Colonel Gurz would let me in,' she said. She was not importunate, imperious rather.

Drawn by her strange music, I shifted the flap, and, looking for her, showed myself.

Melm turned, of course without seeing me, and said, 'These women are only begging. You've nothing to spare. I'm sending them away.'

Recently some of the women from the lower camp, the women of the wagons, the soldiers' wives and comforters, had begun to steal about the officers' quarters after dark, pleading for scraps. The stories were pitiful. They had infants which starved, or their man was laid up from a skirmish, or had a frostbitten foot – only his friends were keeping him walking. Did we have a crust we did not want, some beer – for all the issue barrels were dry – or spirit, which was better to keep the blood circulating – Gurz was not above giving away his supper of stringy poultry, a crock of butter, his wine while it lasted, to any who asked. He had drunk a krater of drink a night in the City, but now went thirsty save for icicles boiled in Melm's kettle.

For myself, my habit of poor appetite had stood me in good stead. I was accustomed to going without, and definite hunger had not yet properly found me.

However, there was nothing left tonight of a very frugal repast. And Gurz, who had eaten it, was attending the General's tent.

The huge white tablecloth of snow, laid with bivouacs, stretched up and down and away to a dull inky skyline. Before the tent door were three women, two of them wrapped in dozens of layers of rags, deformed by their windings, like crow-scarers. The other stood up tall. She was a mountain of shining black bear pelt, above which rested like a moon a fur-hooded face. A Kronian woman, one of that number who had travelled south with their army and now returned with it. Her brows were thick and black, her face white and red with a fierce natural complexion. Under the hood she wore some kind of headdress, an Eastern thing, which fringed her cheeks and forehead with rows of guttering gold medallions. She looked at me and nodded and the medallions made once more their belled-bridle sound. Her Kronian speech, though native, had an accent of the provinces.

'You are mistress to Colonel Gurz. I be Jilza. They know me, even this one,' at Melm a careless aside, 'as the teller of fates. I keep a key to the lore of the lands of Taras Ind, the secrets of the Serpent Kings. I can tell you this and that. You, in exchange, might give me what you believe I earned.' I stared, and a long white arm, naked but for bracelets of painted wood and ivory, rose itself like a serpent, pointing up into the sky. 'Do you see the orb?'

The Kronian word 'orb' was unknown to me – I looked straight up, wondering, and saw that she meant the moon itself, that other moon which was not her face.

A curious phenomenon involved it. The disc was perfectly round, and for miles the sky about it showed clear and harsh, caught with stars. Then a white circle, perfect as that of the moon's, shut off the remainder of the heavens, which were opaque and starless, fading down to blackness and the earth. It was like gazing through a rim into some vast cauldron. I had never beheld the sight before, this wide halo formed of high cirrus and particles of aerial ice. To me it was uncanny, and perturbing.

I looked again at her, for explanation.

She only said, 'I'll enter your tent.'

I let her, for it seemed to me she was in control even of the moon and the darkness, and might therefore help me, though how I could not guess. For Melm, he offered no further restraint, only turned sneering aside to a nearby fire. Her two attendant women crouched by the wall like dogs, to wait.

A pan of coals was burning on its tripod inside, and she went at once to warm herself, though without any rush. She was no age; her unlined skin was dried by the cold, but her mouth had not been cracked by it. 'Sit,' she said to me, so I sat on a stool, and next she came and sat in Gurz's chair, confronting me across the little folding dining table.

She stared at me some time. The impulse was to look away, but I thought I should not be able to. Then, there was a sort of easement in being held like that, by the strength of her gaze, which seemed of a metallic black, all pupil, but for a pair of slender outer rings of gilt, like a cat's eyes by night.

Eventually she spoke again.

'You're a child, less even than your years. Also, you are older. Should you live to be ninety, still you will be older.'

I did not understand, but could not have interrupted.

'I can tell you not so much. But something I can. Believe it?'

I stuttered like the candle before her breathing. 'Ye – yes.'

'Then, what will you give to me?'

Her face was stern and pure, but I knew, through everything, she was a trickster, too. By which, I do not mean a charlatan. Long ago Litty and I had visited the fate-reader at a fair. She had scared us, and we had gone away giggling. Her predictions were incoherent and her assumptions wrong, most of her power had been borrowed from the presence of a large lizard that lay motionless in a cage at her elbow. The woman Jilza was not of such an order. Probably she came to me because she knew I was immature, and Gurz away (as does the wicked witch in the legends). Gossip or the gods had informed her of my trouble. Both, I think now.

Before I could respond, she began to put highly-coloured cards on the table. They had gaudy pictures on them, of beings and beasts, architectures, and the symbols of planets, weapons, and plants. She set them three times, each time sweeping away the previous arrangement into her sleeve, it seemed. The final time, she left only one card, and picking it up, showed it to me. A pale woman in white and yellow on a crimson ground, with a green sun behind her head. Hyacinths spilled from one hand and changed to papers, then to smoke, blood, pearls, and drops of transparent water, as they fell. At her feet the stream became a woven carpet, the design complex but abstract. Her other hand, the right, held up a wand, which lightning was striking. She smiled, but tears were on her cheeks. She had a diamond tiara, though her feet were bare and half the edge of her garment was tattered.

Jilza said: 'This card be called the Heroine, or the World's Girl. Though it is also one of the cards of the She, the goddess Vulmardra.'

Having shown me the card, she put it away like the others. She folded her hands before me on the table top, empty.

'What will you give?' she said, and regally, 'What will you spare?'

I got up, shaking all over, and went to rummage in a box after a small bag of dried figs and another of oatmeal. I brought them. She weighed them in her empty hands.

'I can't—' I said, 'I can't give you much. It isn't mine. It's Colonel Gurz's food.'

'I will take these, then,' she said. 'And give me your bangle.'

Glancing down, at a loss, I saw the coral bracelet. Her wrists were not child-narrow, it would not fit her.

'*He* gave it to me,' I said.

'What do you care?' she asked.

I blushed. I did not care at all. Like her co-conspirator, I removed the bracelet, and handed it over. In some town of the North, it would fetch her nice hard cash.

'But if he asks—'

'He will not. He'll never ask of that.'

'I could say,' I supplied, 'I lost it.'

'As you have,' she said with a hint of humour, for it had already vanished after the cards, the figs, and meal. 'Sit,' she said again. I sat, but now, I did not meet her eyes. Already I felt *flayed*, used and abused, and made a monkey of. Yet, too, her power sang on in the tent, dizzying me.

What she said next came in a jumble through my discomfiture, my partly listening ears – I was now afraid Gurz would return and catch us – the screen a piece of me had tried to put up between her truth and mine.

Nevertheless, I was informed that about my earth-globe was wrapped the fire-snake of Ocean, who imparted burning water. She said that for some, their path was built, for others the building was to come, and so for me, but that I had another self, a shadow or reflection, of whom in turn I was also the mirror and shadow, and thus my way had already been influenced, plaited and incised, scattered with bright seed which might fruit, or might perish, but if so my very soul would itch—

And by now, still not looking at her, I was twisting, writhing on my stool. It was as if needles pierced in and out of the levels of me. I started at them and wanted no more. And as though she had mercy, suddenly, in the middle of the long chanting her words had become, she left off.

'But at this station, you're in much fear. Hunted by one moving after.'

At that, I jumped entirely, and looked up after all.

Her face was like a rock. 'You must cancel his debt.' Her hand opened, and something lay on it. 'For the bangle,' she said.

It was a tiny figure of the goddess, not more than four inches in length, made of some form of white enamel, with ochre on the hair, and the feet ending together on a brief crosspiece of iron.

'What is it?'

'An amulet,' she answered. 'See, this puncture in the hair for threading with a string.'

She rose, and her ornaments jingled.

I, too, got up, as if magnetically she pulled me.

'*But what shall I do?*' I cried, and put my hand on her fur sleeve. It was like touching the living bear. The fur itself crackled and purred with life and heat. My hand flew back. She only looked at me, and said, 'Do nothing. Will come. In that way you will find it is, for you. Remember the card, the World's Girl. Lightning is attracted. Even a flower alters.'

She collected her shining darkness and the singing of her powers and strode to the door flap. There she paused. 'Have you anything you don't want,' she said, favouring me, as if she had had nothing. 'Some warm shawl, maybe.' And I went to the rug bed and took up the shawl there and gave it to her. 'I wish you might see the joy this warmth will bring the poor women,' she said.

The tent seemed to fall in behind her. Outside I distinguished her progress across the freezing snow, her showing of spoils to her attendants. They panted at her, two hungry expectant bitches.

Perhaps the food would not be missed. Or Melm would investigate. Perhaps I should forestall accusation and mockery and tell Gurz my adventure. I had other shawls. Disappointed, dashed; help had been only a mirage.

In the icy night, some of the soldiers had begun to quarrel, shouting and brawling over a shred of meat or liquor.

I flinched at their racket. Tired to death, I slipped the figurine of Vulmartis – too significant to be ignored – under the bolster of the rug bed. And lying there, hoped Gurz would not come back before morning. And my prayer was answered.

3

Gurz's carriage was requisitioned, to carry wounded officers, or men maimed by the weather. Arrangements had been made for several of the ladies to travel together. I was smitten with terror and I was right to be, for the carriage Melm then conducted me to was that of the blonde princess and her friends.

It was a monstrous vehicle, heraldic arms still on the doors. Her own train floundered after, carts of necessities, the private kitchen (now with a picked-over look to it), and the wagon of the fabulous bed. Apparently, from subsequent laments, there had been more, but she, too, had given over transport to the needs of the army.

My own itinerary, packed in its chest, rode with Melm's culinary cart. I imagined he would not be overly protective of it.

'You must thank Tritark Drahris for your seat here,' said the princess to me instantly. She gave me one single flat stare, which revealed very plainly her hatred. She gave and said nothing else to me. She and her companions continued to converse most ably without me. They talked of a million matters. I pretended to read my book, even turning pages to deceive. I felt they might chide me for eavesdropping, though

I could do nothing but hear them, their voices were so brilliant, so intrusive.

Why hate me? What could he have said, her lover, my demon? Was it really possible he was, to her, a man to be adored and jealously guarded? Even had he been human, why should she be concerned at me, a nothing beside her.

Her carriage was warm – from its crowding of five exquisitely-scented ladies – but also from the glow of their quantity of charcoal hand and foot warmers. It should have been paradise, but was, of course, only another hell-on-earth.

The princess wore a travelling gown of maroon velvet, and over that a black Kronian fur with clasps of gold and ruby. Three pearls of astonishing size clung at her throat. They were his gift, she was telling her brunette accomplice. I thought of hyacinths, pearls, and blood, falling from the hands of the World's Girl.

They handed about some candied peel. The troops were starving, and so were they, they said to each other. They would be forced to live on sweets. They also sipped a little white wine. Nothing was offered to me. They passed sweet box and cup across my bowed head.

'Zoli! It's just mythology. Does such a town even exist?'

'Yes, princess. I've seen it on the maps. Ten days, and we shall be there.'

'No, they say it will be fifteen days. The snow—'

They were grave a moment then, these aristocrats of the King's City. Zoli stood against the Kronians, in the grip of an alliance which now actively supported the King. Then, with a flutter, one spoke up bravely. 'Well, we've lost all for love!' And let off, ennobled, they burst out in merriment. Had I better join in? I, too, presumably, had betrayed my country and my sovereign for the grand irresistible passion. Yet no. I was only a slut seeking to raise myself. For me there could be no excuse.

Presently, as I had known must happen, the carriage drew up with a jerk. Kronian officers appeared at the window.

I did not turn, kept bowed my bowed head to my unseen

book. He was there. I must hear the recollected voice. I heard it.

'Are you cosy, my dove?'

She was just a touch haughty.

'I am not distressed, sir.'

His laugh. 'And I see the brat is with you.'

I felt her bristling, all the barbs for me.

'Well,' he said, 'I like you to answer.'

'Yes. As you commanded. She is *here*. With *me*.'

'The smell of dish water and blacking must offend,' he said. 'My apologies. But could we leave her in the snow for common soldiers to tread on?'

'Oh, why not?' said she.

'Girl,' he said, then, 'hey, Gurz's fancy, pop-eyes, aren't you about to thank me?'

A deep luxurious stirring ran all through the carriageful of women.

I would not look. No, I would not.

My nearest neighbour slapped me with the lid of the sweet box.

'The Tritark is speaking to you.'

'She has no manners,' said Drahris. He laughed once more. 'I've already learned as much.' From the blonde woman a ray pulsed like the ice itself. He said, 'Well, darling, I and mine are off to kill Charves. I regret you must do without me a night or so.'

I heard them embracing through the window. She begged him to be wary, and he asked, 'What was that?' She said, before us all, she would die if he received so much as a scratch.

'Yes,' he said, 'I'd see to it you did.' And laughed again, and was gone.

As the coach started up again, surprising me, something slid beneath my bodice. But it was only the useless amulet Jilza had given me.

I felt so sick I was sure I would have to entreat the carriage stopped again, or else lean from the window retching in sight of the marching soldiers, these women stabbing me the while

110

in the back with their eyes. But the nausea died down, leaving only the equally appalling urge to cry, which came and went in a tidal way, until at last, I trust unseen, two or three drops sprang between my lids on to the page.

That night I asked Gurz to let me seek some cart or wagon to ride.

He was scandalised. An increasing impatience character-ised him since the snow, an unavoidable sense of his impo-tence in the teeth of events, which made him testy with us all. Why should I spurn the kindness of these generous ladies, he demanded, my own countrywomen, who had given up their birthright for the sake of loyalty to their lovers. (Nor did he include me in this selfless panoply.)

I said the ladies had snubbed me. I did not dare say more.

He countered that this was only their upper-class air. I was a young girl, and of humbler origin. I could not expect their confidences. He seemed furious that I had forced him to assert, worse, to recognise it.

During the exchange, Melm served us the charcoaled bones of a fowl and some liquescent greens. His hands were in a bad condition from the cold, three of the fingers bandaged, yet he gave off a chime of satisfaction, for all he could not see whom his master addressed. (Nothing had been said of the fate-teller or the missing stores. I found this suspicious rather than otherwise.)

In the bed of rugs, Keer Gurz tossed and turned. Neither had he employed my body since the snow. I do not compre-hend, racked with our different worries, how either of us slept, but at length we did. I woke once to hear him snoring heavily which, at the black house, he had seldom done. He had lost weight on the winter diet of the retreat. His eyes were reddened and sad.

In order to retain his protection, I must shield him from Drahris. But, puzzled, I had begun to wonder why I had ever allowed him to take me from my City. Could I not have fled and hidden? True, I had had no one to go to, yet once the Kronians had marched away, Elaieva's house I might have proved to be mine, through the documents she had awarded me. Had this seemed too onerous, too unlikely a deed for me to accomplish? More outlandish than to be borne off by strangers to the foreign empire of my enemies?

Next morning, Melm came to escort me again, my gaoler, to the carriage of Drahris' princess.

I set out with him, then, in the middle of the white world with its postings of men and sickly fires – by one of which a slaughtered horse was being portioned for meat – I stopped.

He could not see me. He said, 'Come along, now.'

'I won't,' I said. The craziness of revolt braced me. 'Find me a place in a cart.'

'There are none,' said he, obviously resenting so much talk with the nonactual.

'Then I'll walk.'

He spat. 'You'll freeze.'

'I'd rather freeze than sit with – than sit in that carriage.'

He would not look at me.

'You'll have your reasons,' he said however, with poison on his voice. 'Freeze then, you little whore.'

He left me with that. Never previously had he shown malign distaste as blatantly. The last fabrics of all things seemed to be fraying at their seams.

4

I walked, therefore.

For all I knew it would be a test of stamina; compared to the other it had seemed preferable. Indeed, once avoided, the other – the carriage – became out of the question. Yet the walking—

At the commencement, I located myself among some baggage wagons and kitchen carts of the officers, which were also moving off. Before us lay the combered white track, and the great white pine woods were closing in a few miles ahead. There was no wind, if there had been perhaps truly I could not have started out on foot. For the wind cut like a sword. It blinded and slew, I had watched it at work.

All along the way, men were still sitting at their desolate bivouacs, those bloodless fires. The snow was striped in gore, for a general butchery of horses seemed to have been agreed to at dawn. This vision did not affect me, unless I should accidentally identify the head of a carcass. It only occurred twice, but I almost dropped on the ground and at the second view an awful spasm of weeping got hold of me. But I trudged on, and the talons of the cold soon returned me to myself and my own plight.

I did fall more than once, when the baggage train got far in front of me and the earth seemed only glass. I learned to walk in a new way then, putting down my feet in finicky little mincings. Then again, every so often a phalanx of cavalry would approach, and in getting from their path I slithered and slewed, bruising myself on the trees I caught to save myself. Later, batches of infantry, spearmen and drums, overtook me and went by, more wandering than marching. Some supported others less able. Some dragged themselves. One man sang, he had a beautiful bronzed voice; his fellows were muttering that he was off his head. I could not understand the Kronian stanzas of the song, or perhaps he was singing gibberish.

A cart passed me near noon, crowded with frightful men like corpses. Their flesh was purple, and many had no hands, or feet. They seemed not to see anything.

No one saw me. Melm's custom had become universal.

The cold. It transpired I had never experienced cold before. At first it was only intolerable. My eyes streamed, breathing was a knife. My winter boots were too small, and I had not known till now. I could not feel my feet, and imagined they would be sloughed from me like those of the doomed wretches in the cart. The cloak of fur hung on me like lead and I froze inside it.

Perhaps – surely – three or four hours went by. I have no notion how I walked for such a time. There seemed a hiatus, where I had either remained static, or the land itself moved me on. But my condition was intensified. My hands in their gloves were cracked and bleeding. Terrible pains lanced upward from senseless ankles to knees, into my hips and stomach. The white of the snow seemed to be flashing with dark green blotches and curlicues of bilious red. My head ached as if a cap of steel too tightly enclosed it. It seemed I must die if I could not go somewhere else, be in some other place.

When I heard a shout, without interest I glanced up. Some wagons had bunched together by the track. In a clearing there, amongst the pines, a fire was being made. Ahead, the land advanced over a curving shoulder, and open sky showed, formless.

I got there, and saw beneath the march going on and on, among miles of trees and snow, black figures and black vehicles struggling, diminishing, pointless and awful, and miles off beyond these, a smudge on the horizon. I peered at this, and my eyes gradually remade the sky, but could not create anything sensible from it. Instinctively I ascertained I might be looking at Zoli, the mythical town, due to be arrived at long before, or long after, it was reckoned on.

Then I turned aside towards the well-patronised fire. I hoped no one would send me off. But this would have needed energy. I could not go too close anyway. The heat was violent to my surfaces, yet did not warm me through. A man in fur and rags was moving about with a huge copper flask, everyone taking a gulp at it, and eventually he reached me and speechlessly offered. I, too, gulped the caustic spirit. Now my inner surfaces were also burned, but between my intestines and my skin, I was unthawed ice.

As I stood there, I thought of darkness coming quite soon, and that Gurz had mislaid me at last, and would never find me again. I wondered if Melm would admit his part in it, and if he would be blamed.

A man rode into the clearing, a flank sergeant of the cavalry. He came straight towards me, and glared at me. 'You. Your name is Aara?'

I almost shook my head. Then I tried, with frozen lips, to say yes.

He lifted me up on to the horse. It was peculiarly familiar,

for my father and his fellow officers had once or twice done
this when I was a child. The spirit had gone to my head and I
laughed. Gurz had sent this man to rescue me. He must have
been riding back and forth along the line of march, cursing,
searching for my short stature, the fine cloak. I felt I should
tell him I was sorry, but instead I lolled against his uniform
and the furnace heat of his body – which seemed astounding.
I could now feel my feet, or areas of them, and I was
tremendously encouraged by that, as if reprieved utterly.

We were deep in the forest before I said, 'Where are we
going?'

'Silence,' replied my escort. 'There may be Charves about.'

It struck me that indeed this was risky, this rider alone
with a useless girl in the trackless wood. (Though I had heard
the cavalry boasted that, equipped with his mount and
sword, one Kronian warrior was worth twenty of the foe.) I
had assumed Gurz had been found some shelter in an
abandoned cot aside from the main camp. But what a
distance it was. How far the black rider had carried me – at
least another hour was gone. I could no longer hear the army.
Only the great silence ringed us round. Wondering, I gazed
up into the white overhang of the pines which seemed ready
to topple on us. The horse picked on across the thick white
carpet.

When we came to it, the building was a stone farmhouse,
unoccupied for years. A frozen duck pond had been broken
and horses were drinking from it, clouds of steam billowing
from their mouths. While at a fire some soldiers roasted the
flesh of dead horses on their pikes.

As we rode up, a banner major stepped from the house
doorway. He saw me and smiled, showing his teeth, and I
remembered him. He wore his beard clipped as Drahris did,
and had been beside Drahris the day he first came to my
carriage.

Once the sergeant lifted me down, I made a stupefied
attempt at flight, but the banner major already had hold of

me. In any event, I could not have achieved much progress over the snowdrifts and the ice.

I ceased resisting, it would do no good, and I was too dazed, too weak to be effectual. Instead my mind began to hurry about, groping in its attics, finding nothing. 'No need to pretend in front of me,' said the banner major, and took my quiescence into the house, through a stone-flagged kitchen and up a wooden stair. A large square room, panelled, and with a sloping ceiling, once some staid parlour perhaps, was dressed now with a campbed, a chair, a wooden table by the window. On the table, an earthenware jar shone molten against the black and white cartoon of the window-pane, and snow-light caught in the chimney of a glass lamp, and starred a bowl of yellow pears. But Drahris was standing by the table, black on the shadow outside the light.

He looked away into the dimming afternoon, at the duck pond and horses, the soldiers, as if curious about them.

'At your service, Tritark,' said the banner major, clicking his heels, grinning.

'When you leave, see you shut the door,' said Drahris, not turning.

The banner major left, and shut the door.

It was here, that moment, culmination of all dreads. I had known it was unavoidable. Even the witch had foretold it.

Some minutes elapsed. Neither I, nor he, had stirred.

When he spoke again, my heart started like a frightened machine, it seemed it had been stopped before.

'Not care for the gracious carriage, eh? Not keen to take Blondy's sharp pins of looks. You preferred the snow, did you? I'll tell you what she likes, the princess.' He told me what he said she liked. Now, these sentences were only what I expected from him. There was no jolt. My fumbling mind went on in its unprofitable search and I barely listened.

He had turned.

'The door is locked,' he said. 'I have a key. Try to take it? No? Oh,' he said, 'why don't you come here. Afraid I'll hurt

116

you? Come and eat one of these pears, they'll cheer your dingy skin.'

His face was muffled in the shadow, only the eyes of him described by the window light.

'Ugly little scullery harlot. Come here and let me make you pretty.'

He moved. He came for me. I, too, must move and get away from him.

Like dancers, we circled, until the table tapped my waist. Then he reached out, into my hood, snatching at my hair, wrenching it so I thought every filament was torn loose.

The window showed his face now, molten like the jar, and the eyes sparkling.

He pushed at my forehead which threw me back. I fell across the table and pears scudded everywhere, I heard the platter smash.

He leaned towards me. My mouth and neck were drenched in liquor, which he was pouring over me from the jar. He urged me to drink, and to fight him. I could not help myself, I thrust the jar away, and he got my hand, drew me up and thrust me down, and again, up and down. My mind was caught in a whirlwind now, dashed through blank spaces which had no answer—

'*Fight* me, you dirty slut.'

He slapped my face, and not meaning to, knowing he desired it and it must not be done, I resisted. None of my blows landed. He parried them all, chuckling and congratulating, and calling me now names of lunatic foulness, and then he struck me a second blow and I could not breathe, I heard my own screeking for air, and felt him dredge me up as if I had no bones, and felt myself dangling from his hands, and could not do anything. As in the true nightmare then, for an instant, I wanted only to die and have it ended. But he shook breath back into me, encouraging me, saying no, I was not finished yet, and telling me again all that was to be between us. And tearing open my bodice, my petticoat, he was splashing the drink over my breasts, and over something which hung on a string there, saying he would wash me, dirty

117

slut, didn't she like it, and breath was an agony and I fought him as he wanted, and he swung me this way, that way, all ways, and my head met glancingly the wall, the table, he was eating a pear and the juice ran over his jaw and he spat the chewed fruit on my body and there was a sound from the window – a sound from another place – a sound – a sound—

'Damnation,' he said; he had used all the excremental oaths and the blasphemies already, 'What—' He dropped me on the floor of the room and from there I watched him go to the pane and look out.

I put my hands to my flesh. He had bitten my arm and it bled. I did not know that I was not in bits, all strewn along the ground. Some dislocated thing lay on my breast – some broken piece of me.

'Charves,' he said. 'They pick their hour.' He swore more strongly. Turning, he came swiftly back to me. 'I regret, my dove, we must be quicker than we wanted.'

Outside, a jumbled cacophony that might be anything. Horses neighed and a man bellowed. Drahris laughed. 'Open your legs.'

The unbuttoned flap of his breeches fell aside like rent skin, and he came down on me engorged and primed, and it was all to begin again. And in that second, that madness, he pulled me up and kissed me, a carnal kiss, vehement and savage, biting my lips – but only so gently— And getting away from his mouth I began to shriek all my denials, over and over, clawing and striking at him as now he let me, busy with his penetration that was not as he had promised but only in Gurz's fashion, normal, to be accepted, but not, *never* from this man. 'Ah, my beauty,' he groaned. His hand shut on my throat and my screams were stifled, my brain was on fire, and a fearsome pressure began within me, like some unthinkable swelling that must burst— In terror I clutched him and the amulet of Vulmartis came away in my hand for the cord had snapped – (There was a rattle, a thump in the chamber below, but I could only hear my own heart screaming.) – I had nothing else to hit out with, to make him stop, to stop the laval rush inside my womb that was like death – so I beat with the enamel and iron of the goddess, at his shoulder and his neck—

Drahris rose over me, making a choking noise I took for the male sexual apex. Then I saw that blood spurted from beneath his left ear. In a fantastic arc, the scarlet liquid shot across the room. He rolled from me, torn out of me, grasping at his neck, his eyes starting.

I gathered myself on to my side, head hanging, and found that in my fingers, at a correct, inadvertent pressure, a tongue of steel had issued from the feet of the Vulmartis, under her crosspiece of iron. Jilza's amulet was a knife, and with it I had severed the vital neck vein of my attacker.

I felt nothing now as he heaved himself on over the floor, the fountain of blood increasing, slackening. He tried to shout, to call to me. His eyes were wide, then they fixed. I felt nothing. No, nothing at all, even as, in the last galvanic upsurge he strained forward – and crashed down beside two snow-clogged boots now standing in the open door.

5

They were not the boots of his friend, or of a Charve. It was Melm who waited there, his face all blue from the cold, his bandaged hands wrapped in strips of fur. And he stared at me. He *saw* me.

'You've killed him,' he said. And with one of the boots he toed Drahris away. 'I thought all along,' he said, 'you and he – what I'd have expected. But you were calling out. *No*, you were calling. And you defended your honour.' Melm walked across the room, and lifted me, pulling down as he did so my skirts, very decorous, as if he only rearranged some flounce, while I drew my bodice together aimlessly. 'My Colonel said you were another sort. Never believed it. But there. Don't get in a fuss. The Charves have been by and done for the lot outside. And the two who came in here, well, I saw to those. This one, they'll think he got caught in the fighting like his men. Not some slip of a girl, a proper girl, seeing to him.' He raised my cloak and draped it about me as if he clothed a precious statue that could not assist itself. (Drahris he also tidied and buttoned, like doing up a parcel.)

Melm guided me carefully from the room, down the stair. Two slain men in Charvish uniforms that had no import for me, lay on the flagstones. Melm had indeed attended to them. He had been handy with sword and dagger in his youth, Gurz would tell me that. But what a lot Melm himself was telling me. His ratty face, all baseness expunged by the cold, presented two eyes to me, which perhaps I had never been allowed to see. I stumbled on the stair, and he supported me. 'You're safe now, my little lady. It's all right.'

The battle horses were all gone from the pond, the Charves had taken them. Only Melm's horse remained. The flank sergeant who had brought me through the forest lay dead before the dead fire. He who had been so warm. The others rested here and there, among them the banner major in front of whom I had had no need to pretend.

Melm had meant to catch me out. He had picked up early some talk that I was leading on a Tritark, cuckolding my protector. Melm had learned of the stone farmhouse, Drahris' headquarters for this night. My refusal to travel with Drahris' official mistress had assured Melm I would be nowhere but in the keeping of my new lover.

He said, as he unfurled all this before me under the enormous silence of the woods (making his confession), that he, Melm, had also had some compunction in case I should founder in the snow. Gurz would never forgive him if he had let me come to harm. Although, if I had been shown up as a hussy, Melm might have left me to my desserts.

As he approached the farmhouse, the direction of which a soldier's map had shown him, Melm heard the commotion of the Charvish attack. He came up cautiously, to find the enemy already riding off and dead Kronians on the snow. Two Charves had stayed to investigate the building from which they had heard, they said (he knew enough of their tongue to understand), a woman's shrieks.

He followed, killed them in the kitchen, a blade apiece

from behind, then climbed upstairs. Outside a door he heard the strangled reiteration of my negative, that retarded *No*. He opened the door – unlocked, one more hallucination, lie – in time to see me slash at Drahris' throat.

The condition of me, my bruised cheeks, blood and tears, were further proof. (Had he never heard of the Tritark's sensual methods?)

Melm was conscious of the wrong he had done me. He had not credited that I properly revered and respected his master, the Colonel. But I had proved my value and my continence. For the killing of Drahris, Melm stressed I had only put down a vicious dog. I must not fear. My secret was secure with Melm. Let me trust him, he entreated. From this day on (this darkening twilight) I could trust him with my life.

6

A murderess. I remembered her from a story read in my past. A woman in a murky gown, whose long white hands, it was true, had administered poison. I had had bad dreams of the archtype of the Murderess. Now she was myself.

That night, in the wayside hovel which was to house us, Gurz expressed contrition. He had spoken roughly to me, would I forgive him his unkindness?

He saw that Melm treated me more tenderly. Melm had all the virtues, they had been together since boyhood on the estate. Gurz understood I had ridden with Melm in the culinary cart. This was not fitting, however diligent Melm might be, nor did the cart provide adequate shelter. Tomorrow, I must overcome my girlish repugnance, and seek the conveyance of the princess.

He did not say that Zoli was a day's march away, though it was the general rumour of the officers' camp.

Melm went about his tasks efficiently, in the usual manner, save that now he saw me. In the dusk before the camp, he had murmured again that I need only trust him. (Our unspeakingness had grown almost religious in the last of the wood, as if we honoured there some god of place.) He questioned me

121

briefly, and from my melancholy responses, concocted our scenario. That if any from the wagoners' fire should think they had seen me go away with a cavalry sergeant, Melm would maintain that he had asked the man to fetch me. Certainly the dead sergeant was in no position to argue. I had ridden on Melm's cart thereafter. He did not think to ask of Jilza, but a faint glimmering in my brain reminded me the witch could threaten me if she wished. She had foreseen what I could do, though not warned me. Yet, too, she had supplied the instrument – maybe that would stay her.

Gurz was flushed, and had no appetite for the pathetic soup our rations had abruptly come to. He craved wine, and Melm presently went off to ferret some out.

Once, I had saved the life of a man. For that I had known a sacrifice was due. But what sacrifice for a sacrifice?

There was something shameful also. It was not only a rite of blood.

Gurz said I was feverish. He himself now looked distinctly unwell. We got into our bed. He held me. I felt no aversion, instead a sad affection made me nestle into his arms. Asleep, I dreamed Urtka the Bear sat grinning and laughing in the forest, strung with severed heads. By the cloak and arms I dragged the corpse of Drahris towards his god. The labour made me moan and sweat, my muscles shrilled with pain. Urtka would punish me, and then the burden would be gone.

I came to myself knowing that the burden would never go, that it was mine for life. I was soaked in sweat and my protector had hold of me in his sleep, which was noisy and oppressed. Though I longed to draw away, I could not do it. Melm had not returned with the wine. The fire smouldered. All I seemed to see was the shooting forth of blood, but I felt the entry into me, and the bite on my shoulder that I had washed and hidden. Would I lose my mind in the darkness? Would I suddenly dart up screaming?

Just then, this happened. The screams were high and nearly without pause. They were not mine.

Gurz shifted, grunted, and awoke. Melm slipped in at the door. He made a sort of motion at me, then, seeing Gurz was aware, Melm said, 'Some casualties, sir. The woods are rife with Charves. A Tritark and his men have been killed there.'

'But who is that crying out?' said Gurz, like a heavy child afraid.

'His woman.'

Gurz rubbed his forehead. 'My eyes ache every moment. Where is the wine?'

'No wine. A little brandy.'

Melm brought the drink in a cup, and Gurz took it eagerly. Before, he would never have allowed Melm to come so near when I lay in the bed, but these were different times.

Melm did not look at me, though he saw me. Outside the screaming had diluted. She had not the strength to continue. It was more a whimpering now.

'That is the princess?' queried Gurz abruptly, in surprise. He drank the brandy. 'A catastrophe for her. But I never liked the man, if it was he, the Tritark Drahris. His reputation is – not wholesome.' Then he turned to me. 'Drink a sip of this, Ara, sweetheart.'

My ally Melm had gone out again. I took a gulp of brandy, as I had done at the wagoners' fire. It came to me he would not nag me to her carriage now.

We lay side by side, and Gurz held my hand, with which I murdered the man he had never liked. He spoke of the Homeland, and I pictured the blonde lady lying over her lover's body in the snow.

The Vulmartis knife would be in Melm's cart; he had plucked it from me. No one should discover it.

'In winter, at this very time, the lake turns white again with wild swans.'

The murderess nodded.

Jilza said at my inner ear: *Lightning is attracted.*

In the morning I woke, thinking in my head in Kronian. This distressed me. Hastily I said some words aloud, a nursery rhyme of my own country, in the language of my birth: 'The apple tree, the apple tree, her apples green, her apples sweet—'

The day was bitterly cold, but lit by sun to a razorine clarity. On going from the hovel I joined other persons on an upland. We looked out to where the forest ended and the plain began, and where the town of Zoli had grown visible. It was possible to see the pink and white of the walls, the glitter of the guns of the Charvro Alliance drawn up beneath.

I was reckless, and sat in the sunshine on the edge of an empty cart, tapping it with my boot heels until my chilblained feet throbbed. From this vantage I watched the Saz-Kronian legions going down into the plain.

The drums were beating, and they had polished themselves for the battle, so the sun might spangle and crackle on them like flames, showing the fool of an enemy what was coming. Even men who could only hobble, their enlarged and frost-mauled feet in swathes of fur or donkey-skin, had put on their faces the proper mask of war. The bugles and trumpets were to be heard again on all sides.

In such a situation, any act of mine had become one with the macrocosm.

There were other women near me, Kronians, who waved and shouted praise and audacious endearments. Once a soldier broke ranks to kiss us all. His mouth was rough with cold, but his eyes were like a tiger's. Some of the marching regiments sang a battle hymn. I could follow with no trouble the words. (But— The apple tree, the apple tree.)

The cavalry was lustrous and magnificent, their horses too splendid to be eaten, animals which had gone through five or six campaigns, fully accoutred now, with armoured breasts and eyes, and plumes all the shades of burning on their beautiful heads.

I was watching the lancers pass, the spear companies, when Melm walked round the cart, and I was aggrieved at the interruption, or the reminder.

'The Colonel wants you, Miss Aara.'

He took me along the slope, to where Gurz was standing with another man, a groom, who was attending to Gurz's mount. To my surprise, I saw it had been clad for fighting.

Then, I realised that my protector's chest was crossed by the silver straps of a battle-harness. He came to me and led me off under the trees.

'Are you going to fight?' I naively asked.

'I hold myself ready to,' he answered. He looked ill, as he had done in snoring sleep, face and body sagging, as if his bones were not able to support him. His brow was still clenched with the headache he had complained of for days. Who was this man? I did not know him. And as it can for the stranger, a piercing pity moved in me.

'Ara,' he said. The absurd helm of metal and plumes – it was, on Gurz, absurd – towered above us. 'What do I say to you? I should not have brought you here, into this. Oh, believe me, I thought the city would be a more horrible thing. What would be done there. I didn't know what would become of you, so frail, so slender – my little girl.' I smiled, to please him. It felt sickly, false. Surely, I was all Melm had once reckoned me. But he, my lover, seemed touched by that fake smile. 'How can I help myself,' he said, 'loving things so young and innocent. The spring, the buds of the flowers. They allow us to like those, and the fawns that play, and the white kittens. Will you pardon me?' he said. 'Tell me you do.'

I told him like a parrot I pardoned him.

'If I never see you any more,' he said, 'I'll go with that.'

All at once I comprehended. He meant to fight, and might die. The thought frightened me.

'Melm will guard you,' he said.

My ally and accomplice, Melm, enamoured of my loyalty.

Gurz held me in his hug, put me on the earth, left me, went to the horse and mounted in a clumsy, unlimber fashion.

When he had ridden off, I stood there under the snow trees, and became mesmerised by an icicle like wavered faceted crystal, strident with sunlight.

Only a third of the Kronian power had come up by the hour of the advance. Many battalions had been force-marched and were exhausted. The Charves were sufficiently belligerent, Bear's Boy General Dlant had not wished to wait.

I gazed at icicles and heard the growl of drums.

Then I returned to the hillock where the women had clustered to watch the soldiers pass. All the regiments had apparently gone by, and the women were melted away. Ten minutes downhill, the hovel would provide me shelter. Soon, the cold drove me back there.

Melm had followed the skirt of the lines, with such supplies as were in the kitchen cart. He had, though, refreshed the fire in the fire-pan before leaving, as a service to his master's loyal mistress.

Despite all I had seen and knew, I did not for a second suppose the Saz-Kronians would fail in their offensive. They had staved in my land, and my City. And my whole world.

I sat reading a book, the very one I had not been able to manage in the carriage of the princess. When thoughts intruded, I recited loudly the charm of my childhood.

> *The apple tree, the apple tree,*
> *Her apples green, her apples sweet,*
> *Oh give me some to carry home,*
> *Fair apple tree, dear apple tree.*

Guilt and anxiety, memories of murder, they had become *Kronian*. My tongue had no phrases for such things.

> *Oh apple tree, my apple tree.*

They had been firing a long while. As in the old days and nights of the siege, the rolls of this thunder, woven with distance and time, became a lullaby. I had gone to sleep, journeyed away there, and roused because another sound withheld the first.

A wind was ascending through the forest, it had a freakish note. Now it squealed, now, resounding on the trunks of the trees, boomed, itself like some huge, hugely disembodied cannon.

The sun had paled, withdrawn altogether. I went to the door, opened it an inch, and looked about.

The wind came squalling then, as if to have me – I saw the trees at the forest's edges bow down to it, and snow was shaken from them, and they rose up black and broken. The snow along the slopes leaped fuming into motion. I slammed the door in the wind's face.

Out there, the complete landscape seemed devoid of living beings. Some enchantment. The armies were blown away, all men and women ghosted into other regions, of the sky or the earth's entrails. Ara had been left behind.

The fire had gone out. I had no means to relight it – Melm had taken the tinder box.

The army of the wind raced by the hovel, a bannered cavalry, and the timbers rocked.

Alarmed, I paced about. There were so very many terrors available to me. Adult fears, all the superstitions of my infancy. The room was dark as lead now the sun had been extinguished. It might be the overcast of weather, or of the approaching evening. And the battle before Zoli – unseen it had gone by. If sorcery had not dispelled the combatants, what else had become of them?

Suddenly, I could not bear my prison. In an interval of the gale, I fleeted out, and half-crouching, slipping and sliding, began to negotiate the hillock. When the wind returned, it aided me, pounding my spine and shoulders, pitching me upward. I only fell twice, and gaining the crest, kneeled down, tenting myself under my cloak of fur. In that posture, through the occluded atmosphere, squinting and desperate, I tried to see to Zoli, where the pink and white had been and the glitter of the guns.

There was a pillar of smoke there now, windingly shaped, like a tree spreading its boughs into the low sky. Perhaps the town had been burned, or some large emplacement before it. On the ground the smoke had spread, too, but thinly. Through the half-light, in the distance, was movement, as if the wind was softer on the plain and ran through a meadow of grass, but these were the antics of the battle, the ripples of men and horses, flags and blades, charging and turning, wheeling, sheering away. In the rattle and caterwaul of the gale, I saw rhinestone flashes from the cannon, but could not hear them.

The slopes between were strewn with dead or dying men. They, too, were distant enough to seem a pattern on the snow. But I cannot say even their proximity, which I soon achieved, the smothered noises or quietness of their sufferings, affected me. My senses were brimmed over by all such matters, and fate had never spared me the leisure to consider them.

Riderless horses came and went across the vista, and sometimes smaller blacker elementals skimmed untidily out of the gale. The ravens of the Kronian totem banner flapped cannibalistically on Kronian corpses. The winter was wicked, each must fend for himself.

And I, too, I was frightened only for myself. Surely, this descending heaven, this shadow, was the beginning of night, and snow fluttered with the ravens on the wind. There was no other life but the battle to be seen. Gurz would be slaughtered, and Melm forget me.

The wind itself slanting from the east seemed to herd me off the hill towards the plain.

Bent almost double in my cloak, I began to tinker a route along the broad ruts, the path the army had made. Once I was clear of the barrier of the hillock, the lash of the gale smote on my back again, seeming to cut off my hinder clothing and leave me naked, but it appears I had now come to accept the gale, as I had accepted the cold. The unbearable would be borne. My mind was on other things.

I was a girl of the King's City, and meeting Charvish warriors, or some regiment of my own land maybe, out of Zoli, would proclaim myself racial kin. I would address them in my proper language. Scurrying along the track, in the black and white of frozen mud, bundles of dead black uniforms, black lances leaning from the earth, one with a scarlet pennant frayed by wind, a raven perched on an iron buckler eyeing me sideways to gauge if I were a threat (an abnormal wedge of human flesh which moved); yes, on this road I composed a speech to my countrymen, or my King's allies. Then, fearful I should say it wrong, or with a Sazo accent, I spoke aloud. The ravens at their picking and tearing, watched me, heard me out, between the gusts. And there a white face, white as the snow it looked, stared at me over its black beard, accusingly. But I could not help that. Though you died, I am not your friend. I am not a sister of your Homeland, the forests and lakes of swans. Shut your eyes, why must you glare so? None of this is my fault—

And there an emerald pennant, demonstrating once more that other colours do exist.

And I know there is one who will save me, one who is my sanctuary, and in a moment I will see him ride towards me, against the grey-amber of the horrid sky, and a bloom of light clings to him, and I shall be safe, and he, too, safe with me—

I raised my head a little, for now I could hear the metaphysical horseman, the hoofs mashing the ice, and a blurred conjuration was on the dusk.

My eyes regained their focus when he was fifty paces away. It was Melm, riding one horse and leading by the reins another.

As he saw me in turn, he started, and made a gesture at his forehead, some religious protection I had occasionally noted among Kronian soldiers.

'Aara?' he called, and brought the horses on more speedily. 'Miss Aara.' He leaned down to examine me. 'Can you have heard me, all that way?' Then he shook his head. 'No, you were scared, I expect. That's it. Coming to find him. And this – no spot for you.' He dismounted and taking hold of me, put me up on the other horse. 'Don't you worry. Our Colonel's not harmed. He wanted to go back for you himself, but that would have been a daft enterprise. Now keep a tight grip. Not far to go.'

Along the plain the guns pounded. The wind was resting. We both looked back to see, but there was only the paving of ravens and faces, the blush of smoke, and the pillar of smoke that had become a sky.

'Thankless day,' said Melm.

He meant that they, his kind, had lost the battle of Zoli.

He meant, the last actions were being fought under the walls as clockwork sometimes goes faster just before it runs down. The General and his staff had vacated the field. The troops withdrew as they might, closing the rear and flanks, skirmishing for glory, the hero's death. The border was two miles off. There were further battalions of the Alliance purported to be gathered all along it. Getting across was owed to the honour of Urtka, one must live in order to fight again, otherwise how could there be an ultimate victory?

The horses walked diagonally over the plain of the Kronian defeat, towards a monochrome of hills. Snow started to fall thickly and hurriedly, as if to bandage up the mess that had been made of the world.

7

Mistakes were various, concerning the defences of Zoli, her vulnerable points, the numbers of the enemy, the nature of the terrain. Concerning the border, contingency plans had been created. A night's march east of the town, a river lay frozen, and under the shield of a windless, moonless, sunless dawn, a remnant of Dlant's legions crossed it. Islands rose from the plate-ice, and on the other bank, the forest was, the absolute forest of the North.

Some of the Charvish army had also gone across the border. Where they could, they waited on us amid the trees. But farther up the country was alien to them in its mantle of winter. While the forest gods of the Kronians waxed protective. The Charves would say afterwards they saw Wiparvet the Wolf, sentinel black on the white hills, all the stars garnered in his eyes. And Urtka the Bear hunted them, twelve feet high in a white coat, a beast of snow. Bereft of the anchor of humanity, as in suffering and hate and war and love we are, peculiar phenomena become easy to credit; what is always in us, conceal it as we may, causes them to be.

To their own, also, the forests were ruthless, in return for passage they exacted the traditional price, the antique consecration of death.

Melm had been intent on catching up to the rear bastion of the retreat. The coach, the kitchen cart, all such ballast of the march were abandoned or lost. I was the only possession of Gurz's that Melm determined to restore to him. He reassured me over and over our landfall was not far, but even when the battlefield was miles behind, we journeyed on. In the hours before that sunless sunrise, he brought me up with their wake, the remains of the army, and to the crossing of the river. On the gloaming ice, that shattered trail of men and animals, all in the abject after-snow. A brace of wagons was left to them, to crack the river's top. Officers sat their horses. Male faces like those I had seen lying out on the plain: The sole difference, that these still lived. Only once, with a hollow *cuk-cukk* the ice gave, and a soldier vanished without a cry. Comrades leaned over the tiny hole, attempting to fish him out. The naiad of the river had taken a liking to him, however.

Melm guided me across. I never doubted him. The ice beneath looked dense and eternal.

On the farther forest bank he led me through the forward travelling of all the others, and suddenly gave me to Gurz, who, without horse or helm, was walking in the snow.

There were icicles in his beard. He had wrapped his head in an Eastern turban of cloth with ear flaps of fur. He did not seem glad or startled to see me, did not exclaim. But he took my hand, after a moment, and an hour later, as we stumbled on, he said, 'I knew you never would leave me.'

'Melm fetched me,' I said.

'No,' he said, 'I knew you never would.'

I wondered if he had fought, it was impossible to tell. He might have been dying from a mortal wound that had not drawn blood or torn his garments.

And Melm, shuffling behind with no horses now – others had claimed them – gave me a glance which said nothing.

Thus, we walked across the park of winter snow under the roof of foreign trees. But Keer Gurz did not direct me to observe anything, any unusual plant or fossil. Sometimes he took my hand, or my arm to steady me. He himself fell to his knees several times, and Melm and I assisted him to rise as the column of other falling, stumbling, speechless ones went by.

High in the Northern hill-forests, a derelict fort had been resuscitated by our listless influx. It was our hub, now, and on the snow about was our camp. From the little windows in the tower, I could measure everything that was left, a couple of hundred men, some carts, the lean-tos of matting and chopped logs. In the courtyard below, a group of women was tending the main fire, cooking for the officers. The powerful smell of roasting horsemeat ascended, tinctured with the balsam of frying pine cones.

A day and night we had been here, the fifth in the forests of the Sazrath, that ancient kingdom from which this nation, this empire, and this despair, had sprung.

The small round chamber had its own hearth, and in front of it, on a bed of sacking and cloaks, with a broken saddle under his head, lay Keer Gurz.

It was Melm who nursed him. I need do nothing – save be present, always that. When I left the room for unavoidable purposes, Gurz would be troubled.

Melm kept the hearth supplied, and brought soup from the fire for us both. The soup was horse and water and some brandy. The soldiers by the wall were living on blood and snow, or on snow alone.

There had been no encounters with Charves for two days.

The General, Hetton Tus Dlant, was in the fort. He roomed across from us, in the tallest tower. His left leg had been fractured by a cannon shot near Zoli's unbreachable west gate. Once, as I prowled our windows round, I saw his face framed in the adjacent embrasure. The huge stones dwarfed him, and I did not suppose he saw me. He was much changed, and I recalled how he had entered my City with the drawn sword in his hand. But I could not gain any solace from this.

★ ★ ★

'Sweetheart,' said Gurz, 'get up now. Comb your hair. We'll go to the General's room.'

It was nearly midnight, stars in the windows. I thought his mind was wandering again. I looked about for Melm. But Melm was standing ready by the door with my cloak, and he nodded.

'What is it?'

Gurz smiled at me. He had risen already and performed some sort of toilette, a straightening of the uniform, a rubbing of his boots with straw—

'What?' I cried, afraid at this attempt, this everyday thing, as the plain of corpses had not made me.

But Gurz simply looked at me, urging me gently to hasten. His raddled face was red and wrung out with the fever, and radiantly full of love for me. It seemed I had never beheld such a look, such a face before. Had I ever really known the extent of his emotion? It had lifted him from his sickness and now incredibly supported him. How could I dally? I complied with what he said, swiftly doing the best with myself I could, as he had done, asking no more questions.

Melm lighted us down the tower with a pitch torch that set the night reeling, and as the walls jumped our shadows were hurled behind us. At the stair-foot a woman was sitting crying. She got up, continuing to weep matter-of-factly, and moved aside to let us past. None of the women who had survived to the fort appeared familiar to me. I did not guess what had become of any of the rest, the ladies from the princess's carriage, the wagon-girls, the witch herself, Jilza; perhaps *she* at least had told her own fate and sloughing her mortal form, got home another way.

We walked through a passage and under an archway to the second flight. There was a sentry, finally incongruous, by Dlant's quarters. He did not challenge Gurz, only rapped on the door which, warped and part off its hinges, did not any way shut, or properly open.

Invited to enter, we squashed through that door. It was reluctant to let Gurz by. A comic and macabre contest ensued. Dying, Gurz was forced to this extra indignity and waste.

In the chamber, he leaned on Melm, sweating and breathing. While Dlant's hearth, built like a pyre, flamed on us, and on the tableau we assembled.

Against one wall inclined the banners of the raven and the bear, and the fire licked bright their gilt, and showed, too, they were stained and rent. How many battle honours had been stolen from Dlant's legions at Zoli? It was a regiment's death, they said, to lose its standard. And could it be the Charves had captured the *god*? He was not here.

But Urtka-Tus sat, like the anachronism in a dream, in that carved chair of his, his leg splinted and bound and thrust out aggressively as a club before him. Two officers of the staff stood by. In the light of the vulgar fire, these big men seemed rosy and hale, giants of red bronze able yet to conquer the earth. But I recollected Dlant in his window, earlier.

I even saw myself in that room, for another curious vanity of the General's, a mirror of silvered glass, hung on the farther wall. There I was in it, a face of pale angles I had never been shown before, and I was taller certainly, I must have been growing. My hair, so long unwashed, worse for combing, almost black . . . A memory stirred in me, and filmed away. My eyes were like two coins of mercury. They had been enlarged and shaped by *seeing*. Such pain as had remade my face astonished me, for I had not felt it, no, I never had.

Dlant spoke. Probably the mute tableau had been going on too long for his tolerance.

'I'm rejoiced, Colonel, you're recovered sufficiently to step up here.'

'I've held myself ready, hoping you would grant my request.'

He had held himself ready to fight at Zoli. From the fever's meanderings, he had, or imagined he had. But had he never previously viewed the arena of war? How had he avoided it, to take such hurt now from the facts?

'Colonel – my best Keer,' said Dlant, fulsome, without

sincerity, but deliciously flattering with this intimacy, drawing a response from Gurz and every man in the room – 'saving the lady's presence, I trust she'll excuse me – but are you determined?'

'General,' said Gurz, 'I promised to look after her, and brought her into this. What I offer her now – it's all I can do.'

'And she?' Dlant glanced at me, the pastel eyes seeing no one I would ever have known, even in a silvered mirror.

'She will abide by my decision. I've never wronged her.'

'Very likely she will.'

The pastel eyes were back on Gurz now, reading death.

The General made to rise, and his officers promptly propped him. Gurz, too, must continue to lean on Melm. So they confronted each other, and I was poised to one side, a white-faced afterthought, the cause of it all.

I had realised, I believe, in the other chamber. But I had not put my awareness into forms or sentences. Failing in the wilderness, what could he do for me but transform me from a harlot to a wife? My protector was about to marry me.

'Does she speak Kronian? I assume she can.'

'Excellently. I taught her myself.'

'Aara,' said the General to me, 'is that your name?'

'Aara,' I said. Why burden them with fripperies?

'Our custom,' said Dlant, taking time to reassure me, 'during the campaigns, allows the higher officers to act as priests. I am empowered to wed you.'

'Of course,' I said. He blinked at me, thinking me pert, no doubt, and bothered no more. Nor did he concern himself with my years.

'And you will accept these gentlemen as your witnesses?' Dlant added to Gurz.

Gurz said that he was grateful to them. His voice was less strong. Had he forgotten the jeers and snubs, how they had rated him? Needful friends now, at his wedding, and at his bed of death.

'Regrettably we lack a statue of Wiparvet,' said Dlant, 'but we're on his ground. Not only the forest. This old fort was dedicated to the Wolf. That must serve.'

Mystery trod weightlessly along my neck, the hair at the base of my scalp rose. Gurz's shrine was gone, but in my brain, the wolf was there. The lamp had lit the spirit in his eyes. To hear his song was madness and surcease. But the print of his paw brought happy fortune— And did Wiparvet send me Drahris, did Wiparvet feast in the elder wood on the murder done by the virtuous woman?

Dlant was speaking, the terms of the contract which, by their laws presumably, must be rehearsed.

In the mirror, my eyes were black now as Wiparvet's own.

'And you will take this woman to you?'

'I will take her, gladly.'

'And you, Aara, you will cleave to your husband, before the gods and in the sight of men, attentive to the repute of his house and his name, for the length of his life? You need answer only Yes. That's binding. But speak distinctly.'

Gurz would not die. He would endure, and I should never be free of him— Oh, what now must I do?

But Gurz had turned to me, he gazed at me. He gave me all he was, I could not hesitate. He would not live.

'Yes,' I said, distinctly as instructed.

Great heat seared through me, then a draught of cold. My eyes went dark at the rush of blood, and when they cleared, a paper was on a table by the ebony chair, with Dlant's writing on it, and the officers were signing, and Gurz, and next they called me and I, too, signed, but only that piece of a name they had left me. One of the officers had heated some wax. They dropped it in the upper corner and Dlant impressed his seal-ring there.

'And we have even the loving cup,' said Dlant, and the other officer produced a skin of wine, and they drank together, but poured a little in a beaker for me, and some on to the floor, for the god.

'Well now, at Krase Holn, you can marry her again if you want, with all the ritual. Myself, I'd say you're a lucky dog to get off so lightly.'

Beyond the embrasures of the upper tower, a weird silken wailing filled the night. It was a sound of purest otherness.

Like nothing I had ever heard. It rimmed the sky, brushing the stars, and sank beneath the horizon. We had started, every one of us. Even Urtka-Tus flinched round towards the windows.

'The wind,' he said. 'Can we have forgotten the voice of our own country so soon?'

'The voice of defeat,' said Gurz.

Dlant rounded on him with a brusque 'Button your lip, man. What talk for a bridegroom. Off now. Get your rest. The other duties I'll assume you've already attended to.'

Like a huge inanimate object Melm and I took our master away. On the stair he was silent. But in the passage below he wanted to lean a moment by the wall. 'That cry was the cry of the Wolf,' he then said.

'No, sir,' said Melm quickly, 'no wolves in this province. Perhaps one of the black dogs, got away from Zoli.'

'Wiparvet's singing. All who hear—'

'Come on, sir. You'll be snug in your bed. Don't fright your lady, now.'

'Ara, my wife,' he said, just before the sun rose. He stared at me, as on the plain they had stared. What did he want? What could I give? 'I've loved you. You know it,' he said. 'When I opened the door the very first, and there you were, dear funny little creature, like a wild kitten in the dust, and your eyes so beautiful. So kind, my little Ara. And when you came to me, when you gave yourself. I shall never see the lake any more, the lake with the swans. But you'll see my lake. And the house. You'll count all the birds. Sweet Ara. I've loved you.'

In his shrunken face the last vestige of life, the flicker of the lamp, going out.

I had loved my mother so very, very much. How I had loved her.

'Do you believe me, my Ara, how I've loved you?'

The tears came and ran from my eyes. I took his hand and kissed the desiccated skin.

'I love you,' I said. I wept. 'Please stay with me.' He heard me, I was in time. I gave him that. It was all I had, that lie. That good and special lie. That deep, perverted truth.

8

Just as the witch predicted, he never did notice the absence of the bangle of gold and coral. It was Melm who noticed, after some of the soldiers had buried my husband in the white ground under the wall. 'That's a shame.' He did not demand where it had gone, so much had been lost. 'You've nothing really to remember him by. That was a family bracelet. He never wore a ring.' And I cried, thinking how Jilza had robbed me of the family heirloom I had deemed only some trinket from the shops of my City, a bauble I had never valued. 'I'll keep the marriage document safe for you, madam,' said Melm. I only cried, and he decorously left me. His grave approval was evident. Was I snivelling now to ensure continuance of his sympathy and protection? Who could say? It was all muddled and mingled, the pain of everything.

Dlant did not look out on the funeral, nor send me any message. Naturally I was not presumptuous enough to think he would.

The next morning, our third at the fort, he addressed us from the courtyard terrace. Our power had swelled to five hundred souls. We were to resume the trek. He rallied us with prospects of Kronian towns, the capital, the Homeland, the Emperor, consolations for all pangs.

I do not know if his troops believed him. They and he were disgraced.

The great forests went on and on, a desert of forests, having neither beginning or finish. The snow fell.

We were a staggering fragmented wave upon the snow, and then we were stragglers. The separated bands hailed each other through the trees. Voices came back, or did not.

There was a morning, Melm and I, by the ashes of a fire, alone. Or, alone but for one other who had died beside us in the night.

138

'We'll get on,' Melm said. 'You're a clever girl, you can walk.'

Both his hands were bound up, two batons of wool and fur. His mottled cheeks sometimes acquired patches of whiteness, but he would rub his face in the snow, and some of its mauve colour would return. Otherwise, he had not changed. He walked and walked, as I did. I pondered, even then, how it would have been if he had despised me still. Would he have left me? I never doubted he had some secret knowledge of a way through the woods. It seemed he did. He never faltered. He went straight, up the whiteness under the white above. At night, he made fire for us and sometimes by day. We ate some strips of meat he had, and sucked the snow, and there were a few drops of brandy. This can only have been two or three days, but like the forest, it seemed a sort of forever.

I could not feel my feet or my hands. Which did not matter now.

'What songs do you know?' he said.

I sang about an apple tree.

'How would that go in Kronian?'

I translated it. It made me cry bitterly.

Did I suppose I would die? Oh surely, yes. But death was such a commonplace, maybe it had foregone its grandeur, its relevance.

He would not let me sleep. I recall – or it was a fever-dream – we danced madly under the trees, stamping and shouting.

'Come see,' he insisted out of the white haze, 'the road. Come and look, or it will fade, it will.'

And he dragged me from the forest, or on to a wide tract at the forest's core, and the sky was overhead, and an endless space, marked by tall posts that perhaps were the lopped trunks of pines, spread away.

'This leads to a town, can't do anything else. The army might have come through, on the way south. Now the only thing, there may be wolves hereabouts, near a town. But if we're on our feet, no harm.'

He gave me some more brandy. Like a magic bottle it never seemed to run dry.

Later, a large white mound appeared beside the road with a black stalk poking forth.

Melm thanked Urtka and ran against the mound and pounded on it and rushed into it. I stood staring. Melm emerged to collect me. The mound was a cottage, vacated – or put down for us in the snow by the gods. Pine cones and branches lay ready by the hearth. In a cupboard was a loaf harder than a brick, a heap of onions, honey and pepper, salt and herbs, wine in three jars of brown vitreous. Into the cupboard's cauldron – Melm's kettle had escaped – all edibles went, and a wondrous slush was cooked, which we drew from earthenware bowls with our sensitive lips. Behind a curtain was a bedframe, though no bedding but for a mattress spotted with mildew. With the miracle, Melm waxed decorous. He swept the cobwebs and ice from the floor and joists with a long-handled broom. He allotted me the bed, so that, years after, the aroma of damp in linen and goose-feathers kept for me a whiff of unalloyed comfort.

We did not know why the household had voided their home. We did not mind they were not there to receive us.

'I'll rest a bit, and then try for that town. But you shall wait and shelter here.'

That night, I heard wolves, singing their own song, not like mine, or that of Wiparvet. Perhaps they scented our chimney. They did not come very close.

It was four Charves who did that.

Probably they were off course, as we had been, strayed too far without orders into the Sazrath, enemy country. The abandonment of the cottage hinted that such rovers were not, however, unique.

They crashed in our door in the sunrise. As we leapt from sleep, seeming to leave our bodies on the floor or bed, there they were. Four weather-whipped men, two on horseback, two filling the door-frame. Their uniform retained a hint of colour and design. It was neither the regalia of the Emperor's forces, or of my King's army.

'Ah. And see,' said one, in Kronian, I thought, 'there's even a bit of skirt, to joy us.'

Melm drew the sword I had forgotten he had, and wielded it in a baton of fur, I could not see how.

He plunged forward and spitted the man who had spoken. There had been no interval, I doubt Melm was even entirely awake. The Charve dropped dead and the other tried to stab Melm or fist him in the jaw, but Melm cut him down with a little knife in the left fur-baton. He had said he was handy with these weapons.

The two horsemen were off their mounts. Melm stood panting, and I ran up beside him. I had seized the long-handled broom from the chimney corner. As he had done, not pausing, I thrust the broom-head of sharp thorns and twigs into the face of the nearer man. He yelled and went tumbling backward, knocking his fellow down with him.

As they rolled in the snow, the two horses bolted. One of the Charves, with a cry of anguish, leaving us, set off in pursuit. The other climbed heavily to his feet and looked all round, at his slain brothers, at Melm with sword and knife and myself with my broom which had almost put out his eyes, at the scrimmage of fled mounts and vanished comrade, at the winter and his own thoughts.

Then he spoke to us. I had not considered before, the Charvish language was not that of my country. I did not understand a word. Melm, if he did understand, gave no sign.

Presently the Charve, with an idiotic shrug, went loping off along the track of hoofs.

Melm lugged the corpses behind the cottage. We barricaded the entrance, and sat down to indulge in more nourishment from the cauldron.

An hour after, we heard a horse lipping the melted snow by the door.

We had anticipated another visit, but no rider accompanied the horse, though from its Charvish trappings, we knew it for the mount of a foe. We admitted the beast as a neutral, into the cottage, and fed it from the cauldron. It, too, was the gods' gift.

Under cover of darkness, we trotted our conveyance along the road. The constellations blazed in the sky, the snow and the wind slept. Neither Charves nor wolves contended our way.

Up on a hill, we saw the murmur of light below, a thousand lamps within a fence of walls. A mile or so farther on, a patrol of Kronian militia met us from the town.

Part Three

KRASE HOLN

Chapter One

1

We did not go to Krase Holn, Melm and I, until the spring. By then, there were pale violets and wild hyacinths at the outskirts, like a garland. For months, the only flowers I had seen were those made of stiff paper which our housekeepers put out to vivify my lodgings. We wintered in three towns of the Sazrath and of central Kronia, moving always northward when weather and transport allowed. Melm had had twenty gold Imperials sewn into his belt, besides a pouch of money left him by Keer Gurz. Nothing had been given to me, that had not been considered necessary, for Melm attended to everything. His papers, too, were in order, and at his explanation that I was the widow of his master, who had died in the retreat from the south, during which all else was torn from us, I was shown both sympathy and open official doors. I was even able quite often to pass for a Kronian, which simplified matters further. There was a fashion for female blondes in the North, and there were soon few shortcomings in my speech.

At midwinter, under thick snow, in a house on a street called Rope Canal, Melm climbed to my room bringing me a candle to burn through midnight, and a small cake. Apart from that, our customs were dissimilar, or else unpractised.

It was strange, at last, to sleep alone.

Although he was now my keeper, Melm was the soul of respect and decorum. The very extravagance of my secrets – rape and murder, outlandish widowhood, the ferocious

145

progress of our survival together – these had only made him ultimately more taciturn and correct. In his vicinity I was never less than grateful and always somewhat uncomfortable. I had won him by false representations, and accidentally at that.

We did not converse much, either, it was not 'fitting,' as he seemed to say, though never did. What in any case was there to talk about? I could not bring myself to ask him of what he might have liked to tell me, the boyhood of Keer Gurz. On Melm's intentions to get for me my rights as Gurz's wife, I had never been consulted.

However, I did learn something of Krase Holn, the old capital, and what our procedure there should be.

A century before, the ruling family had moved east, with the acquisition of Empire, to the New Capital. The city of Krase then declined into an unending, fruiting autumn. It was a city of buildings, of monuments, a winter palace of the Emperor which, standing on an artificial lake, might be crossed directly in the season of the ice. Temples and shrines lined with their marbles and green porcelain a wide glassy river, where, in the season of the sun, huge salmon were regularly fished.

The Gurz estate began some miles west of the city. It was my home, Melm promised me, as if, by hasty marriage alone, its soil had been sprinkled in my heart.

He had sloughed the smallest and fourth finger of his left hand, despite the visits of a doctor in the first Saz town. He made no drama of this, and had made none, either, of the slough of Keer Gurz. Yet perhaps *I* had become a gesture of an inner grief, the wreath Melm must lay upon the grave.

Reports of the war were garbled, and got the quality of anecdotes the farther north we went. So near to where the essence of Empire sat upon its golden chair, the fleabites of retreats and fatal actions, the dead of a mere two legions paving the snow, were negligible.

The last of our journey was by sailing-sleigh from the town of Jermeena. To this area the gales swept down from the eastern mountains in winter's finale. A highway, still frozen solid, and engineered to a fantastic curve to catch the winds, made a two day run to Krase, or less when the weather was boisterous.

They were pretty things, these sleighs, poised on their high runners, with prows carved like the heads and breasts of horses, geese, swans, painted and gilt, rails strung with bells and amulets, and with the upper sail a shining colour. When the canvas went up and the anchor was slipped, off one went very fast with a sense of flying, a rush of ice, and all the bells jingling sweetly. Very rarely did the winds fail, though there were stories of becalmed sleigh captains and their two man crews, obliged to haul five or six passengers along the road. The sleighs were returned against the wind by teams of horses. Altogether it was a fanciful affair. And there were other routes to Krase. I believe Melm may have chosen this to please me.

It did. I stood on deck, with the rainbow sail bellying above, entranced, cleansed of all thought, this safe cold kissing winelike on my face, the lovely mindless rush and twinkle of a noise in my ears. There was but one other passenger, a fat merchant who kept to the cabin. The captain, his navigator and sailor, reminded me of nobody. We flew, and reached the city in a single extended day. How happy I should have been if we might have gone on for weeks.

2

To begin with, I was lodged at an inn overlooking the river. Narcissus filled the garden that sloped to the water's edge, and between rafts of breaking ice, river traffic went up and down ceaselessly, lit by night to ghostly reflections. Apart from the view I had quickly crowded my room with the old plethora of books and games. Melm attended punctiliously all my expeditions, awaiting me at a short distance where the shop was exclusive to women. He ported my purchases, and made no comment on how the money had perhaps been squandered. Despite the confidence a litter of possessions gave me, however, I found myself at odds with most of them. To play a game of Temples, or the Kronian Sword and Star, to devour chapters of the adventures of others, such pursuits had given up their hold on me. Unfortunately there was not much else to do.

In order to secure my inheritance, I should have to obtain Kronian citizenship. To that end, I must present myself and my marriage lines at the City Hall once every seven days, reiterating to the bored clerks my pleas for an interview. This ritual apparently could go on for months. One was judged it seemed as much by sticking power as need.

Time and again, seated upon a hard little chair in a chill little anteroom, frequently bulging with diverse petitioners, I wondered how I could be rid of my task. The fatalistic looks of my anteroom companions, and their efforts to become engaged in other activities (cards, betting, gossip-mongering, and occasionally even a communal sing-song – swiftly silenced by an entering guardsman), implied the spot was reckoned a sort of club for orphaned hopes, to be indulged in for itself rather than any chance of success.

How to convince Melm to let me off? I could not. Patiently he willed that I gain the estate and had taken enormous pains to bring me so near to it. There were no other direct claimants, and for that reason it might pass to the crown if not to me. The adult values, though remote as ever, I must now accept. I had grown three inches, I was a woman and a wife.

Thus then, on the fourth visit, a month in that city, I planted myself before the fatter clerk, in my one new skirt which was long enough and the gloves a seamstress at the inn had darned.

As usual he inspected the certificate of my union, and requested my signature afresh on a paper.

'And your region of birth?'

I confessed it, once more.

Once more down it went upon the paper.

'You understand, young woman, the Empire is at present in the condition of war with this country.'

'Yes.'

'You have no family there to which you might return?'

This was a fresh question. Although the answer was absolute, I was choked by confused affront. It had cost so much to get here. I did not even desire to be here. Yet, here I was, and my land riven from me by every ethical consideration. *Return?* This fat, smug thing was mad.

'Her only family, sir,' said Melm, 'is that of her husband, Colonel Gurz.'

Always he would follow me into the clerk's office, and wait like a cloak-stand against the wall. Never before had he spoken. The clerk spared him a sneer.

'And who are you?'

'The lady's servant, as I was my master's servant.'

'This – colonel . . . Gurz.'

'His last wish was to see his widow established on the ancestral estate.'

'Yes, yes. But I gather he was part of Tus Dlant's fiasco. A lot of fever. Delirious. Mistaken ideas.'

'As you perceive,' said Melm, 'the signature and seal of General Dlant himself are on the certificate. Or perhaps you never chanced to see them, until today.'

The clerk reddened. Before he could reply, a babble of merry music burst upon us from the anteroom. A violinist had arrived from the sound of it.

Incensed at the leavening of his private purgatory, the clerk rose, scarlet, with froth on his lips. 'Am I to do my job in this – this *lunatic hospital*?' He raised a loud small bell and shook it vigorously. 'As for you,' he added, 'take yourselves off. You, girl, may present yourself again in seven days, but I warn you, the Emperor's government does not take lightly the wasted time of its officers.'

I was struck speechless by this injustice. It was Melm who led me firmly out.

In the anteroom a scene of unsuitable festival was going on, the fiddler playing for all he was worth and most of the petitioners dancing an unrestricted Tarasca.

At the inner doorway the clerk puffed like an apoplectic

toad, at the other the guardsman only smiled, tapping his boot while he let us by.

Out on the street tepid rain was falling and the roads were muddy. But the white buildings shone along the river, and the lettuce-green domes of the observatory and the Temple of the Victories. A foreign place, that had no niche for me.

'Madam,' said Melm, 'I'm going to take you now to the house of a woman. Her name's Vollus. It's all the name she has. But her influence is considerable. I wrote to her on our getting here, and was sent her answer this morning. Please continue to trust me.'

'But, Melm—'

'And, you see, she knew the Colonel. She can make or break a person, madam. It's that simple. I wouldn't resort to it if there were another course.'

A million inferences chased through my brain. To what were we going? Not some harlotry surely (as it almost seemed).

The hired carriage he detained and pressed me into set off, Melm up on the box with the driver. I rattled about the inside, thrown this way and another by our pace along the wet streets.

We crossed the wettest street of all – the river – by Seventeenth Legion Bridge, and jounced down into a grand suburb behind the observatory. What great trees there were in the gardens there, oaks and hornbeams, bare and still green-stemmed from the cold. But every sprig of spring dappled the lawns and urns like softly tinted sweets.

The carriage drew up before a line of dwellings, flank to flank, with rows of lacquered columns, broad steps, and ornate windows that might have graced a temple. The house of Vollus had in addition a tower with a cupola of copper tile, and on that, the decoration on the cake as it were, a weathervane in the shape of a dragon.

We went up to a brass-bound door, and at Melm's knock there came a maid in spectacular clothes – red satin in the Oriental style.

'This is the Lady Aara?' said she. And, not pausing, 'Quite

so. Your man can come in at the side door below.'

Melm accepted that without a pause either, and left me there in the odalisque's custody.

The room was a salon, but large enough to dance in, the Tarasca at that. The paper on the walls represented a forest of blossoming trees, in whose branches sat jewel-like birds. The ceiling had been done as summer sky, with a golden lamp depending from a sunburst. Other lamps were raised torch-fashion in the hands of lacquer nymphs. The carpets were from the Ind itself, and the chairs and sofas and tables, and the cushions and shawls and boxes and pipe-stands and goblets and comfit-dishes and fruit-bowls and vases, which were scattered on them, were carved, embroidered, inlaid, fringed and multihued. It was a tumultuous chamber, that seemed, when empty, to be full of active movement. Everything rang against everything else, but – maybe because it was all in the same vein – without a single false note.

A gold cage at the window housed a gold bird which might have been mechanical. It fluted and chirred, and to this fanfare, Vollus entered.

She was a big-framed woman, with a powdered Northern face, no longer young and going to the bone rather than the flesh. Her garments had, too, a touch of the East, though, unlike the room, they were subdued. In contrast again, her black hair was elaborately done, and I think that she normally wore wigs, for though I beheld her in several different and involved coiffures, there was never a tendril out of position, and a kind of something to them, as if they had been arranged at a distance.

'Well,' she said, on seeing me. And she waved me to a sofa, to some comfits, nuts and apples, and sent the maid to fetch me a glass of milk with cinnamon I did not want.

Her eyes were like the proverbial gimlets. If she missed anything, I doubt I had found it myself. I was reminded of the witch Jilza, in a form I could not quite unravel.

'Be so good as to stand another moment. To turn round.

Just walk to the sideboard. And back. Thank you, Lady
Aara.'

The milk came, nestling in damask napkin on twiddly tray.

'Now,' she said, 'though I see you don't care for it, you
must drink the milk. You've grown too fast on too little
nourishment. That may suit you presently nicely enough.
But we must not give the teeth or the eyes to suffer.'

'Why am I here?' I said, oddly made bold by her boldness.

Up went her ink-penned brows (the inky hair stayed still.)
'Melm is a stalwart,' she said, 'but has left the explanation to
me? Then you'd better know it all. No tweetings of reluctance.' When I only sat there, she said, 'But you do follow the
Kronian language? There's scarcely a trace of accent when
you speak. Excellent. But surprisingly common, I note, in
your countrymen. Clever mimics. Or is it merely that you
think our tongue—' and here she used a word I did not know
at all. 'Ah,' she said, gratified. 'Then you don't speak the
other tongue, this Charvish. That word means *thick, glottal*.'

'Aren't – are the Charves not your enemies?'

'Ours and not yours?' she queried. 'Come, be a proper
Kronian.'

'Our enemies. I – fought off Charves, in the Sazrath.'
(Whatever had been mixed in the cinnamon-milk?)

'Wise. The Charves are barbarians. All men are so, in a
war. We women, too. But, on to our business.' She slapped
one hand down on the other. 'If you get your estate, my
lady-girl, you'll be rich. Not of the richest, but, as they say,
with a melody in your purse. Our transaction, which will be
seen to by lawyers, will ensure I am repaid for my services.
And what are they? I'll tell you, Lady Aara, to get something
it must always seem you have most of it already. You will find
this applies in every walk of life. For example, if you want a
man, the best means of getting him is to show him you belong
to another. And likewise with money and property. Who will
grant a loan to a beggar? It's the wealthy fellow gets that. My
labour will be, therefore, to make you all you are not, in the
eyes of the world, in the eyes, that is, of the justiciary of
Krase. You require legally to be a Kronian, so without

recourse to law, I will make you into one. You require the Gurz estate, so I will make you Gurz's rich inheritor. You follow all this?'

I nodded. The milk had soothed me. I was always ready to obey, if only they would make it easy for me.

'For yourself,' said Vollus, 'you're fine material.' I heard her voice through a warm winsomeness. The creature she told me of was no one I had met. 'In a year or so you'll be something of a beauty. You're not far short of the mark as it is. Like a flower forced in the hothouse. But it was a coldhouse for you. They breeze it about Dlant's to be executed, in the capital, for his failures. Who'd have thought it. Urtka-Tus strung on a pole. It may turn out, that seal of his on your marriage lines will be a bad act done you. But the retreat they dragged you through, that polished up the gloss. Now, our Melm has written to me you are sixteen years of age. If that's the case, I assume you looked a great deal younger when Keer Gurz took his fancy to you.'

'No,' I said, dreamily, 'I'm fourteen. My fifteenth birthday – the autumn Vulmartis feast.'

'Who's Vulmartis? Vulmardra is your goddess here. But for the look of you, you can pass for sixteen, the war's helped you to that. You must have seen a sight or two. Perhaps done some deeds yourself.'

'I—'

'No, I won't hear it. I'm not your priest. I have my own past to tend. Shoulder your own sins, Aara. It's best.'

She got up in a swash of silks, and went about me as I lolled on her sofa. I did not mind at all, not now.

'Dress you out of those little-girl skimps, whiten up this hair—' she took a strand and rubbed it in her fingers, 'yes, it will suit to bleach. And then, when you're in fettle, the lawyers.'

She had sat down again. The bird sang. From nowhere a huge tabby cat had pounced upon the lap of Vollus. It stared at me with gemstone eyes.

'For Gurz, you'd better hear from me. When he was a young man, I was the actress Vollus then, your very age. The briefest liaison. I don't wound you, I suppose? Did you love him?'

'Love . . . whom?'

'Your husband. Never mind. Melm will think so.'

She stroked her cat, which purred, smiling on me as a cat does by partly closing, in a particular way, its eyes.

There had been a cat once, and an apple tree.

'We will have your things sent for,' she said. 'Go to sleep on the sofa if you like. It will do you good.'

3

Into the hour of my death, I think I will carry it so far, that afternoon of the image, white in a lozenge of amber, the moment of my rebirth, the first time that I saw myself as she remade me.

There had been days and days – how long? Six or seven or ten or more – there were caterpillar catkins on the hornbeams in gardens below . . . Days of steam baths in the classical bathhouse, days of oils and tinctures. Days of having the nails trimmed and burnished and the skin pumiced, and measurings for corsets, and for shoes with heels two and a half inches high, and of learning how to cinch into the one and tread a floor in the other. Days of blind initiation in the arts of powder and rouge and black for the lashes such as Loy would have been amazed at. And on the hair a paste that in colour was a most raucous blue, and terror that my hair would turn the same shade, or drop out entire upon the ground (had this happened to bewigged Vollus?) and of Vollus herself, drifting among the slender women of the house, now ordering this, now uttering a sharp tiny word. 'Blue hair? There *has* been such a fad. But you'll see, not blue but pale, like moonlight. But careful of it,' to the hairdresser. 'The texture of the hair is fine. Don't overly coarsen. Nor too yellow. Like the snow-maiden this must be.' No mirror. Even in my bedroom where all my games and books lay transported and were let lie. 'For an effect, use belladonna in the eyes. But sparingly. If you want to deceive, do it then. Never a shoe too small.

Well-made, it will have the appearance of a little foot. Never cramp, for it cripples the toes. Rose, take off your slipper and show your bunion!' And poor Rose obliging, to get the reward: 'But with Rose's face and figure, who should care?'

No mirror, no not even for the makeup of the cheeks and eyes. 'You will have your maid to see to it. Or, later, we can teach you. But for bleaching the hair, be advised. Even on your estate, send for one of my girls.'

And three dresses, paid for against the recompense of what I should come into. One for morning, and one for later in the day, and one for the sequined night.

For diet, the etiquette of the table, and menus ever altering. Vollus, seeing my preference for fruit and cordials, instructing me on essentials that must be taken now and then, as I did not enjoy them, like medicine. 'The skin is healthy, the body discovers what is native to it. But, since you prefer sweets, less sugar and more honey, which has anyway, a better taste. You dislike meat, that's splendid news. Strong men die of liking it. But a thin little fish like this, charcoaled – try this quaint little fish with this gooseberry jelly. That is appetising? Of course.'

She weaned me to wine also, but only the best. She assured me a woman who did not dare consume a pair of goblets for fear of falling headfirst was a dolt. And I must learn the value of vintages, for the Gurz estate itself produced a lovely wine they called the Topaz.

When, emerging from my whirlpool, I asked if I should not present myself at the City Hall for the seventh day pleading, she waved that ritual aside. There would be no need for it now.

Indeed, she seemed very sure she had backed the winning mare, the likely chariot. Her lawyer had already presented papers for our signing. He had made me read the terms zealously. She would not ask a penny if I had no success. He asserted this generosity was foolhardy, but again, he had never known her wrong. I, just loosed from my cauldron of bleach, sat meek and mild.

Melm I had not seen since Vollus received me. Cocooned

in a house of women, where only the fey shoemaker and his girlish assistant got in, I was not sorry. And if the round of dressing and table-manners, the cinchings and powderings, left me space only to sink in swirling sleep, how glad I was. My dreams were forgotten. All of them. Even the very first, my dream of a City and my mother's face.

Then, at our luncheon, my benefactress, feeding a wisp of salmon to her cat (who bore with but never sought me), declared: 'There is the last bleaching today. After that we'll dress you. At five this afternoon I'll unveil you to yourself, my girl.'

There had been sun all day, and they seated me in a shaft of it and began upon me. The girls of the house chattered like starlings. They were trained so to do, for often young women came to Vollus, to be made something of, to be brought forth in flower on the city. Her girls spoke only of pleasant frivolous things, my taste in colours and sweets, such items. Men were not mentioned, for I was bereft. Otherwise no doubt there would have been a flood.

'And the shades for a war widow are dark red and purple,' said Rose, gartering my stockings, 'but madam says for your evenings it must be a white dress, and only violet at the sash and shoes.'

They did not know sufficient it seemed to realise I wept no more for my spouse.

But the white dress was the evening adornment, acclimated for dancing or a dinner. I had only seen it on its dummy.

The shaft of sun had moved across the floor. Two lamps were brought and prematurely lit for the devising of my face.

'A makeup for candles and lamps should be applied by lamplight.'

Extreme measures were being taken with my hair as it dried.

Although I had modelled the white dress once before my patron, it felt most peculiar on me now. But the clamp of the corset I was used to, and the way of the dress, too, would probably become accustomed.

'Oh, stand up, lady,' they cried, and fluttered back,

clapping their hands like happy children who have got up their doll for a party.

They were artists, I suppose, and I the finished picture.

I was led down into Vollus' sitting room where she, herself robed for some opulent event, was playing Red-and-White apparently with the cat.

'Well,' said she as she saw me, just as at the start. 'I am gratified.' My attendants twittered, and she rose up and came to inspect me. When this was complete, she took me forward to one of the large windows that looked out on her garden.

Through the boughs of the trees the sun was westering. It burned upon me and, like an intimation, I felt myself seem turned to gold.

'Bring the mirror,' said Vollus.

They brought it, the full-length lozenge, covered in an Eastern shawl.

'Away!' cried Vollus then, scattering her girls. She, the mistress-magician, took her place behind the mirror and put her hand upon the shawl. 'You will look, Aara, and you will see. You will never forget. That is my power over you.'

She flashed the shawl aside.

And there stood the one they had been speaking of.

She was tall and slim, with a waist like the nexus of an hourglass. The gown lived on her, it had become herself, white with a glim of goldenness upon it, and from the bodice bloomed the pearly shoulders and curve of a bosom of a skin far whiter and far warmer. She was a woman, certainly, there need be no surmise . . . the lines of her figure, and the manner in which the silk curled down her to the narrow feet in their slippers dyed in the blood of a gentian, and the expression of her arms, too, bare from the elbow, lying against the dress, and the hands that were made only of ivory tines with a gauze of velvet stretched over, like two delicate fans of fingers—

Her hair was in the latest mode. Some of it coiled up and some cascaded, with a sheen over each ripple, but it was the colour of – what had she said – of moonlight, or the ice. The face had been sculpted rather than painted. The mouth was barely more vivid than a pink geranium petal, but of a perfect shape. The eyes were large and wild and scarcely even human, for what they beheld was shocking them very much.

'See the lashes,' said Rose, from some other room, 'a foot long they seem. And the waist – no wider than my wrist.'

'Quiet,' murmured Vollus, 'she sees. She sees it all.'

'Grey as glass,' said my mother, 'your eyes are grey as the antique casement-crystal a princess used, to let in her light.'

I went forward and almost touched the mirror, but all my movements, reflecting in it, showed that it was – only I.

Behind and about, the amber room sank into malt as the sun slipped off through the trees.

'Don't fall in love,' said Vollus at long last. 'That's for others to do.'

I frowned and drew back.

Turning from the mirror, I seemed to myself to be a small thinking atom, trapped in an exceptional shell.

To take a step might be to crack the casing. No. I was entire.

She knew. She said, 'Bear up, you won't snap, for all that little waist. It's done. You're sound, for an evening anyway.'

I would need an evening, she said. It was a night when she opened her salon, famous in Krase. The world and his friend came to it, and this time those with discernment should have something novel to discover.

A box was brought, and recalling my ears were not pierced, she selected for me instead of earrings, a torque of purple spinels.

Then she had a bottle uncorked, and all of us drank the health of the Emperor, even the tabby cat.

4

In the vestibule of Vollus' house, Wiparvet had his shrine, and by the front door there was a miniature house-god, more a foible than anything, for the Kronians did not set much store by them. Upstairs, however, in the exuberant salon of tree wallpaper and Indish rugs, a cabinet would reveal a deity of the old Sazrath, Yoba, the god of joy. He was the sponsor of anything congenial, from music and fine food to the amusements of the bed, but neither was he a god of excess or vice. On the nights of the salon, he would emerge upon his tray, a garland of seasonal flowers in his curly locks, and incense tapers smoking from a cup of green quartz in his hand.

Beyond the salon, several other vast chambers gave on each other, the double doors standing wide. They were all incredibly ornate, the room of the buffet perhaps the most unearthly, upholstered in a brocade of golden corn-sheaves, and with three candeliers of black winged horses, every one ablaze with candles. There was also a room for cards and gambling, and several smaller closets for retiring, resting, or intimate talk. The musicians played on a dais in the buffet. A harp, some violins, an octoreed mouthed appropriately by one in the guise of a faun, and a lyrachord habitual to the house, having a wonderful raised lid enamelled with figments of pastoral dance.

By nine o'clock, these apartments were like a bulb of light, straining with impossible noise. The music cried but was barely audible about a pandemonium of voices, the clatter of dice and crash of coins. Outside on the boulevard, the carriages and Saz carrying-chairs were constantly lined up four or five deep, making both road and pavement impossible. Vollus' neighbours must bear with the disorder and din, or else they had been invited.

Despite my early dressing, I was not summoned until a quarter of the hour of ten. Unable to ignore all this rising animation, like an up-pour of boiling water, I was tense. I did not taste my supper, but took to pacing. Then I was given a powder in a goblet of spring water.

My nerves had no definite pivot. It was only strangeness, or some vague memory that social gatherings had not always been lucky.

Then in hastened Rose to tell me I was to go down. A last pollination of rice-dust, a last dropping of scent in my shoes. I did not see what they did. I was half afraid to look again, after the first revelation. Nevertheless I was shown to myself in a glass on the landing. Or, *she* was shown to me.

I descended, under the surface of the noise, the heat, which lapped up through the stations of the building. A man in Vollus' livery pushed back a door for me, and I was into the tree paper salon, twenty heads turning and twenty more having no inclination.

The fire galloped on the hearth and all the candles and lamps in the world seemed to be alight there. The sparkle of jewellery, the visual *commotion* of that room, so full of itself, now full on fullness with men and women, nearly changed me to stone. But Vollus came strutting towards me, to steady me with her authority. And, in the tide of her skirt, the huge cat came strutting, too, on a doeskin leash.

'Yes, my dear Aara,' said Vollus archly, and took my arm. She had instructed me beforehand, I had only to do as she bid me, and to say the minimum. She meant to keep me a mystery – a beauteous mystery, as she described it. Caught in her tow, like the vigorous cat, I relaxed. Any way, I had come masked and in complete disguise.

'Lady Aara is a widow of the Gurz family. Her husband lost his life in Dlant's unfortunate retreat from the south.'

'Woeful business. My deepest regrets, madam. You can't have been married long?'

'Not long.' (Vollus had taught me, too, that useful trick. Lifting up the finishing words, or some interior phrase, repeating or modifying it. A muted tone, sad, or remote. An actress, she was teaching me to act.)

'And that great ramble of an estate. The Gurz possession for centuries. You'll sell, maybe.'

I lowered my eyes.

'Come, come,' said Vollus, tapping my interlocutor with her fan. 'You are usually so tactful, Unitark.'

The rooms swarmed with Kronian military. I had not anticipated that. Yet, there was not a man beneath the rank of banner major, and not one, I would have sworn, from the legions who followed General Dlant. The siege and the

160

retreat, spoken of now and then in connection with myself – though it was never mooted that I might be of the wrong side – were plumed consistently with the adjectives *unfortunate* or *mismanaged*. It had not yet gone to the stage of an *oafish* retreat, or a *treasonable* retreat, as it would. Even here, the chrysanthemum – victory, or death with dishonour.

Vollus bore me forward, gave me briefly to the gaze and interrogation of her guests. To women with high-arched noses and dresses of Indish mulberry-silk. Quite a number of them were blondes; it had not taken as well on their raven black as on the hair I had seen in the mirror. The Unitarks and Tritarks had their black hair and beards at variance, some in bushes, and some topiary-clipped. There was a vogue beginning of shaving off the beard, the effete barbering of the beardless, semi-conquered south, which (shortly) would feel the lash of the Emperor's displeasure.

Gurz, other than a flag colonel of the ruined expedition, had been also a prince at Krase Holn. I had never known it. How should I? If the estate reached me, I would become the Princess Aara.

I was much admired. I had somehow learned the look, the demeanour which proclaimed it. They judged me something valid. My obscure origins might be laid out for vivisection later.

When the Unitarks, the colonels, and the batch of civilian gentlemen became too numerous or fixed, suddenly their hostess would dispatch them on errands. Even a prince she sent to fetch the cat's saucer. Not a man demurred. It was all so good-humoured, so polite, but you glimpsed her supremacy. What Melm had said of her was surely exact. Make or break. She must deem me valuable to do this for me. And she had let them see as much.

There was such a cloud of noise, it was out of the question one should hear individual claimants at the house door. Arrivals simply arrived.

It was as Vollus stood me at the buffet under a winged horse of lights, momentarily alone, that a liveried steward edged through the press to her.

'Now, what's up?' she said, lowering her dainty plate.

'Madam, the Tritark Vils is at your door.'

'Well – he can come in, I suppose. But I'll have a word with him. That debt is quite robust. If the man wants to play the tables again, we must see.'

'Madam, he's brought the Southerner with him.'

Vollus looked surprised, at a loss.

'Which Southerner?' Before the steward could reply, her own brain had supplied her. 'The *traitor*? Do you mean that one?'

'The same, I understand.'

'By the Dog, let them in. Oh, let them in. We shall have fireworks.'

As the servant went off, she turned to me. 'But for you, a hint of difficulty. Or perhaps not. Best be safe. Will you go up on the gallery? I think you don't know about this fellow. But you may find it entertaining. Or he may be dull tonight, and behave. Only memorise. You're now a Kronian.'

The gallery was located over the gambling salon, a spacious promenade twelve feet above the room and lined with giant ferns in tubs. The stair led through one of the retiring alcoves behind the buffet, and the gallery itself proved quite crowded. I pressed to the balustrade by one of the ferns rather larger than myself. Below in the salon there were two main tables, the vaster being devoted to Red-and-White, with a placing for sixteen persons. All the chairs were occupied, and on the centre board, piles of gold Imperials and silver crowns had risen to stairways.

Just as I positioned myself, a sort of current wavered through the salon. They had wind of something new. Heads turned, as they were apt to, and silence ordered the site like the platform of some drama. The music from the buffet grew audible, a soulful air. Outside in the opposite direction the teem of sound yammered on in the tree paper salon. Then through the double doors swept Vollus and her cat, and on her arm now the Tritark Vils, a chiselled young man in his twenties, his black hair worn to his collar, and face clean-shaven to display a high clear Northern colour.

And in the exquisite attentive stillness, Vollus disengaged from him and said, 'Well, we are all known to you, sir, I believe.'

'Because, alas,' he said, 'I'm in everybody's debt.'

Silence had now spread its muffle across the outer salon. Only the buffet chattered and piped on in ignorance.

Vollus looked back at the doors, as if offering a cue to the third actor of the trinity. On the cue, in he came.

'May I present, darling Lady Vollus, my friend and brother officer, Unitark Zavion.'

'Why, sir,' exclaimed Vollus, her brows aloft. That was all. It said enough. But she held out her hand to the Unitark Zavion, who brushed it with his lips and smiled into her eyes.

It was the way a flame leaps in a dull hearth, his way among them. He had real light about him, too, the fair skin a little wind-burned, and gilded hair like a mane of darker fire under the massing candles. But his paleness and his handsomeness, highlit by the black of the Kronian uniform, they were not all of it by any means. There was with him a dangerous and torchlike quality, the well-mannered lion that is not tamed, that purrs, and remembers. They might stare all they wished. If ever he was ready, he could spring.

Vollus was tall for a woman, certainly as tall as my Aunt Elaieva. But he overmatched her. He had, as had I, been growing since that evening on the stair of the black house.

Vollus withdrew her hand, which he had continued casually to retain.

'We have been hearing things about you,' said Vollus.

'Oh, really?' He, too, put up his eyebrows, interested to be told what they said. His Kronian was colloquial, elegant, flawless.

Vollus laughed, liking his performance.

'And what are you seeking in my humble abode?'

'A glimpse of yourself, madam, naturally. And to play cards at your tables.'

'You'll excuse me, sir. For that you will need credentials. Nor is the word of Tritark Vils, fond of him though I may be, of any use.'

Vils grinned broadly.

'Well said, my goddess.'

Thenser inclined the gleaming head of un-Kronian hair. He produced a card whose gold-leaf shone only a notch more extravagantly. He handed it to Vollus without comment.

She studied the card.

She said, 'Such an illustrious name—'

'Which would prefer not to be repeated aloud.'

'Quite. But I see she says I may welcome you.'

'*She?*' queried Thenser.

'The *gentleman* whose card this is will cover your losses.'

'Assuming I have losses, and fail to cover them myself.'

A man's voice boomed out from the stillness of the dice table. 'Yes, he's got rich by it. Spitting on his king's name.'

Thenser turned, and looked. 'No, sir,' said Thenser, 'you have the story a touch awry. I stole my money by deception of the Emperor.'

Utter noiselessness now, the doors both to the buffet and the outer salon blocked with people.

'Or,' added Vils, with good-tempered malice, 'that's the *other* story.'

I could not make out which in particular had challenged him at the dice table. All the men there were glaring on him, some puce-faced, while the women gazed. Then at the table for Red-and-White a Tritark got to his feet.

'I for one, Lady Vollus, decline to sit down with a bloody weathervane.'

Thenser this time did not bother to glance. He had crossed to a bowl of hothouse roses, and taking out one flower, examined it in idle fascination, as if there were nothing else on earth to do.

It was Vils who snapped: 'Very gallant, Lixandor. I would remind you, without this *weathervane*, five thousand further men would have gone the way of Dlant's herd.'

The Tritark Lixandor threw down his cards in a gesture of overly-controlled contempt. He had the short hair and full beard of tradition, but was older than Vils or Thenser, and of the same strong slender build.

'I have no quarrel with you, Vils, save in the matter of your acquaintances.'

'Then you have a quarrel with me.'

'Why so heated for the defence of this southern rat? By Urtka, what is he? If he dupes us, he's a spy and an enemy. I would hang him, but I'd concede his honour. Otherwise, the man's a scavenger, a leper. He may be serviceable in war, betraying his own land and kin, but I would rather share my space with a stinking dirty hog in its pen.'

Thenser looked up again from the rose. Clearly he said, 'Sir, you force me to offer you another alternative.'

Lixandor turned to him impatiently.

'Your meaning?'

'The usual one. At whatever hour and place you prefer. Though, if it's convenient, tomorrow morning would suit me very well. I'm to go to the capital inside the week, and have things to do.'

Lixandor scowled. 'By the Bear. You're offering a duel?'

The wonderful silence of the rooms (even the music had left off) seemed shimmering, and was flecked with tiny diamonds of light . . . these perhaps due to my eyes.

'Well, of course,' said Thenser, apologetic, 'it puts you in a difficult condition. How can you meet the sword of a man without honour? Conversely, if you don't, they may suggest you were afraid.'

'Your honour be damned. I'll accommodate you.'

'Thank you so much,' said Thenser. 'I think we have plenty of witnesses.'

'I'll send notice of the place before midnight, to your lodgings.'

'You know them? Splendid. That's that, then. Good night, sleep tight.'

Someone laughed and quickly got it back down.

Lixandor gave vent to an oath rather more sinewy than Vollus was generally prepared to tolerate. His face had flushed up. He said, 'You southern cur, I'll leave when I'm ready.'

'But you're vacating the table?'

'Certainly, and the room, if you are in it.'

'As I said, then, good night. I have some work to do with the cards.'

Lixandor removed himself, stopping only to nod at his hostess. He strode into the buffet, the pack of watchers hurriedly parting before him.

Vils, barking with laughter, went to Thenser, and threw an arm over his shoulders. 'You're a maniac. And so is he.'

'Oh. Well,' said Thenser. He proffered the rose to Vollus. 'I'm sorry.'

'Not at all,' she said. She put the rose into the neck of her gown. 'They always have it nothing happens at Krase that doesn't echo in my salon.' In fact, she did seem pleased, sleek and beaming, with inscrutable eyes. 'But we think Lixandor has had success in duels before. I've no doubt he'll aim to kill you.'

'Yes, he wants my guts. Perhaps he isn't alone in that . . .' said Thenser, sitting down at the card table. The men there tensed, but no other moved to go. 'For myself, I'll settle for a little blood.' His silvery eyes came to rest on the dealer. 'Might we begin? My time's a trifle short.'

Paralysed on the gallery, so completely motionless a bar of pain had locked my spine, I clutched the rail and watched their play. Possibly his bravura, his sitting down with them and their allowance of it, impaired their judgment. Or Yoba, the jolly god in the adjacent room, admired his style. (There were others who did so. They gravitated towards him and he neither shunned nor beckoned them. Vils leaned at the chimneypiece, drinking frothy wine. Once his eyes came up and found me on the walk above. But I returned Vils no flirting look, and he forgot me in the onslaught of the game.) For Thenser won, and won.

He won enough that the salon steward came forward, at the stroke of midnight, and said courteously that the house must request an end, or the other guests might be discommoded.

'Of course,' said Thenser. 'And anyway, I shall have to get

166

on.' Then, he tossed all the money back upon the table, a glittering reel of coins. 'But I think that cancels what the Tritark Vils owes you? Yes?'

'For Urtka's – what are you doing?' protested Vils, apparently genuinely agitated. 'You can't do that—'

'Done,' said Thenser. 'Come on, or we shall be late for Lixandor's breakfast.'

Lixandor it seemed had gone by another exit, to avoid mobbing. Thenser Zavion chose the main door. Those who had not plied him during the cards now attempted to lead him off. But as he explained, he must hurry as he expected some tidings at home.

When the black uniforms, the pale flambeau of his hair, were through the doors, I turned and went away.

It was as if the lights had been doused all over the building, and as if no one else were there. I passed by the crowd and up the staircase not quite knowing where I was, or where I had to get to, and found the chamber they had given me in darkness.

'It's as well you left. But was it only prudence?' Vollus stood beside my couch in her salon dress, a candlebranch gusting in her hand. 'Rose says, you fret over this duel.'

'Rose – told me you'd go to see it.'

'I may take the carriage out. Such a public declaration invites spectators. The location will be learned or guessed. The preferred hour is five. Half Krase will probably be there. The worse for Lixandor if he loses points.'

'Will he?'

'It's with the gods,' said Vollus.

'And I – must go with you,' I said.

'Where I can go, for you it is inadvisable.'

'No. Let me go with you. I'll veil my face—'

She leaned above me, as I lay on the bed in my costly dress. How could she not observe my eyes were dry but my skin burning? Her shadow towered upward from the candles. It did not much waver. Her hand was steady.

'Very well.' She looked to see how I would take it. Perhaps

I breathed again. 'Aara,' she said, 'I don't ask anything. But I say to you, be careful.'

5

Rose had known it all. She jabbered a portion that night, and in the ebony predawn she jabbered more. She reckoned I had fallen in love with him on sight, this was divinable even by me. And many a lady had, it transpired. Was there not his wealthy mistress, rumoured to be princess something-or-other, who must have spent a sleepless night for fear of the duel.

Although, he had fought before. Twice. Rose had heard. Or, it might be only once. It was his habit to respond to snide inference and plain insult alike by offering the sword. Some had proved craven and made recompense. She could not swear if the other ventures ended in a death.

It was, though, a fact; he had sold himself to the Kronian power in the south, and when the siege was lifted and General Dlant marched away with his legions, Zavion had been kept behind along with five thousand troops and their Quintark, who were to order the city. Naturally this was impractical, and presently, with reports coming in of an advance of the king's battalions and allies on all sides, the last Kronians pulled out.

Zavion had been marked for some while, it seemed, as being of more than average usefulness. For himself, he was alleged to have told them, in return for decent remuneration, he was at their Emperor's disposal. His blood was mixed, and besides his king had never troubled with him; he did not trouble for the king.

For the five thousand he mapped a route to and along the coast, at the edge of the Oxidian. Though they were even able, at one juncture, to espy the enemy king's pet island on the ocean, there had been few skirmishes, as the native foe and the allied Charves had pressed inland.

'The Oxid Sea was frozen to half a mile out,' said Rose. 'They had only to light a fire on it to bring fish and seals.

They fed like gluttons.' Some of the command had, moreover, been got away by boats, and for the shore-bound, on the southern traitor's advice, a cache of enemy uniforms was donned, dug up, of all things, from a graveyard by a shelled fortress, to which he insouciantly led them. 'What a nerve! The ghosts must have wailed. But if there was a challenge, do you see, lady, they could say they were the king's army in charge of Kronian prisoners. He gave them language lessons, too. There's five thousand speak that tattle better than anyone.'

She had never been told my race.

The uniforms came from the fort of Oncharin, I supposed. The cold had preserved them in wardrobes of soil, for Thenser and his cunning.

Traitors, both he and I. It meant nothing. Oh, surely, nothing.

'The Emperor may reward him with a medal. Just look at his status. He told them, they'd have to raise his rank from major, that was all his king ever gave him.'

In my inner vision, something revolved. A reddish sheet of paper.

As I dressed – in my expensive day dress – for Vollus and the carriage drive, I sang under my breath, the Kronian version of a song.

Rose, catching it, joined in, hooking up the seams. We were quite merry, singing of an apple tree.

'But your forehead's on fire,' said Rose. 'You *shouldn't* go.'

The hour was five, the customary hour: First light. Vollus had got the information from subterranean sources, and it was precise.

The venue was a large public park, behind the winter palace and lake. In the wooded groves, a statue to Wiparvet the Thief, a reference to the god in his jackal form and having associations to the planet Quick-Silver . . . Close by, in a sunken garden, they would fight.

Up towards the markets there was a stirring as we went out in the dark. Elsewhere, the city was not much awake. It had a

spectral glaze upon it, all the great architectures eyeless and
dimmed, the river like a bottomless crevasse of mist in the
faint illumine of the embankment. We did not need to cross.
In the narrower streets what sleepers we must have disturbed.

The winter palace rose grey and formless like the rest, the
ice long-thawed from its lake. Black on black the wooded
park, and then a gravel drive, and the statue, a jackal of
obsidian moist and glimmering with dew on the east's
embryo sky.

There were not so many carriages, ten or twelve. Not
everyone, it seemed, was in the know, and not a lamp or a
brand had been lit.

An officer in military cloak came to us courteously, asked
Vollus for her name, almost genuflected at it and said, 'Let
me take you round where you'll have a bit of a view. I've been
asked – no uproar, no distractions. Though I realise *your*
party can be trusted, lady.'

'Tritark Lixandor objects to an audience?' inquired Vollus,
as we began to pick through the dripping grasses.

'*Oh*, indeed. He is not, he insists, a fun-fair. We were to
clear the park. Someone explained, there are influential
people who like to see a duel. He gives in ungracefully.'

'What of the southern boy?'

'Zavion's all right. He said, anyone willing to turn out on
such a raw morning must be a connoisseur.'

At a steep part, the officer guided Vollus, and then took
my arm. I sensed he was curious, but along with my
hooded garb I had wound my hair in a turban, Oriental
fashion, and besides curtained myself with a silk scarf to
the eyes as if against the damp. Not to be daunted as he
handed me up and down, he muttered, 'Two liquid orbs to
sink a man!' But compliments were superfluous, I felt half
dead.

Where he left us was on a wide terrace wall, among some
arbutus trees. They were already in leaf. It was a spot for
seeing and concealing, and perhaps Vollus had sent a bribe
ahead of herself.

Below, the garden, grisaille like all things, with pallid outcrops of stones and statuary, and a cracked fountain, and on the lawn two separated groups of men.

Lixandor's face looked sable with beard and high blood. He was in a rage, expostulating to his companions, cursing and stamping about his end of the turf.

At the farther end, Vils and two other men stood easily and quietly talking as if at the gate of a library. In the half-light, Thenser's bare head showed hair more sombre, perhaps more ordinary.

Rustlings, like nesting birds, went on along the rim of the garden. In spots, a ghostly figure, a pleat of material or a booted leg were to be seen. In another place the uniformed officers stood forth without shyness.

A man in civilian finery trod down the steps; a bell was ringing five from somewhere nearby.

'It's time, gentlemen. Are you prepared?'

The groups on the lawn came to order. Lixandor strode out.

'I'll be damned if I am. Can nothing be done about that crowd of ghouls?' (Some of the ghouls guffawed.)

'But what could be nicer? Make believe we're gladiators in the classical arena.'

Thenser's musical voice, with a lilt to it, struck against me, causing me to start as if at a blow, and a rush of blood seemed to go through me. My feet were soaked in the dew. I felt all my body plastered on to me like the case it was, and I trapped inside, a captive at the windows.

'Now, gentlemen. We must get to business. You are mutually agreed. It's to the First Blood? You will be satisfied with that?'

'No,' said Lixandor heavily. 'I will be satisfied only in removing this man from the estate of life.'

The arbitrator looked at Thenser.

'I will be satisfied by First Blood.' Thenser shrugged. 'But I am ready to defend myself against further assault.'

'Tritark,' said the arbitrator.

'I've told you. Death.'

171

'Gentlemen, you must see reason. One of you must make concession.'

'Never,' said Lixandor.

'Very well,' said Thenser after a moment. 'Death, if he wants. But I'll respect a change of heart.'

'Respect be damned, you arrogant piece of dog-muck—'

The arbitrator cleared his throat. Lixandor checked himself.

'Excuse me. I'm angry.'

The arbitrator bowed his head, lifted it, and said loudly, 'By the code of the Emperor, and the laws of this city, under the judgment of the immortals. Draw, gentlemen.'

They stepped back a pace. The two swords came out like tongues of water. The sun was rising.

'You are now,' said the professional arbitrator with a voice of iron, 'in the scales of the gods.'

He went quickly from them as if they might no longer be touched or spoken to, and climbed three of the steps, and stood there like the rest of us, looking on.

Anything preposterous in Lixandor, anything fly in Thenser – these things were gone. They were two swordsmen, fighting to the death.

Watching their movements, I lost track of the blades. I did not know, for all the educations lavished on me, what to observe in a duel. Thus, it had an uncanny aspect. Things occurred that seemed inexplicable.

The birds were singing, colours beginning in the park.

The two blades blanched and went out, and over the eyes criss-crossed each afterimage.

Sometimes, from the other, knowledgeable, watchers, a mutter of approval or dismay. (Had they taken bets on it?)

This was not the way men fought in war—

They were well-paired. Despite his bombast, Lixandor was able. And Thenser's lightness was deceptive. He let his opponent come on and on, leading him, then, a swift evasion, and he chased him off again. It was almost pretty, the skim and feint, the flickering thrusts that could not mean any harm. The swords collided now and then and drizzled down each other with an emery rasp.

They fought with the left hand hooked in the tunic belt. That was the protocol of this sport, to demonstrate only the sword hand was in use. Across the outer edge of Thenser's left hand there seemed to come and go an odd bluish diagonal – a scar I had almost noticed at the card table.

Thenser was stepping backward again, sword gliding at the stretch of his arm. Lixandor, all black now with his concentration, stalked after.

Abruptly I beheld the Northerner's hand clench to a fist on his belt. Something different was to happen. I felt once more the strange rush of my blood, as though all of me had moved except the solid outer casing of my body.

Lixandor drove forward, ducked as if at an invisible doorway, and from beneath brought up his sword. It jarred against the other blade, sweeping it skyward. Thenser seemed catapulted weightlessly aside. Lixandor slashed. The stroke was no longer pretty. It raked the gilt straps on the tunic of Thenser's uniform, with an audible curious clicking – but the cut did not go any deeper, and the air divided in a lightning-bolt—

The watchers shouted and from the tail of sight I saw the arbitrator slap with his glove against their noise, silencing them.

Thenser stood back, lowering the sword blade a few inches.

'First Blood,' called the arbitrator stonily.

'Ask him,' said Thenser, 'if he will allow it.'

'I'll allow – you pecked me. Damn you. But come on.'

There was crimson jewellery on Lixandor's cheek, above the beard, beneath the eye. A facile wound, a scar he would have to carry now for life. Yes, he would need to murder after that. So, when they asked him, he might reply, *Got from a man I killed*.

Thenser looked as stationary as any of the statues, and in the next instant he sprang. I saw the blades like the spokes of

a windmill, seeming to revolve, cross-hatching vision with
slicings of blue-white and red—

Lixandor cried out. It was a howl of agonised anger. He
was stumbling away, nearly going down. His tunic was laid
open at the left shoulder, and a broach of blood sparkled
beneath.

Thenser left him alone to stagger, to right himself, only
standing there looking.

The arbitrator called: 'Second!'

'Ask him,' said Thenser, flatly.

'No,' raged Lixandor. Straightening, he wiped his forehead, then his cheek, glared down at the crimson on his
palm. 'You cheap showman.'

'Very well,' said Thenser.

A misapprehension. They were not properly paired, for
Thenser was the superior of the two. It had needed to become
apparent. Perhaps he had been slow at first from innate
reluctance, or he had been measuring his adversary. Or it was
something intrinsic, to begin by deceiving, working up to
this.

Lixandor's discrimination seemed done for. He hurled
himself forward, and lanced at Thenser's body, which
departed, at the beautiful clean-shaven fair-skinned face with
its eyes now of something cold and cruel. And the face, too,
danced away, miragelike. The sword came instead and
clipped Lixandor mercilessly, on the forehead – blood starting like a dreadful flower – in the left thigh—

Lixandor roared a curse. It was a terrible sound, it shamed
those who heard it, for his shame.

Thenser stood away again, breathing a little quickly, that
was all.

'Third and Fourth Blood, Northerner. I think that's
enough. You're beginning to bore me.'

No one spoke. The audience along the terrace rim was
slightly put out, at Lixandor's rank humiliation, at the
dishonourable dishonouring sentiments of the winning
swordsman.

Lixandor drew himself together. The blood stole down his

face, striping him absurdly like the warpaint of an antique barbarian.

'To – death – I said.'

'To death. You want me to kill you?'

'*Urtka! Urtka!*' Lixandor was screaming. He charged forward again and Thenser met him. The tempo had altered, I saw as much.

The blades clanged higher, linked against the sky, scraped and pushed against each other, came down and swung free and swung up and clanged again. Like a frightful engine, suddenly one united thing, the duellists pressed along the swerving lawn, coming up against the dry fountain, and on under the bank of arbutus trees, not ten feet below me. 'Eyes of night,' whispered Vollus. I had forgotten her.

I could hear Lixandor panting like a dray beast under its load. As his blade missed its mark over and over, he began also to whine. The note of it sent me cold.

Thenser's face was stern, almost pure. His eyes were no longer cruel. For the bloody redness of the other he had gone very white.

All at once the Northerner crashed full length. I did not see how it had been brought about – the fighting sword, some tree root or uneven spot. The weapon went out of Lixandor's grip. It lay, smitten to stillness in the green grass, and Thenser bent above him, holding the second sword point-down to Lixandor's breast.

Lixandor was sobbing now, hoarse appalling jolts and jerks of exertion and anguish.

Thenser made no further move for some moments. But then, he made as if to take the sword away.

'Do it,' Lixandor choked out.

'What?'

'*Do* it, filthy southern bastard. Finish me.'

'No.'

Lixandor's sobbing grew worse. I was afraid for him, that they must all hear it. 'Finish – finish it— Or I'll come after you again.'

'I'll only put you off again,' said Thenser.

'*Kill me.*'

Thenser seemed to consider a proposal.

'If you insist, Tritark, I suppose I must. But you'd better understand. Dishonourable southern bastard as I am, I'm bound not to kill you cleanly.'

Lixandor's wide eyes, blurred with sweat, water and blood, showed by their motion the face that leaned to them, its appearance and manifest, hidden to me as I hung above.

'If I put the blade in – *here*. You know what will happen?' The musical modulated voice had become an ache, a sickness. One longed that it would stop. 'I've seen several men die from a wound like that. And you? I see you have. Or, here. This is the liver.' (Did he know anyone was above, anyone else to hear this and to watch Lixandor's face?)

'Kill me,' repeated Lixandor. His own voice now was feeble.

'And then, of course,' said the musical voice, 'there's this question of theology. Do you believe in the immortality of the soul?'

Lixandor panted, each gasp catching in his throat. He shut his eyes.

'Because,' said Thenser very gently, 'perhaps there are the gods, and perhaps they will be there to punish you. Torments for your sins. Or, do you think there's nothing, maybe? When you've completed your dying, after you've vomited up your own blood and coughed and strangled on it, do you think the lid of the black void will thud down and shut you in oblivion for ever? Who can know? We are all of us, of course, obliged to find out. Do you wish to find out inside the next five minutes, Tritark? Debate with yourself. Please be quite certain.'

Lixandor had begun to weep. Tears ran from his eyes. I could not breathe. I, too, felt I longed to die.

'Well,' said Thenser. 'Have you decided?' He pulled back the sword, readying it for the down-thrust.

The man on the earth spoke without haste, as if he knew there was no urgency, the raising of the sword being only a formality.

'No.'

Thenser straightened up immediately, sheathing the marked sword. He turned and walked across the lawn.

'The Tritark Lixandor has kindly let me off butchering him. I'm satisfied. I trust we are all satisfied.'

He went to the arbitrator and shook hands with him. Vils and his escort came up, making much of the victor. Some of the other uniforms were already jumping off the wall, with the grey cloak of the surgeon. They nodded to Thenser, going by to Lixandor who still lay there on the grass.

'And have you seen enough?' said the woman beside me. 'Come along then. Let's get away to the carriage.'

My guardian's vehicle had been positioned by itself in a grove of beeches.

The driver handed us in, and shivering I huddled to my corner.

I thought we would start off at once, but Vollus, looking out of her window, stayed the man. Vils was striding over the incline, and had hailed her.

He arrived at and filled the window, greeting her effusively for half a minute, all smiles.

'And you were here then, lady, I should have guessed. What do you think of our hero?'

Vollus did not reply.

Beyond Vils, Thenser said, 'I think she thinks, quite rightly, he isn't much of one.'

'But I mean *you*—'

Vils moved to allow Thenser to fill the window with him.

'And I mean also *me*.'

The shadow of the beech walled off my corner. I was wrapped and shielded in it, as in my bindings, the veil of silk crammed up to my eyes. Through silk-slot and beech-umbra, I looked. This was the nearest of all he had been. Not much of his colour had come back. Sun on leaves gave to his hair a greenish blaze.

'It seems to me, Lady Vollus,' he said, meeting her eyes, 'you were rather closer than I reckoned anyone to be.'

'Who knows,' she said.

'Well, if it's the case, I apologise. But I've had a surfeit of killing men, in this war. And there's more to do there.'

'I form no judgment,' said Vollus. 'The affair's your business.'

'Unfortunately, yes. Then, good morning, madam. I hope the remainder may go on for you more pleasantly.'

As he turned to leave, his eyes passed from hers and into mine.

He hesitated, something went through his glance, across his face, light, expression, pallor – something – it might only have been a movement in the trees reflecting there. In me, the soaring red-hot wave fell spent when, with one more civil nod, he was gone.

6

If Vollus had observed the condition of me, I did not know. The journey was indescribable. Every brightness and darkness, every noise, seemed to pierce through me, bringing an aftershock that caused my teeth to chatter. By the time of our return to her door, I hardly knew how to descend from the carriage, to climb the steps.

We entered the foyer with the tiny addendum of the house-god. I must have dropped. I found myself on her carpet and she was saying, 'The little fool, all my labour and to spoil it—'

But when I woke up in my bed, she was not unkind. No, she was very kind to me. She said the fault was hers, she should never have permitted me to attend such an adventure, after all the other atrocities I must have been privy to. She had known me, she said, upon a wire, could plummet either way. (Not once did she mention him.) Sleep, she said. Drink this herbal posset. A doctor was to come tomorrow, and an alchemist, a clever man, he tended all her girls. One or the other would physic me better.

I strove. I battled and struggled. Against mountains that

moved and skies that tumbled. I could not see. They helped me to drink, and to perform the other functions of the body. The pain of it was unendurable. Let me die. Oblivion was beautiful, and precious. The black lid. Oh, yes.

She hates me. They all do. No one is my friend, no one cares for me.

Why should they care. They are nothing to me. I have no one. My mother died, and my father, too. And here am I upon the barren shore, aground like a shell, and I can detect the sea, for they say it sings in the ear.

There was an apple tree, with enormous branches that spread across all heaven, but severed heads hung among the fruit, and golden candeliers.

Drahris stood over me. 'You bitch,' he said, 'why did you kill me when I gave you ecstasy?'

'You never did.'

'I did. What did you think it was, that sensation? Why didn't you wait?'

'It was fire – you would have burst me open—'

'Lying slut. It was the fire of lust.'

His face was corpse-white, frostbitten by death.

Melm shouldered him aside and Keer Gurz leaned down to me. 'Ara,' he said, 'where is the bangle I gave you?'

'Mama!' I shrieked aloud. And through a briar-hedge of shadows, Rose reached out to hold me. But the shadows dragged me under, and Rose was gone.

I sank a million miles, into blackness beyond all black, and suddenly I was cool, and the pains left me, though I was blind still and the sea sang in my ears. There, on the floor of night, I touched – another.

Who could it be? Not my mother that I had loved. Nor my handsome father, nor even Elaieva, dying in her frozen despair. None of these. But the contact was so profound, so comforting.

So comforting, so perfect, let me not lose this holy and unreasonable moment—

But I woke.

The fever had broken, I had only to recover, now. When I

cried for the dream I could not remember, they soothed me with fragrant cloths, and cordials.

It was several days before I realised I had forgone utterly all my taste for sweet things.

The roses were rioting in Vollus' garden before I sat there again. It was summer.

'You're a miracle,' she said. 'You haven't lost your looks. Well, then. We can turn this to commerce.'

Rose brought me a rose. She was loving to me. I thought it must be another theatrical of kindness, but was grateful.

When I asked, to begin with she would not say. Then she informed me of Lixandor's history in the two months I had been ill.

'He can't resign his commission, because of the war. So then, his friends found him. He was just about to take poison. Everyone talks of it. He's disgraced. And now his health's given way and they sent him to his home province. It would have been a better thing,' she added, 'to have killed him in the contest, and have done with it.'

The Southerner was weeks gone to the capital, miles away. Although the duel was yet discussed, they hushed the name of Thenser and exercised scathing reticence with the name of Lixandor.

One morning, Rose said to me:

'When you're mistress of the Gurz estate, will you take me with you?'

And then I looked at Rose, *looked*, for the first time.

'Madam says I can go. To see to your hair. I've been with her since I was eight. She says she'll give me a bouquet—' (The phrase meant a parting gift of money.) Vollus, placing her envoy in my future home?

But Rose, dark curls, red cheeks, Rose poised before me eagerly. Was she younger or older than I?

'What age are you now, Rose?'

'Nearly fifteen, lady. Your own age.'

'Why do you want to go with me?'

'Oh – lady, it's so lovely there, they all say so. I don't much care for a city. I was born in the provinces. I'm a real country wench. Do you know, I can milk a cow? And I'm a wonder with hens.'

'Shall you bleach their feathers, Rose, and black their eyelashes?'

She stared, then exploded into laughter.

'Oh, you,' she said, 'what a one you are. And not two weeks ago we thought you'd die.' Then she blushed and said, 'Only I'm not meant to tell you they said you'd die.'

'I wanted to die. I'm not sure . . . I don't see why I didn't.'

'There's too much to do and find and look at,' she said. 'It's a messy lovely old world.'

Chapter Two

1

Yellow morning heat smelling of dust and incense, carnations, offal, fish and the sumps of the river, fired out of the sky, fired back again from the facades of white buildings and the cut-glass water, so sufficiently like a blow I put up my hand before my eyes.

The solemn lawyer, and Rose, steadied me.

On the boulevard fronting the City Hall of Krase, people had turned to gawp as soon as the opulent hired carriage drew up.

My stepping forth in a magenta morning dress, with gold clasps and ear-drops of amethyst (the alchemist had recommended the piercing of my ears to speed my recovery), my ashen face, Rose's solicitude – these did not dispel the interest.

'Stand aside, please, and allow the lady by,' said the firm young lawyer.

The building was not icy cold as I recalled, but wonderfully cool. A guardsman came at once. We were conducted to the second floor, into a stuccoed antechamber empty of anyone save an elderly scribe scribbling in his ledger.

'As you perceive,' said the lawyer, as I leaned on Rose, 'the lady is not well. We've no intention of being kept waiting.'

'Have you an appointment?' croaked the scribe.

'You had better make sure that we have. My secretary advised your superiors all of two days ago.'

'Two days? No one can be seen inside fourteen.'

'My man,' declaimed the lawyer, his drama-trained voice

bulging the walls and windows of the room, 'this lady is the widow of a prince and warrior of the city. She has been kept waiting for three months. She will now be seen inside *three minutes*.'

Although it was apparent he had grown, dryadlike, into the wood of his desk, the scribe arose and padded away.

We were seen, certainly, inside half an hour.

I was barely required to compose a sentence. I sat in an armchair, shading my eyes with my gloved hand on which a bracelet of thick gold twinkled. Vollus, as she put it on to me, instructed, 'Make sure they notice that. It belonged formerly to a queen. Meanwhile, don't look at any of them except very rarely. Then, turn your eyes luminous and great, but looking away – so. Yes, precisely. It's a natural look of yours that's both employable and risky.'

The official was informed by my lawyer that my husband had died on the treasonable retreat from the south. His efforts to dissuade General Dlant from treacherous insanity had gone for nothing. His heart broke, and killed him. I was a woman of the South, but having some kinship with Northern families and friends here, for example, the Lady Vollus (the official eyebrows twitched), I had left with my husband, trusting to his protection. After his death, I had endured the most grisly hardships, as anyone who had troubled to glean anything of the retreat's last days could imagine. Having made my way to the home province and city of my deceased spouse, the Prince Gurz, I had been treated like a vagabond. The indignity and injustice had proved too much for my failing health. I collapsed and the doctors had nearly despaired of me.

'This heinous record of incompetence and ill-will it is my intent to reveal in open session, if needful to bring to the direct notice of the Emperor.'

The lawyer, if youthful, was well-known and well-feared. Vollus had chosen him with thought. Though doubtful his broadcast accusations should rise so far as the Imperial Ear, their effect on public opinion via the law courts was another matter.

The official suggested we should not be hasty.

'Three months and more are not evidence of haste, either on our side, sir, or on that of the justiciary, whom I take it you represent.'

'Quite so. But tell me, madam, for what are you suing?'

I looked, luminous and great-eyed and far off, and felt the effect of it upon him. 'Only my rights,' I said softly and distinctly, 'as a widow and destitute.'

The lawyer, inwardly tickled, smoothed my shoulder of rich silk.

'The Lady Aara requires legal citizenship, and thereafter the scope to assume the title to the estate of Gurz.'

'The crown has some interest in that.'

The lawyer drew himself up. He was affronted and disbelieving.

'Am I to understand the justiciary of Krase will seize the inheritance of a frail young girl, willed to her by a loving lord in his final hour, in order to line its own nest? Certainly, I shall never entertain this allegation as being true of the *Emperor.*'

The official wet his lip, and next his pen.

'If the lady will make a statement—'

'I have it here,' said my lawyer, 'with the marriage lines and all other necessary papers.'

The official glanced to see if I would look at him again, but I leaned my brow on my hand and twinkled the gold bracelet.

He asked our indulgence, got up, and left us.

'We have him in a dither,' said my lawyer. 'Watch, he'll come back with something nice.'

And sure enough, he came back only to lead us to a higher and more marbled closet, where some robust and sweating gentlemen, in greater amounts of jewels than I, were read my statement, asked me a handful of questions which the lawyer answered, eyed the bracelet, and Vollus' name on my list of patrons, and said they were disturbed to hear I had been poorly used, that loyalty such as mine in such times of affray was estimable, that Gurz had been a fine scholar and a patriot, that I might return in another three days.

'Is everything to do over again?' I asked my lawyer.

'Not at all. In three days you will get your citizenship. And within a further week, the estate.'

'Is it so simple?'

'Seldom. But you have good friends, Lady Aara. Or, perhaps I should begin to practise the new title. That will have to come from the Emperor, but it's a formality. The old bird signs twenty such love-letters a month, the penalty of his spreading Empire. Chastisements and rewards. I'm a prince myself. Maybe, Princess Aara, you'll allow me to call on you in the country?'

2

How long had I been a Northerner? Ah, it was long before the day they gave to me the sealed vellum with the arms of the Sazrath and of Kronia embraced upon it. I think it must have been that other day, in the snow, when the Charve spoke in the doorway of the cottage: *See, even a bit of skirt, to joy us.* For I had heard him speak in Kronian, but it was not Kronian at all. It was the tongue of my own City, of my childhood, and so I had recognised it. Then, like the apple tree, I turned it round, like the apple tree, the weathervane, a traitor, and *would not know*. Melm put a sword through him. I stood ready with my broom. We fought them off. That was the day, I believe, if not of my Kronian citizenship, then of my slough of past belonging . . .

. . . And Thenser's day?

That was easy.

It was the day, the evening, they brought back the death warrant and the reprieve into Pantheon Sector.

I had changed him into what he was. My pen, ripping out his name from the column of the condemned: *You will note, some names have subsequently been erased, after deliberation on their potential as servants of the Emperor's plan.*

A collaborator.

He had been expecting execution, the rope, the black lid

186

of oblivion or the punishing gods he had spoken of. Yes, he had known that inner debate, had had the time for it, in whatever hole they shut him, as never before in the madhouse of battle. And then, the cell door opens and daylight or moonlight or merely the brand of the guard flows in, and thinking he is at the rope's end now, he gets up, to have his deliberations answered by the crushing of his windpipe or, if lucky, the cracking of his spine. But no, it is not that place they take him to. He is to be their friend. For he is one who is wise in what will be helpful and is glad to share it.

Startled, he wonders if he has been mistaken for some other, if they will suddenly find out the error and bundle him into the yard where the rope is hanging still, like a hungry tongue.

Days pass. Nights. Death, like a distant thunder, sinks away.

Then, he is called on for his services. No error has been discovered. He can pretend to be what they suppose, or renounce it all, and life with it, and he chooses to live. He invents and gambles, he plays a glorious bluff. And the gods, whether they *are* or they are *not*, go with him.

But it was I, I who recreated him, that man in black, the Southerner who must issue the challenge to the duel now here, now there, to keep the slavering dogs from his heels. Tearing out the name of Thenser Zavion, I had written it again in different ink upon something more everlasting than red paper.

'Flowers,' said Vollus, 'and a glass of wine. They are grilling the fish for you as you like. Now, I can't have this, are you getting sick again?'

If I had remade him, she had made me from scraps. She would want something beyond the fee of cash that would be paid. I must not renege on the debt.

'No, Vollus.'

I, too, it was life I chose.

★ ★ ★

My fifteenth birthday was celebrated in the house of Vollus. She could not, I think, have been more lavish for a daughter, and perhaps would have been less so.

Her salon was thrown open. They drank my health at midnight, and again at three in the morning. Though I had yet to receive my 'love-letter' from the Emperor, I was now addressed as Princess Aara. I had been shown documents and keys and itineraries. The melody in the purse was quite a tuneful one.

Melm, too, came to call on my birthday, bringing me a small smooth pebble – off the ground of my estate. It was a traditional token to an heir. Vollus pronounced it a very correct one. She granted us our meeting in the tree paper salon. Decorous Melm said only a word or two and did not outstay his servant's welcome. Vollus approved of Melm. I had forgotten, between, how ratlike his face was, forgotten his devotion to Gurz and beneficence to me.

From the roses and the wine, the men who made ardent, respectful love to me, the friendship-seeking ladies, the birthday presents from strangers – some rather bold ('Who has sent you garters!' squeaked Rose), I descended the auburn stair of autumn with a feeling as if my hair blew in a mild wind, as if my feet, in fashionable sandals, met only the thin pavement of existence, and below churned the sea. But I was not afraid. Not of the way before me, not of the shadow behind. Not of my debt to Vollus. Not of the pale woman with blonde hair who came into my mirror, holding out her hands for circles of gold. I was only sad. It pressed on me, against my heart. It made all other things seem less. It did not turn beauty aside, it could listen to songs, it could laugh, and get into the carriage with excited Rose, and as we started out, look to see the city wheel and fold away, and it could sigh therefore, and smile.

'Ah, you did love him, then,' said Rose in after days. 'Your husband. I knew it, when we set off.'

Poor memory, poor husband. He had not been in my mind at all.

Part Four

THE PAINTED HOUSE

Chapter One

1

Only miles above Krase Holn, the Northern forests again
begin. Yet, in autumnal summer, how unlike the winterscape
I had seen before.

The black-green of the pines was shot with sunlight that
went unextinguished until seven o'clock; then the twilight
stole along the avenues like a troupe of silent nuns. Many
other trees encroached upon the pines. Evergreen ilex and
ambering oak, conifer and wild lime. Rhododendrons,
torched with red berries, shone from the glades.

The journey we had elected to continue day and night,
with one pause for dinner, and another for a breakfast, at two
balconied inns. Before noon therefore of the second day, the
carriage turned from the highway and rolled off along a broad
arboreal track. A few minutes more, and the forest was drawn
aside like a curtain.

'Oh, madam – look!' cried Rose.

An instruction to the coachman halted us. We alighted,
and walked out on the brow of the earth, to see.

The track descended into a valley, the woods going with it
but then swept off on either hand, like the parting of an
ocean. The discovered land was a green just combed to the
tawny pelt of the turning season. There, an alder leaned
burning to a creaming weir. And there, a broad-winged bird
swung across between the two shores of the wood. Held in
forest, the valley break, sometimes raised in trees or rock, ran
on into infinity.

'The princess sees the commencement of her estate. From this point the forests and fields are the possession of Gurz.' The driver spoke from his box.

'From here?' the princess answered naively enough.

'There is the marker.'

Along the track, upon a tree some hundreds of years of age, the heart-shaped shield, a wreath of flowers about a staff, old and bearded with moss, the colour licked off by all weathers. I had seen the device on the documents, and the keys. It was mine.

We returned to the carriage, Rose brilliant as a bride.

We drove down into the wolf-emerald artery of the estate.

Presently the track ended at a stone bridge, by which we crossed the curding water of the weir. On the farther bank was a paved road. A shrine to Wiparvet overlooked the roadside. On his altar lay a wizened plait of wheat, a honeycomb the birds had already fully enjoyed. The harvest might fall later in the North, but a long hot summer brought it on like strong drink, and now the gathering was nearly done. As the road pulled us forward, the fields and orchards appeared in a golden-green afterbloom of sun-switched stubble and leafage. Here and there clutches of tall baskets were still standing, bubbling with fruit, yellow apples, pale quinces, midnight plums and damsons. On the border of the sky the forest travelled with us, but then the vineyards came between, and the plantations of those bushes that yield herbal teas. Occasionally a flash of metal, some scythe or knife at work. Along distant paths donkey and ox carts were moving, piled with the edible effusion. And out of sight, the berry gardens, where the raspberries and currants had already gone to be smoothed to jams, and the hothouses with the persimmons and apricots, while on the acre of nut trees quite soon the hazels and walnuts would come raining down. I had barely assimilated the literature of the estate. Now, the proof of ripeness and excess. Through the open windows soaked an alcoholic scent of taken things, things luscious and bruised, things possessed to be bitten into, eaten, drunk, and *had*. It dumbfounded me. This, too, was mine.

An hour later, exhausted by abundance, the forest drew in once more, gliding almost to the road in cool and savage shadow, indolent and uncaring, fruiting randomly and only for itself. The ceiling of noon sat solidly upon the tree tops, blanching everything else, the stones, the road, one's own flesh, to a vivid living white.

Shortly the coachman stopped a second time. He called that if the princess would be inclined to see the house, behold the point at which the best to see it.

The slope was gradual here, in the narrowing of the valley. I saw the lake, another sheet of blinding noon whiteness. Above, an odd building, like a brick, some two storeys, with four square towers, one at each corner. The sheer flatness of it was all that struck me, and by me Rose sighed, as if disappointed.

The carriage bore us on, the road curving off into the trees again, among enormous pines with red stalks, and every so often the upper floors of the wood emerging in mid air, blue, almost luminous, the haunts of nymphs and fairies. 'Do you see the smoke, madam?' said Rose, who had been giving me swift lectures on the dealings of the countryside. 'That will be the charcoal-burners.'

The road came out again and drove along beside the lake. The water was limpid, rouched by trees on its shores whose mirror-images turned it to onyx. Water-fowl made free there, but no swans. They came in winter, white beings of passage, Keer Gurz had told me that.

The house looked better from this sideways angle, but soon resumed its flat tinder-box aspect as the road straightened in again towards it.

Then I began to see that its pinkish-brownish hue was composed of many collective bands of colouring that went up the walls like a series of tidemarks. There was also a veranda the length of the facade and extended around to merge into some birch trees. The two storeys culminated, however, in the flattest roof, though the towers had cones of terracotta tile.

The road passed across below the front of the house,

ending under the easterly tower at a black pavilion.

Mounted on steps, the veranda had pillars of carved and painted wood. Two leaves of a white and grandly rustic entrance were standing wide.

Our vehicle drew up.

'Well,' said Rose, in high dudgeon, 'will no one come to see to a carriage door?'

She had not bothered with this until now.

'Never mind it,' I said. I opened the door and got out as formerly. The largeness of the house was becoming obvious to me. It balanced on the road, and the building seemed to bulge above me, its towers looming over to look. Then out through the wide entry came pelting a girl of about nine, smiling and very clean. She rushed over the veranda and directly down the steps and up to me, holding before her a vast bunch of flowers, every plant of the estate it seemed, orange lilies and fiery roses, cornflowers, daisies, autumn lotus, jacinths – I accepted this cornucopia. The child grinned and danced away. I beheld all the household filing out in religious procession, a multitude, and coming last of all a little withered woman in a black-purple gown, whom I took for the housekeeper.

Then Melm, who seemed abruptly my oldest and only friend, walked down the steps, in a house uniform of some magnificence.

'Princess.'

I did not know what to say. 'Thank you,' I murmured.

'This is the tradition of Gurz. To welcome the mistress once she has, of her own volition, put her foot to our ground.'

'What pavilion is that?' I asked, flustered, weighed down by garlands and customs, fearing more.

'The black marble? The tomb of a patriarch of the family.'

He led me up the steps. Rose dogged me. The retainers bowed, holding out their hands palms uppermost and empty. I wondered nervously if I was supposed to give them something, but Melm did not indicate it, nor pay any attention. I followed this example dubiously.

We reached the doorway, which was barred by the tiny elderly woman.

'Princess,' said Melm, 'I will present to you your dependent.' That was enough to startle me. But he continued, 'The Lady, my master's grandmother.'

As I teetered, without an idea in my head, the old woman – she was extremely old – bowed like the servants, although she did not lift her palms.

'She is addressed as *the Lady*,' said Melm to me. 'Will the Lady permit me to tell my master's wife the Lady's age?'

She looked up, and her ancient face broke like water into rings and ripples of amusement. She clicked her tongue and said with total coherence, 'Speak!'

Melm said, 'The Lady is in her one hundred and sixth year.'

'Goodness bless us!' cried out Rose.

Perhaps I should have said it.

The Lady, Gurz's grandmother, peered by me with fierce misty old eyes. '*Hah!*' she announced in triumphant approval. And smacked her fallen old lips.

I had been sensible, fearing an onslaught of customs. In the vast hall I was seated in a chair, and two maids came to wash my hands in a silver bowl of water. I was served a greeting-cup, a beautiful soft white wine – not the famous Topaz, but an apple-vintage of the estate. Also I was given a piece of spiced bread to eat. Rose waited valiantly beside me as I accomplished these feats, watched by one and all, upward of forty people, and also two of the large black wolf-dogs, the pack-leaders, for with its stable reduced to twelve horses, the estate still kept two packs of hounds for purposes of hunting and guard.

The hall had an upper gallery hung with shields, and a lofty ceiling, the rafters all carved and coloured into a kind of madness – boughs of pears and cherries, woodland deities, pouring jugs – and other unsure things. But I dared not keep on looking up, for I was meant to concentrate on the human level below.

I had some better view of the floor – which was polished like glass and also scored to opacity from the tramp of shoes. And of a mighty white pillar that went up through the hall's centre, straight in among the carved nymphs and boughs, and by them, presumably into the apartments above. This was, I learned after, the Great Stove, the presiding sorcerer of heat which stayed the house all winter.

The hundred-and-six-year-old Lady sat in another chair, scrutinising my ceremonials with alert complacence. Was it conceivable she knew who I was? Did she even know her grandson had died? She must be used by now to journeying past the rest of us. Fortunately she seemed not to resent me. She would appear to credit I had some right to be there.

My head was beginning to ache, I longed to run away. Quite suddenly they allowed it. The ritual was done, all but the making of a small offering of wine and salt to the Wiparvet by the stair. He was a black marble (like the tomb outside), standing upright as they sometimes do, and clad in a robe like that of a priest. His lean large paws supported the watch-fire, which flickered as I put the salt upon his tray and the wine into his cup. I had never been allowed to make him an offering before, not even at my marriage, as, if it had been performed in the normal way, I should have done. Would he snarl at me – or would that hallucinatory wailing note fly over the forest, impaling us all with terror, as once before—

The god was impervious and mute, the offering accepted. A maid led me up to the gallery, and leftward along it, and into the wall. Rose followed with my flowers. The servants of Gurz, and the Lady, watched us out of sight.

What was I doing here? Of all the rampaging oceans that had swept me headfirst, siege and war and death, surely this was the most awesome and unavoidable.

I must put on again a garment that did not fit, and grow into its form.

I tossed on my bed in a feverish doze as the afternoon went down the window-blinds.

Rose, having heartlessly congratulated me, *oohed* and

squeaked over the oddities of the grandmother, the house, had left me, to play in an adjoining closet with sewing boxes and luggage. She seemed already at home, or at least at home in unfamiliarity, prepared to swim for a visible shore.

But how should I be here?

I dreamed Gurz was standing on the lake, on the water, like a mystic. His beard blew about at his laughter. '*Ahr*, little Ara!' he shouted, delighted in my misery. This was his revenge, not his bounty. I had not loved him. He had died. Now he had tied a carven painted millstone on my back.

The bed, which had blue velvet curtains, and pillars that were the whole trunks of trees so far as I could make out, all ribbed and whorled, cut off with its plum-dark canopy the ceiling-rafters, where candy-pink doves were beaking red and green apples, and bluebirds and indigo ravens carried sprigs of real flowers, picked for my arrival, and shattering their petals on the floor. ('Luckily, those birds won't be letting go of anything else,' exclaimed the heartless Rose.)

I slept again and dreamed Gurz had brought me to the house and was carrying me up the stairs, his flower, along the gallery through the arch in the wall, along the corridor, and up that other flight, into this, the West Tower. Mine was the Mistress Chamber. The Master Chamber – his own – lay in the tower to the east. In marriage, only the Master Chamber was occupied. This alternate female room was for the lying-in, or the illness, or it was the widow's place. Gurz the ghost carried me appropriately here, and flung me on the bed. His face was melting to another's face. It was the face of Drahris, and then, most curious and worst horror of all, of Lixandor, lying sobbing and bloody on the turf of the duelling ground.

Waking with a ghastly surge, I stared about.

Where was I? Oh. Still here.

The blinds glowed milder. Long spillages of shadow were under and upon all things. I was alone. There was no one to call to who could help.

I looked up at the painted birds – abruptly they broke my heart. I cried for them because I had not loved them, their colours and their flowers, the open hands and greeting-wine, the crone, the lake.

Dying, he had predicted to me this chamber. '*You'll count all the birds.*'

Through my tears, I tried to count them.

Through my tears, it could not be done.

2

But I was not truly in a cage. Or not in any cage but that I had already suspected, the physical box that shuts up every one of us.

Vollus, the mere fact of existing in her domain, had taught me something of domestic management. Even my mother's far humbler, rather whimsical, housekeeping, had lingered in my brain. At the mansion of the Gurzes, I had a whole army to toil for me. With the slightest pressure I could set my globe into motion.

Melm was my steward, an elevation his master had ensured for him. Cognisant of the estate since infancy, he knew everything there was to know, and was respected and esteemed by its population. By his treatment of me, and perhaps by his attitude towards me even in my absence (he had been there since the spring), he gave them the lesson that I, too, was to be honoured. I need only pay attention for half an hour each day when stewardess and chief maid came in. And elsewhere be responsive to the breakfasts of gorgeous fruit and new-baked breads, the dinners of woodland fowl and lake fish. I smiled on my minions and tried to remember their names – and for this they regarded me as if I, too, had flowered from their forest. Such generosity was disarming. But it made me uneasy. Had seizure by the Imperial crown been such a fearful doom that I was preferable?

Then again, they seemed to know I had the blood of the south. They must think I had thrown off everything, kin and kind, perhaps even riches, to belong to Keer Gurz. If so, my naivete recoiled at theirs.

But I preferred not to speculate. In a peculiar fashion, I had begun to be happy.

The autumn changed through amber to gold and from gold to crimson. The trees had leaves like paper rose-petals. In the frosts of early morning, in the deep-cored afternoons when the sun still scorched, I went riding in a quaint little doll-chariot with seats and canopy, drawn by plump twin ponies. Melm, or Covelt the under-steward, would accompany me on a fine horse, pointing out the treasures of the landscape. Soon sometimes I would only walk, with no companion at all. It was entirely safe for me to do so. Indeed, the estate liked it in me, that was obvious. Meeting the last workers in the sloping vineyards, ordering the stocks and stripped ground, or men and women from the fields, they identified me, probably from detailed description, hailed me as *Princess*, with hearty courtesy, let me by undetained and unmolested, with long, long lookings.

In the woodland I started one or two deer, once a tree-cat, and later once, in a pewter dawn, a grey fox made of the frost with a snow tip at his tail.

I had been at the house twenty days before the decanter of Topaz was offered my table. Melm did not indicate why I had waited – maybe the wine dictates its own time, or I need only have asked.

That evening, in recognition of the drink, the Lady dined with me, an event I had until then escaped.

How could I socialise with her?

The dinner was set not in the Mistress Parlour (which lay to the west of the Hall), where it had so far been arranged for me, but in the Hall itself. The colossal column of the Stove was not yet into its winter lighting, and so braziers of logs were put about. (Above the table, the breasts and faces of the nymphs were black from centuries of such snugness.)

Rose, my silent adviser on such matters, had brought me a dinner gown of pale red silk, with braidings of black and lavender. In deference to granny I was to be a proper war widow.

The Lady did not arrive until I had reached the dessert.

She was assisted down the stair – her apartment lay easterly in the Quiet Tower. Having acquired the scratched burnish of the floor, she came on under her own sail.

I rose. She bowed to me. I bowed to her. No one had told me what was in order.

We sat, at either end of the table.

I had been dreading seeing her at her food. She seemed to have no teeth, and memories of elderly people in a similar mess to babies remained from my childhood. However, the Lady's dish turned out to be some sweet soup or preserve which, plying spoon and napkin, she demolished with utter grace.

'Do you care for wine?'

This, tossed casually across to me as if we had been conversing for hours, caused me to stammer.

'I have – never – this wine – is new to me, Lady.'

'The Topaz. You won't be disappointed.' Then, astonishing me more, 'They told me how you are called, but I forget.'

'Aara,' I said, 'Lady.'

'Princess Aara,' said she, almost malignly I thought, though it was the malice of mischief not ill-will. 'Now, I tell you. When you speak to me, you must say *my* title as at one remove. As so: My name is Aara, the Lady should know. Or, the Lady must understand, this wine is new to me.'

Perhaps my mouth had fallen open. I collected myself and said, 'The Lady is very kind. I extend to her my regrets that I'm ignorant of the manner here.'

She went into a trill of laughter.

'Pretty girl,' she said. She aimed a merry stabbing gesture at me. There were rings on her hands tonight, for the wine, or me.

No mention was made of Keer Gurz. (Surely he had never spoken to me of her – his talk had been of the forests and lake, the wolves and swans, or Melm. But then. How often did I listen?)

Presently Melm entered with the wine, already decanted in a vessel of heavy crystal. The tint of the drink was what its name described.

The first glass was for the god, Melm had forewarned me, as it was a fresh rack, the first of the five-year vintage.

It was very cold, a cold heat, mellow yet dry. The fragrance was of flowers. The aftertaste was dual, flinty, then very clean, as if it were the water of a pure fountain.

'Good,' said the grandmother, smacking her sunken lips. Her eyes were on me, filmy, *seeing*. 'When the snow brings the wolves, we used to put out a bowl for them, for the prince or king of the pack. Sometimes he had to fight to get it. Then he came and lapped the wine. In a bad winter they claw at the doors of the house, the Hall doors and the doors of the Parlour and the library and the Master Study, that give on the outer walk. Melm will show you the marks. And then there's sometimes a black wolf seen, the god's wolf.'

I shivered convulsively before I could prevent myself. She was gratified.

She did not stay long after that.

The Topaz had gone to my head, and as she got up on to the gallery, I whispered to Melm, 'What a remarkable woman!' I do not know quite what I meant by it, a sort of sentimental gush, possibly, but Melm, discounting my sentence, or accepting it, did not reply.

3

The rose-leaves had fallen, the winds were awake, when I found the temple to Vulmardra in the forest.

When the sun set there would come the long gloaming of the north. Around midsummer I had heard, though I had been unwell then and not witnessed it, the half-light would last a clear night through almost until the dawn. Now, the sun was gone by four, but at six you might wander the lawns about the lake under a sky like the blue paste jewellers make up into false sapphires. The birds sang on. They would soon be leaving for the south and one must store up their voices, like the wine and fruit. The winters here would be silent.

The intimation of winter gave me a faint sense of fear again. It was the after-shadow of the retreat. (The summer, too, would bring its ominous inference – even at Krase Holn I had seemed to scent occasional gunpowder in the smell of wall-flowers or roses.) Yet, even my fears were reasonable, might be debated with and turned off. I walked through waist-high clumps of reeds, and past the bending docks. The painted house reflected gently in the water, now and then dismantled by a whirl of water-hens, reforming undamaged in their wake.

The black sarcophagus of the ancient lord of Gurz did not insist to me on death. Death was a wide field of snow, a garden plot covered with logs, cannon, a blow – I turned death off, and saw, reflected in the lake from the easterly bank of trees, a nacreous thing I had not seen there before.

Having walked around the lake and into the pines, I found a grove of lindens. They had given up their leaves and so revealed the temple.

It was no bigger than the black tomb, but of dove-pale stone, stems of eight slight columns, roof like the upper third of an eggshell. Two bare lilacs were sentinel at the entrance. A frieze of women passed around the column tops. The floor was cracked and plush with wintry moss. Once through the lindens the house was not to be seen. In summer, the temple itself became invisible.

I went forward a short way, up the one broken step. I did not like to enter. An altar, chained with ivy, had had its surface cleared not long ago. The sheaf of wheat leaned there, going to its husk, grapes and flowers had been scattered, and fed the thrushes and the finches.

There was no statue.

I had been correct to her, at least when I must, when she was Vulmartis in the south and I a child. But Vulmardra I did not know. Gurz had said, the peasant women worshipped her.

Quickly I inclined my head.

As I turned to go, I felt as if fingers brushed at my cloak. Within the tense quiet of that spot it was enough to make me jump in my skin. I looked back – the scene was undisturbed.

'Shall I bring you something, lady?' I asked aloud. I found

I was trembling. 'Is something still owed?'

Owed? How not. For the slicing of steel under Drahris' ear, for the First Blood and the Fourth Blood in the garden of swords.

Two giant hands seemed to hold me cupped in them, off the earth, two unseen eyes seemed to stare at me. Had I horribly offended in ignorance? Were my crimes and sins worse than I had thought? Must I be enslaved again by terror and pain to appease her?

I was let go. A vast compression of the air seemed to wash in soft swift pulses down into the ground.

I would bring her wine and honey in the morning. It was, even if I had imagined all of it, no poor thing to show homage to the deities of any place.

4

A morning or so later, a courier arrived, the outer world intruded.

He wore the livery of Vollus' establishment, and for a second seemed familiar and everyday because of it. Then he came across the Parlour and placed in my hands a letter. Covelt conducted the man away to be refreshed in the kitchen quarters behind the house. The fire-boy, who had followed them in, put another log on the fire before following them curiously out.

I did not seem to want to open the letter. There was no reason not to. My financial reimbursement of Vollus, and her stipulated fee, these had been attended to before I left Krase. But of course. I had understood she would want more than that.

With the ivory paper knife I slit the embossed paper.

'My dearest Princess Aara,' thus she started off. Intimate, reminding me, I felt, that if the affectionate adjective was at my discretion, the aristocratic noun she had helped me to.

She trusted I was hale, had suffered no sort of relapse after the journey. That I discovered the estate to be as charming as she had always supposed it. She had been sorry not to hear from me (oh, then I should have written her some drivel, more thanks, safeguards), but my minutes must be filled indeed. It happened now, she would be travelling herself to the coast before the winter set in hard. Her party was a small one, some five or six persons, a handful of servants. Might she stop en route and call on me? Perhaps, after the busy social life of the city, I might even be glad of a day or two of visitors in my peaceful nook. (Her prose jolted me quite. It was as if, in choosing such phrases, she pointed out her insincerity lest I should miss it.) As for her calling here – how could I refuse?

I sat and tore serrations along the edges of the paper.

My stewardess would manage everything. I had only to be present, effect more smiles, remember the way one chatted to citizens.

Finally, I read the last paragraphs. She imagined I heard nothing of the war. The city was abuzz with it, but half the news was stale. One was informed the Charvro Alliance, puffed from its little victory over that nincompoop, Dlant, was completely up in arms, while southern insurrectionists probed the other weaknesses of the Empire. (She spoke scathingly here. Could it be she took extra care, for letters to me might be intercepted – was I not a Southerner?) Certainly, half the legions were flying east and south like the wild geese. They were saying, there would not, soon, be an eligible gentleman left in the old capital.

'Return your answer with my man. He has my orders to leave you at sundown, but will probably dawdle at some tavern on the way. If I am welcome, expect me on the Feast of Urtka.'

The feast of the Bear-god was movable and fell farther along the calendar this year. Which I had known, yet at the mention, my stomach twisted sharply. I had seen it celebrated only once before, among the flambeaux in General Dlant's pavilion.

Had she chosen that, too, in order to unnerve me?

I had hoped to find her a friend before. She had acted the

part well. Perhaps that would continue. Or was this the day of reckoning?

There were three carriages. The second was crammed solely with luggage, another with servants. From the foremost carriage emerged two ladies and one Vollus, and two gentlemen, one of advanced years, and, nearly tripping him with its leash, the huge brindle cat.

There were also outriders, a pair of Kronian officers and their military valets, all in the black uniform and varying straps, stripes, epaulets and braids of gold and silver.

I felt a child, shy and self-conscious. Also irritated. They came flouncing and pouring over at me, up the steps, into the veranda, introductions tossed like unmindful nosegays – even the cat scratched its talons on a veranda post, chided too late naturally – though what matter, when wolves had already scored it? I was partly backed into the Hall. The grooms were bringing the luggage. The crack of hoofs on the road threw birds and echoes from the pines.

'And Melm!' said Vollus. 'How are you, my marvellous fellow?'

She gave him her hand, unprecedented. He bowed to it, not touching.

Rose was waiting in a flowered gown under the stair. Vollus held out her arms and Rose rushed forward, seized both wrists, and kissed them.

The elderly prince, leaning on his stick, commented that his insides had been shaken up by the carriage. He would be grateful to get directly to his room. Covelt stepped forward and conducted him away. The other prince – I had not caught their titles – was inclined to remain, peering at me coyly through a diamond eye-glass on a filigree stalk.

The two ladies, bleached blondes, neither in her youth, circled about, exclaiming at the rafters, gallery, stove.

'What a monster it is,' said Vollus. 'When do they light it?'

'I gather that will be today,' I said.

Melm nodded in complicity at me. I grasped the nod as one who drowned. But Melm loved me for a lie.

The cat clawed at a leg of the great table.

'Sir! For shame!' shouted Vollus and tugged the leash.

'I protest my innocence,' said a young man's voice.

We turned, and there were the two officers, framed in the doors by daylight and sudden rain.

The taller of the two was a Quintark; he stood a fraction aside with the kind of modesty that betokened ego, or power. Both men were clean-shaven, their hair grown full to the collar in the new fashion. The other young man, he who had spoken, was Vils.

'You see, I bring old friends, too,' said Vollus, in her arch tone.

Perhaps I whitened, certainly my hands changed to ice. Vils swept me a bow that caused the eye-glass prince to express laughter. Vils strode straight forward, went down on one knee before me, raised my hands and kissed their backs. His mouth felt burning on their cold. Once – years ago – I had known something similar. Then he looked up at me, glamorous and assured. 'No, we've never had an introduction, princess. But I saw you in the spring, at Krase. How could *I* forget? But for me – you won't have noticed.'

'Yes, I remember,' I said. He quirked his eyebrows, smiling.

'You tell a fib to please me. I am pleased!'

'Indeed, she should be kind,' said Vollus, coming to my side. 'These gentlemen, having seen me safe at the Oxidian Coast, must ride off to their war.' She looked across Vils, to the other man in the doorway. 'Prince Kahrulan, may I present to you the Princess Aara Gurz.'

Vils stood quickly, and stepped away. The Quintark came across to us, his cloak of bear fur swinging from his shoulders by its golden claws. It was the face of a statue, so decidedly and strongly made. Could a beard ever have hidden it? His eyes were blue-green, like turquoise. He bowed to me briefly. Even I knew sufficient to return the bow. The name of Kahrulan was that of the Imperial House.

I had not had to do a thing. My clockwork dwelling, aided

and propelled by the merest unsure suggestions of mine some days before, had evolved into aired and perfumed guest chambers, and brimmed the bathhouse with an endless tide of boiling water. The stove was lit, with some solemnity, in its belly in the cellar, and by sunset the white pillar throbbed heartbeats of heat into the Hall and the adjacent rooms. Garlands of evergreen, forced pinks and tawny chrysanthemums were being hung for the feast. The dinner and the wine were well in hand. And for all this glory I, the mistress of Gurz, might accept smug credit.

Vollus came to my bedroom in the gloaming, when my windows were blue jewellers' paste.

She swept in, and took possession. In the chair before the hearth, on its cushion her wigged head, her black-spangled slippers on the hearth-stone, there she queened it. And the cat prowled the room's drapes and corners, hunting the ghosts of mice.

She spoke of the weather, and of her acquaintances at Krase. (The cat meowed quietly now and then in its own tongue.) Vollus ate some grapes from my fruit bowl.

'The Gurz hothouses?'

'Yes, Lady Vollus.'

'Do dispense with that beginning "lady." You've got the eldritch dame upstairs for that. *The* Lady. *Night's eyes.* She'll be at dinner, too. I recall her when I was on the boards, in her seventies then. But tell me true, little bird, are you chirpy here?'

My cue, now?

'My gratitude to you—'

'Stuff. I was paid.' I looked at her. 'Can it be,' she said, savouring, 'you grow more subtle? Well. That's neither here nor the other place. I'll tell you, you're well out of the city. This war of the Emperor's is inclining to a burlesque. Who'd have thought it? A million malcontents just waiting on a whiff of rebellion. The Charves have waked up half the Empire, it transpires. For myself, I've put my money into gold and am making for the coast. I have a little cot at Port Yast. It will be easy to be off from there, if needful. I see I surprise you,

Aara. At the state of the war, or my frankness?'

'Both.'

'Well, and who knows, perhaps you rejoice to find the North embarrassed.'

'No.'

'Yes, always say no to that. Unless,' she added jollily, 'the southern pack should win.'

'Is such a thing—'

'Is it feasible? A year will tell us. I wouldn't place a bet either way.' She tossed grape pips in the fire from her hand. They sizzled and were gone. 'Don't be frightened,' she said. 'It can't go for you as it did before. Or, even if it does, you fared nicely, didn't you?'

My heart began to hammer.

'But—' I said, and fell silent.

We gazed, each of us, into the fire. What she saw her gods knew, but for me the flames wiped out my sight, my flurried thoughts. I became calm. Yes, it was much easier to dismiss the phantoms she had roused.

'And in the meanwhile,' Vollus murmured after some minutes, 'there is the Prince Kahrulan. We must be sweet and adorable to him. He's from the bastard branch, you see, but his reputation is excellent, especially on the field of battle. If the war goes badly, the Emperor may think it best to haul his rheumatic limbs off the throne. To the granddam in the Quiet Tower he's a baby, only sixty-nine years of age. But they'll say he's senile and he bungled. The way we all now say Dlant was a treacherous villain and a fool. And the Imperial heirs are sickly or incontinents. Of the bastard branch, therefore, one – expects things.'

She spoke freely, for what threat could I be? But I had an urge, bred of some dimly-recollected novel, to tiptoe to my door and check for eavesdroppers.

The cat had manifested on her knees, and now she put him off.

'Let's descend,' said she with amused hauteur, 'let's throw some life into those *males*.' In the corridor she remarked, 'Rose dresses you exquisitely. Are you glad of her?'

In that way, our dialogue was of clothing and the vogue when we went down the stair.

'And the bracelets and hair ornaments are modelled after troves from the mausoleums of the Serpent Kings – snakes and crocodiles biting their tails, or one's throat. *Eyes!* I shudder.'

We could have been in her salon. With relief I let her guide and chivvy our conversation. The two princesses were fulsome to me, and envious. The younger prince patrolled us with his eye-glass, saying, 'Ah, you ladies and your dresses.' The elder prince sat near the stove reading a great book, paying nobody any heed.

When Vils and the Kahrulan prince entered, they brought some sort of magic surge with them. The princesses certainly came alert, and flicked their fans.

Vils again made straight for me, and stuck to me as if leashed like the cat.

Kahrulan, with an easy encompassing grandeur, steady, impartial and cool as a turquoise gaze, assumed charge of the other women.

For myself, I was caught between my strange fear and stranger, less accustomed pleasure. After a glass of wine, for which I was complimented as if I were together grape, treader, vintner and cask, I sent fear off with the rest of the regiment of shadows. The Krasian duel had been nothing to do with me, and was over. But to be singled out by this beautiful specimen of manhood, even shaven as he was in the way of my homeland . . . I think, never really having been so before, I became flirtatious. It was simple. One had watched it performed very often. And he, thankful at last to get the proper response, played up to me until we seemed to sparkle like the lights.

After all, then, a happy dinner. And as dissimilar to the pavilion of the retreat as might be.

Vollus had suggested I press the authority of the toasts upon Kahrulan. With much joy I did so. He, aficionado of countless ceremonial meals and courtly rites, saw to everything with tasteful, perfectly-timed, uninvolvement. He was *so* cool, this man, he must be bored, yet well-schooled not to show it. He listened with attention to all the futile chatter of the ladies, to Vollus and her sallies, to the cuts and thrusts from Prince Eye-Glass, and the whining of old Prince Addled-Stomach. To granny, though, Kahrulan behaved somewhat differently. Catching her glance, he held it, and smiled. It was the smile of a limpid and practised seducer, and to it she replied with such a cackle, I realised they, too, were in some game. That he was prepared to study to delight her, made him more than ever an object of foreignness. With the princess-widow of Gurz he had little to do. Did he guess her an upstart, southern rubbish . . . doubtless someone had mentioned it. He bowed to her over the flowers, he at one end of the table, she at the other. He adorned her dinner party. She would not dare ask more – in fact, would not have wished so much of him had she been granted a choice.

After the second savoury, instead of the final course of fruits, a huge cake was brought in, saffroned golden, with bears of white sugar marching round its rim. If they had been meant to be fierce, they were not. It was a pity to cut them, but cut up they were, and to each of us came a whole white sugar bear in cake – a cookery masterpiece – for which, again, *I* was praised.

'Aren't you going to eat your bear?' inquired Vils fraternally. (Even the Lady was somehow managing hers.)

'No. I don't like sweet things, except fruit.'

'Yes, you eat only enough to stay a butterfly. What built this alabaster skin, dear Princess Aara, and that hair, and those eyes – do you feed on honeydew?'

'I feed – on kind words,' said I. And flushed at my own spark.

For the last toast, Prince Kahrulan poured wine into the cup of the small Urtka statue before him on the table. (The greater one had been lost, with the Wiparvet, the whole shrine – and so much else – at Zoli.) Then Kahrulan rose, and pledged the Emperor. There was nothing special in his efficient manner at that moment. Nor in ours. But, against my judgment and expectations, I remembered how Dlant had

210

done this, before the tall war-bear with the jewelled claws.
Gurz drinking and passing the cup to me. Drahris drinking.
The other blonde princess – where in the name of the gods
was she? Beneath the snow, beneath some rock— She, too,
had had skin and hair and eyes, had moved and breathed.
Were they all now, all those moving, breathing men and
women, *bones*?

The Hall was very hot, and outside the night had grown
lucent and still under a gigantic moon. They were proposing
they should stroll about my lake.

'What is it, Beauty?' said Vils to me very softly, already
tender – and I must present ploy or falsehood, for he, too,
could not be trusted, was no friend, no ally, only a living
shadow between me and the shadow-army of darker truer
things.

'A memory.'

He said slowly, 'You did love him, then?'

I need not answer. Silence would do for my lying now.

He must approve. To one man, the love for another set
your value higher. It showed you could, in the right circumstances, be faithful, and that the next wooer must fight. How
clever Vollus was. But had she ever been able to trust? How
could you live and live and never for an instant be at peace,
save in blind solitude?

5

The lake was all white moon.

The moon filled it.

'What a night!' said Vils. He extolled its poetry, spoke of a
night campaigning when he had seen such a moon across a
marble lake of ice. Then he asked how the hunting was
hereabouts, and talked as Gurz had talked of wolf hunts. But
Gurz had not interested me, and Vils, in his vital beauty, did.
Which itself was guilty, wrong. And be wary, Ara, this is the
adult sport you only begin to think you have come to
comprehend.

Vollus and a princess, escorted by Kahrulan, were some

distance ahead of us. The other princess and Eye-Glass, both patently dissatisfied with their partner, quarrelled about the black tomb. The Lady, and Prince Stomach, had not joined us.

In the pines, the temple to Vulmardra glowed. Vils did not notice.

As we moved through the white and glittering air, his spirits turned to melancholy. He was slightly drunk, perhaps; I could hear his breathing, a thing I had noted with men intoxicated, or ill.

Presently, we were on the shore. The reeds seemed crystallised by cold. He snapped one with a brittle sound, and spoke of making an octoreed to draw the nymphs from the forest. But then he did not need those paltry nymphs, and I should be careful, the woodland goddesses would be jealous of me.

Before I had known he would, he took my hand.

'All leaves to be cancelled. But you make it hard for me to imagine dying,' he said. 'That's good.'

And suddenly I was listening to the other young man's voice, on the landing above: 'I'm to go out again tomorrow. *You* know our danger.' And she, 'If you mean I should invite you into my bed because tomorrow you may die . . . you'd be very foolish, Thenser.'

And, inexplicably apposite, Vils said, 'Do you recall that duel? Zavion, the Southerner?'

I removed my hand. I stared at the lake.

'I didn't mean to offend you,' he said.

'Only by speaking of the Southerner.'

Vils checked. 'But you—'

'I took my husband's country with my marriage.' And who said this? It was a woman, in a woman's voice.

'Princess,' said Vils, 'are you about to tarnish me with that, like all the witless tribe – those— If you've heard, then hear my side, at least—'

He had my hand again. Confused, I looked up into his face, his dark and half-unfocused, anguished eyes.

'Thenser Zavion,' he said, 'threw in his lot with the North

– as, forgive me, did you Aara, my lovely, brave goddess. *He* made a kind of marriage vow. To the Emperor and his legions. And Zavion kept the vow. For himself – why, such a man—' his face brightened, he laughed aloud at something only remembered. Then bent his troubled eyes on me again. 'If I trusted him, so have many others, oh indeed, in far superior and more lofty positions.' (Trust, to *me* – did I not know you could not—) 'Then, if he *has* betrayed us—'

'Betrayed,' I said. Or, she said it, that woman who spoke with my Aunt Elaieva's voice.

'Urtka's buggeries,' said Vils. He begged my pardon. Then swore again, and worse. 'He's off with his battalion, with his Unitark's thousand. Either he's to assist the North or he's over in the Charve lands, giving to them on a salver every considerable dish he has learned with *us*.'

'Thenser,' I said.

'It's disgrace, madam, for anyone who was his friend. So far we keep dumb and march about glaring. I've called out twice and been called out. None of the duels came to swords. As yet. We have tougher meats to carve, in the South and East.' He turned from me, still with my hand in his. He was sober. 'I've said too much. At best, I've been tedious. Will you keep the confidence, sweetling?'

It seemed now it would be a slight to take away my hand. I was sad, as he was. There was nothing to say.

The others were a quarter of a mile off, either way, and we in the closet of the docks. He judged that swiftly, then drew me in and kissed my mouth.

I felt nothing. I searched and hoped to feel. But there was only the warmth of him, the taunt masculine persona brushing against my softness. A gale of longing tore through me for something that did not exist. I closed my eyes in pain, and he held me to him once more, before I must, in turn, draw myself away.

Child that I was, I wanted to bury myself in the ground, run from him. Elaieva, Vollus, kept me in my place, and I said to him quietly, 'Sir, on the eve of battle, even, such—'

'Excuse me,' he said, 'let me off. Or, set a penance.' He

sounded gladsome again. It had taken only that to restore him.

Wanting only to hide, to be buried, I caused him to walk with me along the shores of the moon, towards the crowd of Vollus and her women friends and the kissless Kahrulan.

Vollus said, 'The swans always return to the lake, don't they? And you take to water in the same way.'

She had come with me to my room, invaded a second time my sanctum. My toil, like a task in the afterlife, was never to be over.

She had kicked off her slippers. She ate walnuts in sugar. The cat, which had swum in the lake, had gone to be dried.

'What I mean by that,' said Vollus, 'is that you do everything I would have told you to do, untold. Or is it the early training? If you've had to content a man a few months, that will do it.' She massaged her thick creamy neck and brow, but not her immaculate hair. 'And what do you think of him?'

What to say *now*? 'I was amazed he recalled me, from your house.'

'Eh? No, no.' She laughed. 'You mean Vils. Vils is all very well, but I may have to drop him, since this affair over Zavion. Of course, it could all be fuss and nonsense. Has the traitor-Southerner betrayed us back to the South? There, I'll hedge my bets. But I don't mean pretty black-haired Tritark Vils, who kisses water maidens behind dock-leaves at midnight. I referred to the Kahrulan prince.'

I allowed myself a breath, and let it leave me.

'Am I to think something of him?'

'You should always think something, whether it's said or not is another matter.'

'But I'm to say it?'

'Say.'

Flummoxed, I gained sudden refuge in fancy.

'When I was a little girl, I read a story in a book where a prince had eyes of blue-green. And the witch stole them to decorate her hair-pins.'

'Gruesome brat!' crowed Vollus, hilarious. 'Did he get them back?'

'I forget. It was a story.'

'You must tell him. He would laugh.'

'Never,' I said. 'Can he?'

'For sure. He has a sense of humour and is very well-read.'

'Doubtless he would have preferred to spend this evening with a book.'

'Like old Flatulence? Take no heed of Kahrulan's uninterest. His blue-green eyes are always wide awake. Your witch would have been in a fix trying to disocular that one. And he was in favour of you.'

Exhausted, I could only answer, 'He seemed barely to see me.'

'Again, what he seems not to see is just what he's looking at. Vils he also saw, making ungirdled love to you all night. Appetite whetted, by the lake, he nudges me aside. Is there, says he, some understanding between those two? I replied I had no knowledge of any. But he'd better question you himself.'

I sat upon my bed, my hair loose, for I had been fiddling it from its coiffure. I wished Rose would come to undress me. But no, this Vollus would have organised her delay.

'Well,' said Vollus, 'let's put our cards out in plain view. Don't look scared, or are you only exasperated? It's not young love I'm talking about. You wouldn't have survived to your fourteenth year if it'd been that. Under that milk-crystal and floss, you've a brain. Or is it only instinct?'

'Vollus,' I said, 'I'm so tired and my eyes are aching—'

'Bathe them, salt in water, and *Queen's Jewel* as tea, for that.'

I waited.

'He requires money,' she said, 'and property. Something at his shoulder. Such an estate as Gurz would fit his bill. For you, you're comely and have the grand way with you. More, you have southern blood, and in this tide, that might prove handy.'

She had said I had a brain but what an idiot I was. I had not even suspected. And so *this* was the recompense.

'On your side,' she said, 'unless the sky falls, within two years he'll be the Emperor of the Saz-Kronian Empire. By the hour of getting, that may mean less than it did. But permit him half a decade, mark my words, he'll have cut up the map like that cake we chomped at supper.'

'You're speaking to me of Prince Kahrulan.'

'No, the fire-boy.'

'You're saying he wants to marry me for this estate—'

'Ah, no. Forgive me. You're unversed in all our customs and I forget. It couldn't be a marriage – not of the sort you had.'

'That marriage was makeshift enough,' I heard myself snap.

'But legal monogamous union, for all that,' she said smoothly, smoothing me down like the cat. 'This would be a form of marriage. It's recognised in law, and quite honourable. But you would never be Empress. Another woman would be that.'

I floundered there amid these meaningless values, and heard Elaieva again, like ice, declare, 'You are saying that to repay my debt to you, to make your future Emperor fond of you, I'm to become his legalised whore, let him feed off Keer Gurz's lands, and end with nothing of my own, even the right to wed where I will.'

She said, dryly, 'You have another in mind?'

'Of course not—'

'Hmm, I do hope not. Vils is in dire straits enough, without lugging his smashed heart behind him.'

'And what of the people here?' I said. 'The retainers of this house, Melm—'

'Why do you suppose they were so enchanted to welcome you? Why do you suppose they dreaded going randomly into the old Emperor's coffer? They had some inkling of *this*. Cristen Kahrulan is popular. They'd rejoice.'

Trapped, I was in the snare. I was in the cage. For cage it was. Aradia would have burst into tears. But Elaieva rose slowly to her feet.

'Vollus, I'm sorry, but I haven't the resources to continue our discussion. I can't think why my maid is this dilatory. I beg your pardon, but I must say good night.'

Vollus cracked the last sugar-walnut between her teeth and got up in turn.

'It's I who must beg your indulgence, Aara. Naturally, you need your sleep. We'll talk again.'

I did not doubt it.

As Vollus' slippers clipped away, Rose came bustling. I had her unhook and unlace me, then sent her off without a word. She was Vollus' thing and had danced to Vollus' tune, not mine. Let her sulk, the red-cheeked bitch. I needed the private dark.

Chapter Two

1

Two days after the Bear Feast, Vollus' party rode away to
Port Yast. They left before sunrise of the third day, and from
my West Tower, I heard nothing of it. My stewardess besides
had had, at my request, a sleeping draught made up for me of
potent herbs from the herb garden below the bathhouse. The
two festive days of rides and card games, elaborate meals, and
sessions of reading aloud in the library – even, on the final
night, a charade – had worn me out. To Vils I had not any
longer been able to extend guileless encouragement. Whatever was to happen, I could not involve him further as a
pawn, the backdrop to my attractions. He mused, then
brooded, then went off laughing after the younger of the
blondes, who received him with pettish enthusiasm. Kahrulan
did not pay me the slightest attention beyond what was due
and unavoidable. But Vollus' comment had stayed with me,
that what he did not gaze at was his focus. I had never known
her wrong in things devious and small.

After my long sleep, breakfasting in my bedchamber, they
brought me a letter with the rolls and apricots.

His seal was of a gauntlet above the arms of the Sazrath. It
seemed he was not yet entitled to cross them with those of
Kronia.

'Princess, all thanks for your generous hospitality. May I
abuse it again? In a week or eight days, I will be crossing your
territory once more, returning to my regiment at Krase. I
shall be alone, save for my man.'

* * *

Rose was concerned for me.

'Now madam, won't you try this conserve of berries – whatever can be the matter?'

'Don't you know?'

'What can I know?'

'Get out. Take that disgusting mush with you.'

She stared at me, biting her lip, perhaps attempting to cry.

'Out,' I said. I tried the word, 'Out, you slut.'

She ran.

Temper was my reaction. I blazed with rages over all the little pointless things. Sleeping too long or not enough, the icy temperature of the room because my fire had gone out overnight. The noise the pillar of stove made. Being laced. The dressing of my hair for the long, empty, *awaiting* days.

The north wind blew on the seventh day, the White Wind, and a scurry of snow frosted the land. He, however, did not arrive. So, it was to be the day after.

Kahrulan would find it difficult going on horseback if the snow fell with any purpose. I, of all people, knew that. Did he plan to be snowed in with me? Laughable.

I could not miss the pleasure of my servants, the looks of Melm. Did *Melm* wish me to be unfaithful to the dead in a legal unmarried alliance?

Partly I wanted to take him aside. It was not done. I was no longer an infant, to discuss things with my slaves.

I had dismissed Rose from my person. I gave her only sewing tasks and ruled she could attend to my infinitesimal amount of jewellery (the jewels of Gurz, if any other existed beyond the bartered bangle, remained in the possession of the Lady.) Another maid was elevated to the status of my body-servant. The girl was younger than I, and clumsy with unuse. I washed and curled my hair myself for fear of soaped eyes and scorches from the tongs. Otherwise it went undressed. It had been freshly bleached for Vollus' visit. As well, I could never trust my nervy skivvy with bleach. *Trust*.

To such particulars I had reduced it.

That seventh night I went to bed early, dropped stonelike in demolished sleep, woke after a few hours, in a deadly insomniac inertia.

A tiny bell-clock in the passage marked time with me through the night.

Winter dawn lay years away.

Then I dozed, and dreamed that curious dream which does not present itself as dream but as reality.

I was stretched, not in the bed, but across the lid of the black marble tomb below. My nightgown shifted, and strands of my hair, in the low roar of the wind. I was not cold, only pressed to the marble by sorrow, and – death. For surely I was dead, to be there?

Then the wind flew away, and the architrave of sky turned to the different gloaming blue of morning. Through a break in the pines along the lake, I could see the star Vespal hung low, like a white flower of light. She came up just where the temple must be.

The head of my seeing, living corpse turned again, and I beheld the painted house – poor house! It was a ruin, its stacks and roof all fallen in. Only the Wolf Tower, the westerly forward bastion, of solid stone inside its plaster, had survived. Even there, the conical crown was gone, the windows glassless, channelling the twilight in and out like the currents of an ocean.

Does this mean then that I will die here? That I will bring them their mean glory, which they covet, be the belonging of an Emperor, end here forgotten, at the mercy of time and place as I have always been at the mercy of everything?

My head rolled back again as it had done in the fever, and I saw, along the crushed wreck of the road, a phantom battalion riding. Perhaps ten hundred men, or more, or less . . . They wore a uniform barely distinguishable, yet it seemed unknown. Each man, bloodless like the winter fires upon the snow, bowed to his reins, the horses were like skeletons, I had seen their kind before. The banners drooped, were dark rags. And through the tatters and

221

hollows of this army, the light was passing in and out, as through Wiparvet's corroded tower.

Up to the road's end they came, and halted, rank by rank. Their commander stared before him. His features were so blurred I could not make them out. He was like all the men, but for his hair, which shone and took colour from some nonexistent source.

Leaning from his mount, with a drawn sword he struck a pillar of the tomb five times.

But on the sixth stroke I wakened.

It was only the clock-bell sounding in the passage for six in the morning.

I got out of my bed, frozen cold, filaments of the dream all over me, and went to my west window, my north window, like a madwoman who does not know direction. Then I was reminded of the roof, to which access was available by a narrow stair I had been shown but never thought to utilise. In a trance, I put on some garments, the fur cloak they had added to my coverlets. Something compelled me. In the corridor no one was abroad. I wandered, found the stair, ascended, forced in its lock a stubborn key – I surfaced into stone-silent ice-blue air.

The parapet reached only to my knee. Beyond, the landscape seemed to open so very wide, caught in the glacier of false dawn.

Under its dome, far, far below, no one lay across the Gurz sarcophagus. But it was true, Vespal was rising from the pines like a kite of silver flame. And where the temple stood, occult in the trees, there were other stars, glimmering and moving.

My heart halted, rushed. I shut my eyes and looked again and saw the last stars fading, but I saw them fade.

Not sorcery. It was some winter ritual to the goddess. Were they thanking her for snaring me, for hooking the onset of an Emperor?

The rage came and shook me. I felt wound tight from foot to skull. I drew back from the parapet, returned into the house, ran down and through it. I passed not a soul.

Normally, even at this hour, the women would have been about. Not today.

In the Hall Wiparvet stood with a new garland of evergreen at his neck, and the fire-boy poised in horror at my advent, his basket of logs before him.

'What are they doing?' I said.

'Who, mistress?'

'At the temple.'

He dropped eyes and head.

'I mayn't say. Be a man, mayn't go there.'

'Dolt,' I said. (*Man.* He was a little boy.)

I went past him and unfolded a leaf of the door and stepped out into the veranda.

The light had clarified, even in the minutes of my descent. But no birds sang. There were no birds to sing. The cold was like a blade. Ah, but I knew the cold. Old enemy, we are reconciled, you and I.

There, the phantom army had halted. There the ghost with Thenser's lion's mane had struck the pillar. Traitor. Traitor twice over. Worse than any corpse your name will stink – South and North.

I turned my foot upon a stone. I left him behind me.

Where the pines gave on the linden grove, they had killed something. It was a little black water-hen. I was sickened and tears sprang in my eyes, but the cold tore at them. Alas, one could not weep for the death of a little black water bird when one had seen the death of men. But then, too, knowing the dominion of Death, neither would I have killed you, little bird.

A powder of white blossom, unthawed snow, lay on the sentinel lilacs. Beyond, inside the temple, the women crowded. Those who could not squeeze in there were outside.

They were turning to look at me. All my women, all the women of Gurz. The kitchen drabs, the under-maids. The chief of maids. My clumsy skivvy. My stewardess. And Rose, there she was, with a round morning face, mooning at me.

Would they race to me like hounds and rip me in pieces? It

was an old rite, involving blood. Who could say what they would do?

But then the stewardess spoke.

'See, the mistress must come to her, too. To the She.'

And they moved aside and I saw the altar, and by the altar was the grandmother Lady, in a white robe belted with a sash of gold and indigo, and her hair unloosed, thin as grey smoke yet long to her knees, fraying all over her.

She beckoned to me. She smiled.

She was crazy and the rite was filthy and barbarous. I would be rent and ripped apart, my hair and teeth and eyes pulled out—

'Come, Aara,' cooed the grandmother, 'come, pretty girl. The goddess called you.'

No, they would never kill me, even in religious ecstasy. I was to bring them an Emperor.

Numb with cold, my muscles oddly fluid, so that I might have fallen but somehow did not, I went on. Through the women, up the step, into the shrine.

The *pressure*. The *power*. It closed around me. I was in a globe, like that of a pale golden tulip. It sang and hummed and smelled sweet, not of the incense they had sprinkled, but of honey. Every hair on my body stiffened. My sex, my breasts, engorged. But it was not sensual. It was a cup of lightning, and it held me.

'Here, take, take.'

The grandmother pressed something on me. Her voice sounded distantly. I could not really see her, she was distorted, as if in water – or was it that she stood *outside* the globe of power? I took what she gave. I stared at it. It was a full-blown yellow rose. From the hothouse, where but. Yet, they did not grow roses at Gurz under glass, for such flowers had no scent, and the perfume of this rose was like wine, like the wine called Topaz.

I laid the rose gently on the altar. It broke apart. It was a heap of golden coins. It was a dew of golden blood. It was the tears of a gold statue. It was faceted topaz. It was a carpet, a pattern – I craned forward from a mountain top to see the carpet on the valley-floor, and what its pictures told me, but I was too late. The pattern had been sewn: A field of golden grain.

My eyes cleared and on the altar lay a rose of ochre paper, and the women were chanting. I could not decipher the words. So I sang to her softly, in its mother tongue, the rhyme of the apple tree, which they had said was once a hymn of Vulmartis.

When the women filed from the temple and got out on the grass, the sun was almost up, the sky streaked with brick red. Suddenly, they were house-women again. They hurried away.

The grandmother took my arm. Someone had covered her in a great cloak of grey fox. How many of that fox dynasty I had seen one morning, in the frosty wood, had gone to make her warm?

The star Vespal ebbed, dissolved. The singing power, the globe: quite gone.

As we walked slowly along the woodshore towards the house, behind the vanishing tail of women, two riders came out of the farther pines, onto the road.

Abruptly, catching sight of the traffic crossing to the house, the foremost horseman reined in. All at once both horses were turned, and bolted back into the trees.

The Lady cackled.

'*He* knows,' she said. '*He* knows.'

Prince Kahrulan, accidentally overseeing evidence of a women's ritual, had absented himself, circumspect as the fire-boy.

2

He did not mention anything about religion when I met with him at luncheon. He said he and the servant had stayed the previous night for an hour or two at an inn farther west, then started for the estate at four this morning. 'Not an inn of the loveliest,' he said to me, 'but one is prepared to suffer and strive, when the coming reward lies close.'

If he meant the house, or myself, I might take it either way, perhaps. Kahrulan was another proposition, one to one. All that concentrated wholeness, attentive now *only* to me.

As if he did not concern me, as if I had not been obsessed by him for seven days, I had left him, unmet, to my servants. I went to my bedroom and sprawled in a swimming sweetness, honey and gold, and sleep.

When I woke, I was scarcely bothered by him. I called Rose to dress me, and to powder and paint my face, but only had the tongs to my hair. Let him think this loose style was the new vogue. (It had been in the temple.) Neither had Rose mentioned religion. Her reinstatement she took meekly, maybe uncertain of its permanence.

When I went down to the Parlour, Kahrulan got up from the sofa by the fire. Having forgotten the impact of his self-assurance, a stab of compunction went through me. If I had dreamed of ghosts and gold, if I had been present at a ceremonial old as the forest, here was reality. How strong and definite reality was. It promised always that no evasion, finally, would do any good at all.

'And when must you leave us?' I inquired, as he began on the baked lake fish.

But he looked up, and stretched his closed mouth, merely amused.

He made light conversation throughout the meal. It was easy, through his auspices, to go on with the social and proper.

'In fact, to answer an earlier question,' he said over the marzipan and straw brandy, 'I'm to hurry. I will beg a bed from you tonight and get off again before sun-up tomorrow.'

He had told me, Vollus was safely installed at Yast. The Oxidian streams were warm and the harbour seldom froze, it was a fine spot for wintering. If he knew her true purpose, her access to flight, he did not reveal.

'But for you, all alone through this cold inland weather. The winters here are fairly solid.'

'I've experienced a winter in the North. I wasn't, then, in any comfort.'

'No, indeed.' He lowered his eyes, which were his beautiful feature, though few women, I think, would not have stolen a second glance at him. 'Princess Aara, shall we come to business? You are – what? – seventeen years? And a young widow of a noble scholar who, against his will, involved you in ignominious and appalling suffering. Now, this estate is yours. I understand,' he paused, to make a show of delicacy he did not insult me by demonstrating I should believe, 'that Lady Vollus put to you a certain proposition.'

I met his look, feeling my colour rise, my own eyes darken. 'I'm fifteen. I'm a Southerner. I married Gurz since he wanted it. I took the estate because it was expected *I* would want *that*. Now I'm to want you, and some sham to save my face, and make me into a – a—' I stopped, having no words, then came out with a choice pair from the army, 'a dough-kneader.'

Kahrulan raised his brows.

'Not quite,' he said. 'The type of union is called the Heartgift marriage. Some of the most exalted ladies in Kronia have consented to it.'

'For love,' I said ingenuously.

'On occasion. More often in the way that you and I would contemplate. For security; gain; not I hope without some consideration on both sides. Eventually, I'd suppose, with affection.'

'And one day some other woman to be your Empress.'

'Are you envious?' he said. 'Of her throw at the crown, or her run with me?'

'Neither, sir, since I don't want either. Your crown, or you.'

'That's honest. Like most honesty it's a slap in the face of the recipient. I stand slapped. But won't you think again?'

I left the table. I walked across the room and leaned on a pillar of the hearth.

'Only fifteen,' he said. 'Common sense hasn't shut my eyes to your looks, princess, don't think so. Or don't you care either for that, detesting me as you do?'

Then he, too, got up and came straight to me, as Vils had

227

done. He took me by the waist, almost by the neck, and swung me round. Then both arms and hands became a support, so I could fall back and let myself be taken. Which he did. Gurz had kissed me in this way. To Gurz my blood had not responded. Drahris – was this what had happened, or begun to happen – the force of strength, the implacable destiny that flung me on and would not let me be myself— Or was it that in these men *was* the North, that spirit of iron and brass which had destroyed the one I was, made me the one I had become. This invasion, though only now of an embrace, a mouth, the truth made *actual*—

I pushed from him and he let me and I gripped the mantelpiece for support.

'Very well,' I said, the sentences tumbling out, 'whatever you want. This *Heartgift*. The estate – *have* the estate – do I go up to your bed with you now?'

'Certainly *not*,' he said. (So, he could laugh.) 'Unless . . . No, unfortunately, it wouldn't be the thing.' Smiling he returned to the table and sat to drink the taste of me in brandy. 'Can I flatter myself the unbridled magnificence of my lust is what convinced you?'

'There's no escape,' I said, 'and I give in.'

For a long while, he said nothing then, and when I turned, he was examining the brandy in its glass, untouched. At last he said, 'I can only tell you this, Aara. I'm not a brute and I'm not unreasonable. If I lose my claims to what I expect to get – I'll see *you* don't pay for it. If I attain my goal, you will do well. Yes, I see that means nothing to you now, but – fifteen. Dear girl, in five or ten years, it may. For children, it would be better not. But if it happens, they won't be stigmatised. Once I must make this Imperial marriage you any way disdain, you'll be free in all but title. Any man that you choose – I don't expect you to become a nun. Perhaps even, you and I may remain friends in this dim, distant, half-improbable future I'm weaving.'

I sat on the sofa and took up some embroidery I had begun. It was a poor effort, on all counts. I was neither seamstress nor diplomat.

At length, he got to his feet again.

'I think what would be most sensible, since I'm pushed for time . . . I'll go and take my sleep now. Get off before sundown. There may be more snow, and the better speed I make—' He stood over me and raised my hand. Only his mouth had moved me, his caress did not. 'If you want to change your mind, do it now, and quickly. I won't force you. Not today. But if you haven't put me off before I leave, I count it settled. Can you hear me?'

'Yes.'

'Say no now. Or accept me. If you don't say no now, I won't give up. No love songs. I need the cash and chattels. I can get them elsewhere, but not so simply or, dare I say, so beautifully. I should like very much—' he employed, also, army words, far stronger than my own. 'But I'd like you happy, too. Well?'

'Yes,' I said. I gazed only at my messy stitches.

'Look at me,' he said. I did. 'Well you're no liar. Yes. Be it so. On your feet and kiss me farewell. We won't meet again till spring.'

The second kiss was, if anything, more rough. I gave in, to Kahrulan and my own senses. Part of me stood by and wrung its stupid useless hands and grieved. But for what? For what?

Thus kissed, we parted.

As he said, we did not meet again till spring.

3

The swans came with the snows. The lake had frozen, and I took them for a snowbank. But the bank altered shape, and had wings.

The women went down from the house with baskets of food. I followed. We cast the scraps of fish and bread. These kings of heaven seized them in beaks of marigold horn.

As Keer Gurz had told me, the lake was white with swans, but only for the briefest while. We were some recollected station on their journey south. From ancient times, from prehistory perhaps, impulse had set them down here.

Grooms broke the ice to give them drink. Inside a week they flew away again, like the snowbank lifting.

Sometimes, then, the servants would skate on the lake, but only in the earliest morning, that I might not be offended at the sight of them. I had no inclination to take up the art. I had grown again, and waists and hems of rich embroidery were being added to such of my gowns as could not be let down. Child no longer, I had now too far to fall.

After the swans, they said, the wolves would come. I was not to be alarmed. They were timid creatures that would attack only sheep or hares, or something prone. Past wolf hunts had been for winter exercise or to cull the packs, not from any sense of danger.

Once I heard wolves singing in the forest. But they were invisible just as the seen swans had had no voices.

Three letters came together from Kahrulan. They were friendly, but not intemperate. 'Tell me something of yourself,' he said. 'Of course, I'm in love with you. But don't let me love a painting. Who is this delicious Aara of Gurz?' He signed himself only *Cristen K.*, and recommended where my replies might be sent, to ensure they reached him. He would be on the march by now, he did not tell me where, for the policy of war forbade it. Let me think of him kindly in the winter lands. He did not speak either of battles, gave me no news. With the third letter came a piece of jewellery. It was a silver crocodile necklet, biting its tail and an apple of ruby— Assured now of getting my money, he had spent freely on me and was possibly in debt. I thought of sending to say I would pay for his present. But that was too harsh, too mannerless. I could decide on nothing else to speak of. Could not regale him with anecdotes of me. The note I penned was frigid, my thanks for the jewel, inquiries after his well-being. It reminded me of notes I had been forced to write an elderly relative when I was five or six, after birthday tokens, or a Vulmartia gift.

The winter. There seemed no end to it. It had only begun. That other time . . . We had been within the forest's whiteness. Black uniforms on snow, the struggling horses, the blood of butchery.

There were mornings, evenings, the smell of smoke drifting from the house chimneys or the kitchen sickened me. There were dreams.

Wolves gave tongue in the woods, or the ghosts of wolves, those which had scored the veranda posts, scratched upon the doors like shy lovers: I saw none of them.

I read and read until my eyes were calcined coals and my head ached day and night. I stitched samplers of drunken flowers and deformed bluebirds. Rose bleached my hair.

Winter bleached the world. An illness of whiteness. Will it never pass?

For the midwinter feast there would be some rejoicings, I had gathered, but these did not seem to involve the temple of Vulmardra. Its mostly ruinous look convinced it was not often frequented. A mystery of women. And they had never said what brought on the last spasm. Even the Lady did not ramble on over the affair, though she was inclined now to ramble on, generally speaking, during her now and then visits to the dinner table. I could not be sure how much, with her, was senility, how much some cunning game whose burden I did not guess. She spoke of Kahrulan several times. She called him 'Gem-Eyes.'

The clockwork house continued to run. Granny, Vulmardra, and I presided redundantly.

I would tend, however, to wake every morning at the sixth stroke of the bell in the passage. Should I have this clock-cog of the clockwork removed? No, conquer the silliness. In any case, the light was never blue now at that hour, the dawns came later and later, on many days without a ray until ten.

The morning was black therefore when I woke, left the bed, dressed and put on my fur, as before, and went down through the house.

The women were about that day, and bowed to me, and the boy brought my sturdy boots and the maid my gloves. No one seemed surprised to watch me out into the waste of snow.

I might make my own eccentric devotions. Nor did I hide my path to the temple.

Indeed, it was myself I amazed when, on entering the shrine, I crouched by the altar and wept.

There was no aura of might or significance that I felt there, or had my tears doused it? Nor could there be any solace in the granite slab and brittle ice-blackened ivy.

I rose, chastened, and laid the hothouse flowers and fruit from my bedchamber on the stone. Sad flowers, sad fruit, to kill you more quickly in the bitter snow.

'I don't even know any more what I should ask to have.'

As I came out from the bare lindens, I heard a wolf crying sheer as slender blades passing through the silence.

I paused to attend. Then, when the howling died, went on, to the edge of the pines. And there the sound came. The *Sound*. It was the note I had once heard, and feared would haunt me, that I should hear it at some other time, and in some other spot, yet bound forever to the first, for this note was eternal. It was everlasting and sounded always, but it befell that only at special moments the partition unclove within the ear, and you could listen—

It sank away.

'The wind, the voice of our country,' said Dlant's memory beside me, but it was not the voice of the wind.

Those who hear your song will perish.

And then, I saw the god. I saw him. He was walking, with great care and delicacy, over the surface of the frozen lake. He was a wolf, as they show him to be, and – as they show him – unlike the wolves of the forest. He was far larger than wolf or dog, and of a smooth pelt, jet black. But I did not think for a moment he could be anything ordinary, no wolf, not one of the house-packs of hunting-dogs. I did not think for a moment he was anything but *what* he was.

He stopped close to the near shore, and lifted the long head with its pointing muzzle. His eyes moved across me. They were white and burning.

I experienced no fear. I was in terror. They are not, of course, the same. He might kill me if he desired. To this one

232

wolf, it did not make any obstacle that I was full-grown and upright, if I shouted, if he was solitary, or fed. He was not a wolf of the wolves. He was Wiparvet.

With the niceness of a fastidious young girl, he stepped from the lake, and began to walk a slow canine walk towards me.

It would have been insanity to run. I stood where I was and bowed my head.

I felt, but did not see him come towards me, like a low black wave along the earth.

But he never reached me. I looked, and saw with a wrench of disappointed release, like agony, that he was gone.

'What does it mean?' I asked the noiseless winter wood. But the wood knew and the wood might not tell me.

As I started back towards the house, some warmth, or a tingling sensation, returned into my limbs. I wondered if anyone else had seen the god, or heard his song. It would be important to scrutinise the face of the first one I met beyond the door.

I reached the veranda steps, and glanced back. He had left no pawmarks on the ground, for lupins to grow. Perhaps I was going mad.

In the house was bustle, unchanged. They had neither heard nor seen.

'This does mean something,' I said aloud in my room. 'I saw – I saw the Wolf, the god. What is it? What is it telling me?'

Chapter Three

1

With a succession of great cracks, like the fracturing panes of an icehouse, the thaw laid hold of winter in the forests. I had not ever heard or seen much of it, this battle of two vast natures, two metamorphic wills at war with one another. In the cities, on the roads where Melm and I travelled towards Krase, there had been the thud of falling snow, the slough and slush, mud and rain, the muddy days that were not warm and smelled of fever, the tangling of branches, which, seen close, were rendered into bead strings of buds.

But at Gurz, the snow crashed like an avalanche, from roofs and trees, breaking such quantities of tiles they must be replaced, pulling huge boughs to the ground for dismembered arms and captured standards.

The ice broke also on the lake one sunrise, with a terrific supernatural *twang*, so even in my tower I heard and marvelled at it, as if it was some other transcendent thing, but they told me at breakfast what the noise had been, smiling to find me not at all anxious.

The lawns became a seashore of black sludge, from which the needles of new grass arose as green as mint, starred with snowdrops, asphodel, and glassy violets. Primrose-green, the flowering of the lindens, the birches, initially seeming stripped almost to spikes, then puffed out in a healing pollen of catkins. Beneath the west veranda, shrubs I had never properly regarded leapt into pink flames.

The birds came in battalions, the colours of the blossoms,

and starlings, like rubbed clinker, and nightingales and blackbirds for their music.

Lethargy, depression deserted me. They had outworn me and were no longer interested. Short temper and restlessness took their place in my brain, and my veins were rinsed by bubbling alchemies.

Six letters I had had in all from 'Gem-Eyes' Cristen Kahrulan. I had sent but one. He had not reproached me, nor waxed sarcastic. He said he believed my efforts were going astray, and such was war. He said they sat upon a hill, a plain, within a wood, but not where. He said his horse was a stoic and one did well to emulate the equine fellow's patience. He said I was missed. (How could I be? He had known me less than four days.) He did not ask if I wore the silver crocodile. He did not renew his vow to visit me in the spring.

But spring had come and he was a man of his word. Irritated, I began to see his visit was looked forward to. The whole household, the whole countryside, was putting on its best for him.

In my turn, I took out my lighter dresses from laundry and herb-press. I thought, I might be pleased to have the novelty of seeing someone again.

To receive a letter from Vollus was not on my agenda. I had reckoned he would inform her of my agreement if not the way in which I gave it. Despite her threat that we should 'talk again,' we had not, save in the general discourse. I was thankful to be spared. Probably they had by then colluded on a plot, and left the table to Kahrulan's cards. To commend my wisdom in accepting – I did not think she would risk that much on paper, nor did she. Opening the letter, I found this:

My dear princess, here I am to say, for the present, my adieux. I am going off on that little excursion, to the blue waves of the Temerid, the palms and isles of Sibris. What an adventuress I have become.

She spoke then of the severe winter, her middle-aged joints needing a warmer spring. She talked of the price of cut flowers and blessed my luck in hothouses.

Perhaps you hear something of our war? The news is everywhere

*but maybe not at Gurz. What can the tree-cats and wolves want
with tidings of military engagements? And even you, my Aara,
with your scant knowledge of geography. Search out the school-
room globe if you wish, and when you have located Tuybiz by the
black Sablic Ocean, mark there an immaterial success for our
foes, the Charvish Alliance and certain Eastern potentates. On
the Charve borders, there have been several advances and some
precipitous retreats. Of course, the enemy stand no chance at all
against the strength and astuteness of the Emperor. We expect
triumphs every hour. At Urmantha, on our native earth, the
North's laurel crown went by default, due to the crass stupidity of
the command, which has since, to a man, been hanged. There are
many such stories.*

Then she spoke of the price of fruit, raved over my
orchards, and ended, *Well, I am away. Doubtless I shall hear
the peal of Kronian victory trumpets from the high seas.*

When I had finished the letter, I carried it down into the
Mistress Parlour, and there read it again before the pallid
fire. They had sprinkled rosemary and rose-herb in the dishes
on the mantel, and that smell, fire-risen, will sometimes
bring back a sudden fright and confusion.

Even I, through the lens of what she had said to me
previously, could read the sentences of peril written large
between the lines of optimism, prices, and downright lies.

From what she described, her own departure not the least
of it, the Empire was in utter chaos.

Presently I did indeed consult the library globe.

Eastward, beyond the mountain vertebrae the gods had
drawn up through the backbone of the land, the Sablic Sea
was far enough – it must have been a resounding disaster to
echo in the west. Of the advances and retreats she did not
spell out for me which side was accountable for which. And it
was clear. Her censure of Kronian commanders and note of
the reprisals against them, evinced further lunacy, the
strands of rule and defence giving way together.

No one had spoken of the war to me at Gurz. Some must
have had some inkling . . . or not. Until now the roads had
been largely closed. We were a day's ride by courier from the

old capital, off the beaten track. And only Kahrulan's dispatches had been brought.

My Heartgift betrothed had not thought to warn me. Vollus had done so. Why? Could it be an altruistic deed? Or only another hedging of bets; one day I might, in my oblique harlot's fashion, have more power than she. That was, if anything survived for me. All other items put by, was it likely now my swain would call on me, going courting in the vitals of who knew what defeats?

Like a bell tolling, a distant roar and scream of shells. My ears made the utter quiet into invented noises. Was I in jeopardy? Again, again, would the mindless war chariot go over me, drag me with its dripping wheels?

2

'Are you ill?'

That was his greeting, a month later, as he walked into my chamber in the West Tower.

When I said nothing, he went on, 'It's hardly irreproachable, you know. To meet in the bedroom. That we have agreed on something or other – one or two are in the secret. Which is as it should be. But you have a virtuous reputation, Puss, and for the sake of both our good names, I'd rather you kept it.'

'Then I'll come down with you at once.'

'That would be better. If you're able.'

'I'm not sick.'

'I thought, perhaps . . .'

'Your delay had distressed me.'

'That you might have been worrying.'

'For your safety, Prince Kahrulan? Of course.'

'No. You're too much a baby to care about me yet. For your own.'

I trembled. I said, almost coyly. 'Should I have been worrying for myself? Isn't the puissance of the Emperor enough to keep me safe?'

'We'll discuss that. For now, let's go down to your Parlour.

Or the garden. It's a day of heaven. By the by, my name is as I sign it.'

'*Cristen K.* is how you sign. Then your seal of the gauntlet and the arms of the Sazrath. And once there was a crocodile in your letter. Shall I call you *Crocodile*?'

'By all means. To be given a pet name by you would be encouraging. More so than one page of letter to your maiden aunt wrongly addressed to me.'

His exact concurrence with my inner thoughts on the type of that letter, made me blush. Which it seemed he liked. We went down arm in arm.

He had found me lying on my bedroom sofa, a pencil drawing lying by me. Young veils of flickering green birch tinted my windows and a creeper flowered there, and the pot of camellias had madly bloomed. Perhaps none of this was a repellent sight for him. His seventh letter, delivered two days before, had told me to expect him, and a 'couple of officers, one small mounted detachment.' This had been incongruous to me. All I had ascertained was that, if I watched for him or waited below, I might come to see soldiers riding up the road as in my winter dream. Superstition presently gave me a day and night of headache worse than all the rest. In the afternoon of lazy convalescence, I heard the telltale bustle in my house.

We went out into the enclosed garden to the east of the house.

It was a day as he had said, full of sunny scent and birds. The yew hedges had been left to grow as they would, and massed up black; the paved walk ended at an ancient cedar dedicated to some elder god, and with a tiny shrine below on which a stone frog for ever sat.

'Now,' he said, placing me on the bench there, 'what could be better for a headache?'

'Oh,' said I. Someone, possibly loose-talking Rose, had blabbed.

'It's your age, my girl,' he said. 'You're better off to be afflicted now, than start in to vapours and migraines in your twenties. They are the more difficult to shake then.'

I was embarrassed. He was nearly thirty years of age I supposed, had sisters, a mother . . . to know so much of women. It affronted me. I wanted to be sound and pristine before him. To have myself to myself. It was all I could salvage.

Then he jumped up on the bench and looked over the hedges, like a boy of ten.

'No one eavesdropping,' he said, and sat beside me. 'I shall award you all the information, then you may question me, if you wish. Perhaps you've had some messages of the war – aside from censored letters?'

'A little. A battle at Toy – Toybilis.'

'Tuybiz is now history.' He spoke rapidly at a perfect, almost silent pitch. 'The war's turned on us and is at the Kronian throat. Forget the East, and the Charvro kingdoms. They are over the borders. The Sazrath's gone down. The last report put the vanguard of the Alliance at Jermeena.'

I started visibly. To have a place that I had journeyed through so named brought immediacy home to me.

'That close,' he said. He appeared neither grim nor aggrieved. Perhaps, with his personal plans for the future, he had foretold all this to the slightest detail, and now it was merely falling ripe. 'They haven't as we have let the winter get in their way. But more than that, it's to be feared we blundered.' He lowered his coolly gleaming eyes. The Emperor had made the mistakes, and the minions and high command of that Emperor. Not Kahrulan, for Kahrulan had been forced to serve and to obey. 'Not least did we blunder over a man – you may have heard of him, a Southerner who allied himself to the North. He took the North's pay, and ultimately took the North entire.'

The birds in the bushes seemed to lay their songs, that the garden might not lose a syllable.

'You could have heard mention of this man, a cunning devil, called Zavion. A gambler of some wit I gather, and diced for us and won. What he failed to learn of us isn't worth the learning. And he's given every jot to his king, and his king's Charvro friends. The routes, the vulnerable spots. He

240

has been living in our pockets and not been idle. Urtka knows, however, whereby he squeezed out such gallons of juice. No one seems to have held his tongue. They hung Kronia round his neck for a bloody love-gift—'

'A Heartgift,' I said. I laughed dully. (He would only think me still in the mesh of my female vapours about which he knew so much.)

'Listen, my dear. This is the next move, as I see it. They'll split away towards the capital, that's certain. But also, with the fourth and nineteenth legions at Krase, aside from her munitions, they'll want to pen us in there, too. Do you see what that means, Aara?'

'No.'

'Your eyes tell me you do.'

'Another siege.'

'It's probable. While they hold two of our legions penned, we pin some portion of their forces in return. The watchdog tied at one gate can't steal the chickens at the other.'

Behind my eyes, on stalks as he had said, my vision was of Krase Holn, with the haze of heat on the river, and the green porcelain domes, the winter palace, the parks, the streets . . . and with it mingled other scenes, other domes and parks and streets – until I pushed shut the mind's casement and looked again outward at him.

'What should I do?' It was, after all, fruitless to protest. He would have to help me.

But help me he did not.

'You have a choice, Aara. Take refuge in the city, a chance I'm obliged to offer your servants. I predict few will want it, but those that do you must, in law, permit to go. Krase is well-provisioned and excellently garrisoned. I'm afraid I shan't be there, nor am I at liberty to tell you where I *shall* be. But I promise you, Krase won't go down as your own – as your experience with cities might cause you to think.'

'They'll dine and dance,' I said, 'as the cannon thunder.' I sighed. That was all. 'Is this what you advise? That I go to Krase Holn for the siege?'

'Or we can get you to the coast.'

'Escape like Vollus.'

'Oh, has she? I rather thought she'd sit it out there. One may spy her now and then, circling over a battlefield.' He glanced to see if that comment shocked me. 'Or again, stay here. In my opinion you'll be safe. If and when they squat down at Krase like that toad-god under your cedar, the forests will be stocked with summer game. There are estates and houses all around the city which will fall prey without a doubt. But this paradise of Gurz is three days' march or more, and not famous. I'd say they'll overlook you. Yes,' he added, 'you seem better now. You're deep in love with the estate and don't want to go, being very much out of love with flight and siege and warfare. Poor Aara. I don't blame you for that.'

I composed myself not to be moved. I trembled now with reactions of all sorts. But he should not make me cry, nor cry out again across the gulf to him.

He seemed to respect my effort to be calm and valiant. In his future courtesan, these might be valuable traits.

'Besides,' he said, 'I trust I can assure you, once we have the enemy as our guests, it will be short work, one way or the other.'

He did not explain that statement. At the time, I did not even puzzle over it.

He said, 'Only one more item. We're empowered to take an amount of foodstuffs and other necessaries from all landholdings. The Gurz granaries and cellars are bursting. I don't imagine you'll object, or even notice. But I did think you'd prefer I saw to the job myself.'

I remembered the City Militia coming to my aunt's house in the twilight.

'And must you take the men as well?'

'My dear Aara, your elegant stewards and gallant griddle-lads? No thank you. Not even peerless Melm, though he knows the war-trade. And he certainly wouldn't abandon you. We will make do with our legions, and – the puissance of the Emperor. And you,' he said, 'have had enough. Do you want to go in again?'

'No—'

'Stay here then. Look at your pretty birds, you kitten. Truly, I would see you somewhere else safe if I reckoned it essential. By summer it will be done. We'll have our own ceremony then. Thank the gods for war, or I couldn't keep my hands off. You won't hear a single cannon over your loud nightingales. My word on it. Have I ever lied?'

I wore the silver crocodile for the dinner.

The detachment captain and his adjutant dined with us, a meal at Kahrulan's suggestion laid homespun in the Parlour. The two lesser officers were under his aegis, and definitely in awe of him. (I had already heard the entire detachment and some of my landworkers, cheering the prince over by the stables.) The men had been allotted quarters in the kitchen premises. My gift-betrothed opined I would take a liberal view, there might be some babies with the new year, for men going into battle were inclined neither to moral strictness or care. What a pity, he said, that *we* must be seen as above reproach. But we should shut the Parlour door at least, and the fire-boy had a heavy tread.

What they took for provender I had no idea. My stewardess sought me in the evening, but only to offer details of the dinner, and the second dinner our kitchen would award the soldiers. It took Rose to point the obvious. 'Some of those boys will never taste a good chicken or a ham or a cheese pie or a salad again.' A cake was baked especially for them. I think they dined better than we did, and certainly in more ease.

When the brandy had been broached and I made a move to leave them, Kahrulan caught my wrist in plain view, and the captain and adjutant huffed and puffed and bowed themselves away in haste. He had the grace to brim their goblets before he shut them out.

Half seated and half asprawl on the sofa, able to be decorous almost at once should any knock occur, he went much farther with me than he had. Dim fires coursed through me, and in my breasts under his hands a silver aching nearly hateful, unbearably sweet— Yet I had had no real appetite for food and had little appetite for this. Much more than a year had passed since Keer Gurz had last embraced me. Not to be touched had brought a kind of happiness, as if each month of chastity washed off some staleness, healed some bruise. Kahrulan intruded, for this wakening of sexual desire in me reminded me of pleasure I had formerly known only from my own hands as a child, acts performed in eyeless hidden dark, having nothing to do with men, I had thought, but only with some inner craving which, newborn, blind, and ignorant, yet comprehended all there was to know, and guided me infallibly towards a molten disintegration like a silent scream. I had never questioned it, never believed it wrong, or normal, a magic thing of the dark, a private matter, to be celebrated seldom and always, always alone.

But life, the throes and pantings of men, their heat and hands, their lips and whisperings, began to teach me otherwise. This miraculous adventure I had happened on was common property. It was a piece, moreover, for the duet and not the solo musician. The terrible display Gurz had made of himself, could I, too, be capable of it? I was afraid of that. Afraid that this man, his eyes now extremely like jewels, and greener in his burning watchful face, would take me to that brink and fling me down. Then I resisted the sensual gratification he might, unselfishly, have given me. My malaise assisting me, I turned from the path, and leaning back, gave him mental if not spoken or physical evidence of my withdrawal.

Then, presently, he too leaned back.

'You've been very generous to me. We shall see, Aara. One day, one night. You and I.' Later, at the mantel, he said, 'You'll say you're seventeen when we're joined. And the paper you sign will say it. Am I correct, you will be sixteen in summer?'

'Late summer. The autumn.'

244

'Well, that will do. A wedding requires sixteen, and I'd like our union, though not quite a wedding, to have the tone of it.'

'Would you,' I said, 'marry me in true marriage, if I asked.'

'Don't ask me,' he said. 'I would not, and it would sully what we will have.' He was lighting one of the long clay pipes from the rack. The fragrant tobacco exhaled, a thin creamy blue into the air. 'Is that the trouble? Do you regret *true* marriage so very much?'

'No,' I said. 'I was Gurz's toy. He only wed me at the end.' He frowned. I saw he had not been told. 'Does that devalue me?'

'Not at all,' he said slowly, 'but it makes me wonder again, a little, of what material you're made. But, the Bear. You don't know yourself.'

Then the fire-boy came clumping, and when he was done and gone, Kahrulan remarked that, with such sluggishness, we could have had the full business seen to, but the boy's reporting us at different sides of the fire might raise a few brows in the house, or get him his ears boxed.

We retired. He kissed my hand a pure good night upon the landing.

'I'll be gone before you wake. None of your servants will desert you, by the by. If anything changes, I'll send you word at once.'

'You mean if you change to me.'

'No, opal-eyes. I mean if there's any danger here. But there'll be none. Now go to bed and dream of me, and write some expurgated sentences of it in a letter, which I shall expect within the week.'

I went to bed, and did not dream of him, but of a red darkness, from which I ran, sensing another ran beside me, but I did not call out lest the pursuer also heard, and maybe I sensed only echoes of my own footfalls.

In the morning, he and his men were gone. As he said, he never lied about such things.

3

They unlocked the way into the rooms, at my request. Possibly they had supposed I would ask sooner, the key was all bright and shining, and the lock oiled. I pictured the stewardess saying to her higher subordinates, 'Now the other arrangement's to be, she's taking her leave of him.' It was not that, of course.

I thought Melm might want to come with me. They said he went there in person, to tidy things, and even the girls were not allowed to dust save under his orders. But Melm only bowed and let me in, and departed. We did not often, now, exchange words.

The Master Study lay on the east side of the house. It was a large chamber, opening both from the Hall and from the veranda, although that door had warped and its lock was so corroded it was left alone, except by importunate wolves.

There were endless shelves, stacked with Keer Gurz's books bound in leather and some in covers of padlocked metal. In jars there were also several antique scrolls, carefully labelled, works of naturalists and philosophers who had written in the classical world. It was all as I would have expected. A large desk, with crystal weights, a copper balance, myriad drawers of papers, curios, waxes, pins, a pair of volumes set out – either for show, or pathetically as he had got up and left them, thinking one day he would come back from Dlant's campaign. There was also a work-bench of marble, cleaned and cleared, but with little fine inexplicable tools, and an apparatus for distillations, everything brilliantly polished under a few weeks' dust.

On the walls were boards to which were pinned pressed leaves and flowers with written paragraphs on their being – in a boy's hand, then, in other spots, the hand of Keer Gurz as a man. There were also beetles and butterflies, quite beautiful and horrifying to me, their viridian and verdigris and acid cyanic and yellow markings on them like skulls and eyes, their mummified death. He had killed them because he loved them, to look at them and study them better. On another wall, between two columns of books, a wolf pelt, long, drab, badly-cured. The notation read, *Slain and cured by me. Taken with flint-shot, two flints. I am ten today.*

In one corner was a small harpsilon, which surprised me. I had not thought he could play any instrument, and this indeed was fettered closed. Then I found a note, too, on the lid, pasted on a faded rose: *My mother's.*

It was uncanny, as if he had been about, jotting, to answer any queries I might have.

I climbed the stair from the Study into the East Tower. Midway was an annex with a bathroom, but the water also was shut out. Above, the Master Bedchamber, and just across from it, a chapel. A carpet from the East was on the floor of the chapel, an old, aromatic censer depended with two or three flies enamoured of its perfume buzzing there, unable or unwilling to get out. A niche with gold-leaf showed where the shrine had stood, with the Bear and the Wolf. Wiparvet was ordinarily the house-god of Gurz, and worshipped openly in the Hall by all who wished, in their season. Here, the master and mistress could evince piety, ask their boons, confess their sins. (I had called the estate priest only once, as a courtesy, though he was now and then at the house, to see to various simple rites. I had not said much to him. Melm tipped him, and I stood by.) Then, into the bedroom master and mistress went, and lay down for sleep – and carnality – in the huge black bed, with its barrel pillars carved with branches, trees going back to trees.

The bedding and curtains had been removed, leaving only the magnificent frame. Above the wooden canopy stood the Gurz device, the heart-shaped shield, the staff wreathed with white flowers. The motto was written beneath in gold. I read it: *Both, or Neither.* I understood. The staff was the immovable, an indomitable warrior strength. The flowers which grew from and coiled it were plenty and easement, flexibility, peace, the holy earth.

There had been all this to instruct, yet he had been like an infant wandering. Nothing had taught him. Both or neither. Reaching after both, he had lost everything: Neither.

A window faced the pines, the sky of latest spring. A final

butterfly was lying in a quartz case on the sill. It was an insect of the south, tiny and piercingly blue. I had seen them in the gardens of the old palace at The Lilacs, not since. How strange. Someone must have brought him this, and like a siren it had lured him on.

When I had seen such butterflies, that had been the day I saw Thenser, a prisoner in a green glade.

The butterfly is a cipher for the soul, in classical romance. Why then this compulsion to kill and pin a *soul*? Where is your soul now, Keer Gurz?

My thoughts became too large and choked the room.

I went away, a pilgrim who had touched the relics but felt no relief. I was not cured. Of anything.

4

No cannon did we hear at Gurz. Not one stray enemy soldier marauded in our woods and pastures that early summer, though Kahrulan's letter (the eighth) came with black uniforms. They would say nothing of any import, nor did his letter say anything. It was playful. He did now reproach me. *Either your tender words to me are war torn, or stolen, to be browsed by some other lonely man, or you are a heartless nymph mured up in your stream or bush, and kindly only to it, nor able to write.* It was a fact, I had not written.

The estate was self-sufficient. The work went on about fields and orchards already showing their fruits, the lavish vineyards and groves. The lake swarmed with fish. They said it was a kindness to catch some, giving others a chance to live.

Now and then, infrequently, travellers brought news. Some peasant families fleeing in our direction from the war zone, some horse thieves who had done badly in the vicinity of the guns. Once a carriage of ladies and gentlemen who were hastening *to* Krase from the other end of the land, to have a part in the 'glory of the siege,' as onlookers.

The white lilac guarding Vulmardra's temple had come and gone, when one tenth of the Charvish and Allied army sat down before Krase Holn.

They got up again on Yellow Rose Eve – uncelebrated in the Sazrath – midsummer.

For my part, there might have been no siege, no war.

It was to be called the Treaty of Three. The Eastern Potentality, the Charvro Alliance – now including that country which had been my own, swallowed by friend if not by foe – and the Empire of Saz-Kronia. It was signed simultaneously at the hour of three o'clock in the morning, at Sablic Baslia on the eastern borders, Zoli on the southern, and within the palace of the Kronian capital.

The Emperor's advisers had been vociferous, the subject princes and monarchs of his dominions equally so. Even those who had clamoured for war were declaring that, in order to gain an ultimate victory, there must be truce and respite now.

A month after the Charve cannon were wheeled into Krase behind donkeys, each wreathed in flowers, after the kissing and drinking in the streets, the fraternising and vows of kinship, Kahrulan sent a ninth letter. It gave me these details lightly. He had been at Baslia, and would have a narrative for me, if I liked historical frivolities. Had he not told me all would be well?

Out here in the world we are all in love. Charves with Kronians, Kronians with Charves. How can it be we ever fought with such adorable neighbours? We feast them in all our capitals and carve up the East for their lunch.

His language was unguarded. It came to me, his position had altered, he was in some form of power.

From ill-understood books I had once read, I began to consider intrigues of all sorts. Secret alliances and unpublished treaties. It was all conjecture. But he had known how the scenario of the drama would proceed. If he had not penned it, the authors had discussed it with him. Perhaps his gods had spoken to him, liking his pragmatic duty better than religious tumult.

Kronia lost lands. The Emperor was a smaller emperor, like a figure of tallow which had melted in great heat. He would be simple to melt altogether, and reform into a younger, brighter, starrier man.

And amid all the welter of history, Aara thought only this: Next then he will claim me for the Heartgift. Gurz and I will be drawn in. *I* will be swallowed up by friend if not by foe.

5

In my dream, a woman was shrieking. Was it I? I woke. This was a morning of the summer's last quarter. The light was blue as bice.

The shrieks had stopped – they did not belong in the dream-country, nor had they issued from my throat. Some ritual – had they again been slaughtering something by the temple of Vulmardra the crone-mother-maiden? As the land burgeoned, and harvest and winemaking came near, I caught the waft of some extra preparation, dampened by word of war, by evasion, perhaps through my presence. I had not, the previous summer, come to interrupt them. The day of their Vulmartia fell the exact day of my birthday. I had been in the city, then. But now? Some prologue, some bird or beast cut with sharp knives— Yet, they had been a girl's cries. Surely they did not – could not – offer the goddess human blood—

She took the blood of women. Once every month, and in childbed. And the blood of the man upon the battlefield. Don't think of that.

The images flew about my skull like flies. I got out of my bed, burning hot, went to my west window, the north window, finding only the smalt light too thick to see through.

I must go up to the roof. By the narrow stair.

I threw a shawl across my nightgown. I left the room. No one was abroad in the corridor. I sought the stair, and climbed, and came to the locked door. The key was in the lock. I turned the key. I surfaced. The air was cool and heady, the sky so high it seemed to draw my soul out through my eyes.

At the south parapet, the summer world of false dawn spread before me, the patching of colours all tinged to blue, the smell of blue apples and plums in blue orchards, and blue

grapes from blue vineyards that would wash to green when
the sun wetted them, blue roses, blue wheat, and bluest of all
the lake and trees.

Vespal stood blue-white on the pine tops.

Below, a soft noise, familiar and unknown.

I looked straight down and saw them riding out of the
wood, the phantom battalion.

For a frantic moment, I stared about me. The Wolf Tower
to my right, the Quiet Tower of the old lady eastward –
intact. The roof was firm under my feet. But below, the
cavalry trotted from the forest on the paved road. *Ghosts*. I
could not distinguish the uniform. Only the blued glint of
braid and metal, buckles, harness, swords, helms.

Ten hundred men? Not so many. Less than a hundred.
And there were no banners. The horses were glossy and solid,
the light did not stream through them all in rays and smokes.
Not ghosts, then.

The leader of the column had a black Kronian cloak,
sabred with the bice flashes that would be scarlet by day. A
commander's cloak.

No one lay on the Gurz tomb, not myself nor any other.

Beneath, the house doors had opened, even as the order
was called to halt. Covelt, my under-steward, foreshortened
by the storeys between us, walked out on to the road with
three of the house-men.

Not ghosts, no they were not ghosts. But no Kronians – the
column's uniform was off another palette than dawn and
Kronian black, despite the Unitark's finery at their head.
And the shouted order, for I had heard a sentence of it
spoken now and then, at Krase in jest, was Charvish.

The leader sat on his horse and Covelt stood looking up at
him. They conversed. I could not hear what they said.

A scalding wire ran through me, plucked, vibrating,
hurting me.

I should leave the roof before they guessed and glanced up
at me. I should go to my room and conceal myself. I would be
safe there. Melm and all Keer Gurz's house would protect
me.

★ ★ ★

Rose burst into my chamber one beat behind her knock. She was in her nightgown, her hair in curling rags. She had seen me so frequently, but never had I been granted such a vision of her.

'Madam—'

'What is it?' I was calm.

Rose was almost hysterical.

'Madam – they're here – they're in the yards, and the officers in the Hall.'

'So I gathered. Charves?'

'Oh, it's worse than that – oh, it's so bad—'

'Control yourself,' I said. Poor Rose. Having once enraged me by her alliance to Vollus, she had been giving me lessons ever since in temperament and venom.

'Madam. Yes. But – they say you must go down at once.'

'At once?'

'He sent me up. Fetch her, he says. But my lady's in bed. It's not yet six o'clock. We're to search this house, he says. Oh, the Mother!'

'*At once* is out of the question. Send one of the maids to say I'll go down as soon as I'm able. Then come and dress me. Have someone bring the warm water and my morning drink.'

Rose, compressed by me, fled out and fled in again, along with the water and the mint tea.

The soldiers – Kronians – had gone up to my aunt's apartment. That should not happen here.

'But madam,' she said, the Northern girl, heating the hair-tongs, fetching summer shift and corset, 'it's so dreadful. You haven't heard the worst.'

'But you will tell me, I've no doubt.'

Her face screwed tight in unhappiness or irritation. She said, 'The Southern battalion is here for the provisioning of Krase. And to see there aren't any traitors or rebels here, plotting against the Treaty. Well! And he should be able to sniff them out, that weathervane, every leper can find his own disease.'

I already knew. I had known. I had always known. I had

252

known since I was thirteen and he came up to me, in the
room with the grimy window, and put out the dancing jewel
in my brain, all I had. I had known that I must not greet him
as then, a child in a dirty dress, sluttish hair, without mask or
shield. Yes I must be well-masked today.

Rose twittered in fear. I was taking so long, making her do
so much. She was on the verge of accusing me of prinking
myself out to catch his eye, that Southern twice-traitor, that
leper. But naturally she never dared say it. She sensed the
awful thing which had taken me over, which would answer
her, and blast her with its white steel.

So I washed and perfumed myself, was laced tightly and so
mailed in the bones of dead animals. I put on a camouflage of
grey Eastern silk figured in purple, a war widow's sash of
black and red. The girl dressed my hair with pretend-
casualness for the daybreak. Ear-drops and small rings of jet.
She painted my face.

I watched in the mirror as I was assembled, and at length,
seeing my breathing, I marvelled that I breathed, for never
had I been more like a matchless doll.

There was a faint commotion below as I opened my door.

As I came out on the top of the stair he had arrived at the
bottom stair, next to the Wiparvet, about to mount to my
sanctum, for I had delayed such a very long while.

'I trust you've not been inconvenienced in your rush,' he
said.

The south portion of dawn streamed in from the house
doors, sidelighting each of us for the other.

Suddenly, looking up at me, he went very white.

Inside my manifestation, I could look back at him without
panic or dread. I was safer than inside my room, than inside
my veiling at the duelling place, behind the oak tree of a
king's garden. Surely safer than behind my childhood, which
had only left me open like a wound.

I had grown five inches since then. He would be the taller,
by the same amount.

He did not know me, no it was not that. But I glimpsed
what he was seeing. Elaieva, now expertly tinted for her inner

snows, blonde on white, and above a stair, as at their last meeting.

And he. The wave of light shining hair, the dark pale eyes, differently set and shaped, that was all I remembered.

His fair skin, retrieving its colour, his eyes had shadowed over like metal under cloud.

He cleared his throat and said, quite levelly, amiably:

'You must forgive the mannerless intrusion, princess. I've been told your circumstances, and whose protection you are under. The estimable Prince Kahrulan.' He waited, I said nothing. He said, 'Which means there's no threat to you, nor to anyone honest in the house. But this estate was over-looked, and knowing of it, it seemed best someone should – sift the place.'

'You are searching it for malcontents,' I said. My voice was far away and worked perfectly, like a well-tuned instrument. I felt how I managed it, the breath hitting the voice box.

'I'm sure Gurz is free of taint,' he said, charmingly. 'A precaution. And then, a few stores for the hungry troops at Krase, with your leave.'

'Do what you must,' I said. I added, 'I can't prevent you.'

He stood at the stair-foot, looking up at me, and I, at the stair-head, looked down at him.

All at once, with no warning, something within me began softly to cry out.

Rose had said a kitchen girl, seeing the mounted men in the woods, had screamed. It was this I heard. Yet, too, it had been an omen for me. That outcry.

'Please believe me,' he said, the young man I did not remember, remembered better than all other things, my past, my beginning, 'you and your property will be treated with respect.'

And, as if something pulled him forward, he began to climb towards me. When he was on the seventh stair, I said, 'This is the estate of my dead husband, Colonel Prince Keer Gurz.'

He stopped again. His face changed, became mocking and sour. 'I noted your sash. I regret his death, madam. I hope you realise, I didn't strike the blow in person.'

It had very nearly been the other way. It had only needed Gurz's signature on a paper . . .

My ears droned. The cannon I had not heard here, some imbalance left over.

'But,' I said, smiling a little, 'how can I be sure?'

'You can't, of course, be sure. I am a very infamous warrior, madam. Trust me, half the widows of the North have been spitting on me. A heavy rain for any man to endure.'

'You are twice a traitor,' I said. *She* said, Elaieva, the doll, the demon.

'Yes,' he said. 'Scum. I've heard it through several times.'

He turned half away from me, looked back down the stair. His men were on the road outside. 'You will excuse me. The sooner we begin, the sooner you'll be shot of us.'

He went down the stair again. His stride was sure, gracious. The unseen brightness of him had tarnished. The black Unitark's cloak furled after. It was his flaunting of the badge of traitor, for otherwise, we might think he attempted subterfuge, or forgetfulness. Behold, said the cloak, *here* is what I am. I recalled in Vollus' salon he had said before them all: *I stole my money by deception of the Emperor.*

And it was I sent you to this. My scratching out of a name. You would have gone to death bravely. You were ready to die, you had seen enough of life. I made you live on, as I did. I gave you life, and this I gave you, the widows' rain of hate, the tarnish, the duel in the garden, the cloak of the traitor.

But he was out through the door, pared nearly to bone by the light, and his hair a grey-gold flame like that running on my gown.

How can I call you back? You do not even know me. For three seconds I was one you loved, or thought you loved, when you were a boy of twenty in a ravaged city. But then I was again the stranger, Aara, bleached to snow, Gurz's butterfly pinned upon Kahrulan's sexual scheming.

Thenser Zavion walked off across the lawn, with a Charvish officer.

Horses trotted along the road, obscuring them.

He was gone.

That morning they searched the house, with a minimum of noise, deftly, politely. They came even to my door. I had been expecting it. I was more fragile now, less positive, but crimson Rose, with eyes watering, let them enter at my instruction.

The uniform of the Charve patrol was of a pallid slaty blue with ribs of red or russet. I did not recollect the Charvish colours from the retreat. In the snow at the end, everything had seemed black and white, and besides, some quantities of them had stolen elements of Kronian uniforms, from the dead.

'And what do you think,' squalled Rose, 'my lady's secreting here? A herd of strapping conspirators under her bed?'

The four Charves smiled, and one remarked, in Charvish, that he would not mind in that case standing in for them. I felt myself go pale in my turn, and they and I saw I knew rather more than something of their language. Was it so very unlike that of my own country?

Just then, he appeared in the doorway.

'What in the name of' (some Charvish oath) 'are you doing here?'

They seemed to say they were searching, as ordered.

'*Not* in the lady's private rooms. Out.'

They went. Thenser, closer now, clicked his heels and nodded his blanched set face at me, and was gone again.

They were to make their bivouac in the wood, and we were to have the honour of providing their dinner.

My house raged. What a travesty of that other willing meal prepared for Kahrulan and his men.

I sent for Melm.

'Set your mind at rest, princess. The Southerner, whatever else, has them on leash. Nothing has been damaged, and little disturbed. Covelt sent a couple of our hotheads across to tour the fields, so they're out of harm's way. This pack should be clear by tomorrow.'

'And the Lady?'

'She has the slight chill she caught, and was persuaded to remain in her bed. He gave them orders to leave her rooms alone. And he looked over the Master Chamber himself, so there's no nastiness there.'

Since my alliance with Kahrulan was confirmed, Melm and I had not had such a long dialogue. He seemed affable, reassuring. There could be no resentment. But now, what would he say now?

'Melm, I want to be prudent. The Treaty has made friends of them, however spuriously. This Southerner besides was known to Vollus.' He watched me attentively. 'I think I'll take a page from her book. Will you tell them to lay a dinner in the Mistress Parlour? Ask Zavion yourself to dine with me, at the usual hour.'

Melm seemed to consider. To my surprise he said, 'Yes, I think that's wise, princess. I hesitated to suggest it, but you've had a clever teacher, at Krase. Of course, he may refuse, but I think it will be a relief to him. Not to be kicked out down the steps in the general way. A dangerous man. The good side of him would be the better one. I'll see you're not left alone together.'

'No, Melm,' I said, 'Only the usual service. He's astute. He'll notice if I'm surrounded by a bodyguard. He won't insult me. He knows . . . of my acquaintance with the Prince Kahrulan.'

'Very well then, princess. Your reasoning is sound.'

At eight o'clock, to the stroke, he walked into the Parlour, bowed and said, 'This generosity leaves me amazed. On the other hand, perhaps this is some gambit to poison me.' Then, seeing my face he said, 'Don't think, princess, that's facetious. It was tried at a mansion in Krase.'

Before I could constrain myself, I asked him what had happened.

'The family had lost three sons. I was, unfortunately, sent

to look them over. (Both sides are troubled by me, you see, and give me interesting labours.) The family asked me to breakfast with them. An impulse on their part. Form obliged me to accept. But I was suspicious. I got in the way of ostentatiously offering titbits from my plate to a nice little dog the daughter liked. She became restless. Finally I offered the dog something and she rushed at me with a table knife. We got it from her. An alchemist then investigated what had been served on to my plate. It was a pickle made of wolfsbane. But the girl put her dog's life higher than vengeance for her brothers. Probably sensibly. It was, as I said, a very nice little dog.'

'Which you would have poisoned.'

'Oh, princess. I've sent hundreds of my fellow humans to death and hell. How can you think I'd hesitate over a dog? In fact, it was a bluff. I was only in reality offering it pieces of candy filched from a dish on the table when I first arrived. Everyone was eating those. As you see, I, too, raise a canine life higher than a man's. Animals – they're helpless at our whims. I've seen nothing but dead dogs and horses on the campaigns, and pet cats being fattened for siege food— In gods' names enough of this.'

'Yes, enough.'

I stood and he moved forward, bowed again, did not take my hand. Five inches the taller, yet he was more nearly placed to me than in my childhood. He had been a towering adult then. And now, he was taller, too, than Elaieva had been, fulfilling my silly child's credentials for the hero.

The diagonal scar on his left hand was seemly, the hands themselves had their calluses of sword and dagger, buckler-grip, lance. Long fingers, the newly manicured nails, on the left hand one also with a dark vein running vertically, some other evidence of a blow. His strange eyes, seen so near if only for an instant, were, like mine, of many changeable colours, that blended presently into grey. He had come spruce to this formal occasion, the uniform immaculate, the manicure and hair burnished. Behind his beauty, and his eyes, was a whirlpool of rage and pain, locked in iron, crushed in an armour of scars worse than any I could see upon his flesh.

Melm had entered, and served us the vintage. It was Topaz, but without ceremony, an old rack, still fine.

Thenser remarked on the wine, holding it against the candle flame, the gold lit back into the disc of each iris, briefly, falsely, quenching the shadow there. He had heard of Topaz.

'And of this house,' I said.

'Yes. You'll understand, I had friends among the officers and princes of Krase. Gurz had been mentioned.'

We were silent. The flowers in the empty hearth abruptly stirred, as if a hand had brushed them. Petals of lilies fell along the tiles.

'I see the dead everywhere,' he said. 'Friends dead to me, the phantoms of those who loved them. Is your husband at my shoulder now, with sword ready? Tell him to strike, princess.' And he tossed back the wine as if it were medicine or water, as if to swallow the thing he had said. But then, he spoke very quietly to me, 'I beg you to forgive my mania. Your charity has unnerved me. And, I've been astonished all day. When I first saw you – you reminded me very strongly of someone I'd known. A Southern woman, who died. I beg your pardon for mentioning this. It's in bad taste no doubt. To compare you to the Southern enemy.'

'I have Southern blood,' I said.

'Do you?' He looked at me drearily, sick of the subject he had opened. 'You must be at stretch to deny it.'

This was the closest we approached the truth. We did not return to that bottomless depth. I could not bring myself there; he did not, or would not recall enough to turn its way.

The meal was served, and it was in my mind to offer to have one of the dogs brought in, to act as safeguard for his food. But this had a sportive, ironic edge I did not want to use.

He appeared to trust me, or he longed for poison as for the ghost's blade in his back.

He did not seem as I had ever seen him with others, this

melancholy, the black mood that made him vulnerable. He was with me as he must be when alone, and, as his own company plainly did not cheer him, neither did mine.

We said a slight amount to each other. We talked of the harvest to come, and the vines, of a pair of books, whose titles, authors, and argument, I forget, but which we had both read. Such issues kept us safe upon the road's periphery. We could not discuss kin or friends, the war, the Empire, the future, even the geographic earth, without some hitch or snag.

He thanked me and begged me to pardon him, they would start early in the morning – he was sure I would be glad of that – and left before the hour of ten. Exhausted, I sat before my hearth of flowers. If I could have wept, my servants, seeing it, would have thought no less of me. I would have been mourning for my lost lord, memory cruelly stubbed upon the evening's sensible actions.

But for what could I, to myself, say I wept? For his eyes and the pain in them? For his voice, and the nail with the disfigured ridge upon it? For both our broken hearts?

One might sit down and sob at the funeral of the world. *It* never ends. But tears must.

Part Five

THE HARVEST

Chapter One

1

Thenser was in prison, in the blackness there. A checker-board of light and dark fell from the small barred grating. Kegs stood about, staved in long ago, by Sazos wanting a drink. Outside, in the yard, the gaoler was hesitating, loitering, on his rounds to let forth certain men for an airing. One could not be sure if today was your turn, for the process was random, perhaps spiteful. The gaoler had a grievance against Southern soldiers, some of them had shot off his leg at Hightower.

Then the lock was racked and the door opened. The gaoler's wicked face peeped in slyly and spoke in slangy Kronian long since mastered perforce. 'Want to come out, do you?'

'If you'll let me out.'

'Well, maybe I will. Got anything for me?'

'You know I haven't.'

'No visitors. No sweetheart to bring you treats for the friendly custodian, who is me. Good-looking boy like you, I'm quite cut up about it, that you haven't anyone.'

'I told you. There was only one lady I had an interest in. You said you'd get me news of her, if you could.'

'And I've been trying to oblige you. Trying to discover, asking everywhere after your bitch. But what do I get for my pains.'

'My boot in your face under other circumstances.'

'Nasty talk. *Nasty*.' The gaoler seemed pleased. This

263

would provide an excuse for reticence or mischief.

Thenser pulled himself round hard. 'I beg your pardon. I do have something you might like. Something I saved, sewn into my shirt.'

'An old dodge. Gold?'

'One gold five-penny.'

The gaolor spat. 'That wouldn't buy me a cup of ale.'

'It might. It would depend where you went for it. Anyway, that's all I have.'

'Right. Give me.'

It was given. The last of its kind, Thenser watched it vanish in the man's greasy neck scarf with a sense only of completion. It was with the same sense that he heard the information then awarded him.

'A woman name of Elaieva – the black house, you called it. Yes?'

'Yes.'

'Dead.'

Thenser did not protest or even repeat the word.

'I said,' however determinedly reiterating, the gaoler: 'Dead. She hanged herself. Or some of them said she sucked hemlock, in the – er – *classic fashion*. It was hushed up. It looks unloving, doesn't it, to go and do that, with one of our jaunty colonels about to take up lodgings with her. I had a deal of bother getting it out of her, that bloody little fart of a girl, some maid, with hoity-toity Southern ways—'

When the man was gone, after all neglecting the privilege of the airing which was no longer wanted, Thenser sat on the ground, his back against a broken keg. It was his usual seat, in prison. He watched the checkerboard of light and dark on the floor, and two cockroaches that were scuttering there for game pieces. That was all there was to do.

This dream, or versions of this dream, I had three or four times, and possibly more, throughout the next month. If it was exactly true I have never exactly known. I think it may well have been.

★ ★ ★

The house was now full of disturbing dreams in any event. It purred and moaned like a dovecote, oven-rife with old summer, the fermenting of a year.

And in the country outside the inadequate palisade of walls and towers, the earth pulsed. As the harvest came on, a great slow birth began, as full of pleasure as the sowing. As they pulled the fertile plants from the bursting soil, as they cut down the swathes of tidal corn, there came a long crying out of the womb of the land, but it was not a cry of outrage or pain.

They wanted me to see, the people of Gurz. And, partly to atone for the influx of the soldiers, of my phantom, the South – for which in some odd way I knew myself responsible – I went docilely where they would have me go. As before, in the dolly chariot, drawn by placatory ponies, I was borne about the lanes, between the stripes of cereal and the stepways of vineyards. See, there the yellow grape that conjures Topaz; this year I must behold the wine treading. And there, the rosy grapes and green that make for the wines for the meat dish and the dessert, and there the palest of the green grapes, for the glassy white wine good enough to drink alone. And then there is the grain looking high as the windbreaks of oak and beech, its tassels combed now by the scythes. They labour half-naked, the workers on my fields, the women's brown shoulders gleaming like the gold rings in their ears, and the men's bare backs like new bronze.

They take me to Gurz mill along the weir-stream. They take me up and down, into heights of jade and cinnabar and deep cores of royal purple. To nut trees, precious tea and spice, which are frankincense, and stinging bergamot, and bittersweet wild myrrh.

As I go about under my canopy, Covelt riding by me and now and then Rose or another one on the other seat, girls steal out of the fields and give me bunches of burning poppies and corn iris, and from the vines, knots of onyx which are grapes, to taste, and sometimes they bring their children to stare, wreathed in leafy jacinths, and laughing, or still as figures of brown clay. By the water of the ponds, where the sheep are drinking, the shepherds point me out, as last year, when first I came, they did not do. All this for all the world as if I were some icon of Vulmardra, the harvest-mother, and in this landscape, perhaps I am.

At night, tossing and turning, reaching out to quench my mouth with water aromatic of vintages, or from the dish of apples that holds the blood of the land, my half-dream is laced with molten images – fruit and skin, wine and flowers and burnished flesh, hair like light and light greener than emerald, and dark pools into which I sink.

But sinking, darkness snaps on me. I dream of a black place, with a checkerboard thrown down from a grating.

I do not want to hear bad news again.

But there the young man stands in his ruined uniform, hand wrapped in the rusty bandage, cheek rent, eyes of smoky white.

'You said you'd discover if you could.'

But it is I who am asking, importunate. Thenser now is the gaoler at my door. He does not smile to torture me. He shakes his head. His mouth is grave, firm. He takes my hand. I feel the coldness of it, he has come directly from their grave.

'They're dead, Aradia. It was hushed up. No one told you. Cry,' he says.

I wake crying. But with no tears.

Another letter arrived from Cristen Kahrulan. He did not trouble now to ask why I did not write, did not refer to it. He did not seem to have heard of, or was not concerned by, our visit by the friendly foe. He spoke of affection and made promises to me. It was almost a love-letter. But what essential had been left out, that made it not quite so? Ah, maybe only love.

There was, for me, nothing to do until he returned. He stipulated autumn now. He was a busy fellow, my suitor. No details reached me of his ascent, yet the pages smoked with it, and the courier had a sheen on him, envoy between this mighty prince and his doxy.

I could foresee him as Emperor. All my child's fancy of

what an Emperor must be, how it would harmonise with him.

Stranded on the brim of the harvest, I could only succumb to its present. My future was a blank, as if, although already so indelibly written, it did not exist, or as if I had been sentenced to execution.

The lion limbs of the year roved forward.

They took me in the lion-coloured afternoon into the small vineyard nearest the house, which they called The Mistress. Here the men and women were waiting in their decently-nearly-covered bareness, the bright handkerchiefs wrapping their heads like decorative fevers. I was given a silver knife and, assisted by Melm, cut the first swag of ready wine grapes.

'Very well done, princess,' Melm murmured. 'No lady has seen to that since the master's mother. That's six years ago. It's lucky, for us and for you. They call it the Goddess Bite.'

I sat on a hillside and watched the ants swarming over my fields, orchards, vineries.

They took me again, and I beheld the trampling of the grapes. They named it by a man's name, not, in various forms, unusual in the north: Zandor. He was the fair god in the fruit who gave his life to make intoxicating drink. His slaughter left the stocks dry and withered, but in the spring he would have rebirth in the young shoots.

It was Rose who mooned in my ear that in antique times they had made a young man god for the day, and killed him at Vespal's evening rising, letting the hot red blood mingle with the grapes. In particular vats, to this day, a few drops of the blood of a living fawn would be added. But most lands, even mine, had stories of ancient bacchanals and horrors. I told her the custom was not unknown in the south. I had come to see, from occasional remarks, she had learned my origin. It seemed to me the whole estate must be aware at last of my southernness. But if it was, they did not see it as a crime. With every scything, pressing, basket, bale, or stack or load, they were making me their own. Rather than a young man sacrificed to recompose the vineyard, they were constructing me freshly from their wheat, wine and apples.

I did not wish to have a festival for my birthday. It meant nothing any more to me, beyond the passing of another threshold. I would be sixteen, but even that was an anachronism, for on the certificate of my unmarriage I should be seventeen. And I would seem older. Though unlined, my face was keenly cut. My eyes had never lost their look of shadows, as his had not, my brother in race and treachery, deceit and anger. Thenser—

Thenser, tomorrow it is the Vulmartia, this open secret celebration in which I am to be included in some sky-touching crazy way that may tempt the goddess surely to strike me. But mostly tomorrow it is my birthday. Aradia's last. For in autumn, Aradia truly will be no more.

2

The day dawned clarified and brilliant. Their ceremony began at sunrise, but a great procession, the carrying of the Vulmardras (from the temples of adjacent villages, every rustic image was to come out into the sunshine), would reach the house at nine o'clock. Then I must join it – if I 'would' – and we should go forth with the priest and people and noise to bless the fallow bald acres of Gurz, and thank them for their yield.

Rose dressed me in yellow and green. They were the goddess's harvest colours here, I had been expecting it. The girl pinned cornflowers and leonine dwarf chrysanthemums in my hair. The earthy smell of these was potent as strong beer.

Everyone laughed and beamed upon me. Relaxed, their unprotesting puppet, I smiled in return. We drank the Topaz at breakfast mixed with the juice of peaches. Soon we were lightly drunk. It grew easier to smile, to step forward in the dance.

(Why had Kahrulan not come to these rites? The estate was to be his, they would welcome him. And I – should I perhaps welcome him, too?)

The procession became audible in the distance. Shouting

and songs, tabors, tambourines with a whirlwind sound, jingling sistra, and horns like an outcry of cows.

They came along the paved road, where the ghosts had ridden, and Thenser with his Northern cloak and Southern soldiery.

Hundreds of people in holiday clothing, and the bare shoulders and throats and limbs I had grown accustomed to, and tossing manes of black and brown hair. The Vulmardras also were parading, quaint marionettes with movable arms and necks, from pastoral shrines, painted freshly for the day, dressed in patterned cotton and hung with garlands. Each was green, blue and yellow, as I was.

My chariot approached with the ponies. I petted them and fed them bits of apple and honeycomb. Under my canopy I stood, for Melm had said that was the form of it, that I should be upright to greet the harvest. Rose, my maid of honour, in white, stood behind me. In the close gown her belly was fuller than it had been. Chatterbox, she had proved taciturn on this, but now her body spoke for her. She must have comforted the Northern troop that earlier night, along with the pies and cakes. A baby was in Rose, Rose in bloom with bud. Because she did not annoy me now, in the glow of peaches and wine and sun, I pressed her hand. 'When?' 'Oh, princess!' And she reddened. 'The spring, I believe. He was a fine man, I swear that. He's sure to make fine children. If he lives . . .' her eyes did not darken; she, too, was slightly raised from the flesh towards the sky. 'He may come back to ask for me.' 'Then, he must have you, if you want.' And Rose grinned her pretty teeth, like a glad vixen.

The estate priest greeted me, and I him, as though we were in a conspiracy of overlooking lapses.

The procession started again, with, it seemed, all my house following.

Up and down, round and about. Everything that had been was no more. The tidal fields were stacked with cloven sheaves, the trees were stripped back to the foliage. Even earlier this year than last, the all-taking. Scarcely anywhere was anything left to seize. Only in the apple-lanes did a few lanterns still hang, or here and there a peach or purple cluster of eating grapes upon a wall. The birds were picking in the stubble, and we threw them grain from baskets. The sheep billowed before us in carded clouds.

Our priest rhythmically halted us and blessed the earth and thanked it, and then bottles and jars and leather skins were passed. Rose always wiped the lip of these and poured my portion in a stone cup I had never seen before. 'This? It'll only be used today. For no other mouth but yours, or your lord's.'

How cold, even in the heat of noon, that rock with its fountains of wine.

Sometimes the wine was softened with spring water. The notes rang gold on white, fire on crystal.

They were dancing for sure, in the fallows, and in the pools, skirts lifted to the waist. Bells on sistra rang. Reed pipes threaded the woods. There were gods in plenty today. Fauns and nymphs frolicking. One caught a glimpse in the green shade, a splash of pale limbs, or browner ones. Elemental with human, then.

The procession had completed its tour. The people were less. The Vulmardras in a row perched upon a ridge above the banks of the stream.

'When do they kill the god, Rose?'

'Heaven keep you! They don't do *that*!'

'But you told me that they did.'

'The god dies at his own whim. But then, I mean the other sort of death.'

'Which death, Rose?'

'Oh, what an innocent you are, madam, and no mistake. It'll take your fine prince to teach you. Poor old Gurz, he never did, that's plain enough. Why, they'll be killing the god everywhere, the women, today and tonight. The goddess expects it. It's not infidelity, not for our sort.' I was excluded. I regarded her sorrowfully. 'Even I,' she said. 'My lover's honour is safe,' she tapped her stomach. 'But today, I can please myself.'

Then she was gone.

270

I sat down alone beneath my canopy, for greeted the harvest I had, and now might rest. I was restless, however, and twisted the grey stone cup so cold in my fingers. Where was my steward? Gone away also. Even Melm . . .

The priest was standing at the chariot side, and two girls were by him, one with a pannier of figs and roses, the other twining her fingers in his hair. He was not a young man, the priest, but he was younger now, flushed and boyish, chiding me gently. 'We must find someone to see you to the house. Look. It's only there. You can make out the Wolf Tower roof.'

'It seems miles off.'

'That's only the wine. Are you well, princess? Yes, you're well. What a pity the prince . . .'

I left the chariot. It was easy to do. Did my feet touch any part of it?

'I'll walk there,' I said. I did not want to delay him, since I knew what he wished to be at. It puzzled me a little still, but I countenanced the joys of others, though they had shut me out.

'Well, princess— But if you walk, please pay no attention to anything you may notice. These are the rites of the She. Holy, of their kind. On this day, the Mother is disposed to man and woman both.'

'Of course,' I said. I dropped my gaze, smiling to show I did not object.

Suddenly they, too, were gone.

I was alone, but for the ponies greedily browsing the turf, harvesting their own, pulling the empty chariot at will. On the ground at my feet, for my grazing, apples and peaches and wine in a skin, half full. I poured for myself into my cup. The strange sensation which buoyed me, made me sublime, tolerant, yet also acute with inner sadness, I could not let go of it.

And, though they had left me, yet all about me they were. As in the ancient time, the trees, the tall grasses, the banks of fern, the groves, all thick with whimperings and laughter, shimmerings and shivering, rippling like water under the sun. While through the reeds one of the Vulmardras watched after me, her white face and pink mouth, her eyes of lacquer and wreath of flowers.

In the legend, the god in his wandering was brought to the goddess in a glade. This someone had perhaps told me. Each was struck by the other's beauty, for where he was an eternally young and perfect man, she had upon her the aspect of virgin and queen. Among the sheaves, the vine-stocks, they lay down. He set his hands upon her bosom and between her thighs, she caressed him, his hair, the golden points of his breast, his loins. He mounted her. They strove. She screamed aloud and the sky cracked, and the sweet warm rain descended. At his groaning the roses smouldered red. When his seed was spent, the earth lay still, readied for a new year's fecundity.

In the bushes, butterflies, and arms thrashing, a silver foot kicked out. In the trees the birds, the skeins of a girl's hair, a moaning of doves and voices, 'Again, love me again.'

Endless, the turning of the wheel. The wheel, bearing me on. I went across the grass, treading an unseen path between screened mysteries. At some stage passing the painted house. Up into the wood. Under the roof and pillar tops of the pines. Their crimson trunks, the thick balsam of the undergrowth. Here the rhododendron in its autumn fire. Here the metamorphosis of the oaks. Here, the marks of the hare upon the world's back. I have come through the seasons. In my hands a skin of summer wine, a stone cup of winter, my hair undone streaming chrysanthemums and cornflowers, and somewhere my shoes detached and the green spring mantle, now only the white-yellow tunic, and stepping between stems of blood my heart could break so loudly it was crying—

I stopped. I was transfixed.

It was a glade, green from oaks and citrine from the turning of their leaves. A horse was tethered to a bough, eating the turf as the ponies had been doing.

The god leaned on the tree, but sensing me, lifted his head.

His hair of green-gold poured away from the darker gold of his face and throat, his eyes were jewels without a name. He was clad as a man, for travelling. The disguise could not deceive.

He was wary, nearly sarcastic, seeing the creature which had evolved in front of him, this dryad from the forests. He stood prepared to fence with her, with some well-chosen sentences, cruel or merely indifferent. For though he was in the spell, he had not known it.

Then, he knew.

I saw his face, changing. As if half asleep, he came towards me. Even so he attempted raillery, weightless, with no laughter. 'Princess Aara. I forgot this is the day of the Vulmartia. Stupid. I've seen evidence in every hedge and copse for two days.' Then he stared at me and I at him. He said, 'How beautiful you are, like the leaves in the sun.'

Tilting the wine, I poured it into the stony cup. I held the cup out to him. He took it, not moving his eyes from mine. He drank a mouthful of the wine, and gave the cup to me. I, too, drank a mouthful and held the cup out to him again. Now he drained it.

'I'm on my way to Yast.' He looked at me. 'That doesn't matter. I was drawn off the road by a shadow, like a black dog. And then I knew myself on this estate. Nothing matters.'

He put out both his hands and touched my breasts as if I were unreal.

'Your heart's beating,' he said.

His arms went round me. We were pressed into each other so that all of his body became known to me, its contours, its bones, its lust and need. I was absorbed into his skin. We grew together as the trees had done. His mouth was on mine, filled mine. The scent of him, the pulse of his blood, the heart hammering very fast, his or mine, indistinguishable.

I could not breathe. I clung to him and told him this. His fingers tore at the insane laces of my corset – his knife ripped them – he flung the thing away, its unfeeling bones rattling. Skin on skin now, flesh on flesh. My hands on him as his on me. His hair, the muscles of his arms and back and thighs – unknown, male, yet it was as it had been, my own hands upon my own self, a private thing, this act of oneness, monologue and duet.

Inside me, like the power of the world itself driving me as I drive against him, moving together and together, more nearly into and within each other, the notes of thunder, my body only this, and this, and *this*—

The volcanic wave broke through me, broke and took hold of me. Flung, falling, I let go. I held only to him, my raft in utter chaos and ocean. Crying aloud, falling upward from my flesh into white light and at the crest feeling the surge of him, the single low hoarse sound he made against my ear, and turning, floating down through great levels of dimness and back into the closing eye of afternoon, a mote of shining silence.

'Thenser,' I presently said. 'Thenser.'

'I'm here.'

'No, I only wanted – to say your name. Don't – say my name.'

'I won't.' He held me, tenderly, he kissed the side of my face, my hair, my neck. 'It shall all be forgotten, little girl. This is the Vulmartia.'

And so no more could I say any other thing, could not say any more the truth. Must be dumb, then, for neither must I lie. Not now.

He was constrained then as I. We did not speak beyond murmuring, the dove voices I had heard. Love me again.

His hands were tangled in my hair, his mouth on my breasts, the ascent begun once more, out of soft ashes, melting me, unbearable, so that my caresses of his body, evoking from him the groans of his own pleasure, became exquisite to me, to touch him was to touch myself, and his lips and fingers upon me in turn, turning him towards me, in the vast heat like a burning glass, twisting and shattering, hearing my own voice miles away, pleading, a long pure call, like a sigh made to a song and the sharp catching of his breath, the pause, the death throe of his ecstasy going through and through me like spears and bolts of fire, so I would die to have him die this way upon me, would die for his joy. Would die for him, my love, my only love.

'Don't,' he said, 'don't cry.'

Before, he had held me weeping, letting me weep. But did he mistake me now, think it some shame or fear, or banal aftermath? It is only love, my love. Love too strong now for pleasure or happiness. *Pain*, welcomed like any lover. Fleeting, dissolving.

'Now you laugh at me,' he said. He kissed my mouth.

We lay curled against each other in the warm hollow of the earth, two naked animals, scattered with leaves and the needles of pines.

A spotted snake coiled through the branches overhead, harmless, flawless, paying us no heed or courtesy.

'I could sleep,' he said, 'hold you and sleep on your breast. But. I must leave you. Do you believe, that isn't what I want?'

'What do you want?'

'To stay forever here.'

'Don't lie.'

'So astute, my goddess-nymph. At least, then, until the sun goes. In the warm and dry. The sea is very wet, my darling. I know.'

'The sea?'

'At Yast, a ship. The villain must be off before they catch him.'

I lay marvelling, but at his beauty, not his words. What he said or did could not matter. Only this could matter.

'Stay until the sun goes.'

'I can't.'

'I'll hide you in the house.'

'Too dangerous and dishonourable for you. A waste of needed time for me. Origos, what am I saying. A mannerless oaf in fear of his life, and why should my life be important if I can have you again. Can I have you again?'

Already and again he had flowered hard against me, and again my loins ached at his need. He rolled on to his back and drew me up over him, he worked my limbs gently, teaching me, giving to me the conqueror's position. I hung above him, and saw the pupils of his eyes dilate, the outer rings dark with my shadow, flecked with green suns, his breathing coming and going, the flood of desire. So shrilly sweet, I struggled on his body, writhed and riven, demented, tearing the grass with my nails, blind and dying. And the other sweetness, the kindness of his embrace, holding me as I returned, soothing me as if I had indeed come back from death with him, we two, returned alive.

He left me a little later, with no further explanation or excuse, and I said no other thing to him. He dressed, and took by its bridle the waiting horse. The shadows were heavy now, bowing down the forest's roof. They caught horse and rider in the weft of that weaving, unwrapped all colour and substance from them. He lifted his hand to me, that was all. He turned the horse and rode away, and the avenues of the wood closed over behind him.

I put on my undergarments and my dress. I left the corset where it lay in some bush. There would be many such, I supposed. I took up the stone goblet.

Coming from the trees, I found the sky deepened to the dense mastic of latest afternoon. Hours yet of sunset, after-glow, and twilight, the white star rising. Hours yet of months and years. My festival I had had. And it was over.

Chapter Two

1

'It's a three month wonder, I can tell you,' said the lawyer-prince, my helper of Krase, who had wrung from the justiciary my rights as Gurz's widow. 'Both powers are put out. He knows so much of them all. They've ravaged his rooms, would have taken his manservant into custody, but it seems Zavion gave him money and sped him along; he isn't to be found. The commission was resigned in quite a stable manner, with even a court witness (bribed to keep mum until after, swears he had a fever and forgot who the client had been). A melodramatic note was left, one gathers, rather like a suicide's. Or that may just be tattle. The gist is, he had had enough of it, selling to one side after the other. No one trusts him, his friends are slandered or slander him. Farewell. Indeed, one guesses it was the business with Vils. That note was come on, also, in the fireplace, mostly burned. But I mustn't bore you with this, princess.'

'What was the business with Vils?' I asked quietly, gripping my shaking hands together neatly in my lap.

'Ah. A duel. Over his connection with Zavion. Vils died, unfortunately. I knew him a little. A sterling fellow, an excellent soldier. A Quintark, if things had gone differently. It seems he had a foreknowledge, or simply saw the other duellist was superior. So when he put his affairs in order, he penned a letter of good-bye to the Southerner. It's believed to have read something like, *This man's blade has killed me, but I died under your arm.*' He paused, to see if I were distressed.

(He had exploded urbanely into the account five minutes after our sitting down.) Of course I was. I could not hide it all, nor was it necessary, for he would know I had met with Vils, perhaps that there had been a mild flirtation between us before Kahrulan staked his claim. 'Also melodramatic,' added the lawyer, who had come anyway from Kahrulan with papers to do with the Heartgift marriage. 'A final blow one feels Zavion could not, or did not want to bear. I hear he went to Port Yast, travelling by night not to be recognised, lying up in ditches. Or, if he were caught, I suspect someone will have murdered him, for policy's sake. Our side, or the South; either. A brilliant dog. Like many truly clever men, a complete fool.'

'Yes.'

'And now, madam, your signature here, and your seal. The wax has heated nicely. What a charming rosinium,' picking up the wax-dish, to allow me space to calm my nerves, 'a tortoise with a *hollow* back – quite bewitching. The Gurz curios are normally somewhat staid, I find—'

Cristen Kahrulan would be here on the last day of the month. The lawyers, a few friends, would come with him, and a brace of ladies, to make a seemly, quiet show. A priest would not be needed, though we should make aesthetic offerings to Wiparvet. And perhaps he thought that would appeal to me, its spurious air of religious condonement.

Presumably he had not come to the harvesting to show the world he and I were moral. To give our legal and morally-lustreless union more gloss.

How long ago, years ago, that day. That night of weeping all the tears I had said were spent, the waters of my soul I had not known existed. Heart's blood.

And, it was the only blood I gave the goddess. My monthly female time had failed me. Since then, three weeks. The trees shed their blood-coloured leaves and stood abruptly bare, and old, like hags, on the curtain of the changeless pines. In the lake, the blood-leaves circled, turning sere.

I had only to look at Rose to be reminded of what my

unshedding dryness portended.

I was terrified. What should I do?

I did not speak of my condition. By speaking I would give it power. I went so far as to effect some evidence that I had bled as usual, employing kitchen methods I had once heard tell of, which sickened me. But then, I did not want gossip. I did not want my suitor to draw back. I was to have connections to a future Emperor. (Though he gained power daily, it seemed, still he would need the vulgar cash of Gurz.)

Later, I must convince him that the sowing was his. This would not be difficult, to be some five or six weeks out with a first child – I could organise a slight fall or startlement.

But I did not want the child. Kahrulan would not want it, even thinking it his own.

To carry, and bear. Alone, screaming in agony, perhaps dying, for there were stories in plenty, too, of this – and for what, for what? A dream of ecstasy, a phantom lover in an autumn wood. He did not exist, maybe did not live, was dead to me for ever.

But I would have no choice.

How I resented what had been done to me. I was the baby, taking no care, always cared for, giving myself to one who used me, left me—

Oh, that was not the way of it.

Worse that the precious glamour of it, all I was ever to have, be spoiled now by *this*.

In the week before Kahrulan's arrival, I drank an infusion of herbs I had read of, mixed uncleverly by myself, and took too much wine. I vomited all night. Nothing else occurred.

2

Prince Kahrulan arrived at Gurz two days early. It was unlike him. He apologised, as the house-boys brought in his baggage and a trunk of gifts. 'I wanted the stolen hour, with you,' he said. He looked at me closely. 'You're always so pale when I find you.'

'The excitement,' I said idly.

'Oh, I thought you were pining for me.'

'That, too, evidently.'

He directed them to carry the trunk into my room.

'Let's go up, sweetheart. I want to see you unpack those things.'

'You're generous—'

'At least you'll like these presents. I called on women of taste and gave the task to them. I didn't choose any of it personally.'

He said this so brutally I wondered if it were a game, and looked at him to take my lead. But he seemed preoccupied.

Nor did he mind being alone with me in the bedroom.

In less than two days we would be joined. Probably he had decided not to wait.

I was correct.

They had brought us Topaz, and he drank it and urged me to drink it, but since my orgy of illness, I could not face any wine. Then, as I pulled out the fans of lace, the liquid silks, and three strings of pearls, longer each of them than my arm, he said, 'Will you make me burn? Not even a welcoming kiss?'

I realised what the kiss, now, would mean, and turned about to go to him. The sooner he had me the better, and he might be careless in his first desire, as later not, a handier excuse for pregnancy.

Then, even with my hands on his shoulders, his lips searching my throat, I could not.

'No, no,' I twittered, skipping away.

'Aara. A pair of nights—'

'We've waited, virtuously.'

'Two *days*.'

'Oh, let's be true to the vows,' I said, so scintillant my own voice set my teeth on edge.

But he only sighed heavily and sat back.

'All right, then. If I promise not to effect a breach, at least come here and comfort me a little.'

'But I can't trust you, now.'

'Bloody minx,' he said, with real dislike and rage one second in those gemstone eyes, so I might see what one could get from him, if one balked him enough.

It was stupid to resist. I had given myself to Gurz as a silly virgin sacrifice, without a thought of anything else. Drahris though . . . I had murdered a man, not to give. Be wary, Emperor, whom you seek to take. This minx is capable of savage jungle things. She has claws.

Perhaps he saw this in turn in my look, for he left off cajoling and swearing at me together, got up, and said he would see to his horse then, no other could be trusted with it, and the horse was a gentleman, and I – well, he would not say what I was, but he supposed we had made each other wait. It was my privilege to be a snow-maiden.

Then, out he went.

Fool. Like the clever fool, Thenser Zavion – after whose touch, I could not bear this other touch.

But I should have to.

Dinner was restrained. He was well-mannered and indulgent. It came to me, I had never, since the bargain was struck, denied him, never argued. Now I was proving troublesome. He did not like to have his labours over again. This was his dissatisfied face. The old coolness, faintly contemptuous.

Of course he must be Emperor. He knew, only imbeciles would gainsay him. He had got so far by despising fate, men, everything. His good humour, his good manners, were the badges of indifference and scorn.

He did not offer for me again.

Even had I been able to bring myself to do it, to become importunate now must have been a mistake. Worse than opposition, weakness or indecision.

I was uncomfortable with him. I had been uncomfortable with Gurz. One grew accustomed to such things. He would not often be with me, though his protection would be boundless.

'I hear you had a visit from the Southern military,' he said, when we reached the brandy and confections. Until that point he had not mentioned anything of war or politics, had told me nothing of his own fluid circumstances. It may have been a punishment, or only his discretion.

'They wanted food. And to see if we had pet agitators in the house.'

I was steady. It meant nothing. It had been allowed to mean nothing.

'Did you?'

'If we did, they were away at the time.'

'Splendid. I must congratulate Melm.' He chose a candied apple, cut through its browned sugar to the white flesh. 'And their officer was Zavion. Another historic event. He's run to the south south east, I gather. A ship called *Dvexis*, a notorious galley, pulling for Tulhia.'

'He got away, then,' I said. 'I heard something of it, from that lawyer you sent.'

'Yes, he got away.' He began to eat the apple and the brown sugar. It was not an interrogation. There was no finite thing to warn him of the truth. To Kahrulan, only Kahrulan was important. This had come to be more obvious. 'A man like that,' he said, at length, 'is beyond me. He could have made his mark. I myself would have had a use for him. But apparently some love-letter from a dying comrade, something like a woman's, bane and acrimony, that sent him off. Or else, he's about to sell us all to the Potentality.'

He smoked a pipe, and the conversation closed.

Each of us retired early, and to a separate bed.

Kahrulan went hunting next day, he was off at sunrise. It had all been arranged without a phrase to me. Already he ordered the household as if it were his, and they fell in gladly, happy to be mastered.

I lay on my sofa and tried to draw three women dancing in a grove of laurels. I could not make the women dance, or the laurels grow. It was useless to pretend that life was normal or satisfactory. Giving in, I lay back on the Oriental pillows. I could not even cry. I slept.

A light knocking on the door woke me. The bell-clock was

chiming for three in the afternoon. It would be some maid with a honey-drink, or tea.

It was Rose, bearing nothing at all but the cage of birth under her gown.

'Madam – I've come to ask a special favour. If I do wrong, please excuse me. But you said to me, before, that if – that when—' she faltered and stared at my floor as if some peculiar manifestation went on there.

Since the harvest she had brought me offerings, her namesake rose, or a fruit garnered in person from the hothouse, searched out and inquired for, particular pains taken; she had stitched a tiny glittering purse, exquisite, and given it me. She was loving me, in the former way. I had thought she made up to me again, keeping on my fair-weather side. But perhaps it was that I had been kind to her (tipsy) at the Vulmartia, not chided her for her rounding belly, and said – what had I said?

'You see, you said, if he came and asked for me, he should have me. You see, in law, madam, I can't, not without you say I may.'

'What are you talking about, Rose?'

Rose-red, she looked up again with a flash, impatient, wondering if she was to be crushed and angered, and would have to corset up her anger as her waist no longer could be.

'You see how big I am, madam. It wouldn't be fitting for me to go on in your service. Forward showing, I am, like my mother, large for my time. Unless it's twins, heaven help us.' Getting neither stop nor abatement, she said, 'He's here. Can I bring him in?'

'Your – lover.'

'My lover, madam.'

'To my *bedroom*, Rose?'

Suddenly she burst out laughing, as once she had been wont to do. In the midst of my dreariness, I suddenly caught this mirth. Something which had been dwelling in that room all at once lifted and made off through the window.

'Yes. Very well. The Kahrulan prince has made free of the

bedchamber, why not your gentleman. We will chaperone each other.'

So then she went out, and fetched him in from some back corridor where he had been hidden like a stray.

Shocked, I started to laugh again. Now Rose could not prevent herself. The poor man stood uneasy, smiling awkwardly in the thrall of women, one rich and one his love, and another maybe a bystander, as they say, in the basket.

He was a Charve. Not in uniform, it is true, but full fair-haired and clean-shaven, with grey-blue worried boy's eyes. I half remembered him from the house search. The goddess knew when they had decided to repair their animosity and fall together under some orchard tree. That night I dined with Thenser and he told me I resembled my Aunt Elaieva, it must have been then. As my heart began to break, they made this child together in the summer night. As our child, Thenser's child and mine, was made in the heartbroken gold of afternoon.

With the dark thing gone from my room, I saw it plain for one whole perfect second, the golden miracle within me – then it passed. My depression came back, but I set it aside, told it to wait, until my other petitioners were settled.

'Well, then,' said I to the good-looking, uneasy young man. 'What have you to say?'

He shifted. He had hoped probably not to have to say much.

'Lady,' he said, 'I'll be happy to take her on. To wed her. I'm stationed at Krase. The married quarters are good. And, the way things are, they like us to be on friendly terms with the North.'

'They as good as told him,' chirped up Rose, 'he'll get to be a captain.'

He grinned.

'Rose,' I said, 'is an exceptional treasure. I want you to know, if you ill-use her—'

'*Never!*' he cried, about to call me out to a duel.

'Very well, then. I assent. Must I sign anything?'

Rose laughed, I laughed, the young man, too.

'No, so long as you're willing, madam.'

'What now?' I said, somewhat deflated.

'I'll pack my bag and be off,' she said, alight with love, for him, for me. 'He's brought a pony trap – fit for royalty—'

'Couldn't have you jolted,' he said.

They blushed, in total unanimity.

'But,' I said, 'don't I – you should have a bouquet—' I was thinking of the parting gift Vollus had awarded.

Rose flung up her hands.

'No indeed! I've been with you hardly more than a year. And other madam's present, Lady Vollus – well, I've had that by and not needed to touch a penny.'

They were at the door now, frantic to be off alone.

'Wait,' I said.

I went to the casket on my vanity and took out one of the long strings of round cream pearls Cristen Kahrulan had had others buy me against the revenues of Gurz. Crossing to Rose, I hung it like a garland round her neck.

'Oh, but—' said Rose.

Her beloved gazed, and said, 'Are you sure, lady?'

'Naturally. She can recall me when she wears them, all the times I've been petty and unkind. And if, forgive me, you ever have need – one by one the pearls will bring something.'

'Oh, Princess Aara!' exclaimed Rose. Tears rushed from her eyes. They looked genuine. She flung her arms round me and hugged me roughly, thrusting her baby into my corseting as if to give me practice. 'All the gods be loving to you, always.'

They left me feeling old and wise, burdened by knowledge and despair, as I had often felt in the presence of another's joy.

Freed to do so, my depression came forward, and laid out its case in endless permutations.

Dinner was less restrained. Cristen Kahrulan had had adequate hunting, if nothing magnificent, a weakly deer that was 'better culled,' a tree-cat whose fur would do well for me, to 'trim some mantle.' The undergrowth was alive with hares.

They might be coursed. It was not a sport he 'favoured'
overmuch, but too great a preponderance of any beast would
come to 'tell.' These affairs should 'benefit' from 'attention.'
Meanwhile I looked 'wan and weary,' I had better go early to
bed. On the morrow 'my guests' (his guests) would be arriving.
Tomorrow evening was 'our ceremony.' 'And the night.' He
honeyed a little when he said that, smiled at me with a play of
his eyes I had never noticed before that he employed. 'I don't
mean to be brisk with you. I came here wanting, and, I avow, it
set my nerves on edge, this wait. There, it's your beauty, you
see. But perhaps you were correct. Such things have their own
resonance. We shall make up for delay, my girl. Come, kiss me
good night, Cats-Eyes.'

I let him kiss me, caress me. His hands on my body were
like the hands of a man gliding across marble; I did not stint,
neither did I feel anything.

Soon he put me by.

'Yes, kitty, you're very tired.' His own eyes were like those
of a graven image, so intently did their turquoises rest on me.
He thinks I am sullen, now, to pay him out for absence, or his
offhand way. He thinks I will come round in the heat of
documents, legal promises, wine, lust. 'Aara, my dear,' he
said, as I went from the Parlour towards the stair. He walked
after me and took my arm. 'We can't go back,' he said. I did
not reply. He said, 'In all honesty, to lose Gurz now would –
it would sink my ship. Cargo and all.'

'There is no reason you should lose Gurz.'

'I hope not.'

'Good night.'

'Aara . . .'

I waited. Thenser had stood where now Cristen stood, but
not so near to me, then.

'Aara, I would rather you were truthful with me. Remember that. *This* I must have. But as to you— What you have of
me is your choice.'

'You're saying I may refuse you.'

'The legal union, no. The union of the flesh, if you will.
Naturally, it would decimate me. But I won't force myself on

any woman. I dislike such things unless there is some reason of policy, or state—'

The getting of an Imperial heir, for example. I did not say it aloud. And of course I shall want the union of our flesh. Am I not already in blossom with your child?

'Thank you for your thoughtfulness,' I said. I went up the steps, and left him there.

Night was no longer for sleeping. It was the time in which I prepared for my bed, lay down in it, lay in it, propped myself on its bolsters, read words I did not understand that became, after sunset, written in another unknown language. My candle lighted and blown out. The lamp lit and lowered. About four, I might begin to go around the room, take up pieces of jewellery, play with them lacking other toys, start a game of Red-and-White, lay out the board for Sword and Star – but too dull, too exhausted to concentrate on anything, longing with scorched eyes and numb fingers only for what I could not have . . . sleep.

Sleeping herbs did not assist. They made me by turns leaden and agitated.

It would be a good thing, to lie with Kahrulan. Not for pleasure, I would have none. I should be revolted as never in my life before at this grotesque act which, once I had found its secret, could never delight me, worse, never leave me unmoved, again. But he would wear me out. Surely then I would sleep.

Yet there was something to fill that darkness, a thing I might do, this last night of my mistressdom of Gurz. Was it only my desperation, the drug in the herbs, this sense of some concluding rite?

I would take these table flowers and give them to the goddess in her shrine.

On the stair I thought precisely, I am mad. Since the harvest I have been insane. Perhaps the child will be born insane also.

Wiparvet brings the man to the woman. Thenser had followed a shadow like a wolf into the woods. And I, by the frozen lake, saw the god and wondered what it could mean.

The night was unseasonable, warmly fragrant like a cake cooling from the oven. But soon the winter would return, snows and swans and wolves— How strange it was. I did not believe I would see them.

I would die then, of the child, before term.

The moon was on the western tower, the Mistress Tower.

As I came towards the temple, its moon-rinsed whiteness clear beyond the naked lindens, I beheld the goddess was there before me.

My heart sprang and dropped back. Yet, within myself, I was not frightened. I went on, going only more slowly now, fixing my eyes on her, to see if she would indicate I must not.

She was standing behind the altar, thus only visible from the waist. Not tall, Vulmardra, for a deity, but mysterious, and very white, cowled in the aspect of a priestess . . . And then I saw that she was winged. Huge, the wings fanned out behind her with the smoothness of water, and her amber eyes that were each the autumn moon blinked black, white, silver – she flew up from the altar and straight towards me, trailing the lights and vapours of her wings—

She was a white owl that had been perching there, inside the shrine. She flew over my head on her sails of ammonium, and it seemed I counted every shelled feather, and could have touched the oyster-coloured feet that held fast a tiny dead darkness, her kill.

I went into the temple between relief and lingering wonder, and found instead the Lady, seated on a little wooden chair.

She poked up her head, inquisitive. When she dined or lunched with me in the house, sometimes she would recall me, sometimes not. Now she seemed to know me well, but not who I was. We met without exposition, as if by pre-arrangement.

3

After a few moments, I felt I must say, 'Is the Lady – quite well here?'

'Quite well. Here is the place to be. Full moon,' said she. This gave the proper construction to everything, apparently.

She motioned me to sit, but there was nowhere. I knelt by her chair, having let fall the flowers on the owl's altar.

Then I saw she had the cards of fate, or three at least, which she had set out, facing me, or someone, on the ground.

They were not like Jilza's pack, not the gauds of a travelling sybil. These were from the salon of an aristocrat. The tints were rich, not loud. Each bore inscriptions. The Lady tapped them with her foot.

'The cards of the She. The women's cards. The Priestess, the Heroine, the Hag.'

She seemed to beckon me to look.

Though purified, the Heroine was much as I had seen her, clad in yellow and white on a crimson sky, a green sun; lightning was striking her wand, the hyacinths, tears, papers, ichor, smoke, temple to her right, and volcanoes behind – a nuance I had not noted before. Under all, the scroll read: *Lightning Is Attracted*, and the borders of the card: *The World's Girl, Of the Maiden*.

The cards either side were darker and more pale. The Priestess had the dark card, blues, purples, and bloodied greens. She stood upon a shore and the ocean came to her with its molluscs, fish and creatures. An azure lunar disc formed her nimbus. Her legends read: *The Moon, Of the Crone*, and *Calling the Sea*.

The third card was the Old Woman, or the Hag. The border said: *Of the Mother*. The scroll under her crabbed feet told me *Dispatches From the Towers*. And at her back such towers ascended like charcoal sticks on a heaven of embers with a red-blue evening star.

'Wisdom and justice,' said the Lady, showing off the Hag. 'Neither of us can claim this card. I am old, but young beside this one. My card is the Priestess, the Moon. Changeable. Tides, shadows and harsh lights. But you are here,' and she pushed at the Heroine.

'I've been read. A woman once, with the army.'

'Lightning,' said the Lady, her owl's claws scrabbling on her lap. '*Seize* it.'

She was the owl. Somehow she could transmogrify into a bird. Or was she the goddess? Had Jilza been the goddess?

I stood up suddenly and a pain rose with me like a serpent twisting in my abdomen and belly. Something tore, like material. I felt the gush of scalding blood. It came so fast, it poured through my nightgown and robe, dappled the stones, and stained me as if after some disastrous rape.

She saw. She looked impartially on. She said, 'Given sacred to the She.'

Late, my time, or some swift miscarrying. The pain already easing to the thick, heavy, and familiar ache.

The goddess took the shackles from me. She gave me liberty. She *stole* from me. She *robbed* me of his seed—

'I must,' I said.

But the old lady only sat shuffling the cards with her foot, like a contented child.

Doubtless she was often there.

It was not always ritual, but communion. She was so ancient, almost out of the world. And I, so inadequately young—

I ran towards the house, holding in my blood, meeting no one, meeting nothing, entered my chamber and saw to myself with the practice of womankind.

And when I had seen to everything, as if after a murder, I fainted.

Near dawn, rising stiffly from the chill floor, I went to bed, and I slept.

Kahrulan would lose his night of union after all. Or perhaps he would not mind; some men, I had heard, did not.

There could have been no life in me. It was so soon gone—

I felt purged and weightless, only the weight at my groin anchoring me to the bed, or I should have flown away, where the owl and the goddess and the moon had gone, over the forest tops, towards the western sea.

4

It was a small party, two Quintarks and three ladies; a trio of princely lawyers and their disposable clerk; Cristen Kahrulan and myself.

A girl Rose had been training (far better than my own choice) attended me. Two of the ladies stood as my legal witnesses. One was a princess of an old clan related to the Imperial House. She would, now and then, give Kahrulan a certain look, indescribable, undemanding, potent. They must have been lovers, once. Like him, she had the name but not the money bags. She was the soul of charm to me.

The ceremony was not a ceremony as such, but he had seen to it it should rather resemble one. It was conducted in the Hall, with all the upper servants present in their best, victory chrysanthemums in vases and the antique brackets high on the gallery walls holding fired brands, to augment the thickets of candles. Ochre and ruddy light ignited shields and carving, a scene of barbaric opulence.

We wore garlands, and were smart. The men were tricked out in uniform, my partner with the fringed scarlet sash of his rank, and the gold Kahrulan sunburst at the pectoral.

He gave me a ring. It was heavy silver orbed with a heliotrope, something he – I – did not have to buy, it was in his family. Perhaps all the men of that Kahrulan branch gave it in turn to their official mistresses, retrieving it at death.

Our vows, which concerned my loyalty and obedience to him, his honouring and defence of me, we repeated from a paper the lawyers held. We signed three documents, and one of them was then pressed upon both of us, with the justiciary seal and the signatures of our witnesses.

Then Topaz was brought. We made, he and I, an offering to Wiparvet, also Kahrulan burned incense to the god and asked that he be taken under the god's eyes as physical protector of the estate.

The toasts were drunk, our own, the ancestors of Gurz, the Lady (she was absent, I did not know why, if it was form or insult), the Emperor – not one of us smiled at this. Lastly the

291

attending servants were given each a charged glass. Melm stepped forward, to present a symbolic key, always the property of the male incumbent, to Kahrulan. Melm then kneeled and placed his hand under the foot of his new master.

This rite he would have performed for Keer Gurz when both of them were adolescents. But Melm seemed sanguine, his rat's face alert only to deference and solemnity. Kahrulan raised him and clapped him on the shoulder. Handing to him, also in the way of tradition, a gold Imperial.

The servants applauded, downed their glasses, and went off to what the ladies titled 'peasant merrymaking' in the lower house.

The lawyers' clerk and my maid went after, and we were served our dinner in the garish Hall, with the taste of torch smoke in all our food. There was no talk of treaties or tolerance of the foe, beyond a comment or two on the quantities of Charves and general Southerners on the streets of Krase. There was no such thing as war tonight, just as there was no such thing as true marriage.

After the cake (decorated with sunburst and flower staff), the brandy and liqueurs, my new protector thanked our guests, rose and held out his hand to me.

I had no choice but to rise also and take his hand.

The adjacent Quintarks were restrained but vigorous in their noises, and the ladies flapped their fans. The wine-steward, at the door, bowed smiling. Two maids strayed up with more sweet dishes, watched us, glowing, as we approached, yet hand in hand.

The Wiparvet dipped and straightened his flame.

We took another route tonight. I had almost forgotten that we would. With brooms, balms, and bedding they had been preparing it all week. Our nuptial chamber was to be, in accordance with custom, the Master Bedroom in the East Tower. The room of my dead.

On the large black bed, that I had last seen undressed to its frame, my lord sprawled himself, eating apricots.

'These are very good,' he said. Three hours ago it would

have been praise of me, but now it must be self-congratulation. 'And you,' he said, 'are like a beautiful image. What a jewel you are, my love.'

Going through the Study, he had run his eye across it briefly. No doubt he had observed these rooms earlier. The bathroom had been restored for our convenience. The chapel he glanced at.

'We must have a new shrine. The other was lost, you said.'

'In Dlant's retreat.'

'A pity. It sounded a fine one. But we'll do better. And shan't you want a niche for Vulmardra up here? Or do you prefer the holy groves down by the lake? For certain things, they would be better.' I recalled how, coming on the exodus of the female ritual, he had turned his horse not to encounter it. He would allow me my woman's sacraments.

But I had not answered. He did not press for reply.

Flowers decorated the bedroom. Everything was polished, draped. They had taken away the blue butterfly from the window sill and hung an embroidered blind.

Would the ghost of Keer Gurz arrive, to stand over us as we lay together under the armorial mottoed shield?

What had the other marriage been but a rag and a bone? Then, the Wolf-cry in the woods, that unearthly noise – should I hear it tonight? What had it said to me but *wrongness*. It was the voice of chastisement, and regret.

'I can call my man,' Kahrulan said all at once, 'or will you help me get off these damnable boots?'

I assisted him, they were scoured and burnished; he held my waist to prevent my falling over, then pulled me down on top of him. 'A service for a service. I'll unlace you.' He began to kiss me. His body was ready, a weapon honed and from the sheath. 'Both or neither, Aara,' he said.

I put myself away from him. He said, not realising yet, 'What now?'

'You said, sir, you would prefer the truth from me.'

Complete stillness came over him. He lay on the bed, and said to me, 'All right.' And then, breathing deeply, 'But you'll have to sleep here for show till morning. I won't put a finger on you.'

'No,' I said, 'you don't understand. Will you allow me – to try to tell you – it's very awkward for me. I don't know that I should trust you—' the words spilled now, overflowed— 'should I just give in, and when you sleep, run away—'

'What on the gods' earth are you—'

'We've signed the contracts. I'm bound to you and Gurz is yours. You have everything you want, and if you want to have me I won't prevent you. It would be such discourtesy on my side, when you've been so considerate of me. I have no reason to object – except for one physical matter, but perhaps you may not—'

'*Aara.*' He sat up, caught my wrist and shook me a little. 'I don't want to listen to nonsense. If there's something you must say, I will hear it. If it's urgent enough for all this, I will hear it through. You have time. Now.'

And so I sat down in the carved chair, by the hearth where a log was sonorously burning. I said, 'My reason is a foolish one. You'll think me a fool. Probably I am. From the beginning, or from my thirteenth year, I've had no say. I've been caught up and pulled and pushed, ridden over and dragged by wheels. And now, doubtless, this is only another sort of choicelessness. There's a man I love.' I paused, to see if he would make some sound of derision or disgust, but he did not. 'He was my lover at the harvest. I thought I was carrying his child, but I've been saved that fear – that chance—' Drifting, I snatched myself back. 'For me, I expect, he has had no second thought. But then, he doesn't know who I am. He thinks I'm some Northern aristocratic widow, the property of Prince Cristen Kahrulan. But he knew me as a child, he comforted me when my parents were killed. He was in love with a woman of my kindred. *I saved him from death*. I'm a Southerner as he is. Besides, besides. If he wants me or not, I can't – I *won't* belong to any other man. I was Gurz's. I've played that role. Not again. Not with you. If you wish to have me, I give myself, freely. For this night only. Tomorrow I'll leave Gurz to you. I'll go after the others, where everyone goes to escape the treacheries of being on two sides at once. South and east. The kingdom of Tulhia. I read about it once in my lessons. Sunny lands, mountains, golden gods, and a blue sea.'

'Prick of night,' said Kahrulan. 'And you're still a school-girl. What a speech. I knew, there had to be something. No. Go through it again. I'll have the details now. You are fully a Southerner, you say?'

'Yes. I was born in the very City Dlant conquered and lost. My father and mother died at Fort Hightower.'

'Very well. Continue from there.'

I felt a terrible weariness knowing that suddenly all my confession, all this life of three enormous years, was now to be given him.

For I had interested Kahrulan. There was some worth in that.

And so, while the guests drank, and slyly envisaged us, below, in the paroxysms of appetite and desire, we sat, icon to icon, and I told him all of it, with a draining and sickening sense of release.

How long this took I shall never know.

When I had finished, and he had questioned me, and I had answered the questions, not stinting even the names, he seemed to think for some time. It must have been then I drew off the heliotrope ring and laid it on the arm of the chair. Then he got up and drew me to my feet (I was half paralysed), and led me to the bed, where he put me, alone. There I fell almost instantly into a kind of stupor. My last sight was his shadow at the window. He raised the blind and stood there staring out at a great opaque moon. His silhouette was more couth and slender than that of Gurz, yet in my trance, Gurz he became, looking away from me into the night, looking away and away.

When I am very old, I may boast that an Emperor was kind to me. I have some cause. But then, he was not yet quite an Emperor.

He let me sleep, and I think took some rest the other side

of the great bed, fully clothed. What a night for this Heartgift marriage.

Early in the morning he got up and began to arrange my affairs, for I was not yet free to take on my life.

About seven he woke me. Some breakfast had then been served at his request. He made me eat something, although I was muddled, dismayed, nearly ill that I had told him so much, thrown myself on his mercy. Could he *be* merciful? Well, I had caught his interest. Perhaps he might be clement once one had proved oneself a live human thing, beside him on the plains of the world.

'The carriage will be ready at eight, plenty of hours before those sluggards' (the guests) 'stir themselves. A letter came for you at sunrise. One of these tenuous Northern high-blood families you are related to here. A sickly cousin, childhood friend, calling for you. You will go, of course, then the poor bitch will die and you will be kept over for the funeral. By then those that know us will be getting used to our separation. I will take up with someone else. There will be a wholesome, amicable parting between you and me. Here at Gurz I'll put in a proxy master, I know of a deserving fellow who can see to the estate for me, with Melm's connivance. He has, too, a delicious wife, who will in time make up to them for their loss of you.'

'And what *of* me?' I whispered.

'This packet contains my letter to a useful port official at Yast. He will think you are on business for me and will be extraordinarily accommodating. There's also money there. You must now go over to the West Tower and pack. Take everything you think may be needed and that is possible for barter. Otherwise you must by now have learned to travel lightly.'

'But,' I said.

'You reckon me overkind? Recollect, I'd have none of this if it hadn't been for you. Legally you retain some rights to the property as well as I. Did you think you signed over every coin and cog, like some chieftain's daughter in the Black Ages? *Urtka*. What a little idiot.'

'You've been very—'

'Benevolent.'

'And I can only say that I'm sorry—'

'For putting hell's pincers on my balls. And so you should be, you jade.'

'If I've embarrassed you—'

'Not at all. These sorts of embarrassment are nothing. It's only the shames of the field and the council chamber I seek to avoid.'

Set firmly in my place, I rose to leave him.

He stood by the dead fireplace, elegant and indifferent now, amused, so I felt tousled and stupid, the object of contumely. But it did not matter.

To what I went I did not know. But I might go to it. Not even as a fugitive and pauper. I ran away, if not with his blessing, at least with that flaunt of his eyes, that bow, a courtier's pressure on my hand. I should not have liked his malice.

'Aara,' he said, as I was in the door. I waited for some ultimate jest. 'If you find that man, and make him cleave to you, you may wish you'd stayed safe with me. From what I hear, he's a creature of the water and the fire.'

'So am I,' I said. 'Oh, so am I.'

The carriage waited for me. Kahrulan's own man came to escort me down. The coachman and outrider were also his. No query was made. I was bound for Yast en route to my sick relation. Speed was of the essence. And if they thought anything else, it was that I was on Kahrulan's business, some secret toil I undertook from loyalty and love. I said farewell to no one.

I had no trouble.

The forest was not yet done dying in copper and rust on the pines' backdrop of wintering black. Foxes bolted from the track and pigeons flew before us. I was going away, drunk with liberty. Going away and towards.

Rush chariot, fly, wheels not touching the earth: Be winged.

Going towards, towards.

BOOK TWO

Part One

THE SHIPS

Chapter One

1

The ship heaved and pitched. The other passengers lay dying in their cabins. The captain was cheerful, having endured seasickness, he declared, for his first five years of service; he felt therefore both pity and elation on the sufferers' account.

I was not myself ill, felt no nausea, only sometimes giddiness. Such a passenger in a high sea became something of a pet.

The waves were of a hundred strains of green, like strange fluid marble. The crew assured me, though we were tossed, the ocean was not dangerous. Yet now and then there came a curling scarf of water that overtopped us. I remained unconvinced we should not drown.

We had put out in the lull, the eye of the winter gales that crowd the waters between the Kronian North and the Oxidian entry to the Temerid. *This* was no gale, they said, when it began. But the ship's guests soon staggered to their cabins and fell down there. Their groans were often audible above the crankings of the vessel and the boil of the ocean. I was passionately glad I had been spared their malady. Though puzzled as to why.

Perhaps my clothes had saved me. Or the rash folly of my acts. I had come to recall a line in a novel, in which a philosophic vagabond asserts that, through casting himself possessionless and planless on the breast of life, he has found life will succour him at every turn. In the book it was quite true. Whether in real life it should have been so I could not

303

swear. But here I was – if not destitute, then certainly not well prepared, and if not planless, decidedly with a scheme I had dared tell no other after Kahrulan, for fear of disbelief, or the villainy of those thinking me a fool.

Cristen's letter to the fellow at the port had procured me a recommended lodging, some credit in the way of money against my sale of various articles, and reliable news of the shipping. The agent also gave advice.

'I suggest, madam, that you purchase some male attire for your crossing. It will be all told a voyage of two and a half, or three, months. Ladies who take on such a venture find masculine garments more convenient. It's not reckoned improper. Almost, you might say, it's become the fashion.'

And that had been proved a fact, for of the women who travelled very many went boldly clad like their menfolk, or at the least preferring trousers over a skirt.

So I was got up in the mode, with some grey breeches, hose and boots, some cotton and woollen shirts, an elegant dark mantle-coat – that was then every dandy's wear – and a thick winter cloak of sombre sky-blue. My hair I declined to cut, but, having waited in port one month already, my bleached locks were altering to a copy of the light-brown of my childhood. These tresses I wore long, uncurled, and down my back, indeed, like many a warrior of my former country. As a result of all this, on boarding, I heard a man exclaim, 'Why *who* is that beauteous youth?' Then, catching another angle of me, for my figure was not much disguised, 'Damned and bloody tricks of the Bear!' I believe this gentleman bore me some bad-will, but since the rough weather grabbed us on the second day, and he succumbed with the rest, he had no immediate chance to work it out on me.

The *Sea-Fey* was a two-master of sinuous design, with a green nymph at her bow and greenish canvas aloft. She had a crew of twenty, aside from the two mates and the captain and a brave and clever ship's dog named Lion's Heart. This dog, of the black wolf type common through Kronia, had a dash of some other breed, that gave him curious ears. Pointed, they stood out sideways from his long head, lending him a world-worn expression. But he had sailed through thirty voyages, and even once gone overboard, because he would run up the rigging – I had been told. I did not think it possible until I watched him do so, but this was at Candier, in the harbour there, when the water was calm.

Due to their indisposition, I saw little of the other passengers, but they were made up of some men and two ladies, the latter with their husbands. They had wanted my story at once, and the more reticent I contrived to be, the more they had been at me, the women especially, eventually cracking little jokes, 'Oh, she's a close one. She has a secret worth knowing, if one only could.' When I had explained the by-now familiar tale of my ailing relative, they seemed to sense a lie, for they tried more and more for details, or to trip me up. I blessed the storm.

The captain and two mates, with whom thereafter I breakfasted and dined alone in the saloon, were content to flirt with me. Each was married and had, it transpired, girlfriends galore on the side. Though they might have been happy to add me to the list, they could do without me in that way, and seeing I had won my spurs with the sea, they offered my decorum their kindness.

At Yast, while I waited, I had obtained news through the agent of the galley *Dvexis*. She was of that faction of ships that go by oars, in the ancient way, but the oars-stations manned solely by condemned criminals. Discipline is strict to the point of inhumanity, and it is said a sentence to these galleys is scarcely less than a sentence to death. Some men do survive, if their stint falls short of twenty years (men doomed for twenty years seldom continue that long). But the conditions and punishments, and the posture which the oars-bench forces on them, loose these up to freedom crippled in mind and body. One might see a few cases about the northeastern ports. It was a superstitious matter among sailors to stand such men food and a bottle. The sailor's name for the prison ships is *Hell's Galleys*.

Hell's Galley *Dvexis* plied to and from Yast, taking her black way to the kingdoms of Tulhia and Khirenie, sometimes on and up into the Potentality (where such ships are common.) She carried cargo, and passengers who had the stomach for it. It was normally thought that, saving Orientals, only men desperate or on murky business selected such transport.

She was months ahead of me. Where the swimming *Sea-Fey* danced, there the smouldering, bloodflecked spume of *Dvexis* had lunged before. Both had taken the outer route, through the islands of the Oxidees, for though war was packed away, the southwestern inland shores were still visited with caution. (From our larboard, twenty-two days out, I had glimpsed the mainland through the ocean's roll and plume. There were tiny carven mountains, like a wolf cub's puppy teeth. There, behind that screen, the fortress of Hightower must have lain, the picnics and the hunts, which now I considered with a bewildered lack of agony, a dim dismembered ache.)

Kahrulan's agent at Yast had told me the *Dvexis*, variously bound, would pull back into the Bay of Candier on her return. The *Sea-Fey*, too, would be calling there. I must get off and sit down again and wait. The agent seemed, by his eyebrows, surprised Cristen had entrusted me with such a spiky task, this contact I must make, apparently, with a galley of hell.

The worst of the ship was, for me, monotony. At first, the colours of the waters, the sea birds which sometimes sheltered on our rails and mast-arms, the antics of Lion's Heart, the great skies and towering sunsets, entranced me. But the crew's care of me, their conversation, though undemanding, began to oppress. I had remained uncomfortable with other people, and with men in general, though now I was, perhaps, too practised to show it.

Sometimes there would come a clear evening, when huge stars hung molten on the shell of heaven. Some of the passengers might totter forth, but were overly feeble to be a nuisance to me. The mates would sing in coarse, but pleasing, voices, ballads of the Kronian theatre, or of southern lands, for I would hear suddenly a peculiar language that

I knew . . . (And I would remember then how Thenser and I, in making love, had spoken only the tongue of the conqueror, as if neither recollected the usage of our home.) The dog would lay his noble bat-eared head upon the second mate's knee and sometimes howl in perfect pitch, too ridiculous to be anything but admired.

I had a few books to read, my sketching, when the motion allowed it. I would sit under the awning on the upper deck, amid piles of rope, baggage and chests, and there draw things which had nothing to do with the sea – buildings or women – setting them perhaps as an afterthought on a backdrop of breakers. Then from their tales over their brandy at night, I drew drowned sailors whose heads rested on the scaled laps of mermaids, monstrous sea-beasts, distant sinking galleons from which skeins of pearls and guttering lamps drifted, and here and there a pale face and long hair like a cirrus moon in the water.

But the recurring storm was beyond my artistic powers. It was too volatile. And even of this, once I found we did not go down, I grew tired.

One morning five Charvish vessels passed across our bows. The flagship hailed us, and we saw the cannon in her sides. But the Treaty was holding, and *Sea-Fey* was plainly a creature of commerce not battle. We hailed in return and there was no more to the incident.

On the fortieth day, the weather abruptly altered.

The coldness became a coolness. The waves reclined, turned soft, with rollers of blue-green lining. Fish leaped by, sea-coloured with glistening sun on their backs. I looked to discover a mermaid in their midst, with her comb and mirror.

We were passing into the Temerid, the Middle-of-Earth Sea. Such passengers as could, came out on deck. The sailors assembled, and libations of wine were poured to sea gods given arcane names, and a great dragon of Kronian myth.

That night a splendid dinner was served in the salon. Most of the passengers were still unable to face it, and I of course did not do it justice, but the mates, the captain, and Lion's

Heart sat long over the dishes.

In a day or so more, coolness became a gentle humidity. The streams that flow in this sea are often warm. They tell you, if you swim there you may pass in five minutes through chill water into bath-hot and back again. And they also have stories of catching fish already cooked, but that I never beheld.

The land was now clearly visible to larboard. It was not like land I had seen before, which maybe gratified me. Long shores rose into mellifluous hills, which then altered to rough-hewn and crenellated cliffs, the contrast between the three types of terrain very marked. Upon the cliff-heads were snows like powdered salt, which the sunset turned to car-nelian crystals. It seemed then the landscape of another world.

Presently, some days early, we moved in between two enormous promontories they called the Thews of Cand, and entered the vast Bay of Candier.

Here the windless water was like heavy glass. Though it stirred, the motion was nothing, and the ship required all the skill of her navigators to bring her round towards the port.

There are ruins at Candier of an elder town; they are scattered all through the modern city, which has its own classical High Mount, dazzling white, fish-scale-blue and gilt in the sunlight, with temples and public buildings. There are freak orange trees in the groves there that reach seventy or eighty feet, with fruit small as golden coins – and, they said, as hard. But the slums of the city are appalling, and the wharf district is not to be gone into by night even by four strong men together, if they can avoid it.

Once our passports had been inspected on board (I was fearful for mine, got by the Yast agent, but it was seemingly perfect), I was to be put off into the town. Finding me a novice, who had no idea how to proceed, the captain sent the second mate with me and an escort of two sailors and Lion's Heart, with my luggage. The dog was too princely to carry anything, but stayed at my side and growled at any unknown man who glanced my way on the street. When we got above the lower town into the mercantile quarter, the mate asked with blunt kindness what friends I had, in order to know where to take me. From the sale of Kahrulan's silver crocodile and some sundries, I had gained a respectable amount. I told him a decent lodging was not beyond my means. So then he escorted me in a hired carriage, the sailors trotting after, but the dog naturally in the chariot with us, up to a wide avenue with tall pastel houses netted in balconies, and with urns, and sometimes even trees, on their roofs.

I was lodged in a guest house in a pair of pleasant rooms. A Kronian woman ran the house and was accustomed to being a mother, she announced, to unaccompanied young girls. I was rather daunted, but the mate only smiled. He led me up to my room with the sailors, and 'mother' permitted that without a blink, only looking askance at the noble dog.

My bags and myself installed, the second mate embraced my hand, asked if he might call and on having been told that, my business being next with family sickness and grief, I could not allow myself that joy, he told me his heart was broken and went whistling off. I did kiss Lion's Heart farewell – I had by then seen him ascend the rigging and grown enamoured of him. He wagged his tail politely but was anxious to be off with his friends.

So they went, and left me.

Soon up came mother to ask what I should need and to try, by the way, to find out my whole autobiography. But I had already made Cristen a confession, and was impatient. I gave her a gold Imperial – the coins of the Saz Empire and a dozen other places were legal tender in Candier – and told her I was in mourning and could not bear to speak of the matter. With such ease and such a great loss of money did I manage this caring parent.

2

I lived at Candier some weeks, waiting on the return of the *Dvexis*.

This time, a ship becalmed.

The view from my window was attractive, taking in the impressive High Mount. (I think I paid more for this view than the clean sheets and hot water.) The weather was fine, very mild, the winter as it was, here. Snow, beyond the caps of the mountains, had not been known for a century. There was a dry wind in late autumn that was hated, but I had missed that. Though some trees stood bare, others were eternals, blooming without surcease. And there were flowers along the hedges and in the urns.

I felt the balm almost instantly. No winter here could be mistaken for that of the retreat, let alone the winters of home and infancy.

Further east, at Tuli, where he had gone, it would be more unlike. If Tuli had been his destination . . .

What I had heard of the *Dvexis* gave me nightmares nights in a row. But I was cut adrift, and though I was troubled by my new aloneness, as I had been at Yast, the light burned before me. The light I had made from Thenser, and which perhaps, when and if finally I might come to him, he would quench.

And sometimes I thought, too, of that. Weak silly tears dropped from my eyes. I was a child who loses its kin on the street and cannot be comforted by any other. It was very foolish, to build up this welcome. I would not. Must not. Aside from anything else, I did not know him, he was so scarred and battle-torn – that other dream, the battalion of ghosts – *that* was him, my lover, not the golden god in the harvest wood. He had wanted to stay with me but had been bound to leave me. To what had he gone? To what did I follow?

Towards the wheels had cried, and the foxes running.

A linnet sang in the guest house mother's room downstairs, and its song pierced through me. It was a southern song. I supposed then I would never be quite free of it, that dream of my beginning.

My information on the comings and goings of the harbour

was got now by morning and afternoon attendance at the public offices on the quays, where the boards were put out twice daily to show what traders could be expected. In the markets and narrow streets round about, much dealing and conniving went on. Now and then I saw Oriental sailors, who surprised me by looking so much like their representations on boxes and shawls – slender, yellow-honey skinned, with impenetrable eyes. Even in daylight bands of drunk ruffians were about, so I must always go in a hired carriage, with the coachman's tough boy to walk behind me.

I was spending my funds very speedily, and after supper in my sitting room would make lists of what I should best sell next. I did not want to ask mother where to go for fair prices, either. Guessing me on the edge of penury, she might shove me straight out.

Then came an afternoon when, standing before the facade of the Port Authority, my blood turned to fire, and my heart raced. Seeing me turn so red and then so white, the coachman's youth cast fierce looks about to be sure no one had in any way insulted me. I stayed him almost merrily. Up on the board, cause of my emotion, they had just slotted in the name *Dvexis*, and the token she should be at anchor beyond the bar by midnight.

I was not really merry, more hysterical. I felt a loathsome fright, as if I might put off the vital interview now at hand. To approach such a vessel was the act of a simpleton. Anything might occur. I should have to make the best provision I could.

Turning to the youth, who spoke smatters of all the argots of the port, Charve, Danuv, Tarasi, Tulic, and Kronian (plus many further elements), I said, 'Tonight I must get aboard the galley marked up there. I have to speak to her captain.'

The boy pulled an awful face, but it was only the face they made at the port to avert unluck.

'Slave galley, her,' he said.

'Yes, I know. I am willing to pay you well to escort me.'

'Not on slaver, no, I.'

'Yes. How much money do you want?'

'No. Hell's stinks. The gods hate them. Not go near.'

'Yes.' I added, 'A gold Imperial.'

'With Emperor's face?'

'Of course.'

'Why you wish you go in hell ship?'

'You will come, with the carriage, to my lodging at eleven o'clock tonight.'

My return was like madness. With some sharkish instinct mother sniffed my affairs were on the wing. She emerged to stay me at the stair, but I got by with a gabble.

In my rooms I paced, undecided on everything, even as to how I should dress for the occasion. To be too fine might cause animosity, or danger. To be too shabby, which was now easier, might bring on danger through contempt.

The *Dvexis* was contained by law through her very nature. The law itself consigned to her those living dead who powered her. But I was so slight a thing I might sink without a ripple. If half the tales were half true—

But it was a stupidity now to think of that. My course was mapped. *Lightning is attracted*. Very well. I must expect a strike, and turn it to my advantage.

I dressed plainly but well in female garb, but without any jewel or adornment. Not a ribbon.

Then, shaking all over in excitement and fear, hope and oppression, as sunset began to scorch the windows, I did not see how I could last until midnight.

After a mouthful of the communal supper, I arranged with the hall porter that he should let me out, and in, for some silver. Up again in the bedroom, I was suddenly clasped by a need for sleep. I lay down in a rigid posture, not to crease my dress, and fell a hundred miles.

I dreamed then . . . of her.

To begin with, I only sensed her, in an inexplicable, familiar way – the way I had been accustomed to know my

312

mother, if she should come into my darkened room at night. Even in sleep, I had been conscious of her presence, and so with this.

Then, from some dark that was also a nothingness, she started to move towards me.

She was a child, about six or seven, slim and small, with long blonde hair and unusual eyes. She wore a white dress and a sash of silvery stuff, little-girl clothes, and a white doll was in the crook of her arm, dressed as she was.

She looked at me, with witchcraft eyes. She was all that look. Nothing too canny or unkind. Only all *looking*, all her *seeing* of me.

There was nothing else.

When I woke, the three-hour candle I had lit was almost melted down, and next I heard the bell of a temple on the Mount ringing for eleven o'clock.

Initially, springing up, running to the window and seeing the carriage there in the shelter of some trees across the street – signalling quickly with my light to them – flying about the room to tidy myself, I did not recall the dream.

Then as I combed out my hair before the mirror, and drew on my cloak, I thought of it.

I knew instantly what I had seen.

She was the ghost of one unborn. The child who had left me in a rush of blood, or whom the goddess had cast out for my sake. I should have been heavy with her now. To that, the graceful blondeness, *his* colouring and his eyes, she would have grown. But in some other earth, on some other plane of time, already she had been carried to term, and born, and become. There, I was her mother, she my daughter. But here, only a ghost-girl in my dream.

There was nothing horrid or hurtful in it. I could not even regret this robbery of her life, for *somewhere* her life had happened.

But I was disturbed at the dream, for why had she come to me now?

3

Like a devil ship the slaver looked, too, reared up in a black wedge on the lesser black of sky, the red torches at her bow burning down through the water like two stains of blood.

The long boat, procured by the stalwart coachman's youth, had put out from its shed on the oily umberous sea, with sullen looks and grumbles from the rowers. There had been altercation formerly, in argot, as to why the madwoman could not wait until tomorrow, when at least there should be sunlight. Such vessels as *Dvexis* did not put in inside the bar. They were pariahs of their kind, but also did not care to risk escapes from the slaves. Although the chance of that was extremely rare, for the felons at the oars were normally shackled both day and night.

My generosity to the boatmen and the threats of the youth had prevailed. By one in the morning, we were going out into the Bay, answering only once to the watch. This seemed to have no interest in my business, after a bribe was handed over. In the ways of such things, the agent at Yast had been a useful tutor.

The galley stood well off, like a plague ship.

She showed no flag, her rigged sails were swarthy, the mark of her tribe. Her figurehead was a rodent thing, with hideous bared teeth. In all forms she fulfilled her promises.

My rowers hailed her.

At first, not a flicker of response. Then came a clumping one around the deck, and from the rail glared over a pock-marked face and dirty lantern.

'Yes, we are *Dvexis*. What you wanting?'

'I have a lady here to come aboard.'

The face was amused. The largest pock-mark, a mouth, devoid, unlike the rodent's, seemingly of every tooth, created a laugh.

'Lady? Not for ladies here.'

The rowers turned to me with shrugs of satisfaction. If they had had a row, I had spent my money on them for nothing.

314

I stood up in the boat, having kept my sea-legs, and addressed the face.

'I have business with your captain.'

'Ah,' said the mouth-pock. 'Who says?'

I flinched, but I had not lived as I had without learning, in my parrot-fashion.

'Do you say I have *not*? You may be sorry when he hears of it.'

'Ah,' said the pock-mouth.

Then he disappeared, and my heart plunged.

'Don't expect no civility from their likes,' said one of my uncivil rowers.

'I do expect it,' I said, in a flare of temper, which was a relief.

Just then, a man in naval uniform, of a sort, appeared at the ship's rail and gazed down on us. From his appointings he was a first mate, and from his eyes and insolent manner, a habitual drunkard, pickled hard.

'You,' he said, in my direction, 'may tell your business to me.'

'No, I may not,' I said. 'I will see your captain.'

At that he lit a pipe, and leaned on the rail calmly contemplating the ocean of black morning.

I stood balanced, and waiting, keeping my eyes on his face.

'The captain,' he informed me, 'is abed.'

I took my chance.

'Then entreat him to get up.'

We had spoken in Kronian, which had not astonished me, as the ship had her origins in the North. His accent, though, was of some other land. I felt my plight to be hopeless, the rowers restless and audibly complaining, my guardsman youth scowling, the man smoking above, the night and the ship looming over me.

That galley stank. It was of no odour I could name, except perhaps it resembled the battle-stink of hatred and fear – yet even that was animal and not unnatural in its way. While this was something from the sinks of human existence. The oar-ports, had they been opened, would doubtless have let

out human stench enough, for the poor wretches were half
the time chained in their own filth, and the positions besides
constantly awash with bilge. But this other effluvium hung
over and around the *Dvexis*, soaked outward from her planks.
Any who had contact with her must be contaminated.
Vulmardra. Let me turn round and go back ashore.

Exactly then, contrary, on that vast inner level wherefrom
so much mortal commerce is conducted, unseen, unheard,
and sometimes unfelt, the first mate of the hell's galley
shifted.

'Well, if you're so importunate, on your own dainty head
be dashed his wrath. Get ready. There shall be a ladder.'

Soon it arrived, and clinging to its brass joints in terror of
falling on the escorting youth who followed me without
another word, I climbed into the full miasma and the lantern
light.

When I was up, not having helped me, mate and Pock-
marks gave me a good scrutiny. I bore it with a mask of cold
disgust, looking away from them now.

'I'll tell you,' said the mate, 'he may not mind seeing you,
after all. And he's not in bed. Not a man for early bedding.
Unless in company.'

Then I made myself look at him. I thought of Kahrulan,
and gave him *that* look. But he only smiled a crooked smile
and led me off to the captain's cabin under the upper deck.

Here he rapped loudly, and a man's voice without delay
replied, 'Yes, first mate?'

'A *lady* is here. She declares her affair is with you.'

'Send her in then, first mate.'

'Your boy must remain this side the door,' said the mate of
the coachman's youth, 'within call.'

The youth positioned himself. The mate then opened the
door with a flourish, breathing his pickled-stone brandy-
breath on me, eyes and teeth like those of the figurehead.

What I had expected next I could not say. All that was
putrid, doubtless. But the cabin was orderly and clean, with a
raised and screened sleeping-place, and a desk where a large
lamp burned on some books of accounting and perhaps the

316

log, and pens ranked neatly in a tray with two pewter dishes of ink and sand.

The captain of the *Dvexis* was a black-bearded Kronian. He wore his uniform, but in his ears were golden rings from which hung unrefined chunks of gold, and on his left hand were three coils of gold and silver, tarnished, almost grown, like barnacles, into his flesh.

There was nothing about him, in his looks or demeanour, to indicate evil. As I entered, he nodded though he did not rise. He sat in his chair and observed me across the well-kept desk, and a pen of coloured enamel, an artistic thing, was in his fingers.

But I became aware that, though the cabin was hot and well-lit from the lamp, there was a chill upon it, and its impression was of darkness.

'Good night, madam. What, then, is your need?'

He might have been a lawyer, or gentleman of Krase.

I had my scenario, and would cling to it like the ladder.

'Sir, I'm seeking my cousin. I have been told he had passage on your ship, on the last voyage out towards Tuli. He may have used the name Zavion, or possibly not. A fair-haired Southerner, perhaps you may see a likeness . . . He is my only kindred. I'd be obliged to know at which port you put him off. That is the sum and total of my business with you.'

'Is it, by the Bear's Hide,' said he, and something had quickened in his narrow eyes. I did not care for it.

Because I said nothing, he missed some response, and waited, watching me. Then he said, in a friendly way I cared for less, 'He did use that name, Zavion. An officer from the occupying army. I supposed him, he gave me to suppose, he was on secretive affairs for the command at the capital. But I've learned since he was in a scrape. A traitor to all sides. By the hour of hearing, I wasn't amazed. Shall I inform you why not?'

He waited still. I could only say: 'Any information—'

But he interrupted. 'Your kinsman, madam, did me a foul turn. And he did the law one. So I guess that's what he is best at. Illegal matters, betrayals, the inconvenience of others. I shall have to pay a heavy fine besides, due to your *cousin*. He is not, you will gather, beloved of me, though perhaps of you, for he was a dashing fellow. For myself, I'd like to see him take a stint at my oars. And confidently I look forward to that pleasure.'

'What,' I said, since I must, 'was his crime against you?'

He got up. He was a tall man, and had to bend his head at the cabin's roof.

'I will take you to see something,' he said.

I grasped what it would be and a rush of fear went over me. Could I protest? I was for the moment in his sphere, and should do better not to oppose him.

We went out and all along the deck to the hind sections (the coachman's youth following blankly). A trio of watchmen, Pock-marks of their number, were standing at the three masts with their lanterns. They saluted their captain as he passed, and leered at me. But I was engaged holding myself in a vice not to tremble.

'I believe I know your intention, captain,' I haughtily said. 'Is it necessary to subject me to this?'

'Not at all,' he said. 'But I have a grievance.'

'This is to punish me then, in lieu of Zavion.'

'Perhaps. But if I'm to tell you of his whereabouts, and if you should catch up to him, you may remind him by what you saw, for he, too, has seen it. As I said, I expect he will one day come to it. Let him look forward accurately.'

He took my arm, not at all roughly, and drew me on. At this, two of the watch ran up, and bending to a hatch unbolted and raised it.

Heart's gods, what an air rose out of it. The human stench I had rightly predicted, and the miasma of all deathly and deadly nonthought, compressed, unconsciously feeding on itself.

'I won't request you to descend,' he said. 'You'd faint, and then I'd have that on my hands, and women's vapours are not my province. Lift up that light,' he added to Pock-marks, who lurched ready. 'And now, lady, feast your lustrous eyes.'

318

So I looked, where the light fell, into that cavern of decay and death like a breached grave.

I saw very little. The shine of troglodyte limbs, of water like a nest of snakes, a glint upon huge chains that might have confounded bulls. I heard a soft moaning, and one shrill thin scream like that of a mouse under the claws of the owl. But that was all. Yet, like the odour, there was a sound which went on continuously. A kind of throbbing like the galvanic of an unstillable pulse.

I shrank back.

'I looked,' I said, 'and have seen enough. Be satisfied.'

'No, I am not,' he said. 'But it will have to do.'

He signalled and the two men clamped down the lid once more on horror. Not one of the doomed below seemed to have registered its going or return.

We went back to the cabin. The door was again shut on the escorting youth. I felt reprieved, as if I had come through some ordeal. But the gods knew what the black beard had planned for me next. Nothing, maybe. He adhered to the law. I could speak if I wanted of safeguards for my person, left by me at the Port Authority, and of a connection to the Imperial House. But this I did not desire to do unless pressed. I imagined it would not, at this quarter of the earth, have much weight aboard *Dvexis*.

The captain did not reseat himself, he went to a cupboard and took out a decanter of grog and two fine cups of Easternware.

'You'll drink?'

'No, thank you.'

'But, after the experience I forced on you?'

'If it will content you to have me drink,' I said, 'I will drink. If you offer out of courtesy, I need nothing.'

He showed his teeth, rustily stained from chewing Red Leaf of Taras. 'I'll drink alone then.' He did so, and nothing else for several minutes.

At last I said, 'As you feel I'm in your debt for my cousin's actions, I conclude you want recompense.'

'Your meaning?'

'I'll pay you for the facts you're withholding.'

'I'll allow that.'

I bit back my nervous anger, and took out my last three Imperials.

'This is all I can offer.'

He looked at them, on my hand.

'There's much more,' he said. 'You could sell some of your clothes. Or yourself.'

'My clothes and myself are not for sale.'

'Not yet. I see you've never known hard times, my lady.'

At that I laughed. Something made me say, 'You'd be startled then to discover what I've known. Men like you, captain, lying dead in hundreds on a battlefield.'

His conventional face uglied.

'A threat?'

'My only threat is that I can withdraw the offer of money and leave you. Perhaps others may give me this simple piece of information that I seek. Your own trader's itinerary, once it has been entered at the port. A bribe to some clerk there, who would settle for less than you, and not insult me either.'

This was a vain hope, but anyway he said, 'Fine lady, a list of our ports of call won't help you. Your kinsman was off *between* ports.'

I felt the life rush out of me. But it was only blood going from my heart. I heard myself say, as if across the room, 'Do you mean he was murdered and thrown overboard?'

It was the captain's turn for mirth.

'And if he was, the bastard earned it, but do you think I'd tell you?'

I leaned on the wall, could not help myself. Either I would lose consciousness or I would kill him, and I determined, of the two, it should be the second.

'I will say now,' I said, in a voice found somehow, 'and only once, does the name Kahrulan mean anything to you? Yes? Then reckon that I know it better, and more intimately.'

'What, doxy of princes and here, like this?'

My illness had oddly inspired me. Nothing mattered but to have the truth.

'Perhaps it is a test of you. Had you considered that, captain? Or are you so flighty with the law and the Emperor of Saz-Kronia you needn't bother?'

A pause. He drank his grog. He said, 'Zavion wasn't touched, though if I'd foreseen what he was at, I would have hanged him myself. No, he got off swimming. And he took one of the oars-slaves with him. A great boar-bear of a man, Irmenck – we recalled his name, there was no other like him, he had kept alive seven years in the rowers' station. Zavion was interested in my rowers, so he said. I thought he was a queer one, for he lost his colour, went green at the very mention of the rowers' deck, then he would see it, and I'll say he had some fine jests about the offal down there, he made us laugh. Then, he asked histories. Well, they're a wholesome collection. Don't waste your pity, I'd say. No man gets sent to that but he earns it. There's one man, he killed three women, cut off their juiciest parts – and another, he was a robber, cut the throats of more than a hundred travellers on the road. But then there is Irmenck. And Zavion stood over him, there in the stench of the station, and watched him. What's *this* man done? said Zavion. Now Irmenck had always protested the story, which is he slaughtered some holy priest. When I have done, Zavion says to Irmenck, as if he can see this one is still rational, *Now, your version.* You can imagine, the villain speaks up with his own tale, which has it the priest regularly terrorised the poor of his village, preying carnally particularly upon young children of both genders. And one morning, hearing screams, Irmenck found the priest astraddle his little brother, eight years of age, and the child facedown in blood. And the priest regaled Irmenck with the vow that this was the first of many such visits, at which, taking up his smith's mallet, for in such trade he was, Irmenck brains him. But the village is too afraid of the temple to talk out, and Irmenck has no evidence, for even examination of the child fixes this assault on Irmenck himself, who they say the priest caught in the act and not the other way about.' The captain poured more grog. 'In my experience, young boys are often the readiest to bring this kind of venture

321

off. In the Orient, they're trained to it. Who knows. The great bullock was convicted and sent to me, and has powered *Dvexis* exceedingly ably. I had belief I should keep him for the full twenty years, and saw to it he got good meat, and even wine on feast days in which to toast his priest. Zavion, hearing Irmenck's rendition anyway said straight out it was rubbish, put his handkerchief to his nose as if suddenly noticing the smell, and turned on his heel for the upper deck. Irmenck had such a look then, like a girl who's been slighted in love, I laughed myself.'

The captain's voice went on, greased now he was into his own tale of grievance. I recollected the start of the narrative later, so I had heard it, but not with an entire mind. I was busy at first in the knowledge Thenser still lived, drawing the fragments of myself together again.

I had done so by the juncture of the captain's launching into a recital of a drunk dinner, at which Thenser had come on like an actor and showman, having the captain's table roaring with merriment. Then, about two in the morning, though the captain himself had retired and the first mate was overseeing the watch, the drink yet flowed, and Zavion persuaded the second mate to bring up Irmenck to the table, to supply a captain in the captain's chair. The other ship's officers being idiots, and all of them intoxicated, the game was agreed. As what would be more ridiculously entertaining than the stinking galley slave addled with brandy and in a garland fashioned of flowers of paper torn from an account book, and being asked for the orders of the next day, and so on. With some subterfuge, Irmenck was released and brought to the saloon. Sometimes slaves were let up for an airing, and the privilege had been accorded the giant before, to keep him healthy the longer. He came in shackles, of course, but once installed, and after some more rounds of drink, Thenser had got the second mate to unlock the irons. The officers subsequently maintained, and the captain partly agreed, that Zavion had somehow doctored the brandy with a powder.

A number of japes were then indulged. Finally Thenser

rose and staggered to the saloon ladder. He said they must all go aloft to see the stars, and Irmenck must be brought, too, to see if he remembered what stars were. By now they were used to following Thenser and to follow him bodily seemed nothing. Up they all went, and on the open deck Thenser overjoyed them further by flinging off his mantle-coat and boots and saying, as he led Irmenck like a garlanded bull to the rail, 'Can you swim, dear heart?' Irmenck had presumably got the drift, or already been in mind of something on his own account. 'Enough,' he was afterwards said to have replied.

Then both men were onto and over the rail and gone into the sea below.

The drunkards left behind raised a rowdy cheer at this ultimate joke – which fell off in confusion.

'The Tulic shore was about a mile away,' said the captain to his cup. 'They may have drowned, but I think not. We put out the boat but found no one, and in the morning a party went ashore at the town there, but not a trace was to be found. Nor did I expect it.'

'And the name of the town,' I said.

'Yes, you can have it. For they'll be well gone by now. It will do you no good. Genchira is its name.'

I put the three Imperials on his desk and left him with no other word or gesture.

Outside the youth came forward and caught at my arm.

'I'm well,' I said. 'Has the boat waited for us?'

'Yes, but must be hailed. Were sent off twenty lengths of the ship.'

Putting to use our voices, we had them back before too long.

I was sentimentally grateful they had not abandoned me and lavished on the rowmen some silver pennies in excess of the fee. Also on the coachman's youth.

Now, with a sale of my elected possessions, I would have enough for my passage to Genchira, in Tuli. Beyond that point I could not see.

Chapter Two

1

Smooth as mermaid's hair, the blue sea bore me south and east, in the cradle of the *Nileni*.

My passage was a funeral gift. That was, in order not to alarm my landlady, I had informed her I must sell certain items to procure an offering to the relations of one deceased. The shop to which she recommended me was sound, and the agent honest. The ship herself was a small craft with only four passenger cabins, the other three unoccupied.

We were never out of sight of land.

The gilded coast went by, luminous by day and mystical by moonlight. Flights of astonishing ring-doves settled on the rigging and purred to us before they flew back to shore, and on the thirty-third day, platinum-backed dolphins leapt from the water, and later speckled porpoises, to give us friendly escort. Sailors seem fond of both animals, and flung them titbits. I was persuaded to feed the dolphins myself, holding out fish to them from the rail which they took with an apologetic snatch, never once harming, let alone frightening me.

They tell stories of shipwrecks and drowning mariners saved by dolphins. Even if Thenser and the slave had foundered, would they not have been rescued by these intelligent beings, apparently human in all but form and habitat, and surely having human souls: The Ambassadors of the Gods, Tulic sailors call them. Already – at once – I had accorded the slave my complete trust in his integrity, for

Thenser's sake. Thenser had judged him. Yet, this was so like all else. This man I did not know – if someone had begun the captain's story and asked me to finish it, I would have concluded it in legend as it concluded in fact. Perhaps with the proviso of bringing them to shore.

What shores they were, as we sailed towards the kingdom of Tulhia.

Groves of wild orange trees crowned the hills, sweeps of turquoise wood came down to the lapis lazuli water. At times the very scent of the land drifted out to us, sweet and resinous, fruit and flower and acres of the dancing glimmering substance known as air. The only argument to be had with the weather was the lack of wind, which made our going leisurely.

The harbour at Genchira, where the *Nileni* was to call, was not a marvel. Shipping preferred the better, larger port of Tuli a week or more farther south.

The town of Genchira was old, a backwater, tapering off from its silting harbour. They said the elderly preferred Genchira and the young went away. Do not, they warned me, look for dances and dinners, chariot races or gambling or theatre, at Genchira. It is promenades and parasols and quiet suppers and staid readings.

But the dolphins certainly liked the town. They returned on the forty-first day to guide us in towards port.

2

The young second mate of *Nileni* had taken so great an interest in me, I had been forced to confide I was to meet my betrothed at Genchira. Then, finding this man had made no provision for me in the way of accommodation or security, my incensed admirer, Emaldo, had had to be given a rigmarole about my betrothed's government business and my anticipation of letters.

Luckily, Emaldo was a Tulhian, and our language difficulties saved me much trouble while giving him large amounts. I had already, by listening to the Tulic crew, begun inadvertently

326

to pick up their speech, but pretended to be more backward than I was. My facility for other tongues I meanwhile laid at the door of early exposure to Kronian. This I had learned mostly by mimicry and observation, and the gathering of as many individual words as I might – in fact, learning as a child does. My grammar and syntax I corrected later, and in much the same way. This stood me in good stead, but with Emaldo I faltered, failed to grasp all the more intense avowals and outcries.

After the pilot had come aboard, Emaldo came to me brushed and beautiful, his yellow hair and blue eyes like jewellers' work, in a mantle-coat of white satin, and pledged he would accompany me ashore.

To do him honour I put on a gown of green muslin, and seeing this he entered such transports I was unsure he would live. He can only have been a year my senior; he had definitely seen more of the world than I, perhaps less of its shadow side.

The poor harbour required us to be taken in by the pilot. Standing with the exquisite Emaldo, I got my first sight of Genchira.

It was as lovely and as picturesque as in a fairy tale. In the dying basin, a lotus pond was forming, choked with skeins of water hyacinth and bog lily. From these charming vampires, the ships must daily cut themselves free. Only two or three small vessels were sitting squatly there like ducks. Above their spars rose ancient water steps, with guardian sea gods in greened marble holding out their arms. Then the old town, with some huge palm trees before its face like feather fans. I saw houses in cages of balconies, walls dyed rose and rouge, yellow as Emaldo's hair, impossibly even bluer than his eyes, or the colour of the peacock's rays. Over the walls were gardens with massive camphor trees and lesser terebinths. On a ruined red tower above the harbour black and white storks flapped about their nests.

'You *see*,' said Emaldo, proudly, having invented the town for me.

'Pretty!' I cried in Tulic, and the conjuror bowed.

'But it is the town of age,' said Emaldo, in Kronian. 'Yet, this the good thing. Your safety. Now, you shall lodge my aunt.'

I looked askance, considering if he meant I was to put her up or she to put up me. Also wondering if in the latter case I dare accept.

'Yes, yes,' declared Emaldo. 'She will care for you. You are nowhere else.'

'But she may not—' I cast about for the proper Tulic expression for nonliking.

'You love, she will adore,' said Emaldo. He pressed my hand. 'As do I.'

It was out. No forms now to protect us.

In the sunlight he blazed. I would be the envy of every girl in Genchira and of many not girls. If I had any sensitivity to pleasure or reality, I would admit his suit. All I had otherwise were phantoms.

The house of Emaldo's aunt was in a shady street, three storeys of tan brick, and over the door in wrought iron a four-masted galleon. Emaldo told me the sea was in his family. His uncle had been a captain, owning his own vessel. Even the house locally was called *The Ship*.

It seemed the aunt did take lodgers, and beckoned me in. She was in her later years; even the maid was in her fifties. Neither spoke any Kronian, let alone any southern tongue. Emaldo was interpreter. I could see both ladies understood the situation perfectly, that he 'adored' me, and that I was rather older and a conniver.

I could not much help that. But I begged him to tell them that I was in waiting for my betrothed.

I think he did. But then their looks were, 'Oh, but we have heard *that* tale before.'

My first idea, once Emaldo had gone back to *Nileni* (stating he would return at sunset), was that I must get further funds.

I had two dresses left and my man's garb, besides some shirts and underlinen, a pair of sandals and one of boots. Not a glove, scarf, veil nor bow to my name. It seemed to me I did not want to sell anything else in that department. But I had a string of the pearls Kahrulan had given me – having left the other behind. Now, as I had advised Rose, I should cut the string and sell the creamy orbs one at a time. Again, however, where?

Armed with the two chosen pearls, I went out to quarter the town.

A delightful walk ensued, along winding side streets and wide boulevards, under poplars, palms and turpentine trees. In a little park was a long-haired goddess of stone, naked but for shells. And in a sunny square of shops, a temple on the west side. I did not know the god, but had some notion of going in to offer thanks for my arrival, when I saw a jewellers in an arcade.

I entered the shop, which was empty save for the attendant and a large spotted bird in a wicker bird cage.

The bird squawked, the attendant bowed.

In immature Tulic, I tried to explain my errand, and produced the pearls.

He, taking out a glass, came to look at them. His inspection involved only a few moments.

'Quite fine,' he then seemed to say. (The bird repeated it, so it was a standard.) Then he made his offer, which I did not comprehend. Smiling dryly, he held up his hand to show me each finger – the thumb withheld, and next removed from a box four Tulhian lild, about the equivalent of eight Southern silver pence.

In anguish I clutched at the pearls.

'*Real*,' I exclaimed, and in Tulic, '*not* fake.'

'Yes,' said he.

I thought he was a maniac, and leaving the cash fled with the pearls, to the bird's irritation.

Across the square, a small market lay against the temple wall. I stared at the heaps of fruit I could not afford, the dead chickens and jars of flour or jellied sweets. Seated on the earth, a butter-coloured Oriental was playing a pipe, and in the dish of tortoiseshell before him, a wonderfully-patterned snake was coiling and swaying. In one ear the Oriental wore a pearl. At that second it came to me that, of the many elderly ladies I had seen parading the pavements with maids, sunshades, small dogs, most had had a string of pearls, pearl broaches, rings, ear-drops. One of the dogs had even had pearls in its collar.

There was a glut in Genchira. Two of them were not worth the price of a night's lodging.

In some dismay my nice walk ended back at the door of the ship house.

I would have to ask Emaldo what to do.

3

'The oyster beds,' said Emaldo in Tulic, 'filled the town with good pearls.' He looked on me sadly. 'This betrothed who provisions you so ill,' he said in Kronian. 'Forget this swine. Let Emaldo protect you.'

I thanked him, colouring at his ardour, which he valued. But I spoiled it by saying I had made vows that could not be broken. How was I to support myself until my circumstances improved? Was there, I asked timidly, any sort of work that I could do, and which would be tolerated in a woman of my class – perhaps a companion to one of the hordes of old ladies? I offered this uneasily, for I had no empathic feeling for the old as none for the very young. To be interested and patient with them embarrassed, distressed me, I could not have said why.

But anyway, Emaldo threw up his hands in horror.

'No! I will tell you. There is something to be sold here by you.'

I looked at him defiantly. *What* would come next?

'On *Nileni*, always, you are at the drawing. Such quaint scenes of gardens and damsels. Sell that.'

Stunned by something so simple and so utterly unthought of, I stared at him.

'But are they good enough? Would anyone want to buy?'

'Old ladies – they like these sceneries, which relaxes them.'

Indeed, the Lady at Gurz had once or twice stolen from me a crayoning of mine, which, Rose got from the maids, then joined a magpie trove in the Quiet Tower.

'Well, if you really suppose—'

'Yes.'

'And perhaps even I could offer to draw their pet dogs . . .'

'More better yet.'

'But how shall it be done? Must I knock on doors like a peddler?'

'My aunt,' said Emaldo, 'knows the soap-seller.'

This did not enlighten me. He took pains explaining that my work should be displayed in the soap-shop, which would take a commission on sales.

A day later, it was done. Several crayonings and pencils, of just such scenes as he had stipulated – girls walking under pines, one reading a letter as she leaned on a fountain basin, maidens and a lion in a flower-meadow, with a sea of nymphs behind. I even ventured an unsuitable *un*relaxing motif from *Sea-Fey*, a sinking brig and fair drowner. It was actually this picture which sold the first.

Every evening for a week Emaldo dined with us, his aunt and me, at the ship house. I see in memory the sunset shining on her glass and snowy napkins, the water bowls of blue eggshell. The habit of Tuli was for reclining, though the aunt did so propped on cushions, Emaldo like a forest god in his crown of vine-leaves – there were vines all over the walls and in his honour there were always garlands at dinner and always genuine. He bloomed for my successes. I came to love him in a way. He was so ardent, and handsome, and he was there.

But, the week done, his aunt reconciled to me he believed, and the soap-seller clamouring for more work so my fingers ached, and were ingrained with colours, *Nileni* was to go east to the port of Tuli, and thence up into Tulhian Khirenie, a land of mountains that grew from the water. He would be gone some months he feared. His lakelike eyes mourned our parting. Would I not give him some assurance against his return?

'You'll meet some other, I expect, on the voyage. Some Khirenian girl with golden hair, who is free to give her love.'

'Where your great lover? Show him me. To have such as you and not to be seen—'

'Emaldo, I've told you what must be. Would you like me dishonourable?'

'Where is he, the dog?'

'I don't know.' I do not know, Emaldo, and truly my heart is sore at it.

But I had said I was betrothed so often now I half believed it, as I half believed at Candier that somewhere a sick relative of mine had died.

We went walking his last evening, and, it was a fact, received some stares.

On the harbour wall, we looked at *Nileni* among the lilies, and, for the evening was clear, saw out to a far blue cloud in the southwest which was the foreshadow of the island of Kithé.

Kithé was exotic and he rhapsodised it. Did I know that men flew there, like the gods? I thought this was some fresh story, until he contrived to let me know a sort of kite-ship was sent off near Port Tuli, the winds being favourable at that point to land an air vehicle on the island.

'Now, if I had time,' he mused in Tulic, 'I should have escorted you to Old Genchira. That is a place you would like.'

When he said this, a strange chord seemed to sound within me.

'*Old* Genchira? Is there more than one town?'

'Some miles inland. The first site of the harbour, but the sea left it.' In Kronian to be more direct, he told me Old Genchira had thrived in classic times, had great colleges, schools, and massive buildings of law, state and religion which, though ruinous, were still used. 'A mighty temple there to the goddess. Yet sanctified. The Vulmartias are held there.'

Despite its fane to the unmet god, Genchira had not seemed very deist. In the ship house there was not even a house deity, though when wine was served a toast was drunk to the wine god of Tuli, Zandoros, or, more colloquially, Dornoy.

'But,' sighed Emaldo, 'at dawn tomorrow we shall be gone.'

'But you will return,' I unwisely opined.

'Yes, and will you be here for me, Ayaira?'

I had grown used to this – yet one more version of my name. I accepted it and said, 'You know I can't – I *may* not.'

He dumbfounded me by bursting into tears.

He leaned on the harbour wall and sobbed.

What could I do? I was between laughter, remorse, and shame.

'Oh, don't cry, Emaldo. It's such a needless thing to cry for—'

'For love – you think that needless – your heart is a rock.'

'Yes, but how can you love me—'

'At first sight, I loved. Now you spit upon me. Leave me to weep. I will jump into the sea and perish.'

Suddenly laughter won. He was a compendium of it all, Thenser upon Elaieva's stair, myself upon this foolish journey.

I put my hand on his shoulder, to shock any old ladies who might be passing.

'Dear Emaldo. I value your love, but can't you allow yourself to know I love also, and so can never go back on my vow?'

He raised his head, eyes wet like blue flowers in rain. He looked magnificent. To waste such passion on me seemed a pity.

'Then only promise this. If *he* fails you – here am I.'

'If he fails . . . If I'm here when you return, he will have failed. I promise I'll be your lover, then.'

'I will wed you,' he said.

'No. That I won't promise.'

But his eyes gleamed. He accepted my refusal of his gift charitably, for he thought he saw me in the net. Doubtless to slake his lust would quieten all the ardour. Should I give in now? No, though he was of the best, and the finest. I would not unless I must.

The last dinner was festive. The aunt, too, wept at their parting, and he wept again, calling her his second mother, so I saw, as I had guessed, tears were easy with him.

He kissed me farewell. The kiss was warm and sensual, but nothing, nothing.

He strode away into the hurried gathering of dark and stars.

I dreamed all night of Old Genchira. I did not see it, but somehow felt its stones, the cool of its deeps and heat of its surfaces, and heard night strum upon it like a harp.

It seemed I had known it was there. I had only to ask the way. Probably it was the sense of something so close yet undiscovered that gave me to imagine—

Even dreaming, I reasoned with myself. Yet before me, also unseen, the presence of another moved about the streets.

The pursuers from *Dvexis* had not coursed so far, or else, he had been away, was now returned. What safer place than one they had already tried?

It was as if I had known he must be at hand. For I had affixed myself to Genchira's port, though it was empty of him and I knew it empty.

The aunt took it as an insult that I would go to Old Genchira and lodge there. Now I could not get scheming hands on her nephew, she realised there was no value in her house – this she did not say, but fired at me from her eyes.

I took her flowers, and paid her for all I had had. I sang her praises in inept Tulic. To no avail.

Good riddance to the Kronian strumpet. Let her walk to the old town every day and back with her drawings, let her get rheumatism from the damp marbles of the ruins.

The soap-seller told me the way. There was a road up above the town, a road itself old as Old Genchira, overgrown, which only the goats kept cleared. Olive orchards I should pass, and three windmills – most scenic, I might make some sketches – and a fallen shrine to Dornoy by a stream. There were ancient tombs also I should note, along part of the route, some very ornate. For protection from the sun, sunshade pines and conifers stood like sentries at the roadside. There had been no robbers in the area for a hundred years.

So, with my possessions on my back in a bundle, like a woman of the fields, and in my poor frayed sandals, I climbed the hill above the town and looked out on all he had described, with additionally some strokes of distant mountains. Going down through the tall grasses, I stepped on the old road.

Part Two

GENCHIRA

Chapter One

1

As I sat in the shop of Master Pella I was conscious of my newness, my novelty, not only to the town, but to myself. Around me lay my utensils of work in immaculate order, each group with its box wherein to go to sleep at night. On a tilted frame the latest creation in its birth throes, and in exact light from the wide window – and when the sun glared on the sheet in its going by, they would lower a sail of blind to dim my paper. My chair was one of the most upright and comely in the place, padded with rose brocade. At midday Pella himself would usher me from my labour to lunch with him and his students on soups, cheeses, fruits, and whatever meats and fishes he had that day fancied for us. This meal did not cost me a penny, and often I, with the students again, was loaded with leftovers, the housekeeper religiously saying to us all: 'You eat them, else they'll only go to waste.'

In the shop front, my drawings and paintings – I had been elevated to water colours and found them amiable – were displayed with some of the work from Pella's studio above. He had remarked at first, 'It is too late to teach you anything. You would have had to come to me at seven years old. But for all the faults there are marvellous virtues, child, which the gods don't bestow randomly. Your invention, too, though it sometimes outstrips your skill, is worth paying for in itself. And I see you are not afraid of a blue tiger. Honour your art. You will learn by practice in the very act. At thirty years, I daresay they will reckon you taught in a better school than mine.' I was overwhelmed, for I had only gone in out of brazenness, having seen canvases in the window, and arrogant with nerves, bridled at the long perusal of my crayonings, and the first talk of my 'faults.'

Once displayed, my efforts sold steadily. And I was a curiosity, since on most days I was the fixture of the shop. Sometimes people came in and watched me, which, if they did not speak, was no bother. *If* they spoke, Pella or his assistant would courteously request their silence, unless I gave the signal which meant I did not mind. On days I did not feel inclined to draw, I might sit reading there in the sunny window the books of Pella's studio, which reproduced the paintings of the great. Rather than consign me to proper gloom at my inadequacies, these gems inspired me madly. No sooner had I done mooning over some picture than I had all my boxes open and, from my own brain, began to invent some like, though dissimilar, scene.

On other days when I did not go to the shop, yet I was invited to lunch there.

After days when I was not seen at all in the vicinity no mention was made of my disappearance.

'If you are in any need,' said Pella, 'you may send me word. It is a rule which I apply equally to my students. They come and go as they please. No one is to be forced to exert himself. If they don't wish to study, they may go fishing for all I care. Although, if a student is absent more than four weeks together, without word, I return his fees to his sponsors.'

There were at present a dozen young men, and two girls, at the studio, ranging from thirteen years to twenty. The girls were diligent and remote, each one in love with a different heroic painter hundreds of years in the ground, and dressing in a bygone fashion to please him. The young men were sometimes loud, and less given to toil, all but one, a grey, grave boy of about fourteen, who was always the first to enter the shop and climb to the studio in a kind of trance, descending the last. Sometimes Master Pella kept the boy to dinner, too, and then I might be included, or some other. From this one, almost speechless being, plainly much was expected. The boy was poorer even than I, barefoot on the warmer days, and in threadbare unsuitable boots on days of wet. One painting of his, which was not for sale (Pella had already bought it of him), stood always in the window. It was this painting which had initially drawn me to stare in. It was of a single fruit, an apple, hardly in the way of an apple at all, more like a piece of emerald with a velvet nap upon it. It rested in pale mysterious space, and was so beautiful one wished to drink it or drown in it at once.

'Dorin sees another earth,' said Pella. And that was all he would say upon the matter of his genius, a fourteen-year-old orphan with a sixty-year-old face.

To enter Old Genchira was to enter the old world. Out of the stone buildings, some black with antiquity, others dyed in the manner of their youth or scrubbed to blinding whiteness, it was a surprise to see men and women emerging in contemporary clothes. For though the classic influence is nowhere stronger than in that elder town, a corseted female waist and tight breeches for the gentlemen remained the vogue.

Behind the pillared Forum, terraces of massive architecture, the basilica law courts and the great temple of Vulmartis Isibri, the snow-pencilled mountains would come and go depending on the weather.

There is a public well under a palm tree they say is a hundred feet high, and looks it, and a horse trough where three stone camels stand forever to be watered.

And to crown all, as they do crown it, the colony of storks is here even more prodigious than at the port.

It is a magic place, hidden behind the other Genchira ten miles away.

It is here, too, the young must come, as well as to Tuli along the coast.

They fill the colleges and the library, the studios of artists and artisans, and crowd on the streets in the brief bright sunset when the wing of night comes so swift and suddenly, like birds let from aviaries.

So young, they seemed. Sixteen year olds whirled past me on the walks, chattered from their seats on the steps of the basilica, stole kisses in groves of the temple. I was not too elderly for them. They thought me eighteen or nineteen. And in my sillier moods I was a child beside their serious discussions of art and existence. But, as if they knew I was *too old*, they held off from me, as from Dorin (who never I think saw them, or he saw their inner lineaments of the other earth.)

I did not seek companions, and few sought me. Once or twice a man would make his address, but my vagueness – or in unease, my coldness – soon turned him off. It was a flower garden of girls. Why hesitate at the unbending one?

And everywhere I looked after another. In vain.

The chord had sounded in me. I had dreamed of it. Upon the avenues and alleys, the stairs and colonnades, I sensed him to have walked before me. He was already gone, then. I had arrived too late.

I will be calm therefore. I will make my life in this spot, at least for the present. Never before was I so independent. What support do I need beyond the kindness of Master Pella, of my buying patrons, the familial atmosphere of the studio. And what beauty and adventure, beyond the town, the buildings and the mountains, the three goblets of coloured glass, blue, red and green, shining like temple windows, which I keep before the casement of my little room, with my pot of camellias.

I believe I am happy. Yes, I am happy. Nothing threatens. They do not speak of war here, or murder. No one assaults me. No one coerces. Let me look forward to Emaldo returning, to becoming his lover, his yellow hair spreading on my breast, his sighing in my arms. How beautiful he would look in love, like the god . . .

Let me save up my coins and take a larger room with the privacy of my own closet, a bath of enamel and a bedframe with curtains. Let me adopt a cat who will be independent as

I and yet let me give it unstintingly my love.

I need want for nothing.

Nothing.

Nothing.

2

I had lost track of the season. It was a winter like a warm spring, now and then a cloudburst which the mountains brought on, some days a little colder or more heated. But then came the midwinter Vulmartia.

From the path of piety I had decidedly fallen. I had not even entered the imposing temple, though I meant to, having admired its grandeur from without. In Tuli the goddess is most often called Isibri, for Sibris, the isle of her Tulic inception in the form of the nubile woman. They say she was born of the mating flowers.

Master Pella invited me to the ceremony, which at Genchira starts early, and then to a festive breakfast at the studio. It would be churlish to refuse.

The procession begins at first light, about seven. One wears light colours so I put on my green dress. My hair had by now grown back into its natural tone, straight and satiny, no worse for bleaching. At Old Genchira both men and women grew the tresses long, and sometimes effected ornate and classical hairstyles. I had added flowers for this morning, the winter violet which is the bloom of Isibri.

One walks towards the dawn into the temple, for it faces east. The light then begins to enter to meet you through a thousand eyelets in the upper stone. There are no stained windows in this temple, it is so ancient, only the bare openings where white pigeons are allowed to roost.

Her statue, twice the size of a tall woman, is almost shocking, for she is nude. But lovely, and pearly white, unpainted, with the only gilding on her hair and green jewels in her eyes, so she seems to see. She holds a shell before her loins, not coyly, but with divine occultism. Her other hand is held open, and flowers were laid there, and her head, too, was crowned not with a diadem but a garland of violets and myrtle leaves.

Otherwise the temple was so crowded I could not see anything much, beyond the pillars going up to dolphin capitals.

The priests came and burned incense before the statue, thanking the goddess for her protection during the winds and storms of winter, and for the hope of her spring.

Then a hymn was sung with poetic words – and Pella's housekeeper passed me a copy of them that I might sing, too. In the song she is called the Violet of night's purple hour, and the white Violet of morning, and told all the world is hers since she rose from sleep among the flowers and walked across the sea, attended by zephyrs and leaping fish, and doves that flew out from land to gaze on her.

Then an old priest was helped to the rostrum, and I was afraid he might be wandering and infirm, but he spoke out in a ringing voice, reciting from a holy book before him, enjoining us to virtue and trust.

Finally he advised us that we should, for the space of a silent minute, offer a personal prayer, to ask her for one especial thing that we required.

This custom was unknown to me. It made me start. I felt abashed, as if Genchira had looked into my mind.

But when the silence fell, I offered my duty to her, and then found my heart and thought were crying out together, loud enough to deafen me – only his name. And tears flooded from my eyes and poured down my face.

As I came back to myself with the singing of another hymn, the housekeeper, along with the words, this time passed me a square of clean linen. They had never asked any history of me. Perhaps it was unnecessary. Did every line of my body tell my secrets?

When the ceremony was over, the throng began to go from the temple, already vocal and lively. I asked Master Pella to allow me to catch up to him and his students. I would like to glance over the emptied temple, I said.

I sought the comfort of the goddess. Only in tribulation did I run to her, she must be sick of me. But the gentle amorous wisdom of her face was not aloof. Of all her aspects, this one surely would commiserate my need.

I lingered then. I put some of the violets from my hair on the table before her, where countless other flowers and objects had been laid. Setting down a coin I took a candle and lit it. I kneeled and bowed my head, while the softly-murmuring priests and pigeons went on about their affairs.

But I had nothing more to say. And she, to me, anything?

I stared up into her face. She looked beyond me now.

I got to my feet, and went away across the floor of polished marble, now all petals and children's handkerchiefs – and there a dropped toy, a rabbit with floppy ears. I took it up, unthinking, sad at its plight – and just then back into the temple ran its four-year-old parent, in tears as I had been.

'Here, here – don't cry,' I said, hastening forward to end her pain and holding out the rabbit, careful to handle it as if it were alive.

She looked at me with such wonder and joy and then stretched up her hands and took. We wept together then.

'Yes, she loves that rabbit. Someone jostled her or she'd never have dropped her,' said the mother, who had just reached us. 'But you. What is it? Are you ailing?'

'No, not at all.' Behind my fountain I cringed, and would have gone on, but her hand took hold of my arm.

'Tell me,' she said. 'I can help you.'

I dashed the tears from my eyes and frowned at her. She was a woman shorter than I, dumpy and unnoticeable, with the eyes of a lioness. Almost frightened, I shook her off.

'I'll tell you anyway,' she said, 'you were good with the child. Take a pink candle. Anoint it with virgin oil of the olive and with crushed violet, before midnight, on a goddess day, as today. Think of what you would have. Repeat his name while the candle burns. Burn the candle down until it dies. It will only bring him if he consents.'

I felt foolish. I fumbled now for another coin.

'No charge,' she said. 'I'd do the same for anyone in your

state. Come,' she added to the child, who had forgotten us in intense conversation with the rabbit.

The three of them went away and I was left.

Absurd. I should not do such a thing. A pink candle – the shops were shut today but yes, I had seen such candles with others in a drawer of the Master's dining room. Easy to take one and replace it tomorrow, when the shops had reopened. For the oil . . . I kept some for my lamp. The violets were in my hair.

Our meal was festive. We laughed and drank wine from the hard-boiled eggs and succory to the Vulmartis cake with lemon curd. It seemed I had never laughed before. It seemed so to them. One of the male students crowned me with more violets the Lady of the Feast. The girl in love with the longest-dead painter declared she had feared me but I was a jolly sort after all. I told them jokes. They howled with mirth. I told them tales of *Sea-Fey* and mermaids and they demanded more. Then everyone told stories. The jugs had no bases and were filled up by Zandoros Dornoy who lay drunk and glorious under the table. Into Dorin's face even came some light. He said to me he would like to paint me and had not wanted to ask. 'It would be a few long sittings. And then, you might not like how I did it.'

'You would show me ugly,' I said.

'No,' he said, 'but I would paint you older, and then, I would want to make your hair very blonde.'

Too tipsy to blanch I said, 'You have second sight.'

'You also,' said Dorin. 'It's more common than they admit.'

The breakfast broke up about seven o'clock in the evening. The night was downstairs and the students had claimed me for a dance that was to be. I declined and no one paid heed. So I went with them to some house in Old Genchira and endeavoured to recall steps my mother had taught me, and to learn new ones, and recalled and learned and was pranced about with, and we all laughed and drank wine, from the Promenade to the Tarasca.

Thus, one hour before midnight, like a princess under a curse, I remembered why I was happy, and rushed away.

The town was full of lights and lamp-lit faces and claimed kisses and garlands hung and braziers to roast apples. Through a cordon of Isibri's love I got to my lodging. No one else seemed in the house. In my room I let down the blind and kindled my lamp. I took out like the thief I was my pink candle. I prepared the elixir.

What did it matter if I was foolish. *I am a fool for you.* Besides, it was aromatic, luxurious almost, the preparation of the oil and the fragrance of the violets, the wax when lit like burning sugar, filling the room with its aroma. All over the town perhaps, women are at this work. Tomorrow the streets will be crammed with consenting lovers.

I had stood the candle in a dish of water, and as well, I slept before it had half burned down. Murmuring as I must, for the spell, his name.

The morning after the Vulmartia I woke with a sense of sweetness, fulfilment. Then I looked about, saw the wreck of the candle, hated what I had done. Hated myself. Took failure in like a destitute, and made it welcome.

3

In the afternoon, I would sit for Dorin, one or a pair of hours. Having somewhat confided in me, and I somewhat in them, Pella's students were now far friendlier, although in the five days since the festival, we had drawn on again thin coats of difference. When Dorin quietly asked his sitting from me, anxious to pretend I had made no overture to the Infinite, I agreed.

The fifth afternoon, after Dorin's sketches, I returned to the shop, idle and restless, not wanting to work. I sat before my own paper, partly remade to a poppy field with sphynx, and was drowsy. Pella's assistant read at his counter. The street door opened suddenly. Light flushed in and was eclipsed. The man in the door was no less than a giant.

He bent his head to enter, and that, too, brought memory—

'Pardon me,' he said to Pella's assistant, 'in the window of the shop is the painting of an apple – or perhaps a jewel cut like an apple—'

'Not for sale, I regret.'

'Then, is there any other thing by this artist?'

'At present not, I'm afraid. He works very long on one painting.'

'Yes, so I would have thought.'

The giant stood in a ray of sun from the window. He had a fine face, a shock of black hair, and bore himself like a king. However, his shoulders and upper back were hugely developed. His workman's tunic seemed about to split at every breath. Conversely one leg, the left, appeared a trifle crooked and wasted. He limped on it.

I had risen, not realising what I did. Some of my pencils fell with a clatter and at once a rush of black lights went over my eyes. I put up both hands to shield them, and in that moment the giant came to me and said, very softly, 'What is it? Do you know me?'

'Yes.'

'You know who I am?'

'Yes.' My vision cleared. I looked in his face and whispered, 'You are Irmenck.'

'How do you know me? Have I met you before?'

'Do I seem familiar?'

'In a way.'

'We have never met. I never saw you. But the captain of the galley described you to me.'

We spoke in Tulic, each with a differing accent of otherwhere.

'You're very white,' he said. 'What do you want of me?'

'Nothing. Except – I wish you no ill, only good. I'm *glad* you are free – of *that*.'

He sighed faintly. He smiled. One could see, as Thenser had seen, he was not a man to love butchery, or lies.

'My thanks. You turned my heart over.'

'And you mine,' I said.

And he gave a tilt of his brows, wondering if I flirted with him.

'This is very unexpected,' he said.

'The man who freed you – did he free you?'

'Yes,' he said, his face solemn now.

'It is – is he with you?'

'Not here. Not in the town. But I know where I may find him. Who asks?' he said, protective of the protector.

Suppose, as in the classical myth, they are lovers. Suppose this one has preempted me. I did not even know what this was, this idea, not fully. A gleaning from the language of the salons of Krase . . . enough to make me falter. But I had burned down the candle and She had heard me. I must go on.

'I'll send him a note by you, sir, if I may.'

'You may.'

I sat, shuddering, and tried to hold a pencil.

(Pella's assistant, seeing we were engrossed in dialogue – though I had not thought to give the favourable signal – had returned to his book.)

I gripped the pencil and could not make it move. Suddenly Irmenck put his giant's hand across the table and laid it on my own. He was very warm, but in the way of land – earth – more than anything animal, and from him came a calm that mastered me. I breathed, and then I took the pencil again and wrote: *Thenser, if you recollect me, I am here. If you would see me, I am here. If not, unread these words. I never wrote them.*

'You haven't put down your name.'

I raised my head. His hand had given me such fortitude. I said, 'Will you tell him? *Aara.*'

The afternoon moved slowly. Few bells sound in Old Genchira, but a day-candle was burned up in the studio. At six, down thundered the youths and padded the maidens.

Dorin did not come down. He was still working. Thank the goddess: Then Pella would not yet appear to bid me go home or bid me stay to supper.

The assistant, due to keep the shop until eight, began to tidy a little, fussily.

I went out into the back courtyard, hurrying, and drew a cup of water from the pump under the fig tree. Returned, there was no change in anything. I did not need to ask if anybody had come in.

The assistant had not questioned me. I had said not a word once Irmenck was gone.

The light failed. The assistant lit the two lamps, at the counter and the door.

I sat in blessed darkness, watching a sky of cinnamon become a sky of ashes, and of the hue of grapes both green and purple. The buildings across the wide street faded into the sky, then put on their raiment of windows.

Soon after Pella descended and finding me, said, 'My dear Ayaira, what are you doing here? Go along with you. Or can I persuade you to supper with Dorin and the girls?'

And so I excused myself and went out of the shop on limbs of lead. There was tomorrow.

As I was turning into the Forum, a ragged boy ran up and handed me a folded paper. It said, *Moonrise at ten. The Leopard Tomb.*

I stood bewildered and almost frantic. Was it some note from another *to* another, mistakenly delivered me? I had never seen Thenser's handwriting to know it. I did not even think it was his hand—

On the walk to the town, long ago, about a mile outside the wall and gate – there were many tombs among the cypresses, and surely one with leopards of stone upon it. There, then, at moonrise?

Abruptly excitement came back to me. Not in pleasure, in fear.

I flew towards my lodgings, for in these streets young women, as children, were permitted to run.

For her assignation the hopeful lover dressed herself most becomingly. She knotted up her hair and put on man's clothes. Though there had been no crime on the old road for a century, I did not want to establish a centenary. To go out in the wild alone at night as a girl was to tempt men and gods. There was no moment when I considered I should not go at all.

I got through the town without incident, passing the two taverns on my way, not even meeting a patrol of town guard, and along a cobbled avenue to the gate which straddled it. Above on the arch a chariot of stone raced over an arch of clouds. There was a weightless wind, the sky very blue and tall – rain might fall later, but the moon would rise in a minute. I had just time to walk my mile.

It was a fraction farther than I recalled. The lunar globe was in the trees like a white paper lamp . . . I went faster and was afraid I should not find the place, or had dreamed it – then there it stood, powdered by moonlight, the tribe of leopards on their high box, black cypresses behind.

No one was there. Only the tree shapes moved, and the moon steeping the tomb sides.

I went forward hesitantly. Had some trick been played on me? Had some unguessed enemy lured me here?

He was here. As if I scented his life, heard his breathing in the race of air and leaves – I *knew*. Thenser—

Then I was seized from behind, taken with such incredible ease, and I felt the warm touch of the giant, remedial even in near violence.

'No resistance,' he said. 'It wouldn't avail you.'

'I know that,' I said.

He swore. He called quietly upward, 'It's no man – it's the girl again.'

I tipped back my own head, and it lay on the giant's ribs. Among the leopards, another, upright, leopard, the lean figure of a man, hair like a flame of silver and iron.

'Oh,' he said down to me, 'and are you this one you say you are?'

The moon was behind us, the giant and I. Thenser was stage-lit, but I a shadow.

'No, I'm not the one I said. Not Aara.'

'I thought not.'

He prowled between the leopards and came vaulting down. He landed light, took hold of me at once and swung me round from Irmenck to the moon. Then there was silence.

Truly, I was not as he had seen me before, bleached and curled, painted, sunlit. I was more of the earlier mould now. More the frightened child. I trembled between his hands, not with love, nor any longer fear, but with anxiety. With anguish. For he was only human. He was only real. And close to me now. In the world with me.

'Thenser,' I said at last. 'You do know me, then.'

'I know you. You're the Princess Aara Gurz.' There was no change in his face. He looked negligent, ironical. 'Where's your escort? Are they standing by to enjoy our reunion?'

'Escort?' I said. He believed I had been used to take him in a trap. So he had devised this meeting here.

'There are no others,' said Irmenck. 'I'd have seen, from the tree. Just this one girl. Ssh,' he said to me, knowing I shook, 'he won't hurt you. But the truth now.'

'Oh the truth,' I said, 'the truth is always so easy.'

'I can't flatter myself,' said Thenser, 'your Saz-Kronia has reached this far for my blood. You're an adventuress. I congratulate you. But what is the plot of this drama?'

Then I saw the way. For a moment the door of my brain would not open on it. Then the key turned. I found the firm trunk of the apple tree. In the language of our birthland, his and mine, I said, 'Kronia was the enemy. I'm not Kronian. I married a man of Dlant's army, for protection. I had no one else. I was in the great retreat, the treasonable retreat. I came to Krase a widow and they gave me the estate of Gurz. Like you, I played both sides. Like you, twice a traitor, and a lost child.' Then the hammer of my heart stopped me speaking. And I had seen his face change, its mask come unravelled, and the beauty of his realness and his hurt cut through me.

'What in gods' names are you saying?' he said to me, in Tulic.

'Speak in our own language,' I said, through the painful beating in my breast and throat.

'This is some ploy of *theirs*, then? That bloody king on his island of lechery and moral filth. That beast,' he said, in our language, 'that fat bloodsucker who left us all to die for him, sold us – traitors – the King's the traitor—'

He had let go of me. I put out my hands and gripped his arms in turn.

'The King is nothing to me. None of it is anything to me.'

'Who are you?' he said again. 'You look like Aara. And she looked – like another. Another of the beast-King's victims.' His eyes burned hollow on me.

I tried to speak, and now again could not.

Irmenck, forgotten by us, had stood aside, as if we seared him by great heat or cold.

'Listen,' Thenser said to me, in the language of the City of our birth, 'I don't know you. You begin to seem like every woman I ever met with, lay on, saw on a street.' He took back his control, and smiled at me. 'Save me from madness. Reveal yourself.'

His spurious calm (his eyes were savage as the blown moon) enabled me to find myself again. As before, through the medium of him.

'I'm not a spy. I'm not in league with anyone.'

'Splendid. And you don't claim to be Aara?'

'I was Aara, at Gurz. Here they call me Ayaira. You knew me by another name in my aunt's house.'

'Which aunt?' he said casually. 'She had better be named too.'

'Elaieva.'

'Yes,' he said. He shut his eyes. Against my hands the muscles of his arms were locked, but all the substance of him had gone away.

'But I,' I said, 'I, *I*.'

'You.'

'Of course, you will have forgotten. I was a child.'

'You were Aradia,' he said.

All strength went out of me. I, too, was a thing of dust.

How long we were together there, in that timeless nonexistence,

I cannot say. It was the man Irmenck who brought us back from it. He said, flat and low, 'You'd do better to take her down into those trees. Who knows, there may be others out. I'll watch the road.'

'Yes,' said Thenser. His eyes cleared and he saw me, and all things.

He indicated a little path running through the cypress trees, and we went along it into darkness out of the moon.

'You see how fugitives go on,' he said softly. 'Never at their ease. Perhaps I earned such a life. He did not.' We came to another tomb, small and overgrown, and here he spread his cloak like a courtier and indicated I should sit. 'He tells me the fiend of *Dvexis* gave you his story. What did you think?'

'That if you reckoned Irmenck was unjustly sentenced, he had been.'

'Still such a child,' Thenser said. He touched one of the loose strands coming down from my knot of hair.

His comment offended me. Not the truth of it – a child I still was in so many ways – but that he should dismiss my belief in him as a childish lack of judgment.

But I did not dispute that. I only said:

'I am Aara, too.'

'Like the goddess, having many forms. I remember Aara. She was a flower life gave me when I expected only thorns. I never deserved Aara that day of the harvest.'

Did he intimate by this that he was done with me? It seemed so, he was so grave and gracious. He stood beside the tomb, and looked away into the night.

'Did you know then—' I said. I did not finish.

'I didn't know you for who you are. Aradia. I took you for a Kronian. And I saw the other. I saw Elaieva. You're very like her in curious ways.'

'Do you dislike me for that? To be like her but not to be her?'

'She's dead.'

His words knifed through the dark. I said, 'She killed herself and left both of us.'

There was a long pause. Then he told me something of the prison, and the gaoler who brought him the news. It complemented the dream I had had. It would have unnerved me if it had not. I did not mention this.

'And then,' he said, sighing quietly, 'you were taken away by the Bear's army. *Eyes*. You were only twelve—'

'Fourteen. I had an expiation to make.'

'So young. What expiation could you have had? Did you love him, the enemy soldier, and think you sinned?'

I did not know whether to speak. The *final* expiation. To tell him how I had crossed out his name from the executioner's list, how I had meddled, made him, broken him, in that one unthinking deed of rescue.

Before I could decide, before I could speak past the onbeating scourge of my heart, which tired me and wrung me out, he said, 'I only knew you on the road above. I remembered, then. The quaint little girl you'd been, with her long silky sunny hair. It was I told you of your parents' death. My gods, how you must have hated me.'

Presently I said, 'Won't you allow me to love you now?'

He shook his head. 'Aradia . . . No. Don't make me avowals. Don't, for the sake of the gods tell me you made this journey following me. I won't let myself think it. It's a fantasy, beautiful and idiotic. You're capable of it. I saw you at the harvest. You were like a shy doe that came out of the thickets, trusting, half thinking to fly, but with the eyes of the goddess, so you see the doe is magical and has the soul of the fire – Aradia, don't make me say these things. The harvest of Vulmardra – those couplings are for the summer's end, and then forgotten.'

'Forgotten by you, but not by me.'

'Not forgotten in the sense which you mean. A jewel of memory. Now let me go.'

I said, 'I have visualised this meeting, and that you would say this. You only met with me at all to defuse a trap. But instead of a snare, this woman is here you don't want, clamouring over a love scene in a wood, best put from the mind, to you only the scratching of an itch. To me—'

He laughed. 'Your days with the army, I see, have taught you a choice phrase or two.'

So again I could say nothing else. A shield was raised against me. He took every sentence as a sword-stroke, and turned it. My arm was numb from the shocks. I was exhausted as Lixandor when he fell bleeding and crying under the strawberry trees.

I slipped from the tomb and began to go up the path through the cypresses. Every atom of me cried out, as if I tore myself away from him by the skin and hair. But the night was soundless.

'Aradia,' he said, but I did not turn, or halt. He would offer me escort to the town gate. I did not want his protection. What I wanted he could not give.

Irmenck stepped forward as I reached the Leopard Tomb.

'No dangers,' he said, 'but will I see you to the gate?'

'That isn't necessary. Tell me one thing.'

'Perhaps,' he said. He looked at me gently, noting I was wounded.

'Why did you come into Pella's shop?'

'The painting of the green fruit. It shone at me, clear across the street.'

'Had you been in the town before?'

'Not often. And not for some time. At first not at all. I'm distinctive. And any who know the signs would know what I had been.'

'Did Thenser request you to go into the town today?'

'No, but recently he told me to look out for Pella's shop. He said,' Irmenck hesitated; he resumed, 'the pictures displayed I might like to see. And that the shop was notable for a fair-haired girl who sat there prettily drawing in the window.'

I shrank back. Thenser had seen me then. Seen, by me unseen. Perhaps not to know me, my head bent and face part turned away – yet, if he had loved me or wanted me, would he not have known me? Could he have gone by? And I, should I not, with my dreams of him and sense of him, have

356

known he passed, *but I did not know*, his shadow only one of a hundred others coming between me and the noonday sun.

I walked along the old road, uncaring what occurred, but no one molested me, there was no one alive on earth.

My eyes were dry and hard with bitterness.

It was all finished now.

I would stay here, for where else was there to go? And he would be away in the summer, who could think anything else, moving his camp to be sure of avoiding me. I had no claim on him. To need was not to have a claim, as to love was not to have one.

My footfalls were heavy, and nearing the town walls, I often stumbled on the uneven paving. I leaned a little while in the gate arch, as if borne down by a garment of granite. I longed for sleep but could barely find my way to the lodging house. I had no home.

Chapter Two

1

For a day Master Pella's assistant had been unwell, and I was asked if I would oversee the shop. I should be paid a wage, indeed, said Pella, I should already have been paid one, for I had become quite a feature of the place.

I had had a mind to absent myself. The instant I got in the shop a rush of melancholy almost pushed me to the floor. But Pella's inquiry I felt I could not refuse. What did it matter?

Sternly, as I sat there, as I chatted to the occasional customers, and I lunched with the Master and his brood, I held myself in check. I had not wept. There would be an appointment with weeping. Perhaps I was not convinced. Perhaps I hoped that, with a passage of time, the man I had set my heart on would relent. But I could not imagine it.

Instead I began to imagine a new lodging, or at least green blinds and a rose-red lamp. I must make a home, since I had none. And I must walk to the port one day, and ask at the house of Emaldo's aunt – ashes. Nothingness. Well, then, I was not obliged, but at least I must forget the other.

The harder I thrust him from me, the sooner and brighter he sprang back into my mind. I saw him in every way, the glamorous captain, the tarnished warrior from the siege wall, the condemned man, the scintillant duellist and gambler, the ghost upon the twilight road, who drank Topaz wine, the lover, the shadow who rejected me.

The second night I lay on my bed and waited to sob and cry. No tears came. I was a dry gouged well. Neither could I sleep. And so, sensibly, I read a book. And went out next morning with grey-hot cinders for eyes, thirsty like one gone insane in a desert, buying a pound of grapes at the market to quench my throat, meeting Dorin, who fell into step with me.

'You're so early today, Ayaira.'

'I didn't sit for you yesterday. Are you done sketching me?'

'No, but now your looks have altered.'

We shared the grapes. I said, 'You're not alone. I have visions, too. Didn't you tell me that? How old are you?'

'Fourteen.'

'So they said. But are you older?'

'Inside. And I . . . remember other things.'

'Don't say!' I cried.

'No. I won't say. I would rather not.'

We walked across the Forum.

'Ayaira,' said Dorin, 'I don't think Bolmo is sick.'

Bolmo was the assistant. For a moment I did not know who he meant.

'Oh, no?'

'I saw him at sunrise on the street, with a stranger. They stepped into a doorway. Bolmo thinks I see nothing, so I saw nothing.'

'Well,' I said. Suddenly his words came in to me. 'A stranger – what stranger?'

'Like a sailor, I think, from Genchira port.'

'Where was this?'

'I room near the Chariot Gate.'

Both of us had come to a standstill at the entrance to Pella's street. 'The night before,' I began.

'I saw you, leaving the town,' said Dorin. 'You wore a man's clothes. You're quite tall, and looked like a young man. But it was you. Then someone followed you. Far behind. I thought he meant something bad, but then I thought you'd asked him. It was Bolmo.'

'*Oh, the Mother.*'

'He walked so soft you never heard him. He kept far behind. Perhaps he knows nothing.'

'I wasn't going to a tryst,' I said. I floundered, and said, 'A man's freedom—'

So shapeless and obscure, the fussy assistant of Pella, I had forgotten his name. He had hung about at my lodging and then slunk behind me. He had seen, from some deep cover, my meeting. The big man had alerted him, entering the shop, though he paid no apparent attention. Irmenck was his quarry. *Fool* not to have thought of it. The landing party from *Dvexis*, they or theirs could have penetrated to the elder town, offered some reward, maybe left some man or other at the port as lookout. Until now, the escaped slave had evaded detection. But I, by my selfish need, by my sorcery even, had drawn him out, the entrapment he and Thenser had looked for, after all.

Had Bolmo followed them, in turn? Certainly they had not noted him, for he survived to lurk in the doorway this sunrise, with this stranger.

I stood wavering, not knowing what to do.

'There's half an hour before Pella will want to open the shop,' I said, thinking aloud. 'Where does Bolmo have his rooms?'

'He has his mother's house, the white one, on Temple Steps.'

I could only think of going there.

I left Dorin looking nearly as he always did. The very fact he had told me so much made the import tremendous, since he was a psychic.

Back in the market I bought more grapes, two glossy apples and a few flowers. I climbed up the stairway above the temple, where the modern houses stand on the terraces to either side as if self-conscious, for the stair is so ancient and they so young, they are afraid to cross it.

The white house was obvious, rather little and mean and grubby. I rang its bell and thought no one would come, but then a housekeeper came. I inquired after Bolmo's health. She said he was up and in the garden room, I darted past her with the apparent speed of delight.

'I'm so happy you are recovering,' I exclaimed, bursting

upon him. The garden room was spare and looked out on a
spare plot of weeds and one urn of rainwater. Bolmo wore a
cotton house robe, and was at pains to be ill, hurriedly flat on
his sofa with an angry look.

'A touch of colic. The weather brings it on,' he said. 'Soon
better.'

I loaded him with fruits and flowers. He took both in
dismay until the bustling housekeeper entered and saved him
from them.

'You are very kind,' said Bolmo, 'we've never been
intimates.'

'The worse my remorse,' I said.

The housekeeper, tired of attempting to catch some inference, went out. Bolmo scowled upon a book he had obviously
been reading. I could now see only one means of tackling him.

'But I had another reason for coming here,' I said.

'Ah – yes?'

'The other night I left the town. You went after me.'

'*I*?' Expecting my accusation he was all ready with over-
done affront. 'If you *will* roam at night, very probably
someone may have – but not I.'

'You. I won't debate it. I was pleased to have your
company, for I thought I might need help. In the end I did
not, but neither did I achieve my goal. The wretches put me
off and I dared not follow after my excuse was disbelieved. I
trust that you *did* follow them? And then sent your message,
or went yourself, to the port.'

'Whatever can you be—'

'I am intent on revenge,' I said. 'Both men have done me
an ill turn. I won't offend you by relating it. Tell me, are you
also in the pay of the captain?'

Bolmo's jaw fell. He pulled it up again.

'Well this is a fine pot of fish,' said he.

'My own reflection exactly.'

'You mean to say that you also have connections with—' he
hesitated— '*the galley*?'

'What else? But we waste time. Only answer. Did you
follow them?'

'A part of the way. The hulking slave was continually hearing me and searching about, though you had got the other in a stew by the looks of him. I went far enough to determine their direction.'

'Which was?'

'Why should I tell you?'

'Because already you've told others and I wish, for my own sake, to see those two pigs taken.'

Bolmo lowered his eyes.

'I don't want any of this to reach the ears of Pella. I'm not the only man in the town to have been approached, some turned up their noses, but I'm not rich. Pella, though, is of the *virtuous* mind. He employed me for my dead mother's sake, but if I annoy him, I'm out.'

'The same applies to me, since I've also accepted money from *Dvexis* and long to see blood.'

Bolmo gave me a withered smile.

'Well, what a revelation you are.'

'And so are you. Speak up, or am I to inform the captain I caught you out trying to defraud him?'

'Would he think so, after I assisted his agent? Ten of them will be on their way by now.'

I almost screamed. My voice came out cool as water.

'The captain will believe what *I* tell him. He likes me better than you, I daresay.'

'You trull,' said Bolmo. 'Give me twenty lild, and I'll tell you.'

There went my shoes. I flung some coins in his lap and jingled the rest.

'The Villa Gencha,' said Bolmo.

'What is that?'

'Anyone will tell you. A rich man's farm. They'll be employed there. A track leads over the fields from the tomb where you met him. Four, five miles.'

I was about to throw him the other ten lild. Then I changed my mind. I flung instead one of the glossy apples off the table and blacked his eye. Leaving him yelping, I ran.

2

My feet were my transport. Only carrying chairs and an infrequent horse were seen on the streets of either of the Genchiras. I had never ridden alone, and reckoned a chair would be dilatory.

Soon, with a scalding stitch in my waist, I wondered if I had been wrong. I went forward running where I was able, or at a running walk.

I had returned to the shop only to cry up to Dorin that I must go out again. From my work table I took the knife with which I pared my crayons and sticks of water colour. It was very sharp, for I had had it honed only yesterday. I felt remorse, even in this extremity, at failing in my duty to Master Pella. I did not know what I could do; did not know what I was doing.

But as I struggled over that hilly route among the olive groves and seeded fields, I met no one beyond some wandering sheep and their boy, who did not understand my panted Tulic concerning ten men, and who only ambled off as I dashed on.

The low red roofs of the villa came in sight, and I was sick and weak with dread. Holding my side, I staggered through an open gateway and in among a jumble of sheds, by a press-house smelling of vinegars and vintages, through a wall of orange trees. The farm seemed just as far away, and probably I went in circles, but in the panorama below I saw a house and haylofts and a serene pond under an old cedar, and nowhere the show of force or even disagreement. Perhaps it was all done. Or – horror upon horror – had Bolmo *lied*?

The way lay downhill now, and downhill I nearly tumbled. In the fields round about there was, here, some activity, and as I hobbled by people turned to look at me and I thought crazily of the Gurz estate. But I was no princess now. I was the harbinger of rotten fortune.

From a barn, into my road, came striding a tall and mighty man, limping a little on the left leg. He carried a massive load of oats, three times the normal weight, and seeing me, stopped, as if forgetting altogether.

'Irmenck – Irmenck—' I reached him, crowing for breath, trying to marshal explanation. By a miracle it seemed I was in time.

And I did not need after all to explain.

'Men from *Dvexis* are coming?'

'Yes, yes – I don't know – why they're not ahead of me – ten men—'

'Drinking in a wine-house,' said Irmenck, 'getting up their courage for it.' He said this with such regal power I suddenly realised what a match he would be for them, even if they were armed.

He swung off the load and set it neatly at the wayside.

'It's my fault,' I said. 'But also, the man in Pella's shop—'

'Don't fret,' he said. 'It had to come.'

'What will you do?'

'We have horses here. The hills, maybe. We were there before.'

'Do it. Oh, quickly, Irmenck.'

'But you'll have to come too,' he said.

I was amazed to find I had anticipated the invitation.

'If one of them learns you came to warn us, or thinks it, they wouldn't be kind to you.'

'I'll burden you,' I said.

'Only a little.'

I was embarrassed and said, 'But I can't come with you, for Thenser's sake. You must go, the two of you, alone.'

'Don't be a silly girl,' said Irmenck, half playfully. Then, he said, 'And anyway, there they are.'

I turned in abject rage – I had delayed him yet again with my stupid frivolous twitterings.

'*Go*, Irmenck. Leave me here. They won't hurt me.'

They were trotting on horseback down from the orange trees, where I had come staggering. Not ten but twelve men. They looked like a black smoke. One of them had seen us. He pointed with an odd scarlet flash – his sleeve – but it was like blood.

Irmenck had my arm, he was pulling me along with him in a lurching stride, and calling in a colossal bellow as he went, for Thenser.

In the side of a whitewashed building a bank of shutters flew wide one after another. Out leaned young men, some with fencing swords, looking like any students of Old Genchira. And then yet another with his shirt open at the throat, and I saw the one I had never thought to see ever again. There was a fencing sword, too, in his hand. He looked along it at the hill. 'Turds of the Bear,' said Thenser in Kronian. He glanced down at Irmenck and shouted, 'Get the horses.'

Then he was gone, and his fencing class about him, all the sons of the farm he had been teaching the arts of duelling, who now howled after him in excited loyalty, getting in his way, delaying him as I had done.

Irmenck dragged me around the wall and in at another yard and through into a stables. Here he got two horses, which would have to be ridden bareback, though he slung up saddles and bridles in a bundle across the withers of one, and lifted me on to the other. 'You can't ride, I suppose. He'll take you. And here he is.'

Before I knew what was happening, the huge living horse under me, Thenser had vaulted up and brought his arms around me to take the animal's mane.

'Hold on to me if you don't want to fall,' he said. 'Hold my wrists. That's better. I won't crumble.'

The horse started off at his kick with a neigh and a type of flaming fire that surged all through its body and mine.

I had not got my bearings. We were pelting out of the yard, taking a hedge at a leap. Irmenck was just behind us, and behind Irmenck the pursuit.

The white track flared out in front again. It sprang up at us and we thrust over it. Then the track was gone and tall grass broke across the horse's breast like spray. I clung to Thenser's wrists, not able to do anything else. They felt like flexible steel, so alive, almost supernatural.

He and I had not been pressed close as this since we made love. I had not held him, or touched him, since he told me my name. He did not want me and I had been forced on him and twelve avengers were on our heels – but the exhilaration!

We were cantering up the slope of a hill, and as we came on to the crest of it, Thenser looked back. 'Good,' he said shortly. He reined in and swung about, and Irmenck, coming behind us, did so, too. Down in the farmyards the horde of riders had become muddled with much animal life, goats, geese, a great brown pig, and several piebald hounds. 'I said,' said Thenser, 'they might let out some dogs. But they were more inventive.' Irmenck gave a brief laugh. The fencing youths were galloping around below with a huge display of apology and inquiry, getting in the way. Women were hastening over, flapping their aprons at the geese. 'To the cross-stone,' said Thenser, 'and if they're still with us, best divide. Meet again at the usual place. Do you have your knife?' 'I have it. You?' 'Knife and sword. Ah, me, there goes the pig. She was always partial to a horse.' One of the pursuers, his mount butted by the brown sow, was falling from his saddle.

Thenser turned our horse's head and we sprinted off again. To me he said, 'I should have left you at the farm.'

'I'm sorry. I told Irmenck so.'

'Yes, you'd have been safer, if they're all to come after us. The farm wife could have put you out of sight. Never mind it. Too late now. Hold tight, girlie, I don't want you off in a ditch.'

Over the running hill, the landscape of up-country opened wide. The olives like static dancers on rising platforms, a vineyard and a white wall, and then the untamed patchwork of lifts and descents, powdered mauve with anemones, and with poplars and stone pines on the straight ridges, and over all, the higher hills of ruled basalt only dusted with greenness, supporting sky.

I should have stayed at the farm. I was a trouble to him.

If I let go his wrists, I would possibly fall and be left

behind. But he would not leave me to the mercy of our followers, it would only be another delay, and I might hurt myself unnecessarily. And I did not want to be sloughed. Let me keep with him while I might, and think only of the rush and flight, green and tawny and pale purple hills, and clouds above—

We reached the place he had called the cross-stone. It was a monolith, leaning and of great age. But looking back, apparently they had come on again, the hunt.

Wordlessly, Thenser roared at Irmenck, and Irmenck roared back at him. He and we parted precipitately, each racing diagonally along the hillside in an opposite direction. We came on another road, hardly a sheep trail and strewn with boulders from some slip above. The horse plunged this way and that, and Thenser held it through and took it suddenly off again, upward.

I had difficulty in seeing back, and was content not to, only to be held so close I had lost the sense now that we were separate. But Thenser said, 'Eight of them went after him. Scared, and well they should be. That leaves four for me.' A few moments later he said, 'I shall have to kill every one I can. Leave no sweets in the box for *Dvexis*—'

Into a wood we plummeted. Trampled like wine, a perfume of leaves and crocuses and infant saffron washed through my brain.

I must have made some sound. 'What is it?' he said. 'Are you afraid?'

'No.'

'You should be.'

'I know I should.'

We dived over a fallen tree and a glittering stream of broken mirrors beyond, and swerved into the face of the sun.

At the next ascending ridge, looking back, he said, 'What bloody unsubtle wooers they are.' Then, 'The horse hasn't much left in him. Up there, I think, those poplars – we get off and send him on alone.'

The horse was gasping from the pit of its lungs. It could have gone farther if it had not had to carry two. And

Irmenck's mare – how had she fared with a giant on her back?

We came among the poplars, and in their fretted screen, he was off and lifted me down. He slapped the horse's side and it fled like a shot bolt.

'Climb the bank,' he said to me. 'Lie down in the high grass. Don't let them see you. If by any chance I am – discommoded . . . well, you'd better run. Do you have anything to defend yourself?'

'A small knife.'

'Clever Aradia. Use it if you must. Don't scruple. This kind is the excrement of hell. The world's well rid of them.' He sounded casual. He was not convinced by his own argument, but rallying me.

I protested nothing but went away and climbed the bank. I lay down in a stand of anise.

Thenser had seemed to vanish into the poplar stems, like a tree divinity.

The afternoon, after our cascade of movement, was throbbingly still. A wind fluttered through the poplar tops, and the sun there splintered and scattered. Somewhere a chorus of tree-frogs was singing in a timeless many-throated voice *kex-coak coa-kek-kek*.

A hawk swam in the sky against a cardamon cloud.

Then I heard the hoofs of their horses.

The first men – two – four – of them, went hurtling by, breaking branches with their impact. They were continuing after the horse, not yet aware it went so fast from an unloading.

Two others followed rather more slowly, either doubtful or tired.

Part of a tree, in a green-gold slide, seemed to fall down on them. Both men crashed off their mounts, one with saddle and stirrups attached. They rolled into the roots of the poplars, the shadow, making a noise which finished as abruptly as it began.

I could make out nothing else, only the two horses backing off, revolving their eyes, stamping and blowing. Then there came a gleam of Thenser's white shirt, and of his hair. He surfaced, rising up. Another light, from the knife, and he stood away. He had dropped on the pursuers from the tree. They must be dead now. It was a Charvish trick much used in the snow forest.

I felt a terrible joy – I acknowledged it was terrible— But next instant there came the other hoofs again, returning.

Back along the slope they tore, the four together – no, there were five of them. And the first shouted, in Kronian with a bizarre accent: 'Here, the rat's here!' Then he squawked and flew up from his saddle like a bird, and going over on outstretched arms sprawled down in the path of all the others. Thenser's knife protruded from the man's chest, as sudden as if it had burst out, not in.

I felt a wave of sickness. It seemed to me the illness was Thenser's own.

All the horses were rearing. The second man was trying to hold his mount as the swordsman came at him, leaped like a cat, ran him through.

They were shouting, shrieking in blind fury and murder.

Not equipped with swords, these men, but with long knives, long as any sword they seemed, flailing through the air, each cut a gout of fire.

Between the crazed motion, the flickering strings of leaves, I could not see what was happening now.

I stood up on the hillslope, and was spun off it. I had the wicked artist's knife from its narrow wooden box. As I came around the trees, I distinguished a man ahead of me on his feet – it was the man with the red sleeve. I flung the knife-box at his head as hard as I could. It struck him, and he cried out and slewed around, staring at me. I thought he might laugh, but he did not. He turned his back to me again, as if to look had only been a promise for my future. So then I darted at him and struck him in the side with the knife.

It was a ghastly sensation, so easy, yet so difficult to retrieve the little blade, for he pulled away and nearly took it from me. But I had somehow got the knife free of him, and next I slashed at his blood-red arm. Then he turned on me and I saw the cleaver of metal go up, and knowing from my first lesson how it must be done I, too, raised my knife high and sliced open his neck just beneath the ear.

He went reeling off even as his own knife came down for me – missed me, and was discarded in the ferns. I did not behold him after that, for I rushed at a horse that seemed to materialise, and grabbed the booted foot in its stirrup. The foot tried to kick me away. I scored the leg, which was that of a doll which could bleed. Cursing me, a living man reached down to kill me, but Thenser, standing on the fourth dead man, called him away with a mocking 'Ah, *come* now.' And before the fifth man turned from me, Thenser was on the horse with him, and on the bucking, squealing mound of it, ended the life of the rider as quickly as if it did not matter.

The birds and the frogs had stopped singing. And then, as though they had no need to observe any terror or dreadfulness of ours, they began again. *Kek-kek kex-kex-coak*. And from the hill, a nightingale—

Thenser had seized me. He shook me.

'You bitch, you're covered in their blood – is it yours? Are you hurt? Why did you do it? You're like a mad thing—'

'There were too many of them—'

'Yes, yes. But to kill – you don't know what you've done. Dear gods I'd rather anything than to have made you do that—'

'I killed before. I killed a man. *I killed him!*' My voice came thin and distantly. We struggled with each other, as if beating off invisible flies.

'Aradia—'

I covered my face with my hands. I would not look and see any of it. I would not look at him. He recalled a child playing with flowers and toys, not able to kill for him in blood. He hated me.

'Aradia,' he said. 'Calmly. Don't.'

'I'm dying.'

'No. Not a scratch on either of us. You see?'

'I can't see. I can't breathe.'

'Hush.' His arms went round me. 'I remember that cry.

371

The venomous corset with its yellow ribbons. I'm here. Rest.'

And so I rested against him, and all my panic left me, melted. And there was only the green light, the sound of insects and frogs, the singer on the hill, the scent of aniseed, and of his skin, no tang of blood or hate. I was calm as he had bade me be.

'I'm sorry,' he said. 'I always forget you were in that siege, that war— You look as if you stepped from heaven. Thank you for your help in need.'

'Hold me a minute longer.'

'Of course. Poor little girl. All your bravery and then to be reviled.'

'Only a minute. Then I can leave you. I can find my way to the farm.'

'Forget that,' he said. 'There may be others of that scum about. We don't yet know how Irmenck fared. But I've seen what he can do. I don't quail for him.'

I drew myself from his arms, from the delirious comfort. This now, the last time, and for ever. But we should not part as we had.

'I'm better,' I said.

Even so, I did not look at him. If I should look at him, into his face, his eyes, I could never look away. I should be fixed to the earth. Bound. I should say things he did not want to hear.

'What,' he said, 'do you go back to?'

'My own life.'

'Which is?'

'Ordered and quite happy.'

'Which is?'

'I can't explain.'

'You told me that you loved me,' he said. 'This was true?'

'Must I say it again? Thenser, you told me then, you didn't want me.'

'No, you misunderstood. I told you, I thought, my life – my damnable sullied life – how can I offer to make you part of that wreckage?'

On the ground, dead men lay in the ferns, and between the roots of trees the horses were cropping crocuses. How strange, how strange.

'Aradia,' he said. 'Answer me. Tell me how.'

I looked only at his mouth, which I had known, which spoke to me. I said, 'My life was damned when yours was. Everything I did, in some way, a bleak echo. Deception and betrayal, and lies, and all the confusion. And homeless. As if I'd been born in the thin air, living where I fell to earth, now in that place, now in this. And no one near. Nowhere ever to rest – except just now, against you.' Then I looked at his eyes, into them. He was very serious, intent and listening. 'Without you, what will become of me?'

'Be with me then,' he said.

'Not as a penance. Not out of pity. Not unwanted.'

'No penance, no pity. I want you. You see a poor fool smitten by love in a Kronian pine wood. Irmenck will tell you, I spoke of Aara often. And after I'd met you again, probably I drove him mad, going over and over it.' He smiled. It was a smile of sorrow, or regret. 'But Aradia, to have me is to get something flawed. If it had been between us then – in that – in the City, where we were born. At some dance. If history had left us alone. Why, what a fashionable couple we'd have made, they'd have fussed over us till we were vulgar with it. But the wine was spilled and the rose torn up by its roots. The bargain isn't wonderful. I'm no catch. The dead ride behind me, Aradia, a battalion of ghosts in the morning before sunrise.'

'I know, my love, my love,' I said. 'I know.'

And putting my arms quietly about his neck, quietly I kissed him.

But the nightingale sang on, as if there were no love in the world, only beauty and music.

Chapter Three

1

Three tall stones in a weird, interrupted semicircle, marked
the usual meeting place. It was a hill of trees, the stones not
visible until we came up with them in the levelling afternoon
light. A stream flashed down the rocks, garlanded white with
bellflowers. There were crevices and caves in the furred sides
of the upland. In such a cave they had sheltered first, hunted
hares for food and drunk at the stream.

There seemed no real doubt in Thenser's mind that
Irmenck, too, would have victory. Although my companion
was very silent. We were both very silent, restrained now, for
there were no longer any customary barriers between us. To
be so open was partly alarming to me. Beyond the one short
embrace in the wood of corpses and sunlight, there had been
no tokens.

The horse had returned to us, which Thenser predicted,
and he had kitted it from the gear of another. The rest of the
horses he left, along with the dead. He said something to the
effect that later there might be a burial. It was nothing
religious, let alone compassionate. He said he did not like to
leave, unnecessarily, rotting cadavers to scare sheep and farm
children.

He seated me on the horse and led it. In that way, we did
not thereafter touch.

At the stream I bathed, decorously in the tent of some
myrtles. I was oddly embarrassed, as I was restrained. I did
not know how we should go on now.

There had been a flask of rough wine along with the taken saddle. This, with the fresh water, was our sustenance.

After a time he stretched out on the ground and slept.

He looked like any young man asleep. Only his closed eyes did not quite lose their shadow. I wanted to kiss his face, but did not know him, did not know how lightly he slept, did not want to trespass or seem to incite. I had washed the blood from my skirt, the material slowly dried in the sun. A few dark bees were gathering from the bellflowers. The standing stones stood on in their perpetual remote significance.

I felt empty. Not happy or unhappy. It was as if I were alone, and yet my sense of him was so complete. It seemed nothing had ever happened to me before, I was without a past.

Irmenck appeared when the sun was setting.

His mouth was firmly shut until he opened it to say, 'A waste of life.'

'All?' said Thenser.

'And you, too.'

'Yes.'

'Perhaps Meia's people will see to it. I can lead them back.'

Irmenck's mare was still with him, he had been leading her, and now she nuzzled the gelding and cropped the grass with it by the stream.

'If we walk the horses,' said Irmenck, 'we can get on. An hour or so will see us at the village.'

'Aradia, can you walk a few more miles?' Thenser said to me.

I said that I could.

With no more to-do, we went over the hill and down into the cauldron of the sinking sun. The lower sky was every shade of red, but in the east the darkness was beginning behind us. A wild aroma came from the trees and the ground. The crickets whirred and ceased, and whirred again.

Suddenly, in a break between two hills, the sea appeared under the sky. The sun was just slipping into it, for a moment was there, glowing and enormous, and then in another moment was gone. And all the fires began to fade and the light died from our faces.

'The village is below,' Thenser said to me. 'Village Genchira. We fetched up there first, Irmenck and I.'

'That was a night,' said Irmenck, and they both laughed.

I wondered if they would speak of it, but they did not.

Instead, Thenser added, 'Tell me then, Irmenck, what do you want to do?'

'I think I'll take up her offer. I think I'll try Khirenie.'

'Yes. Meia isn't a fool.'

'And for you?' asked Irmenck.

'Some otherwhere,' said Thenser. 'It seems to me Kithé might be of interest.'

They said nothing else.

We walked down the darkening land towards the sea.

2

Village Genchira was mostly a ramble of fisher cottages going down into a bay. On the rocky headland above, a square had formed with a small temple to the sea lord, and three or four fine houses. A fifth house, standing back a little with fields and a vineyard, was the house of Meia.

The details of how she had met Irmenck were not revealed to me. Perhaps very simply, in the market, or – in more romantic fashion – walking on the shore soon after he had come from the sea, like one of the sea gods himself, this finely-made giant with his black hair streaming salt water. By now, certainly, they were lovers.

Meia herself was Khirenian, a Troan to be exact, from the old provinces about the River Trojos. She had estates there, but some connection of her family had set her up, too, at Genchira, where she had lived years like a nun.

She was striking to see. Her hair was gold as gold itself, and her eyes a pale honey colour, a manufacture of golden-ness with the summer's gilt still lingering on her skin. And she was tall as a man, taller than most. Irmenck towered above her. One could see she might have liked that at last.

We needed no more than knock at the gate to be taken in.

The house was airy and pastoral, built all round two courtyards with only half an upper storey for the lady's bedchamber and offices.

Yet she had three estates. Not only did she look golden.

I was inclined to be uneasy, and Meia made me shy. She had a queenly way and cared nothing for anyone when she saw Irmenck and kissed him before us and all her servants.

At supper he and she discussed his going as if it had been planned before. She would have one of the sturdy fisher ships take him off, for the weather was settled, around the shores and away to Trojos. And in a while she would follow him. They smiled on each other.

For Thenser, she said she was his slave, he need only direct her.

He said again Kithé might be of interest.

She said she had heard that it was. How would he get there?

From Port Tuli, he said. He saw no difficulty. The *Dvexis* had shot her bolt, and missed.

'Apart from me, he's safe. It's I would show him up,' said Irmenck.

'Yes,' she said, 'you're not to be hidden under a sunshade.'

Nevertheless, she said, Thenser would do better to effect some camouflage. He was known in the area. And was the lady to go with him?

The lady (myself) looked away from Meia's eyes as if guilty.

'Yes,' Thenser replied lightly. 'She'll go with me. Aradia is my wife.'

This utterance stunned me. I did not know if it reassured or frightened me more. It was a lie that could never be a legal truth, the union with Kahrulan had seen to that. And then again, was this some sop he offered me, to gladden me? Still, I did not really know what promise we had made each other.

Meanwhile they talked on, and the lamp shone yellow on the table, and coming back to it I found we were to have peasants' clothes for our journey.

'Do you want to send any letters back to the town?' Thenser said to me. 'Are there things you want brought from there?'

'Everything I own is there. It isn't much.'

I had a vision of some male stalwart of Meia's household rifling my linen, packing up for me my other corset and my stockings. How could I ask for such a thing. I would have to make do. And for the next tenant, how useful the items might be. And the tinted glasses in the window, and the camellia in the pot . . . and a string of pearls in a muslin bag. A treat, a gift left behind.

But to Master Pella I must pen a letter, he was kind enough to be concerned at my vanishment. This one thing must also be done circumspectly. I need not mention Thenser.

Meia's man went off with the circumspect letter inside the hour. Other men were sent to see to the burial of our assailants. Everything was to be tidy at our going.

Meia herself took me aside and said, since I had come away with nothing, she would send someone to me presently with a selection of undergarments and other essentials. She feared her own wardrobe would be too fulsome for me, but she had a personal maid whose clothing was decent, and perhaps I would make do with that?

As I was Thenser's 'wife' I assumed we would share a bedroom. Meia next dispatched me to it, saying I looked 'like a little girl kept up too late at a dinner,' and I was swept away by the haughty personal maid who deposited, on a broad bed in a pink-washed room, heaps of lace and rosettes and ribbons worthy of the princesses of Krase.

Alone, I sorted out a few of the most plain items, hoping not to deprive. Then I drank some water from a crystal glass beside a crystal pitcher and looked out of a small window with a grating, into the branches of a magnolia tree. I counted its buds. I forget how many there were. I counted them anyway more than once; the number was never constant.

He did not come to the room for a great while. When he

entered and shut the door, the lamp on the table by the pitcher flared up and guttered down.

'You see,' he said, 'five minutes with me, and already you are involved in deception and flight. Do you care to visit Kithé?'

'Of course.'

'Why of course? Because you will be with me and you've given yourself to me, therefore that makes all perfect?'

He did not sound angry, or even scornful of my lot. He sounded as I had felt myself to be, empty, at a loss.

I said, carefully, 'Thenser, if I'm to add to your difficulties by going with you, I must be left behind.'

'This was discussed,' he said. 'I want you with me. But if you are, I behold you caught in such a whirlpool.'

'I'm accustomed to that,' I murmured.

'Very well.'

'Why,' I said, as he seated himself and began to get off his boots, 'did you say I was your wife?'

'For convenience. But it can be made a fact.'

'It can't ever be that. I'm contracted in a sort of marriage – a Kronian custom. It means nothing, except in law.'

'I see. Well, then, my wife in all but name.'

He was offhand. Perhaps it troubled me he was not more put out, a silly girl's reason. Or it was only his easy, half-indifferent way. When he had held me under the poplars, among the spilled blood and light, I had been sure of his commitment. I supposed now everything was settled, and I must be as placid, as offhand. I went behind a screen and began to undress, and my hands trembled. I felt no desire, had forgotten what it was. Would he desire me, even? He did not seem to.

Finally, I put on a silk nightgown of the maid's, and stole out of hiding.

He was still seated by the table, his boots off and shirt undone but otherwise dressed. His hands rested loosely on the arms of the chair. He looked into nothing.

A dreadful oppression came on me. I went quickly and soundlessly to the bed, got into it, and slipped from sight among its pillows and covers. There I lay like a stone. He should think me asleep.

Here I was, straying again among the avenues of the adult world. I had mistaken him for another. For the one he might have been . . .

Long after, I returned from a state not sleeping, nor fully aware, to the sensation of his body in the bed at my side.

At once – everything – the cumbersome rolling motion of Keer Gurz, the couth Cristen and his clever lovemaking on sofas – even Drahris, my devil, returned, shaking and punishing me into feeling.

This was like no one else. He had slid into the depths of the bed as if into smooth water. I heard his voice, low, a living murmur in the depth with me, 'Only some coils of mermaid's hair on the pillow.' His hand came and curled itself upon my hip. 'And she is armoured in silk against me.'

At his voice, his touch, all the wanting in me awakened. I could do nothing but turn to him, a mindless sea-creature in the swell of the oceanic bed. When he ceased kissing my mouth, he said my name over and over, he spoke it to my throat, and pulling up the folds of pointless silk, to my breasts, to the length of me. I lay lapped in the nightgown, naked to my shoulders, and felt the exquisite caresses over every surface of my flesh. And did not know any more where I was, only that we seemed buried together in some deep white darkness. And when he filled me, pressing me into the mattress, holding me, for his pleasure and my own, I could not see his face but only felt his body against mine and the heat of him, the inrushing wave, and the dissolving sinking down again into the cool black sea.

I lay in his arms. The night had stopped its movement, yet I could hear the sea still, the waters of the world, and in my ears the tidal whisper of my blood.

'Aradia,' he said, so softly I barely heard him, 'better be warned, sweetheart, sometimes I have bad dreams. Don't – let them dismay you.'

Who are you, this unknown known stranger, this fellow human of another gender, another race of the world, this pleasure-giver, this burning warmth that holds me, rocks me, through the seas of night?

I slept and did not know what dreams he had.

I slept as if I need not wake.

3

In the dawn, I woke and saw him. We lay and looked long at each other. There was no amazement for me that we were together. Although I had not forgotten the doubt of the previous night.

Then he smiled and drew me against him. He kissed my hair and said to it, 'No dreams. What a sorceress you are.'

'Did you but know,' I said.

'That you put some spell on me? How could I fail to know it.' He held me stilly then and said, 'Work your magic. You may save me yet. If I'm fit to be saved.' And again, after a silence, 'For what I've done, some reparation must be made.'

I said, 'Was Irmenck an act of reparation?'

'Yes. An offering to the gods. The life of a purely good man, got out of earthly hell. You see what he is. He can even kill blamelessly. What do I mean – the gods know. But I'm thick with it. With death. Oh, not the soldiers' killing, not the war, but those other lives.' He broke off, and outside in the magnolia a bird was singing. 'On Kithé,' he said, 'will you let me tell you those things? And you must tell me your own story. I don't know it. You were a child, and then a white-haired princess, and now – now you are yourself.'

'But last night, you would have been glad to be rid of all of us.'

Even as I said these words, their falseness jarred on me. I had not meant to commission him with falsehood, but did not know what else to say.

'Be rid of you? To be rid of myself, I think. I have these moods. I told you, I'm worthless. What a wretch you've won for yourself.'

I did not want to leave the warmth of him, the texture of his flesh, and the hair falling on my arm, but thinking of my attentive mother suddenly, said, 'Shall I get up now and call the maid for tea?'

He started to laugh.

'Afraid no doubt of what will be done to you if you remain. Well, you're too late, madam, in that.'

And next the nightdress was tossed across the room to drop against the door, where the maid actually tripped upon it, in bringing me my breakfast later, after Thenser had gone.

Thus the cloud was sent off from us in the way lovers send off such clouds. They hang upon the horizon then. They are visible, but at a distance.

At noon the Khirenian woman was admitted to the chamber. She glanced idly all about, as if to see what I had done with her property, whether improved or disarranged it. Then she said, 'Thenser not yet returned? He was to see a man in the village.' She paused, and added, 'There is a boat will take him over to Kithé, but not, I'm afraid, a woman.' I looked at her. 'A superstition,' she said, 'on some of the smaller craft. I've found it inconvenient myself before now. But then, a very dirty rough passage, and nowhere to sleep. On the other hand, it was the way we had planned for Thenser. He'd do better to take it and get off quickly.'

Everyone seemed in on the secret but I.

'If it would help him, to leave me, I've already said to him that he must.'

'Oh, you gave him your permission?' she said. Her pale yellow eyes examined me. I had the urge to shake myself like a cat. 'Well, that's good. He'll feel free to take the best chance.'

My heart, my very blood sank. But I did not protest, and finally she said, 'Then there's you to be got over. I could send you in a cart to Birds. That's the least obvious way, in case any are out watching. And you shall still have your disguise as a village girl.'

When Thenser came back, he found me dressed in this costume, my hair in a striped scarf. He kissed me and put on my marriage finger a fisherwoman's brass ring from the market. 'Well, wife. Now thee's respectable.' Though the metal was inferior, it was a delightful thing, in the form of two dolphins, which curled about each other, and were thought fortunate. As I played with it, he said, 'Did Meia tell you about the boat?'

'That you are to go one way and I another.'

'It's the wiser plan.'

'You had not planned on me.'

'That's true. Surprising as the spring in winter.'

He held me and spoke love words to me, and in their midst explained the means of departure and that we should meet on Kithé. The awkward pills were all got down in the sweet wine.

He left before sunset, and I set off in the cart before dawn. It was for me a four-day journey, and the boy who drove the cart was not talkative. I had time for elation and unease. Forty miles or so outside the port of Tuli lay the settlement known as Birds. There was a reason for the name, for from this point the uncanny air transports, of which Emaldo had once spoken, winged away for the island. They were a fact not a legend, safe as chariots, safer than a boat, so Meia had insisted, for there had not been a single wreck in all the years she lived at Genchira. I wondered if she was sending me to my death, so Thenser might be rid of me.

The road above the village was a good one, shaded with windblown cedars and windowed by endless sights of the blue sea, with Kithé an image upon it, now solid, with bold heights, now faint and transparent as a bubble. At sunfall the island turned black with fire along her backbone. (Was Kithé feminine?) Her unusual quality began, despite my worrying, to be borne in on me. What might she have been in the misty past, this entity which drew close and wafted away without ever changing her position? Did the ancients believe she could float or was enchanted?

By night I slept in the cart, with the boy inflexibly on guard at Meia's instruction. If I did not sleep, I lay in a sort of limbo, and the scheme I fancied drifting in the air of the

Khirenian's house – the scheme in which Thenser had some
part, and indeed all of them, but I – that came and flitted like
a bat, teasing me to guess its name. Or I thought for light
relief that, in the window of Pella's shop, neither Irmenck
nor Thenser had seemed to notice my blue tiger and dancing
maidens. A minor point. My talent was small. Dorin's
painting had attracted – but then, in Irmenck's possession, at
his lady's farm, was a store of artefacts and books, 'the taste
of the connoisseur,' Thenser had said. It was silly to be hurt
by this, for I knew my place in the world of art; it was a tiny
one. Yet I remembered then how Thenser had gone by and
seen me, too, in the window, and not known me.

The boy and I met no one on the road but some shepherds
with their flocks, and once a rider clad like ourselves off to a
junketing, who greeted us in a burst of Tulic I must smilingly
pretend to understand.

On the fifth day we reached Birds. It was a cluster of cots
dominated by a great green cliff which rose up against the sea
like a leaping comber changed into land.

We ascended mossy steps where terebinths grew out
sideways, to a stone platform. There rested three colossal
butterflies, each with a single ribbed sail.

The gangs trained to operate these craft were busy all
about, at ropes and wheels and with obese bladders, one of
which was being ported to the air ship with the hyacinth
wing.

Six people sat on a bench, some with baskets on their
knees, one with black hens in a coop.

My boy paid another boy who had come up, then went off
and left me with my bag.

'Eh, master,' shouted the new boy, 'here's the last passenger.' He toted my bag, considered it. 'Will do. You and that
make her up to eight. Seven or eight she must be, or it's not
worth our bother. And no more than ten or she goes down.
Though,' he added presently, 'did once go down with eight.
But that was the day a wind blew.' And as we went on he
added again, 'Though she must have a wind, do you see. To
lift her up—'

He seemed to approve my lightness of person if not of heart.

Soon the hyacinth-winged ship was ready.

I and two others stepped bravely on to the deck, which was oval in shape. A series of struts held up the kitelike wing. The monstrous bladder squatted amidships.

The other passengers filed aboard. Everyone looked as if going to a funeral. Near the cliff's edge was a little god in painted wood, holding painted birds up in his hands. The sailors touched him for luck. They seemed spry enough.

We passengers were told we must on no account, once the ship began to move, move ourselves.

'Eh,' said one, 'knew a man hurtled to death for a sneeze.'

The sailor said this was an exaggeration.

Seated, the oval wall of the ship stood above one's head. Even so, a long-haired woman was asked to bind up her locks, and I with my scarf was pointed out as an example.

Then we were rolled along the cliff towards the drop.

Something was done to the bladder, which began to hiss. It had been squeezed full of air, some of which was now rapidly going out: as it did so we suddenly lifted up off the ground.

The sensation was indescribable, and two of the women screamed, and all the hens clucked. A breaker of fear went over me. But as we keeled off from the cliff in an unrolling snap of ropes, and gush of air and ether, there was instead an utter abandonment, and fear could only leave me.

I put back my head, and as the vessel dipped and yawed, the lovely butterfly wing unfolded like a flower, and filled with sky, bore us up.

'On to Kithé,' cried one of the sailors.

The hens muttered. A streamer of gulls flew by, parting to avoid us. We were in their country. It was incredible.

When we were in a steady drift out over the sea, taking to all the proper currents that would push us forth, draw us in again to land, they allowed those who would to open little eye-holes in the ship side and so gaze out and down on a blue sea under which moved green and turquoise braids.

At length above the rail we began to see the tops of the

island coming near, with the sun on its brow. No one spoke, beyond the sailors now and then. Even the hens were silent.

Suddenly I was supremely happy. It seemed the world had been made for me, like the paradise the gods give to those they love, at death.

I could think of nothing more beautiful than this, to fly across the sky towards the haven of re-meeting. Here my life began.

Neither did the bumpy landing at Kithé destroy my illusions. As I stood on the high beach, on the enchanted isle, a man walked from behind the almond trees, and it was Thenser, here to meet me as he had promised.

Part Three

THE HOUSE BY THE OCEAN

Chapter One

1

Half a year we lived in a house by the ocean. In all honesty, mostly I lived there alone.

At first it was a sort of dream. To be with him, and to have him tell me where we were to go; to go there and find it as he said. To ask how he had secured such a place, and to hear that already he had 'friends' on Kithé. Naively I moved within the magic spell. Despite everything, I retained an unconscious belief in fairy tales, happy endings, idylls.

The village was called Steps, it was built all about a great decaying stairway that ascended from the beach. From the main artery, other stairs had more recently been constructed, two or three hundred years ago. The whitewashed houses, and the houses washed with ochre and vermeil, clambered as it seemed on each other's backs to get up, and between were wedged gardens and orchards, two temples with their squares and groves, yards of washing, old walls pebbled by cats and huge tortoises. Steps lived through the sea, from its fish, and by diving after its sponges. Thirty circuitous miles inland lay the town of Ebondis, almost another planet now, though in bygone times it had planted a villa or two on the headland.

The house was one of these, a stately palace of palest yellow edged in leads of faded white stucco. It was embraced by riotous gardens, topiary, that had withstood the winter gales and human neglect, to become dark labyrinths that were the tenements of birds, the treasuries of small animal bones and the arms of shattered statues.

The upper floor of the villa was nearly derelict; one went up there at one's peril, and in the winds, they said, bits of the roof whirled off continually. The ground and mezzanine were let for rooms, mostly now uninhabited.

Our apartment was on the lower floor, two large chambers and one eccentric inner stair that gave on a final room between the storeys. This had the charm of a long window that opened to a private terrace of cracked pink stones. One dry fountain stood there, with a sea girl still pouring from her barren conch shell, not melancholy at all but smiling, so obviously to her eyes the water still jetted forth.

From the terrace was a painter's view, wild garden and slender cone-pines, framing the village of Steps, the beach under it, and the sea.

Behind the house there stood back, beyond the sweeps of woods and olive trees, pastures and hillsides, the heights of the island. They were not, in fact, tall enough for winter snow, and yet they seemed massive, as if touching the sky, and one might watch the clouds come down them in the morning like heavenly sheep.

The almonds blossomed, and then came the green blossoming of the olives; the slopes blushed red with fire-anemones. Sudden terrifying storms came, frequently by night, slicing at the island's tops with lightning lances, and fearful sentient thunders seemed to hunt down men, so they fled into shelter. And indeed they tell you on Kithé, the lightning searches for its prey and kills again and again. It is one of the most common deaths. In their dialect, which describes an older form of Tulic, they even have a word for death which means also lightning, so they can tell you straight out so and so was *lightned* – struck by lightning and killed.

The village was very poor. I think I knew this at once, but evidently I only accepted it. I had had much teaching in the acceptance of many states. I saw the old women with their toothless mouths and faces wizened small, picking at rags, and I saw the thin bodies of the children and the young men, and the faces of the young women when the sponge boats set

out on that uncertain sea one hour cerulean, the next a kettle
of waves. But I saw, too, the flowers growing in the broken
walls, and the cats sunning themselves, the colours of the
washing as well as its darns and patches. It was again my
naivete, or I was wrong. Or was it only that I saw things in
that way.

'Even this little place,' he said, Thenser, 'pays tax to the
government of Tuli.'

Tulhia was a kingdom. I had known that. It encompassed
Tuli and Khirenie, and such outlands as the island of Kithé.
To me, this was a backdrop. It did not impinge on my life,
less than the geography.

In the first month, we were together.

To the furnished rooms we added that we thought necessary, having to send to the town for such things as a bookcase
and the books to go in it, hiring bed linen from the
caretaker's wife. But pots and dishes came from the village,
lovely heavy redware with designs of black octopuses and
white shells. Our domestic arrangements were simple
enough. A girl in the house saw to the cleaning and washing.
She plied a broom of twigs, and scrubbed our dining table
with local sponges. The washing she took to the stream with
the other women, and there Thenser's shirts and my petticoats were pounded on the stones while the goats looked on in
scorn. Food we got from Steps, hot swarthy bread brought
up with fruit and fish in the mornings, milk and curds about
midday. I learned the easiest of cookery from the cleaning
girl. You merely put everything into one of the red dishes,
layers of fish, onions, mushrooms, spices, garlic, poured in
some yoghurt or wine, and took the whole down to the bakers
in the village, where all the women went, to cook supper and
dinners at one of the thirty-six ovens. Alternatively, once one
had acquired a stove, the same ingredients could be fried with
olive oil and pepper in a black iron pan. Otherwise we lived
on cheese and oranges, olives, figs and wine, and on a sticky
porridge they make and sell in slabs, thick with honey and
raisins.

Beguiled by this food, I was often hungry. And love, too,

393

made for me a complementary appetite.

The beginning days were all of this. Landscapes, food, love. We might have been without care. (To sleep with him, too, was a joy to me. To wake to him, or to his touch. Of the nightmares I had been warned of there was no evidence.) But perhaps I hid myself within the thicket of joy, perhaps I was afraid. For now and then we would speak not of the moment, but of some past element, which seemed then to move close, a shadow lacking even a name, having no shape.

Our confessions we did not make. We apportioned our histories a little at a time. He spoke less than I, of that. His concentration seemed on some newer, sterner matter.

Yes, I must have been afraid. I did not question him.

He told me that this was our holiday. But that in Kithé there would be things to do. He had been on the road to them when I caught him up. He lay with his head in my lap and said, looking up into Kithé's blue sky, 'I can't be idle for ever. You see that. I shall work out my sins here. The sin of living when half the world was mown down round me. It *is* a sin.'

Unspoken between us, so much. It seemed now I never would tell him of what I had done, how I took his name from the book of death.

I accepted his talk of reparation, for surviving, for betraying and betraying over, though another man would have reasoned away with logic and sophistry all such notions. Because he did not, I did not think he should, did not think of it at all. I accepted this, as I had accepted the poverty of the village. All the medley of existence.

At night, when lightning struck the crown of the island, I sometimes recalled the Heroine card, her wand exploding at the lightning-strike. But the bolts of heaven did not fall upon the house.

Three vessels of the sponge divers had been lost in a storm, and a terrible keening rose from the village. It began soon after dawn, to hear it was horrible. Immediately the beauty of the view from the terrace became grotesque. I ran in and down the stair into our sitting room.

A man was there with Thenser, a rough brown man who sometimes with his cart made the trek to the town. He had brought a letter it seemed, which Thenser had been reading. Now, turning to the carter, Thenser said, 'When do you return?'

'I must go back tonight.'

'Will you take a passenger?'

The man said he would and held out his hand. Thenser put a coin in it, and the bargain was established.

I stood transfixed, and watched all this. When the carter had gone, Thenser turned to me and said, 'Aradia, I've spoken of waiting on someone.'

'Who?'

'Let me tell you the name another time. It wouldn't, I think, mean much to you any way. Though in some quarters it might.'

He began to put together things for the journey, and I saw from his choice he would be away days and nights. I asked him how long, he said he did not know, maybe a week. But I would be safe here, for now I knew my way about, and was at ease with the Kithéan dialect.

I felt like an infant abandoned by its family. But at last I had the control neither to display my misery, nor speak of it. He could have seen it in my eyes, no doubt, but he kissed me and took me to bed, which happened often enough in the daytime. There we stopped until it was time for him to leave me.

This was the first division, and the end of the idyll. He was gone a month, and sent me one letter, very affectionate, extremely sensual, written in a high-flown style that had set itself to lave my privation. It was a letter to be kept into old age, but I did not keep it. With a sudden ghastly pang, it recalled to me the last letter I had had from my mother before her death. They were not remotely similar of course. But I burned the paper in a spasm of animal terror.

At his return I knew only need, sexual delirium. When they were appeased, I found myself upon an empty beach, and there, at my side, he began to tell me where and to what he had gone and why and to what in future also he would be going, his motives, the requirements of his life. I felt the passion of his social and political commitment. But I could not grasp the fire. It seemed alien. But then, too, I trusted him, and what he willed and hankered for. Gradually, by listening, suspending self, I became Thenser. And so began at length partly to experience this great desire of his, perhaps more potent than carnality, for the spiritual and intellectual goal.

2

Thenser had not been without money, and from the town I had even ordered a pair of dresses, but as such things do, though made to my specifications, they did not fit very well. I clumsily reset the sleeves . . . Now he told me to order a dress for dancing.

I said it would not fit, like the others, and with whom was I to dance, the sheep?

At that he took me by hand and waist and danced with me a gracious Promenade, there on the terrace of cracked stones. An elderly man, one of the other tenants, leaning on his sill above seemed to watch us with sad pleasure. Some boys from the village, pilfering the garden, went crazy, two dancing round and round in imitation, the other lending us a tune on his pipe.

I was overwhelmed by the silly sweetness of it. My lover could dance – but of course, he and his fellow officers had known the ballrooms of the City as well as Origos Field. A glimmering haze of the Good Past – as opposed to the Shadow Past – hung over our action.

'Light as thistledown,' he said to me. 'Well, there's to be some dancing at Ebondis.' And the other shadow came, the stern and concentrated present.

He said the dress should be ordered, but I would be in time for a final fitting in the town.

We went back into the rooms and the piper turned a

cartwheel and the elderly gentleman resumed his nature vigil.

'You'll like to see the town?' said Thenser. 'It's a pretty place, but for the slums, although you won't notice those. Or you'll think them curious.'

This shamed me. I said humbly, 'Am I so unfeeling?'

'You're all feeling, Aradia. That's why you see the sky between the broken bricks. The child's bright eyes and not the scabs on its feet.'

'That isn't true. If you want to condemn me, I admit that if I see something awful I try to look away. What can I do?'

'Yes,' he said. 'If you can do nothing, there's no reason to agonise over it.' His face was very fine, as if firstly carved then changed at a word to flesh. He turned his eyes on me and said, 'It isn't only a dance we'll be going to. That's the excuse. You'll see Retka for the first time. I wonder what you'll make of him.' He said this so thoughtfully I saw it did not properly matter, for what I made of him was superfluous.

'Retka?'

'We've spoken of him, but not by name before.'

This was true. I had known instantly who he meant.

Thenser moved about the room, not seeing it. He said, 'In a month or less, Cristen Kahrulan will have hold of Kronia.'

'He intended to become Emperor.'

'He'll have succeeded. I never knew if I was free to speak of that to you. What he'd been to you—'

'He was nothing to me,' I said.

'But this legal marriage union that was no marriage – a Heartgift, I think? That was with him, was it not?'

'For his convenience.'

'What was your part of the spoils?'

'I don't – I had his protection. I don't know.' I was listless and dismayed at this confusion, the past not quite Shadow, but certainly not Good.

'Well, then, he used you, and you say you had no special liking for him; you live in a dream, Aradia. Are any of us actual, do any of us exist for you?'

'You.'

'You don't convince me,' he said. He glanced out from his

thoughts and saw me, and said, 'Who is it you behold when you look at me? I'm sure he's very wonderful, your eyes tell me that.'

I could say nothing to this, but I was hurt by it. I fell to a rapid self-questioning, and all the underpinning of my emotions seemed endangered. He accused me not only of ignorance of him but of mistaking him. Was it so? He was examining a book now, and I went near to him, and watching him across the table, I said:

'When you looked at her, who, what, did you see?'

'At her? At whom?'

'Elaieva. You look at me and see her now. Isn't that true as well? But what was she? To me she was cold as ice. The day she killed herself, she apologised to me for not loving me. And now you do it.'

'Not love you,' he said, 'I love the air you breathe.' He reached right across the table and took hold of me. 'You beautiful little cat. Your eyes, your skin – when I come into a room and see you there, it's like a light. Come on, believe me.' He held me. I waited. He said, 'She isn't what I see when I look at you. I was infatuated there with what I couldn't get. And then she became the symbol of all of it. The way she died.'

'She needn't have died. It was her choice.'

'Ah, don't be harsh, little girl. You don't know. You felt the coldness of her. She had to live the coldness. She stayed a nun of the goddess.'

I waited again, but there was a long silence between us. He caressed me and let me go.

Then I said, 'What has Cristen Kahrulan to do with us?'

'Nothing. But one predicts, once he's in the Imperial Chair, the treaties will be torn up. Kronia will be awake again, stretching out. And Cristen Kahrulan is soldier and strategist. He knows what's to be done.'

'Another war,' I mumbled it dully. Surely now it would be far away.

'You're not supposing,' Thenser said gently, 'that if he begins to carve for himself, he'll rest until he has it all.'

I remembered Vollus' words, everything cut up like a cake.

'The entire Temerid will be dragged in,' he said. 'He'll bite towards the East. I shouldn't wonder if he didn't put a tuck or two into the equator. Tulhia can't hope to avoid it. She'd make too acceptable a base.'

'How long before—'

'One estimates. Time is the only thing. A year? Before he gets so far, Kithé must have her freedom. Tuli can do as she pleases, her fat king, accede or fight. But to push Khirenie and Kithé into the squabble without a word for themselves will cripple, will *destroy* them. This pastoral little village, Aradia, with its elegiac poverty – they live off the bone now. Imagine them under the onslaught, the Saz Empire and Tuli at each other's throats, and half the Temerid in smoke behind.'

'And Retka is the leader you'll follow, to get liberty for Kithé.'

'He had a Khirenian mother, a Tulic father. His granddam on the maternal side was an Eastern princess of Taras with green-black hair. That's how he speaks of her.'

'You met him at Meia's house?'

'Oh, no. But I heard of him there. I met him here.'

'The cause of Kithé has become the reparation,' I said. My tongue felt heavy in my mouth, my lips were stiff. I stared from a window at the garden and the sea's bow-curve beyond, and tried to know they were Kithé, of which we talked, whose liberty must be obtained.

'I should never have said that to you, Aradia. Reparation. What does it mean? I want justice, wherever it can be got. However it can be wrested away from these slovenly gross kings, these grasping empires. And yes, Zulas Retka is the central pivot of what's to be. When you see him you won't doubt it.'

'Hearing you, I don't doubt it.'

I saw him looking now at a drawing I had made, for solace only, they were too poor to need such things here. It was the usual kind, two girls conversing in a strand of fig trees and vines, with a tame lion at their feet.

'That isn't how I see the world,' I said. 'I know it isn't like that.'

'So you make it over, you try to make it better,' he said, 'and that's what I want, too. The gods, if they created anything, left it too much to determine itself. It's become a monster. We smash the mould and begin again.'

The light from the window was on him, like fire all over him, as if he burned. At such moments the Shadow left him. How could I argue with that?

3

I stood in a gown of strawberry silk, while the dressmaker went about me with her pins.

'The waist is a finger too wide. It must be taken in – here, and here. I assure madam, we followed her measurements exactly. Perhaps she thinks herself plumper than she is. Or has taken to tighter corseting?'

But I would not assume responsibility for her errors, or even my own. I waited dumbly, looking at myself in the long mirror. I had not been sure the colour would suit me, but, with a little rouge, it would. It was the colour Thenser had wanted. Probably he was sick of my eternal greens and blues. The petticoat was a strawberry-crimson, and would be a revelation in the dance, and I had silver slippers and silver earrings which had been bought for me that morning in Ebondis, the way one buys a toy for a fractious child. He had wanted to buy me a ring also, but I would not give up the dolphins.

Sunset was falling on the mirror as the dress was finished and put on again for the last time. I thought of my first showing to myself in Krase. Where had Vollus gone to – where were they all? It was an awesome truth, only Thenser had stayed a reality for me in absence.

When I had seen to the painting of my face, (now so easy, practised), and the hairdresser had arranged my hair with little scented false strawberry flowers, I went downstairs to the hired carriage.

I was as nervous of this festivity as of any in my life.

Thenser was waiting on the steps of our lodging, glamorous in the height of fashion, breeches like a second skin, shoes of blond leather, a mantle-coat of silk the colour of the evening sky.

'A goddess,' said he, getting into the carriage.

'You are even more gorgeous than I.'

The darkness was coming in slow velvet upon the high housetops of Ebondis. A temple passed us with a towering of pillars, lit with eyes of agate. I had not been prepared for the size and modern richness of the town, expecting something more of the type of Genchira. But the paved roads were wide and the roofs went up like cliffs. The governor of Kithé was presently in residence at his summer villa here. To this palace we were going.

Flambeaux were burning above the bank of stairs. Even the gardens had put on necklaces of tinted lanterns.

'Witness what one gets,' said Thenser, 'from a proper respect for kings.'

A hundred windows flamed on us from the facade.

Guardsmen, and a male and female deity, protected the head of the stairs, uniforms and marble wreathed with roses.

Fire-lizards of stewards in golden livery ushered us through.

The night was very warm, and I was glad of bare shoulders under the five great candeliers. There had been a little dancing at Krase Holn, but not on the gaudy scale of this. The Kronians, I believe, see the act of dance rather obliquely, they would rather put in a gambling table. The dances of Kithé, too, were wild. In the first hour came six Tarascas, and a Tulic Caion, of which I had seen the Steps villagers dance a version more tame—

To commence, Thenser did not leave my side, though he was greeted by the most substantial of the men, in elegant coats and gold rings. These took my hand and brushed my fingers with their moustaches, the Kithéan mode. Their ladies smilingly inspected me through the tines of fans. We danced more than we sat by. But I took absolute fright at the careering Caion, and this we sat out. Then came a young man with a chrysanthemum moustache and a beautiful embroidered coat over a matching tunic – a garden of flowers on legs.

'Zavion, may I escort your wife through a Promenade?'

And Thenser, looking at me gracefully, said, 'Take pity on him, will you?'

So I consented. I had already noticed any man might ask any woman to stand up with him, it was the way here.

The Flower Garden led me into the Promenade, dancing in a limber weightless waft that was unhelpful as it gave no lead.

'You are the most fetching creature here tonight,' said the Flower Garden. 'Have you seen the governor's wife? Done up like a bundle and badly tied. I shall have to accord her one dance at least. Take pity again and promise me another of yours in recompense.'

Thenser had told me this man's name, and position, which was something of importance in the governor's party, and naturally I had forgotten both. We glided up and down, and I promised him another dance, wondering how we should manage if it were a fierce one, I should not know where I was with him.

When he returned me to my chair Thenser had disappeared entirely, but a crowd of ladies clustered about who welcomed me like a lost sister.

'Your husband has been called away, to the governor's corner, no less.' That, from a golden-haired woman in a striped gown. There were so many native blondes at Kithé I might think myself dowdy.

'But we girls shall close ranks against the *wicked* men,' said another, in puce, with living-dying oleanders in her coiffure. 'To go and leave us so. It's too vile.'

They flapped their fans until the breeze disturbed their curls, at which they left off.

Another dance was forming, and another host of men came upon us. Despite her militant words the puce blonde was the first to spring away. I found myself with a gallant in a gallop, a dance of few steps that covered much ground.

At a pause, when we could speak, he cried, 'You're the choicest female in the room. Who is your escort?'

'My husband,' I replied.

'Husband? Were you wed in the cradle? Who's this fortunate devil?'

I told him. At once he changed, turned deferential.

I was learning by inference. But in vain I looked about, as we rushed here and there, for Thenser. The governor's corner was an alcove, golden seats draped by brocades, a constant to-ing and fro-ing of liveries and those arriving to be presented, and a flare of women's dresses like fireworks, they were so thick with spangles.

Tulic, lacking the Kithé dialect, was the speech of the ballroom, and presumably of the governor's court. (For that, Tulic was the speech of my home. He and I never spoke our birth-tongue, though sometimes a phrase in Kronian.)

'There is the governor now,' said my partner, as we scrambled through a riot of other dancers, the skirts of the ladies slapping each other so I wondered how many sequins were scraped off. My dress had none. One sequin of any worth cost fifteen lild.

I turned, and received a flying curl across the forehead.

'Excuse me,' I panted, 'I must sit down.'

He escorted me to a chair, anxious that I was faint. I sent him to fetch some chilled wine from the supper salon.

The governor had vanished again behind a human fence. The room surged with stabs of light and maelstroms of motion. It was not my element. I had enjoyed dancing with Thenser, but for the rest it was the usual uncomfortable, trying thing. I was out of rapport with the world; like my made dresses, though constructed to the proper measure, I did not fit.

Besides, what went on? Some pantomime of intrigue, some secret meeting behind a curtain . . . the closed room of male diplomacy. Or, had he found some woman he preferred to me? This thought startled me. It was not vanity that had prevented my thinking of it before, only some rightness, despite all hesitation, in our dealings with each other.

'Permit me to present myself, madam,' said a man's voice above my head.

It seemed to ring inside my skull, so resonant, a huge power kept easy hold of. And a shadow fell across me, covered me. I looked up, and into his face as he said, 'I am Zulas Retka.'

At Genchira sometimes, and on Kithé, I had seen Orientals. Never before had I seen a man who combined the xanthine complexion and oil-black hair with the features of an Oxidian. Now I did see it. The apparition was astonishing. In the light of the brilliant candeliers he looked like an idol of yellow bronze, the large black eyes and smouldering brows like jet, and the wealth of hair, which curled, a profusion like an eruption of black foliage, ivy or some other tough and glistening, irreducible plant.

He wore blood red, the coat thickly embroidered with gold as any of the women's dresses. In one ear was a golden earring. His costume added to the barbarousness of his looks; perhaps he had designed it to do so.

He was ugly; his body, though tall, coarsely developed, and overlaid with slabs of muscle. His face seemed hammered out, dented and distorted. Only the eyes were wonderful, like the luxuriance of hair.

Putting forth a hand of yellow bronze, he took one of mine, and bowed to it, not touching. He had no moustache.

'You were simple to track down,' he said to me. 'He could only have a wife like you. Eggshell porcelain. Well, if you like, I'll take you to find the dog.'

He had mesmerised me. Not wanting to, I found I had risen. He put my hand on his arm, and took me through the press of people at the floor's edge. They made way for him as if before a colossus.

The governor was seated on a chair in satin and medals. He was laughing and joking and drinking with a pair of others, if anything, more spectacular. He was a little man, the governor, although possibly Zulas Retka emphasised this impression, for I gazed on the governor after staring at a strong light.

'Ah, Retka,' said the governor, glancing up the way a schoolboy might at someone he admires and fears. 'Who have you brought me now?'

'The most lovely lady in the room,' said Retka.

The governor beamed upon me. I made an obeisance.

'Yes, yes,' said the governor, 'enchanting.'

'The wife of my friend, Zavion.'

'Just so,' said the governor.

Then Retka led me directly by the governor, into the back of the alcove, which opened on a corridor. Here various servants were moving up and down with trays, and guardsmen stood at waxwork attention. A door of the supper salon was to be seen, ajar, and Thenser was standing there in talk with some other men.

I thought Retka would call them over, to heel as it were, but he did not. Instead, turning to me, he guided me back again, past the governor (in parenthesis), and to the dance floor where the twelfth Tarasca of the evening was forming up.

'What blockheads,' said Retka. 'Let them have their debate, since they want it. You and I will dance.'

I wanted to refuse him, but could not find adequate grounds. He did not seem likely to heed me.

He took hold of me firmly, flexibly. As the music started, I found at once his bolstered, slabbed body moved like silk rope. He was an exceptional dancer, and there could be no doubt of his lead.

At supper I saw Retka's mistress, she was pointed out to me. She came as the wife of another man, a forbearing husband in the justiciary. They called her Sydo, which was more of a nickname, for it was a play on the Tulic word for a silver goblet. She had donned silver, too, cloth-of-silver with white embroidery, and looked, in the candlelight, like a visiting moon. Her hair was coal black, and she wore it seemingly severely, pulled fast away from her face of classic bones, but then from the top of her head it splashed, in a cascade of flowers, to the backs of her knees. Sydo's Whip

they called *that*, and when she danced, she would put this
paragon of hair safely through her girdle.

The governor's supper was served in a private room
beyond the salon.

Retka took me in, and I pondered in bewilderment if
Thenser was excluded, but he appeared, and Retka, with a
laugh, went away. He sat down by the governor's wife (the
bundle badly tied in a bag of satin), and began to make her
laugh in turn.

Thenser said nothing to me of my meeting with Retka, or of
his absence. He talked with me in a witty social fashion, as with
our neighbours, and where I could I flighted along with them.

The supper was very dainty, very unlike the tasty peasant
food of Steps. Kraters of wine went about, changed to the
colour of vacancy, and were replaced.

Outside the rooms, the rhythms of dancing continued. For
us, it transpired, there was to be some private music in an
upper chamber.

We went up, and the ladies were seated on the plush
divans, and the three musicians came in and took their places
by their instruments, a lyrachord and two harps. At the first
notes, the gentlemen went discreetly out of the long windows
and trooped away.

It was so discreet it barely seemed odd. No comment
certainly was made upon it, from the unwieldy governor's
wife on her sofa to silver Sydo plying her swanlike fan. Only I
had been taken aback.

The men had gone to discuss business, while to the mind of
dancing Ebondis below, they were seated in the music-room
attending to a lyrachord and harps. A well-tailored ruse.

The music trickled on and on. I was glad of the cool
windows left open at my back. The chamber was very hot,
and stifling with the scent of unguents and flowers.

4

Almost an hour later, when the lyrachord showed no intention
of stopping, I reached such a pitch I, too, got up silently and

slipped out through the windows on to the terrace.

I felt at once vast relief, and some compunction. I, like the others, had been supposed to sit quiet, wrapped in the mild coma of tinkly melodies and formal developments – which to me seemed all alike, one variation played on forever. Rather than soothe it had driven me mad. Escaped, I hesitated to see if my truancy were to be noticed, but no one came after.

I walked to the railing of the terrace, and looked down. On this side were only the gardens and their lamps, a pair of guards on their rounds. The roofs of the town rose beyond the walls.

The night was fresher, and smelled of trees, and murmured with human traffic. I missed the sound of the sea. Then came a noise of voices raised.

Looking along the terrace I saw a spear of light cast out on the tessellations. The curtain of another room was imperfectly drawn there – the chamber of masculine discussion.

I went carefully towards it, and as the women's music pattered away, I heard the men roaring again more loudly. Their business, then, was getting heated.

I was curious, but experienced, too, a sort of aversion. The spy, probably, has always both an advantage and a handicap.

The curtain had fallen back, or been dislodged in a broad strip. In the vertical yellow segment, I saw instantly the governor sitting like an angry baby now on a velvet chair, tapping his foot so the shoe buckle coruscated: I think there was a diamond in it. At his side another man came in and out of vision, waving his arm, rumbling a volley of denials, all the negative words, No, Not, Never.

Then the blood coat of Retka poured across the entire window, its shoulders to me, yet even so I started away.

'Oberis, let the governor speak for himself, if you please.'

The redness stood there, blocking the light, and waiting.

The waver he had named 'Oberis' I heard to say, 'I beg the governor's pardon. I understood him to be—'

'Oberis only speaks my mind,' said the governor, in his reedy irritated tones.

'Ah, then it *is* "no." '

'In this climate, at this hour. Retka, be reasonable.'

'Oh, am I unreasonable?' Retka's voice was caressive and dangerous. He moved across the window again. As he did so, three other men came into view. Thenser was one of them. He was leaning against a carven chest, in his blue coat, his eyes fixed on Retka and his face grimly composed. 'But you see, I thought,' said Retka, winningly now, deadly, 'that the king could not possibly object to an army on Kithé. It will save him such a lot of fuss and bother when the Kronians unsheathe their claws.'

'There is a treaty with Kronia,' said the governor. He was not merely peevish but alarmed.

'There is a Kronian treaty with half the countries abutting on the Temerid,' said Retka. 'Do you think that will hold them? There's a trade treaty with Candier, which they will use to get in. The burning up of the other treaties will provide illumination for the making of their next battle plan.'

'Kronia. Always this terror of Kronia.'

'Always this Kronia on the march. The Saz Empire, sir, makes war as the fisherman mends his nets. A matter of course. You may speak to Zavion, if you want that much confirmed. He, as you know, spent time in both capitals of the North. He's observed this fledgling Emperor. Don't imagine because Cristen is new that he's green. He was on the field since nine years of age. He knows a thing or two of the council chamber as well.'

Suddenly the governor stamped his foot like a fretful girl, and the diamond burst.

'I've heard enough! Do you suppose his majesty of Tulhia will grant Kithé the right to a patriot army?'

'Tuli,' said Retka, 'will have her hands full presently.'

'Yes, I know the drift. We arm, and then we get loose.'

'Did I,' said Retka, 'mention such a thing?'

'You never mention anything. You allude and you propose. I've had sufficient, Retka. The ideas are very invigorating. Now, let's get back to the ladies.'

The governor rose.

408

At that moment, Retka said, 'The ladies are already here,' and turning again across the window he abruptly flung it open, casting off the curtain, and stood regarding me. 'One, at least.'

No excuse would do. I could only put back my head and meet his eyes. They were not unfriendly. He seemed amused. After all, what threat was I, in my pink frock and pinker flush.

'Aradia,' said Thenser.

Then I did quail, sure I had offended him. But as Retka drew me into the room, Thenser, too, seemed only humorous.

'You see, she misses you so much,' said Retka. 'These young wives.'

I should have been glad to get off so lightly. But something made me say, 'I beg your pardon, gentlemen. I came to see why you were shouting so loudly.'

Retka broke into an enormous laugh.

'Well, there we are in our places.' He bowed to the governor who was looking at me between pique and query. 'I ask your leave, sir, to return to the dance. Zavion, come on. And Oberis, fetch Sydo, she must be haggard with sitting.'

So we passed out of the presence. The governor let us go, with only a diamond twitch.

Oberis came after, and caught Retka's arm on the terrace.

'You don't do well, Zulas, to annoy him.'

'I know, like a stalled donkey. A kick and he refuses to budge.'

Oberis scowled. He was the forbearing husband, grey-haired and big-bellied, with strange, youthful boy's eyes.

'Tomorrow morning,' he said to Retka. 'We had better talk of this.'

'Very well. Your preferred time?'

'Ten o'clock. Now . . . escort my wife, if you'd be so kind. I must get off. The justiciary has an affair on tonight, a case of bribes.'

'My honour and pleasure, Oberis.'

Oberis nodded and hastened along the terrace and around

the wall. In the yellow room they were arguing still. I made out the voice of the Flower Garden and saw him strike a pose by the window, before the governor bade him shut the drape.

'We're in disgrace,' said Retka to Thenser. 'We've moved too fast.'

'What next?'

'I'll canoodle with Oberis in the morning, and we'll get things going that way. Kithé will have her army, and with warriors of your calibre to train it. The governor will go on with his racing and marzipan. He's had his chance.'

I walked between them, and as we reached the windows of the music room, saw the concert was done. The shining Moon turned her head as if at some sorcerous signal, and rising, came straight to Retka's side.

'He regrets, the justiciary,' said Retka. 'You and I, Sydo, must console each other for our loss.'

They went away along the terrace, the last light clinging to glimmer on her gown.

Thenser said to me, 'The lady at the window.'

'I'm sorry I—'

'The governor will reckon you're in the pay of the Kronians.'

'Perhaps he may, if he knows my history.'

'We have no history for the governor. Let's go down and dance.'

We danced in the bright room under the candeliers. He would not let me go, even to the Flower Garden when it, too, came down to claim its promised turn. He wanted me to himself, he said.

Retka and his moon goddess had vanished away.

Not until the morning, in our lodging at Ebondis, did Thenser tell me he would now be staying in the town. He had a post on Retka's staff. He would need to be at hand. And surely I would be happier out of it all, by the sea which was so good for me, which kept me so beautiful.

I wondered if I should make a feminine scene, weep and wail and throw things, like a distressed mistress in a drama.

But that seemed pointless. The scene would only muddy and sour a parting that was now presumably inevitable.

A passenger coach was going from the town to some area farther along the coast, it would let me off on the old track to Steps, an afternoon's walk. He and I had often walked so far. The weather was summer, and two peasant women that I knew from the cooking ovens were going on the same road. I elected for this means of travel. Since he did not want to be cumbered with me, I wished to be away from him as soon as I might.

I sloughed my travelling companions with the coach. I told the women I meant to call on a witch known in the village, who lived up on the hill slope over the track.

They did not seem amazed. From their knowing looks I think they believed I was pregnant, intent on a confirmation or riddance.

But I had no such reason, not any reason to go to the witch. She could not assist me. I had been puzzling on it. There was no answer.

I had wanted his love, and perhaps I had got his love. Yet still we were separate. There was the sustenance for me of his body. But the mind, the heart even, went on behind a shuttered window. I could peer through the crack into the light, glimpse things, but not be part of them.

It was always this way. Nothing I had ever seen could tell me otherwise. Even my own mother, who had followed my father into the towered cage of death, even she had been forced apart to live with me when – oh, I could not doubt it – she had wanted only and solely to be with him. She had borne her deprivation with fortitude, with charm. Would I learn to do this?

I dawdled on the track, oblivious of possible hazards, or uncaring.

The day deepened, everything was gilded. Hares sported through the grass. Once I thought I saw an ibex high on a ledge, a great distance off, visible in a clarity of gold. Wild mint and lavender and saffron smoked on the hills, I heard

411

the running streams. An eagle went over the sky like a god. The beauty of these things made my hurt more poignant. At each start of my spirit towards delight, the reminder came, like a pang of loss or of foreboding.

And yet, I had lost nothing I had ever had. I could not dread what I had always known must be.

I sighted the village when the sunset came. I was glad enough after all, for I realised I should not be out alone on the hills by night.

Still I paused to watch the sun drawn down into the heights, the line of ocean the other way turning brazen, then dark.

After sunfall, one knows the otherness of the island. Her age stirs like an ancient snake in a cavern far below. The air trembles with it, and with little amorphous gleams, the leftover glowing fragments of high clouds, a trail of phosphorus upon the sea. Vespal rises, the star of Isibri, a dazzling liquid pearl.

I lay down on the hillside and cried, until the wind came, stroking at my hair, telling me to be gone, to go home, for a home I had and a lover I had. And I must be content.

But when I had got to the house and gone in and found our rooms, so empty and forlorn as if we had been away a year, I did not know what to do there, in the darkening of night, did not remember how to live, and could only sit at the table in the black and listen to the sea, tracing with my fingers over and over the forms of the dolphins in my ring, or a knot of wood in the tabletop.

Chapter Two

1

Full summer had come, so parched and hot even the sea looked dry. The crickets struck their tinders day long, and through the night combined with the sighing of the ocean. I took to bedding on folded blankets on the terrace, where sometimes fiendish unseen insects feasted on my blood as I slept – until I found an ointment in the village which they did not care for.

I had begun to sleep again, too, through the day. I hated the habit's return. I knew what it expressed, my sense of lethargy and powerlessness, the useless vista of my life. My daydreams also were often terrible and bizarre. All my bad memories were creeping back. Sometimes I dreamed I had been parted from Thenser in a towering city, by night. Crowds pushed at me and struck me aside. They would not tell me where he had gone to, and yet I knew that I must find him. I never did.

I ordered myself out on rambling walks. I plucked flowers and fruit and sometimes the savage herbs of the hills, which went home to store for seasonings. Frequently I was happy as I walked in the sun, never seeing anything quite exactly through the haze of light and dust. When I thought of him, the happiness was shorn.

He came to me now as my visitor. Riding a well-groomed horse currently in his possession, and stabled in the town, he would approach the headland once or twice a month, and if the affairs of his working life prevented his arriving, always

413

there would be a letter. He brought me gifts, beads and bracelets and gauzy scarves scored with golden thread. The girl who cleaned would make a showy dish for our supper. She would scrub the table until it was raw, and broom the ceilings, and as we made the bed she would gaze long at the pillow she supposed to be his. She envied me my handsome husband. Why not, when her own man, if she had one, went out with the fisher boats, was gone months at a stretch, might never return if the sea spoke for him.

The first hunger of my desire, after abstinence, embarrassed me, but he welcomed it. He would guide me, weak and moaning, mindless with the need for him, away into the heaven of ecstasy, from which I fell back delivered of all hope. Thereafter I was never at peace with his visit. It would be over in the morning, he would never stay longer. By noon he would be gone.

He told me I was beautiful. That I was well out of Ebondis, for he lived in one room, and he knew I was more comfortable with space, and the services of the girl, and the fresh sea air. The town was like an oven, had no air at all. It was not worth our while to set up together there, for things were moving.

I asked if the mighty Retka was having, after all, a success.

'Can you imagine he could fail?'

No, I could not imagine that.

Thenser gave me portions of their scenario. It was far away, the wheels and cogs of it that seemed to perform so well. The governor, having had his say, turned a blind eye, it appeared. He was afraid of Retka, who had for a fact gripped such social and financial power on Kithé, one did not cross him. The governor had instead made off to another summer retreat, another of the provincial towns of the island. Over his shoulder, as it were, he had countenanced the training of young men for a defence, should it ever be needful. A little enterprise, Tuli need not be troubled with it . . . But men were coming in from the villages and farms every day, and from Khirenie they were coming, too, for Khirenie had her own stake in independence.

At the capital of the Kronian North, Cristen Kahrulan had received the Imperial diadem.

Everywhere about, the world teemed on.

'What will you do?' I asked Thenser, as we drank wine on the terrace in the minutes of dusk.

'You see Kithé's inland mountains? What better spot to learn the knack of war. The heights are dotted with old forts. Eagle fastnesses.'

The Eagle Regiment had been his own, in the City. He had stayed a warrior, used to commanding men, to order his days in a certain form, lacking only a leader worthy of honour and trust. Like any soldier in any battle, he had wanted to know where he could render loyalty, put his back against the rock, before he stood to fight.

I wished then he would talk a little more of Retka, his pride in Retka, but he only said: 'Come here and kiss me.'

I wanted his love. And that was all I was given. Frail reed, he would not lean on me. He tried to protect me from all I feared.

2

There is a summer festival for Dornoy among the villages of Kithé. I did not know how it was celebrated, but gathered it was lawless, to do with the god's marriage in myth to some princess of the island. I heard the women singing in the hour before dawn, a strange echoing lament – the princess professing loneliness – that broke at sunrise into a paean of shouts and whoops and the beating of gongs. None of this was to be slept through. I put on my clothes and went out on the terrace to see. Up the stairways of Steps the young men were running, minted brown with summer as the copper gongs, and the honey girls with grapes in their hair and wands wreathed in vines and ribbons, flowers and pine cones. Everything that is something of the shape of the grape cluster is sacred to the god – cones, hyacinths, the bees' comb— The god was going, too, with his black-purple grape curls, riding on a wooden panther on wheels that bucked at every step.

The hymn they sang now had an Eastern tinge to it. The handcarts went after with the wine and loaves and fish, and half the dogs of the village ran behind. They streamed away into the hills, from the groves of which, after a time, I began to see strings of blue smoke go up, the fume of burnt offerings, rising from stone altars which I had come on in my walks. And now and then I would hear music or a primal cry, like that of some frenetic natural thing, a bird, the wind even. ⁀

I thought of the Vulmartia at Gurz. I would have to keep to the house today.

The village seemed deserted, and after I had looked at it, I went down into the sitting room, the coolest of the chambers, to take up my own round of meaningless indolence.

About midday, when I was dozing, insane thumpings shook the house. I was frightened, half not in my body, starting from my chair— Then I heard the housekeeper go along the corridor, the rattle of her keys and her grumbling. Twenty years before she had had one family to care for in the villa, and a tribe of servants to enact her will. Now, to open the lemon-painted doors to an intrusion of callers, adjuncts of these migratory guests (people who, in the old days, would have had to come in by the traders' entrance), stabbed at her soul.

Callers at the front of the house were indeed rare. Those few who came to interrupt the tenants' solitude had mastered the side entries and outer stairs.

Presently the housekeeper tramped back along the corridor and rapped on my door.

'There's a gentleman from the town to see you.'

I gazed stupidly at her accusation. I did not know what she meant.

Just then, I was enlightened. In her wake along the corridor came a fantastic image upholstered in gilded silk, with a chrysanthemum mane upon its head and more of the tendrils along the upper lip.

'Dearest Aradia,' he said. 'Long a motto of mine – always

spend the Dornoya in the country. And where should I fetch up but here—'

The housekeeper betook herself aside as he drove forward. He swept into my humble abode with his servant stalking after, toting a basket of food, a clutch of wines.

'Ah, their bucolic retreat. Exactly as I pictured it. To live so simply – how I envy you.'

I turned to the housekeeper for support, but disapprovingly she bent her jaundiced eyes on me, and walked away.

'Sir,' I said, 'I didn't expect you.'

'A surprise, eh? But how adorable you look, not a wisp of paint on your face and your hair all loose—' he swivelled and gestured at the servant. 'Go and see to the horses. No running off, either, with some village tart. They all have the itch.'

The servant went out, and shut the door, and there we were, the Flower Garden and I. I did not, even now, recall his real name.

'Don't look so astonished,' he said. 'Do you want to know how I found my way here? Is that it? My inquiries were *very* discreet.'

'My husband is at Ebondis,' I said.

'Naturally,' he said, 'I'm aware of that.'

He made for the table, pulled out a chair, and seated himself. 'Do bring some plates and glasses,' he said. 'I'm famished.'

His face was utterly devoid of any intelligence. It did not seem worthwhile to be afraid of him. I went to get plates, a glass, and put them at his disposal.

'And for yourself,' he said. 'Now don't be fractious.'

It was all very ridiculous. I placed a glass, a plate, across from him at the table. Then he requested me to unpack the basket, and opening a flask, asked me if this were not nice.

'Drink a drop of the wine. It will perk you up. How hellishly lonely you must have been. He's never here. And during a Dornoya, too. You know, those peasants of yours are at all the exercises of the flesh on the hills.'

He had had one dance with me. He had been refused another. And here he was, to claim the ultimate dance.

I did not drink his wine. I said, 'Somehow, you have misunderstood.'

'Yes, what?'

'I don't know your name,' I said. I hoped that might stand for a euphemism, but he only smiled, riffling the petals of his moustache.

'Firiu is my name. Prince Firiu. Attached to the governor. But Retka finds my services more valuable. Zavion and I – two heroes in his chariot, you might say. But then, *Zavion* will be going up into the mountains soon. With the toy soldiers. And then you'll see even less of him. But I – if you're polite to me, I might often chance this way.'

He began to eat. He had called himself a prince, but he ate like a greedy road sweeper, snatching and champing, with none of the poor man's excuse of hunger. Probably this was his method for the bed, too.

I could not see how he had thought me available. Perhaps only because I was by myself here, and he, being so wonderful, must be like a boon of the gods to any woman.

However, his idiocy had kept off fluster, even outrage. I was quite calm, and sat down to face him over the pastries and roast chicken.

'You may, of course, eat your meal at the table,' I said. 'If that is what you mean by the word "polite." But as to your chancing here often, I don't think it would be suitable or acceptable.'

'You're too cautious,' he said. 'Even in town we could have managed it. In a fellowship, there's no harm in two men sharing a woman. As with a lovely lily,' he said, looking at me amorously with ludicrous calf's eyes, 'all should be able to inhale its perfume.'

'All?'

'And a few, a special few, to touch.' He drank in a huge gulp. 'Think of Retka, and Oberis. Oberis is flattered to give him Sydo. Now what a woman *she* is—' (This, too, was part of his lovemaking, to extol the glories of another.) 'I should gladly slough ten years to sample Sydo.'

'Then you had better get on with it,' I said.

'Pierced a nerve? Jealous are you, you chilly thing?'

I stood up again and so did he, and leaning across pulled me on the table and pushed me flat. He craned leering over me, his hand in my bodice. 'How's *this*?' he cried in glee, and I picked up his glass and dashed what was left there in his face.

He straightened, spitting and complaining about his eyes. I flung him a cloth, a painting rag of mine, and let him wipe his forehead to a bright blue smear. But I did not laugh, he was stronger than I had reckoned, and in his oafish way, he meant to be doing.

'I've misled you not meaning to,' I said, as levelly as I could. 'Please believe me. I only want my husband.'

'Then you go wanting, don't you. Where is he?'

'You know where he is. I'm sorry to have thrown the wine at you. Let me fill your glass. Then you must go. Of course, this never happened.'

But he was leaning across again, and he had my left wrist and was trying to bite my neck, all the while saying I was a bitch, and I had spoiled his shirt, wine stains were impossible to get out.

Then I must have lost my temper. I had become rather scared, he would not hear reason. I hit out with my fist and caught him on the target of blue paint. He jerked back, giving an odd mewing sound, and sat down suddenly in his chair.

He had let go my wrist. He shook his head, cursed me, and poured himself more wine.

'I wish you would leave,' I said.

'You like some opposition,' he said. 'You can have it.'

I too sat down, slowly. I had set a knife on the table for his convenience. Now I took hold of it. He regarded this gesture with annoyance.

'Prince Firiu,' I said.

'Oh, put that down. I don't want you thrashing about with that blunt thing. You'll bruise me.'

'It's quite sharp,' I said. 'I know how it can be used.'

Over his glass, he did then give me a slightly altered

glance. Then he wiped his lips and said, 'You don't fool me. I know what you want.'

'Once,' I said, steadying my voice, 'a man raped me.'

'Did he? You liked that?'

'No, but he liked it less. I killed him.'

'*You?*' He smiled again. He started to pick his teeth fastidiously. But his eyes had completely changed.

'It was in a war,' I said, 'in a lonely place. He insisted. While he was doing it, I cut him in the throat—' something made me swing forward. I tapped the edge of the knife under Firiu's ear and he leaped away and the chair went crashing. 'Just there. Did you know, it's a sure means, usually. The vital vein. He was a strong man, far stronger, Firiu, than you are. But he died choking and helpless.'

He balanced on the floor between the table and the wall, his mouth open and his eyes no longer those of a lovesick calf. I felt in these seconds a most peculiar power. I was tired of being victimised, it seemed. I wanted my own back.

I came around the table, with the knife still in my hand, and Firiu minced away.

'You revolt me,' I said loudly. 'How could I want something like you? Get out!' I began to scream. It was not hysteria but hatred, rage. 'Get *out* you filthy *offal*—' and groping behind me I got a plate from the table, still loaded with chicken, and I flung it at him. It clipped his head as he turned yelling in retreat. Then, as in the most ribald theatre, I chased him. I pursued him – hurling his food, his basket, his flasks of wine – and when he was through the door and in the corridor, shrieking I ran after him – I had dropped the knife by then, but I think if I had got hold of him I might have caused him some damage. I felt I could tear him in pieces.

Squealing for his servant, running full tilt, this Prince Firiu left my home. He went out by the main door, hung ajar, and this, reaching it, I closed with a bang and leaned on it, abruptly exhausted. As I lay there, down the central stairway of the house came limping the elderly man, my neighbour, with a huge rusty cavalry lance from some decades-ago Tulic campaign. Neither of us spoke, though we looked upon each other warily. At length, without comment, my neighbour and his lance shuffled up the stair again, and I wandered to my rooms and shut and locked the door.

Then I was consumed by paroxysms of laughter. After which I wept with fury.

In that mood I sat down to write to Thenser. I began this letter five or six times. Some ethic was getting in my way. I did not know if it were correct to reveal what had happened. For Firiu and he were at work upon the same labour—

I remembered how I had not dared tell Gurz of the threats of Drahris. Had I really got no farther? Had I, even now, no surety?

Finally, I swept up the smashed crockery and chicken bits with the torn leaves of the letters. I tidied everything in the rooms, and then, as if it were only an extension of my tidying, began to put together my clothes and such items as were immediately moveable.

An hour later I sought the housekeeper in her den. I explained I had been called to the town. Would she take care of such furniture and books as I must for the present leave? She started to argue with me about our rent, which had been paid for some further weeks. She insisted she could not give it me. I insisted I did not ask her for it. We seemed likely to come to blows.

In the mid-afternoon, carrying my bag, I went to the carter's house in the village. I thought he would be gone on the Dornoya, and I should have to wait until dusk, perhaps return in the morning. But he was at home, chastely mending some boots. There had been enough ready cash in my possession I could offer him a fat fee for taking me to Ebondis. He seemed glad to get off from the empty village – why he had not joined the festival I could not guess.

At any rate he got out the cart and took me to the town, over the glowing secretive hills.

I was half afraid we might catch up to Firiu on the road, but we did not. He had had a horse, and must have ridden like a blue-browed whirlwind to get away from me.

3

It was sunset of that prolonged summer evening when I stood by myself in the Isibri Square of Ebondis, under the shadow of the temple. The carter had been eager to prescribe for himself at some tavern that he knew of; recollecting, I thought, this square, I got down, fancying I would take my bearings from it. But now everything looked altered in the last red moments of the sun. How swiftly the day would desert me. Already the eastern sky had cooled, the temple's shade had crossed the square. Our lodging, when we had shared a couch here after the dancing, had been in a street leading from the Isibri. But now I could not imagine if it wended to the left or right of the fane. In any case, the street to which my letters had been sent, where Thenser currently roomed, was over by the justiciary building, past which I had been driven, and which I could not at all visualise.

I should have to ask my way. This might prove hazardous. Buoyed up by emotion I had not had the prudence to arrange my hair, and my dress was not elegant enough, or drab enough, to protect me. Men would think me a country girl, or worse, a whore. Women might even suppose I was a beggar, at best some itinerant. I would have to be careful how and whom I approached, and be concise in my questioning.

A stiffness from my hours in the bumping cart, a dazzle on my sight from the hill skies, made me seem to myself more than ever inadequate. The bag of clothes and necessaries weighed heavily.

Night came, and at the porches of the buildings the last lamplighters were busy. Only on the central thoroughfares I had learned were there street lights, elsewhere each house was responsible for providing a lamp. I approached a maid-servant with a taper, and tuned my voice to accentless Tulic.

'Can you direct me to Lute Street?'

Her look said she thought me doubtful, but she answered mildly. Her instructions were complex, however, and though I started out valiantly, soon I could not discover one of the byways she had described. I wondered if she could have mistaken the name.

By now I had lost the Isibri temple, too, which I had appropriated as a landmark. I went up and down several ornate boulevards, one even with lamps on poles, and trusted I was near the main thoroughfares. But then a twist and turn or two put me into a shabby warren of alleys and dilapidated houses with no lights beyond the narrow grilled windows. In this quarter I went truly astray. And a parcel of men coming from a drinking shop sent me scurrying.

As I hastened furtively and frantically on, devoid now of any sense of direction, I came down among steep dark runnels of masonry, thick with deeper stenches. Scarcely any lights were visible, and no one about. Above, the pale black sky had put on its stars. Here and there, at a great distance it seemed, the high places of Ebondis rose from this trough. But having got in here I thought I might not get out. I had tried to retrace my steps even, and become yet further entangled. It was a labyrinth, and no one could guide me to safety.

How absurd, I thought in amazement, resting my weary arms and shoulders from the little bag under some wall, I had sent a dozen letters to that street of the Lute, they had found their way but I could not.

It was as if a sorcerer concealed it from me. As if my lover had barricaded himself from me with tortuous alleys and the architecture of night.

Like clockwork I continued to walk, aiming without much energy now for the areas where flushes of light lay along the roofs and sky. But I could not seem to get to them. There were always these black obstacles between.

I passed a knot of women hurrying, who paid me no attention. I did not have the courage to inquire of them. The very name of his street – an instrument of music – was inappropriate in this nameless underland.

At a public fountain whose water was ice cold, I laved my hands and wrists but was afraid to drink from the crusted tap.

The night was close and still. From far off a temple bell rang out – for midnight.

I was at an intersection, and everything about was black save for the stars. Was this still Ebondis?

Then came a bright ignition, around the clumps of faceless buildings, and all at once a patrol of Ebondian town guard appeared, one with a lighted torch. This flare of fire in the black was threatening more than reassuring. They were the first human things I had met for an hour. As they swung towards me, perhaps not even seeing me, I nerved myself to accost them.

When I stepped out, they halted. Their faces did not seem human, more like masks.

Meticulously, in my loveliest Tulic, I asked my way.

They allowed me to do so. Then one turned to another.

'She's out late.'

'Wanting a street.'

'There's no such place,' said the torchbearer.

This fitted perfectly with the nightmare. Yet I said, 'No, my husband is there.'

'She has a husband.'

'A husband in *every* street,' said the torchbearer, 'likely.'

What I had feared had come to pass. Of course, what else could I be but a harlot. I was there to be used or maybe arrested, for the prostitution of the avenue was unlawful.

'Well, birdie,' said the nearest guardsman, whose uniform I recalled so well from the dance, 'you'd better come with us.'

I had put off Firiu to reach this. I had run to Thenser and into this.

'You had better know,' I said, 'I have a message for the Justiciary.'

'What can that be?'

'Her message is *Give us a kiss!*' said the wit of the party, and they laughed.

I said, 'I've news for Zulas Retka.'

It had an effect. They looked at one another again, and at me again, and one said, 'Improbable.'

'What are you doing down here if it's the Justiciary you're after?'

'I was misdirected. I don't know the town—'

They laughed some more. Not know the town, one such as I?

I said, 'Too much time has been wasted. He'll be angry.'

'Yes, no doubt.'

'He will be angry. Tell me how to reach the Justiciary.'

'First it was Lute Street.'

Something within me gave way. I turned from them, and dragging my leaden bag back to the fountain, I stood there, wondering dully what they would do to me. I heard a discussion, and then one of them came over.

'I'll take you to Retka,' he said.

Now I did not believe him, would not stir.

'Yes, come on,' he said. 'But if you're lying, it'll be the gaol for you.'

So I went with him, leaving the other two with their torch.

I could barely put one foot before another, I was stupefied with exhaustion. Nor was my fright done with, for how could I trust anyone or anything, and besides, I had summoned up in desperation the only name I could think of they would respect, and could I swear he would remember me? Even if he did, he would be enraged at my deception.

In a tower of the Justiciary building, he had his apartment there. Ebondis knew his windows, too. The guard, looking up as we negotiated the wide roadway, said, 'You're lucky, he's working late.'

There was a courtyard. There were more men in uniforms, a foyer, a flight of steps of veined marble that went on and on and up and up, and I pulled myself by will alone, and the bag with a similar stubbornness.

The new guardsman conducted me into a corridor. We reached a pair of ebony doors, on which he smote. After a long wait, during which I tried to catch my breath, a leaf of these was opened by a valet.

'What is it at this hour? Something from the governor?'

'No. She claims to have an urgent message.'

The valet scanned me. He was in his house-robe, with a candlebranch in his hand.

'I think you are jesting,' said the valet.

The guardsman said stiffly: 'Rather than send off a genuine petitioner, and receive the blame—' He cleared his throat. 'Not the first time Zulas Retka has had a visit from a lady at a late hour. Nor the first time a message has been delivered after midnight.'

'Very well,' said the valet. 'Have you searched the woman?'

I heard myself say: 'Don't dare lay a finger on me.'

And then there came the bronze resonance, the notes of that great voice, through the sounding chambers beyond the door. 'What in the jaw of hell is going on out there?'

The two men drew themselves into profound attention. The valet turned and called, 'Sir, there's a girl here—'

'With a message,' came back the voice. 'I've been listening to your play. Now bring her in.'

The valet beckoned me, the guardsman moved aside. Beneath my body a reflection swam over a polished floor, and the candles flickered ahead of me and below me, and there was an opening into a large green salon with curtains of bloodiest red – and he, Retka, standing before them. He was so tall and large, so uncouth in his magnificence – he seemed made of tarnished gold now in the florid light – I, too, ordered myself for the confrontation, to placate him, if it were remotely possible.

'Ah, yes, Dara,' he said. And to the valet, 'It's all right. You can get back to your bed.'

Next instant the door shut, and I was alone with him.

'Dara—' was all I could say, 'no, I'm not—'

'Not Dara. Of course you are not Dara, Aradia Zavion. But considering this unorthodox nocturnal arrival, don't you prefer they should think I'm receiving someone else?'

All I could think was that he did not seem enraged, and that I must put down my poor little bag before it broke my spine. And as I did so, I saw my hand upon the strap – and that my hand was ringless.

The bag fell. I was barely able to prevent myself crying aloud. I was so demoralised, so pathetically bewildered by this last intolerable horror.

When he set the wine cup to my lips I drank obediently, as he told me to, and then I said, 'My ring – I think it was when I washed my hands at the basin – the cold water – it must have slipped off. It's been loose for weeks, I don't know why—' And perhaps I half turned as if to rush straight back there, to search in the darkness. But then he had put me into a chair, and he said, 'Whose fault is all this?'

The question brought me to myself. It was unusual, or so it seemed.

'No one's fault, or mine.'

'Then Zavion's not responsible.'

My eyes cleared, enough that I could see him over by his desk. There were papers, pens in racks, a huge book with several markers, a lamp, a silver wine-flask. These things seemed only extensions of Retka.

'You see,' I said, 'no one would help me. They thought I was a – was a whore, because I was out alone. And in my panic I could only think to use your name. Please forgive me.'

'I'm glad my name has been found serviceable,' he said. 'And why were you out alone?'

'I came to the town to find Thenser. It wasn't planned. He didn't know. I couldn't discover his street. A stupid affair.' The wine had restored my balance, or only swung it to another angle. I was now attempting to be casual, light-hearted even. I wanted to get away from him, though I had nowhere to go. The power that streamed from him, eating up or forming objects in the room, was indescribable. How had I had the temerity—

'And,' he said, in the quiet of that *voice*, 'why such a precipitate race to Ebondis, unexpected, not even sure of the relevant street?'

I had not meant to tell Thenser anything, I had meant to rave of loneliness, unspecific qualms.

'At my lodging I had some trouble. Someone tried to force himself on me.'

'Because you were by yourself there and your husband here.'

'Because of that.'

'Who?'

Could I not have said a fisherman of Steps, or some raffish tenant of the house? The words spilled out of me, as if they must be spoken, 'A man called Firiu.'

'Ah, yes. Firiu.'

I wondered, too late, if I had now properly offended. Retka stood regarding the book on the desk, as if reading from it a passage of importance.

In agitation I got up again from the chair, and stared anew at my empty hand. Within the drain of the fountain, the twisted brass dolphins would be lying, perhaps some girl would notice them. They would be hers then.

'The ring was valuable?' he said to me suddenly. He seemed to read not the book but my mind. Why conceal anything?

'Not at all – but it was my marriage ring. I didn't want another. A fisher ring from Tuli— A bad omen, surely, to lose that.' I smiled, my face hard with its effort to become an adult woman's face. 'It would be just, I suppose, if I'd given up my virtue. But I pushed him off, Firiu. I told him I'd kill him.' Wanting to silence myself I could not, the words came out again where I had managed to keep back the cry. 'He was afraid I meant it. He was surprised. He thought me easy prey. Obviously Thenser doesn't want me, that was the reason he put me away in the house by the sea. I should have left him alone. Now he feels he must take responsibility for me. Was that why I couldn't find the street? I was frightened that if I went to him he would let me see that he didn't want me there.' I stopped. I said, 'Again, I apologise. I'm not thinking what I'm saying.'

'It's common practice, you know, on the eve of a battle,' he said, 'to put the things one values most into a safe hiding place.'

I hung my head, ashamed of my outburst, ready to agree to any proposition which would restore normalcy.

'Of course.'

'But of course,' he said, 'you are feeling neglected, not prized. It isn't my part to explain his reasons to you. But I think you underestimate his care.'

He took a piece of paper and began to write on it. Was I meant to leave? But it was he who walked out, and at the ebony doors called up a guardsman. Returning, Retka added to the wine glass, and again handed it to me.

'I've sent word to Sydo. Her household keeps late hours. You'll be able to stay there, until your situation is more settled, or indefinitely.'

'I couldn't,' I said.

'Oberis maintains the house for her splendour,' said Retka. 'He himself prefers his modest rooms here. A large domicile. A guest won't inconvenience Sydo, or I shouldn't ask it of her. You trust me just a little, Aradia. Or what was the point of your throwing yourself down on my doorstep?'

I sought refuge in the wine.

He said nothing else vital to me as he waited for Sydo's acquiescent carriage to come and collect me. We talked of weightless things, songs, I believe, and the climate. His questions did not delve after my past or present, my aspirations or dreads. He was an immaculate host, pretending everything was quite mundane.

Then the carriage had arrived and I was conducted down to the courtyard by a guardsman, and handed in to a large equipage with an escutcheon on its sides.

Above, as we rattled off, the windows of Retka's apartment burned on in their dark scarlet. I should know them in future.

4

Sydo wore white or black by day, black or silver by night. Half reclining on her divan in the courtyard, under the apricot awning, her arms and feet were bare, her quantity of tresses confined in a snood of silver thread. Even this assemblage hung to her waist. Her skin was sun-kissed but not browned. At the inclination of her hand, some servant would appear to do something, to refill our goblets with the juice of limes or pears, to bring a dish of fruit and confectionery. Now the girl in Sydo's livery turned a page of the novel, and began on its third chapter.

For the space of two days I had been Sydo's 'guest.' She had neither welcomed nor repulsed me. I was an accepted fact from the moment of my entry, in the small hours. A maid conducted me at once to a second floor bedchamber, where, lapped in comforts, I slept poorly. Next morning everything I could possibly need was put at my disposal. I might always have lived there, the attendants of the house treated me so respectfully.

At luncheon, I was invited to join my hostess. On seeing her, I thanked her for her hospitality, perhaps fulsomely. I anticipated some reply on the lines, I am doing *his* will. But she answered, 'Think nothing of it. The house is big enough.'

The house was indeed on a generous scale, packed with marbles and curiosities in bronze and gilt, which seemed well-dusted but otherwise not much attended to. In the courtyard where her translucent feast had been laid, two fountains flickered in porphyry basins through a breathing air of flowers.

She said, 'I spend hours here in the court in summer. You must do the same if you wish. Or if you prefer solitude, you won't be pestered.'

'Thank you for your kindness. I'm afraid, nevertheless, my – abrupt arrival – is an imposition.'

'No, you have said all that,' she responded then. My nervy fawning bored her. I resolved to be quiet.

Truly, she did not converse with me. We sat in silence, and then the maid came and read. The blown-rose Tulic of the text sometimes lost me, as ordinary speech seldom any longer did. My thoughts were free to scurry about, clawing into corners. Apparently listening to the tale of piracy, high romance, and witchcraft (did she have such lurid tastes or had the volume been chosen to suit *me*?), I achingly questioned myself as to what had become of Thenser. Though I might have assumed Retka would advise him of my presence, I had taken no chance. On waking I had loaned from Sydo a messenger and dispatched a brief and contrite note to the elusive street of the Lute. Doubtless he would not have received this letter later than ten in the morning. Yet now the temple bell of the Isibri had sounded three in the afternoon. Decidedly, he must have other business more pressing than mine.

I spent a wretched afternoon, not dreaming I could refer to my predicament, and relieved not to be interrogated.

The hour of dining came upon us. Sydo informed me a few ladies would be present, but no men. The beehive of dexterous maids had already unravelled my clothing from the ported bag, and pressed me my strawberry dancing gown, which was all I had at all suitable for a dinner.

Sydo appeared in a fluted black pillar of silk, roped at the waist with cinching silver, and without any jewels, so I was glad not to have put on my earrings. The three other ladies, wives of men who served in high positions at the Justiciary, wore sullen or wispy white and looks of anxious solicitude. They had come clearly with the idea of making much of Sydo, and were not prepared for me, did not know how they should behave to me at all. Sydo rendered them no aid, merely introducing me as the wife of Zavion, Retka's associate. From this however, and my advent in the room, the ladies took me for a thing of potential value, and waxed more and more imploring as the meal went on.

But my mind was elsewhere of course. And then, concluding I was, after all, an uncertain quarry, they left off their antics.

They hung on Sydo's every utterance. They begged to know what she thought of the season's wines, the latest style for the height of shoe-heels – did she not find them a cause of pinching? And later they were bolder, criticising the governor over taxes and blind adherence to the king on the mainland, the while watching for her reactions (always minimal) to see which way they should jump next.

But the duellist's meal passed in a blur for me. My own tiny concerns kept their hold.

At eleven o'clock the entry of Sydo's steward almost brought me to my feet. I believed word had come from Thenser. But the steward only proffered to Sydo a slip of paper from the Justiciary. Whether sent by Oberis her husband, or Retka her lover, she did not vouchsafe to tell us. She yawned behind her hand and said, 'He toils interminable hours.' The ladies nodded but were unable to elaborate, ignorant as they were of which man to praise and censure. I could not suppose she did not do this deliberately.

When the trio had contrived to depart, Sydo herself bade me good night, and went away into a music room, from which soon came the plangent twang of a lyrachord.

Going to my bedchamber I spent a second mostly sleepless, muddled night. In the morning I rose sore as if beaten, with burning eyes and a darkened heart.

There was no news.

The day looked set to progress as previously.

Sydo, a late riser, appearing at luncheon, made no comment on my lack of appetite. She made no comments on anything. The novel was brought.

For the first time I realised the book was intended to represent the island of Kithé. Perhaps a century ago . . . my mind wandered yet farther off.

The steward came walking over the tiles, and I gazed at him without finding him meaningful. He bowed to Sydo's ear. She turned her head and said to me, 'It seems your husband is here.'

I stood up with two extra hearts drumming in my temples.

'Follow my man to the Turquoise Salon. You will have privacy there.'

He stood under a slanted mirror in a tortoiseshell frame. He wore the dark civil clothes of a secretary, in which he had sometimes come to the house by the sea. He had never looked anything of the sort, and did not now. He was waiting there

regarding me, not speaking to me, and the mirror reflet
him from above, the flourish of fair hair, his absolute
stillness.

I had no inkling of what he thought, if he were angry or
startled, reproving, sympathetic, or indifferent.

I had never known him. That must be true. I did not know
him now.

Then he did speak to me. 'I received your note three hours
ago. Various matters took me away at dawn yesterday. I had a
summons to the Justiciary this afternoon, to see Retka, and
then came straight here.'

'Did he . . .'

'He mentioned your plight.'

My plight. It was a scathing word, and a tone devoid of
expression.

I said, 'If I've angered you, I'm sorry. I was afraid the same
thing would happen again if I remained where I was, alone.'

'Firiu,' said Thenser. 'I doubt it.' He seemed to study me.
He said, 'You've stirred up quite a devil's nest, Aradia. Tell
me, why did you run to Zulas Retka and not to me?'

Told now it seemed too trite, too silly to be believable.
Even so, told he must be that I had tried to find him and not
been able.

'I see. Then having reached Retka, could you not have
asked to be conveyed to my door?'

Such a thing had not struck me. Retka had not postulated
the plan. And – I had been afraid of Thenser's rebuff.

'I didn't want to trouble him further. He suggested that I
stay in this house. Have I done something wrong?'

'You acted in your usual fashion,' he said.

'I take it you are reprimanding me.'

'Well,' he said, 'you might have gone about it rather
differently.'

'You mean permitted Firiu to rape me, and written you a
discreet letter with the details to come in by the next cart.'

He raised his brows. 'If he'd had the metal to rape you he
would have done it. You outmatched him. He has chanced
himself that way with half the women here. I doubt if two

entertained his suit. For the rest a positive "no" sufficed.'

I had begun to shake, with my own anger, and with the sense I had that the story I had been a part of was not the story Thenser credited.

'*No* was not of any use. I threatened him with a knife, before he'd leave me alone.'

'Perhaps you overestimated his ardour.'

'I was *alone*, and no one to help me—'

'The old familiar outcry, Aradia. Because I abandon you, you suffer these terrible calamities. I can assure you, the village was safer than this town is likely to be. But too late now, you're here. As for Firiu, he was informed you had gone directly to Retka. He's taken fright and made off. He was not incompetent in the scheme of things. Otherwise, of course, society here now supposes I am as complacent as Oberis, that I loan you to Retka, my patron, who is therefore your protector. And if they had any doubts, your being in this house with his *woman* will settle them. Two under one roof. He's a master of economy.'

'But she,' I said, 'how could anyone think *her* complacent?'

'She's frequently tolerated his whims with other women. She means to keep his regard.'

'Then I must leave here at once.'

'Again, rather too late. The harm is done.'

'But if he intends—'

'Did I say he intended anything towards you? I'm only giving the opinion of the town, that you're his fancy.'

'But Retka must have known all this,' I blurted out, awash with humiliation and affront, and sickness under everything at Thenser's manner with me.

'Yes, probably. I doubt he considered it. You interrupted him, he needed to put you off somewhere. I'm valuable in my own little way. Not, I should think, irreplaceable. So let me put up with it.' His face was cold. I could not see how deep it went, the emotion, or quite what the emotion was.

'Then what do you want me to do? Do you want me to go back to the villa at Steps?'

'At which Ebondis will say you have been discarded.'

'I don't care what's said.'

'So much is clear. No, you'd better remain in her house. At least you'll have some protection here from these infernal scrapes into which you propel yourself. You see, Aradia, I can't spare the time for this. I'm to leave for the mountains tomorrow. I'd have ridden out to you today, to tell you so.'

I gathered up the scattered images that seemed to break apart within my brain, and put them aside.

'This is when you leave for the mountains.'

'The army of Kithé, you remember,' he said. 'What I'm good for in this adventure. Training men to kill each other.'

I glimpsed it then, but did not grasp what it was, his dissatisfaction, the bitter kernel of some vision he had had, the reparation for blood for which more blood must be let. Surely he had known from the start. He had said, in war, it was not damned or foul to kill for survival or liberty. But the way he spoke of Retka, too. It was more than my undertaking which had abraided Thenser. He had found some other thing to doubt in the great idol of gilded bronze.

I had all at once noticed the diagonal scar on his left hand, as if never in my life had I seen it before, or any others on his body.

His eyes were the hungry hunted eyes of something which hides, cannot sleep, is starving. I recalled them from the enclosure of a dusty room, a glade of a king's garden. My misdeed had not caused this in him. It was only the tickling of a feather on an open wound.

'Well,' he said, 'I leave you in the fair Sydo's keeping.' And he turned as if to go away at once.

'Don't leave me like this,' I said. 'How long will you be gone?'

'Months,' he said. 'How do you want me to leave you?'

'Not as if we were parting forever.'

'I've given you all the proofs of love I can,' he said. 'You untie them till they come to bits and then you cry for more. I warned you I was a poor bargain. I can't give you anything else.'

I thought, perhaps it is true he did love me, for now he does not.

'Will I see you ever again?' I said.

'Of course you'll see me. When I get down again to Ebondis.' His eyes deepened as he looked at me. 'Don't be so sad, sweetheart,' he said, 'you're well shot of me. You love me too much, or you think you do.'

We had come to the pass of speaking to each other, both, in a language the other one did not know.

As I hung there, in that turquoise room, trying to translate for myself what he had said, trying to apprehend the enormous rift, like the cracking wide of a floating raft of ice, I felt the hopelessness of all my ventures. I knew he was lost to me, though I had never really known the second when he was mine.

Each of us said goodbye courteously, and he mentioned then certain monetary arrangements he had made for me, and added, at the very door, as if it could happen, that he would see me before my birthday, before the Vulmartia, before the summer was done.

Then he had gone.

I walked about the chamber for a few minutes, up and down, sometimes examining the curios, seeing none of them. In the mirror my upturned face was whiter than a napkin. My face knew better than I what had occurred.

Finally I returned to the courtyard. Sydo was lying on her divan, the customary bees were sprinkled like trembling furry beads amid the vine. The book girl turned a page and read out stonily:

' "And thus they entered, separately yet hand in hand, the House of Night." '

Part Four

THE HOUSE OF NIGHT

Chapter One

1

On midsummer eve, Sydo's party, of whom I was one, went to the open-air theatre. The play was very stupid, and it had unmelodious songs, as everyone remarked. But the purpose of the theatre was to be seen there, and Sydo was seen. A scent of restlessness, of embryonic excitement hung over Ebondis, a tindery musk like the foretaste of a waking volcano – so I had heard it described. We took an early supper at nine o'clock at the house of one of Sydo's acquaintances. By ten, the light was levelling, the treacle sky thick with dust. All day they had been watering the streets, and through the heat even immersion in an old well had not kept the wine cool. Beyond the windows of the opulent little house, a public garden of palms seemed the promenade of half the town. The streets were noisy and active. No one spoke of this. The talk was of vapid things. (I had been told that sometimes, in the back hills, when a woman was giving birth, it was thought to entice ill-luck if her labour should be referred to. She continued at her tasks as best she might, everything else went on about her, despite her pangs and groans, until the ejection of the child.)

At last we climbed up to the roof, the guests male and female, the men in their satins with their vaporous pipes, the women in embroidered dresses flickering their fans as if we were beset by huge butterflies . . . Sydo in her silver veiling, I in my only evening wear, and escorted by a talkative gentleman of the Oberis fraternity. The purpose of the roof journey was to watch the sun set, which it did every night, although one would not think so.

'Oh, look! Oh, see!' they exclaimed.

The ether was ablaze, cities burned there, enormous mountains of engorged purple cloud fractured on a reef of butchered redness. The palm trees and roofs, the towers of the Justiciary building, hid the final gasp of the solar orb, its peridot afterflash visible on clearer nights. Yet it was midsummer, and the dying frenzy was marked. Even in the public garden and along the street the townspeople of Kithéan Ebondis marked it, and read there what signs they would.

Beside the balustrade of the roof were flowering hibiscus in earthen pots, and at one corner a narrow low altar to Isibri Blue-Mantled.

'Now, come and learn your future,' said my escort, and led me to a lacquer pannier set out by the altar, into which several ladies were dipping with squeaks and decorous curses.

'Well, I declare!' cried one of these, a nervous intimate of Sydo's, straightening and perusing something from the pannier, behind her fan. 'Well! I'm sure I can't repeat it.'

'If it comes to pass,' said another lady astutely, 'we shall all be able to observe the event, in any case.'

My gentleman urged me to join in the merriment. This was a peasant custom, he said. How divine of – he named our hostess – to borrow it.

Great flocks of ladies were now settling on the pannier, almost snatching from each other. I saw that what they were drawing out were small nacreous shells which crumpled at a slight pressure, each revealing a scrap of paper.

Rather than resist, which would have cost me some effort, I took my turn, and soon came up with one of the shells.

'Now you must read it,' said the escort. He was thin and sly under his volubility, and had glued himself to me to see what I was worth. Finding me mostly voiceless, and slow to display concealed allegiances, rather than quit me he had stayed to try a bombard.

I cracked the shell, and nothing came forth from it.

'Why, what a wretched thing,' said the gentleman, peering into my hand. 'One that they missed. You must fish again.'

'Then there may not be enough.'

'Yes, but your turn was void.'

'Perhaps that is my future.' At the risk of giving him an insight, I then excused myself and went downstairs.

The huge sky had made me dizzy. My head had been aching for days, I could never seem to be cool or to take more than a shallow breath. I went into the retiring room our hostess had put at feminine disposal, rinsed my hands and face with lukewarm nauseous liquid, repowdered my face and tinted my lips and cheeks. For though the sun had gone, we did not know how long the night might be.

In the salon I took another glass of tepid wine, but its taste turned my stomach.

The other guests were filtering through the room again in spirited shoals. Sydo appeared and beckoned to me. Her gilded arm made the motion of a swan's neck over water.

'How irksome it is,' she said. 'We shall leave at once.'

Oberis was not with her. The key men of the departments of law and order were none of them here.

'Sydo – are you deserting us already?'

But at her inclination to the door, the entire houseful seemed surging up to follow.

We poured into the street, and bystanders saluted us, some pointing out the silver woman to each other, her glissade of black hair.

The heat, now the light was gone, was more than ever stifling. They were lighting the streetlamps, and the moths were rushing to them in their usual nightly holocaust. Not a star could I see. The air was too dense to inhale. Was it perhaps only this which woke me in my bed again and again, strangled, crowing for breath, my lungs paralysed, cast off from sleep as if thrown back from the wall of a precipice? This night atmosphere like syrup . . .

The two black horses trotted down the boulevard. Here and there, the faces turning to regard her shining carriage, the escutcheon of Oberis, and then a hand waving, a voice calling out: 'Kithé! Kithé!' And suddenly all the street exploding with the cry – and then again the hot silence, only the hoofs and the wheels.

'This waiting,' said Sydo, and unwove the night from her face, once, twice, with the plume of her fan, on which after all the stars had come out in brilliants.

When we turned into the broad street before the Justiciary, the crowd was packed tight. The carriage got through with difficulty and slowness. We drove around the block of buildings, which were alight from ground to roof with lamps, into the square behind. It was normally sleepy, this square, shade trees, a fountain, a modest temple on the farther side to an obscure deity. Tonight the square was thronged with carriages. We came in and nothing on earth could get us out.

'Oh, this is worse and worse,' said Sydo. 'We shall swoon from this heat.' And opening the door she stepped on to the running-board and stood there, a beacon, looking about. The crowd here, too, knew her instantly. She called imperiously into the layers of it: 'What news?'

It was the first salvo. Something which had been expected was about to happen, and Sydo acknowledged it.

A man from the crowd cried to her, 'If *you* don't know, lady, you can be sure *we* don't.' And they laughed good-humouredly, liking her since she was the wife of one figurehead, the mistress of another, and none of it a secret from them.

Sydo sat back in her carriage. 'Their insolence,' she said.

She was not disturbed. So many of her reflexes seemed superficial, her own intent, lizardlike life going on far beneath.

Of course, I knew next to nothing, only what I had gleaned from phrases let fall by guests in her sitting room, from the feverish quality of the town, its volcano tang.

The open carriage door let in a few wheezes of laval air, the murmur of the crowd, an occasional shouted dialogue between two other vehicles. Twice gentlemen looked in on us to greet Sydo. Not one appeared to know anything. Besides the heat, the smell of the people of Ebondis was quite strong.

The pomades and perfumes of the well-to-do mingled with the terrible refuse smell of the poor, who had been pressing round the Justiciary since midday. There were also odours of food, street vendors with sugar-apples and skewers of charcoaled cheese and onions. I had begun to feel very ill, yet very calm. For more than a month my depression had been so great I expected nothing but further misery. Nothing else existed. As the rocks were piled on me, I greeted them.

Then suddenly there was a terrific shock of sound, a concussion. The floor of the carriage shook and the horses started. Women screamed. The sound came a second time, and a third. Now the crowd was roaring. 'The guns from the fort,' said Sydo. Alert, she stepped out again on to the running-board. Beyond her delineated profile, stretched forward like that of a snake, a spray of scintillants burst on the sky. Up on a nearby roof someone had ignited fireworks.

The guns were the signal; the old tired cannon from the ruined emplacement half a mile up a hill above the town. They had been repairing them for weeks. Not fired, they said, since the last brush with the Potentality, fifty years ago.

The crowd was bellowing, for the island, for individual names – which presently formed themselves into one name alone, that of Zulas Retka.

'He will come out now,' she said. And turning away to her driver, 'Help me up to the box. I will stand on the roof.'

The guard of Ebondis had all gone over to him, the influential men, he had made himself the spearhead. Word had been conveyed to the governor, cowering in his other villa to the east.

Sydo ascended sinuously, the carriage barely moved. The crowd cheered her, too, her boldness and style. But I stayed by the window, which I desultorily opened, because not to do so was not in keeping with the world, this thundering, firework, shouting world of excitement and daring, this dramatic world of breaking chains and self-avowal, which was the square behind the Justiciary of Ebondis.

I felt nothing, only the throb of my nausea. If I fainted now they would think it was passion, it would be allowed.

There was a dim memory swirling behind my sight. The other square, the crowd, and the women on the carriages with their plumes and wine – my City in its throes of war-delight, promising the Kronians defeat. Nothing changed. It was all a wheel, endlessly gurning on along a way of stones and fires. War, conquest, rebellion, flight, death, and the death of love.

Would they know in the mountains this exact moment? Yes they would know. The training army of Kithé's liberty, the commanders in the eagle perches of the forts. Was he near enough to hear the noise of the cannon?

They were throwing wide the long windows of the balcony three storeys up. The members of the justiciary and of the town council appeared. I saw Oberis looking indigestive with portent. Then Retka came out of the windows like a torch in a yellow silk tunic, coatless in the heat, raising his arms as if to embrace the crowd. Which answered him by flinging up hands and flowers, lifting its scared, wide-eyed children to see, and screaming. When the first uproar sank, I heard that bells had started ringing from half a dozen temples and towers. With ease, he pitched his voice above them.

'People of Ebondis, tonight, for the first time in three centuries, you may call yourselves Kithéans.'

It boomed, that voice, like a brazen thunder-sheet, the very kind they had used to such unfortunate effect in the theatre. But the result here was quite different. The hugeness of the voice increased the volume of the crowd. The carriage shuddered again at their cries.

Retka held the tumult in the air with his hands, then let it slowly down, and there was an incredible quiet under the clanging of the bells.

'There is a school of thought,' said Retka to us all, 'we have heard it often. That we should await an engagement of the Tulhians with Saz-Kronia, the Northern Bear. And then, like jackals, creep in to nip Tuli in the flank with our defection. But this supposes Kithé to be a breeder of cowards. Are we cowards, my friends?' His hands moved upward, orchestrating them, and they shouted that they were no cowards, not they. Until his hands let them sink once more to quietness.

'The cowards' way then is not for us. Not for Ebondis, not for the island. What then? We tell the king of Tulhia flatly. Sire, we honour you, but we are not Tulhians. Give us our liberty – or we *take* our liberty.' The crowd thundered back at him. Retka smiled and his smile was for everyone. His address, so vast it filled the sky, remained personal, he spoke softly in our ears even as the organ notes peeled round the square, its adjacent splay of streets, the windows and roof tops packed with watchers. 'You are in agreement,' he said. 'You want your freedom, my children. What living thing does not? An end to slavery, an end to their tithes and their taxes, and their mainland laws. If we fight for them, we do it as free men. Under our own captains and our own banner.'

For some while they were out of his hands then, howling and singing some song that had been adopted for their cause in recent days. It had a cheerful tune, simple to remember. Even I could have sung it with them, though I did not.

When they fluctuated again, he produced a letter. He said it had come from the governor. He read out this letter, which was short, terse, a wealth of meanings between its lines.

The governor had every confidence in Zulas Retka. He entrusted the town of Ebondis to his care. In the matter of independence, he would be guided by Retka's acumen and zeal.

Then the guardsmen forced their way out on the square and presented arms, and the key of the town was ceremoniously proffered to Retka, who took it and laughingly told us it weighed more heavily than his heart.

I sank back into the carriage seat. I was wrung out. Power was what this man wanted, he would loose the island from Tuli and rule it himself. He did not mind a war, or the methods of kings. Such themes interested him. For he might take up the trade himself.

Was this what Thenser had seen, which had disgusted him, flawed the golden image of the chosen leader he would follow through hell to the purity of victory or death? How could I tell? Thenser and I were strangers. Though he had mentioned his return, I had known he would never return to me. I had understood the real horror of those husks of politeness.

The horses of the carriages were neighing, the crowds surging and shouting, the bells tolled, the fireworks cracked and tattooed the night with rose and antimony.

I recollected the route from the square to Sydo's house. This was ironical, but perhaps just. Not far to go.

I descended from the carriage, and began to push my way among the hundreds of men and women, too sodden, too unaware to bother with the work it cost me, the insults and dalliances.

At length, penetrating through the forest of flesh, I came into some slanting streets boasting a handful of streetlamps. They were nearly vacant, though half the doors were open and the windows lighted up. The door of Sydo's residence was shut, and one at least of her servants remained to let me in. This boy's eyes were bright, and on seeing me he exclaimed, 'Where is madam? Where is sir?'

'They will be along,' I said. (Did he mean Oberis or Retka?)

There would be dancing in the streets that night. Already, as the bells tapered off I could hear a band in a garden playing a ruthless Tarasca.

I did not think her capable of annoyance, Sydo. I could, if necessary, excuse my absence legitimately, it was my female time. My showing was slight, as had happened in the siege, and during and after the winter of the retreat . . . the very barrenness of my votary to the goddess seemed to increase my illness.

In my room I prepared myself for bed and lay down on the couch to suffer again my nightly encounters with the stunning rock-face of oblivion.

But the noise of the town kept me awake – the music and cheering, the carriages, even the guns once more from the heights. And I remembered the City nights of the siege when I could not slumber if the cannon were dumb.

2

'They have their frugal troops at Kisara, a battalion more at Hermion. In the northwest there is the governor's pet castle – he has withdrawn his guard and there are no Tulhians there beyond the master. That is the sum of the Tulhian force at present on the island. I've been reliably informed, the two garrisons are already subdued without bloodshed, by the civilian populace.'

Retka stood before the tortoiseshell mirror in the salon where Thenser and I had parted. It was afternoon, a solidity of honey-coloured heat stuffed the chamber full, and piercing lights from the vine-wreathed windows slit at our chairs. We were an important gathering. Most of the pillars of Ebondis were there, with their wives or women. We were a party gathered to drink mint tea and cordials and water-white wine. But in a trice the conversation had become a political debate. The ladies mostly kept silent. Retka, keeper of the town, and of the house of Oberis, held forth at stage centre. As questions and doubts darted at him, he parried them superbly, and with a professional thrust brought home his point.

'The Tulhians,' said Retka, 'have for a very long while relied on abject acceptance of the unacceptable. We have made Ebondis the hub of Kithéan rebirth. From here, we have sent notice of the new state of affairs.'

'And Tuli fails to reply,' said the most prominent of this afternoon's opponents, a man in a black linen coat.

'We must allow the messengers a little time,' said Retka, smiling.

'Time has passed. More than enough. For the message to cross the sea, to reach the king's ministry, the king himself.'

'Then he must deliberate,' said Retka, 'upon what bargain he's prepared to strike. Oh, gentlemen, we'll hardly get the goods without some haggling. That we knew. Our promises of brotherly love, our preparedness to fight shoulder to shoulder with the mainland, should any – unspecified – threat be made against Tulhia . . . those are hardly a proper recompense for losing Kithé.'

447

'What demands can we accede to then, if we're to have freedom?'

'Almost anything,' said Retka. 'Never was a word of more moment – *liberty*. Let them grant us that. The rest will follow.'

'You are saying,' said another man, the pinched, clever-looking secretary, 'that Kithé will continue to be taxed, continue to give her first fruits to Tuli, after a state of Independence has been declared?'

'If necessary. This is not, naturally, what one tells every-man and his wife. One swears down for *them* the skies.'

'You vaunt the word liberty. Where then is the profit?'

'That will come. Free, we are free to make bargains elsewhere. The island is strategic to both the Oxidian and the East. Begin by soothing Tuli, eventually we can dictate better terms.'

'She may be aware of this, Retka.'

'She may. In which event, gentlemen, she may send an army here, to shut us up for good and all.'

There was an angry susurrus. The women began to flutter madly with their fans like birds trying to escape.

Were we all perhaps trying to escape him as hopelessly? He had somehow caged us in his will. We should never fly away.

'You, I believed, Retka, reckoned such a catastrophe was unlikely,' said the man in black linen.

'It may be so still. The Kronians are biding their time, exercising at Baslia, picking quarrels with the Charvro Alli-ance. Tuli seems to see this as happening on the face of the moon. She's lazy, refusing to mobilise. Now, we might have waited a pair of years to have her occupied in that way. Did we wish to wait? No, we took our vote on that. Consider, if Tuli won't prepare herself against the Saz Empire, will she stir for us? Does she wish, moreover, to be looking even now two ways at once? Over her shoulder to the North, and forward out to sea? Don't miss another possibility. Lacking the magnanimity of Tulhia, we might appeal to the Northern Emperor. We might ask for Saz-Kronia to come to our rescue.'

There was some noise. A man or two got to his feet.

'That would upset the entire balance of the area of the Temerid,' said the secretary dryly. 'Not to mention ensuring our fresh servitude, to *Kronia*, gods help us, for the next three centuries.'

'Obviously,' said Retka. 'But what do you think Tuli would make of it?'

This silenced them again. They perused it, there in the Turquoise Salon of Retka's mistress, which had become a chamber of council. The sunlight clotted. I heard a delicate little click, the setting of one of the lady's porcelain cups upon its saucer. I saw Sydo blink her long-lashed lizard eyes, basking as if mindless in the power of the slave-master.

Did I think for myself? Not at all. I had given up any idea I might have control of anything. Even my individual freedom to leave the room, let alone the house of Sydo, seemed illusory.

'Then, again,' said Retka, 'and I will only speak shortly on this venture, we shall soon have our own army. What it lacks in adroitness will be made up in enthusiasm and patriotism. And it will possess at least one commander of considerable talent and bravura.' And across the room he bowed to me, so some heads turned. Retka was honouring my husband.

'Very well,' said the secretary. 'But—'

'No, gentlemen,' said the smiling idol. Turning his battered metallic face to all sides, anointing them with his friendliness, the gentle rebuke, 'I consider now we must recollect this is the salon of a beautiful woman. We are wearying the ladies. Let's talk of other things.'

I was walking in the cloister of Sydo's courtyard, like that of a nunnery, up and down, in the summer delusion of open air.

A bird whistled sometimes in the fig tree. The climbing fig along the wall was fruiting . . . nothing else seemed remotely alive. Even the town had lost its tongue.

In an hour the sun would set. I should not be invited to dine with her, for Retka was in the house, as nowadays he often was, with no subterfuge. He took dinner with her alone, and remained through the night. It was Oberis who never set foot on the premises.

'Aradia.'

He had imbued the house, Ebondis, Kithé – it was no surprise that Retka was also here. Like some large men, he could move about soundlessly, a habit shared with the tiger.

'I hope you're well.'

'Yes, thank you.'

'You seem very pensive.'

What to say to that? I said nothing, examining the purple-green globes of the fig.

'A pity you could not,' he said, 'have gone with him up into the mountains. But you're not that sort of woman at all, are you, the Amazon in boots, holding a knife in her teeth.'

The timbre of his voice, the soft purr of it, vibrating in the enclosed space, tingled the leaves.

'You miss him very much,' he added.

This was a fact. I said, 'Yes.'

'And letters are infrequent. Besides, a square of paper is no substitute.'

Thenser had sent me no letter. I had expected no letter from Thenser.

I touched the leaves of the fig.

He said, 'You don't take the sun, do you. What a white little hand.'

And then he reached by me and plucked a trail of the dark leaves, and threaded it into my hair just above the right ear. His fingers did not brush my skin, but at the contact with my hair alone I shivered.

'I don't frighten you, do I?' he said. 'Remember, you came to me in your distress.'

'I haven't forgotten,' I said. Hurriedly I amended the words, 'Your kindness, and hers, leave me in your debt.'

'I should like that. You as my debtor. But I can't claim it to be true. For Sydo – I doubt if you disrupt her life.'

I turned from the fig and looked into the westered sunlight of the court. The fountains did not play today. They had lost their beauty with their song.

'Then it must be,' he said, 'that you hold a grudge against me, for sending him to shape an army.'

'That was Thenser's choice,' I said.

He said, 'There's a quarrel between you.'

I was embarrassed, and sickened, as if again I had blurted out my secret to him. But how could I deny it? In time he would come to see the proof of his assertion.

'A woman's error,' he said, 'though I have seen men make it, too. You create one man into your universe. You concentrate only on him. Therefore, you imagine, he is yours. You've assumed the right of ownership only a god can lay claim to, or a goddess. What you have made must belong to you. How can any of us bear that, or live up to that?'

'It would hardly trouble *you*,' I said. I was stung.

'So you think it has been done, with me? By whom? Not Sydo, I trust. Sydo is a creature of watchfulness. A gleaming serpent on a warm wall. When the winter comes, Sydo glides away.'

This was so exactly my own perception of her, put so succinctly, I stared up into his face.

'There have been a few perhaps who built their worlds of Zulas Retka,' he said, 'but I discount such women. They were dross. The business is only troublous, Aradia, when carried on by a strong and passionate will such as your own. And who with such a will, do you think, would make her landscape from me? Such hideous clay, such a ruined edifice?'

The overpowering icon of him was poised above me, the looming mask evoked some shade – perhaps of Keer Gurz, swayed down his height to my immature vision – or only of an elemental thing, the clashing darkness of the sea, the pylon of a burning building—

From the jungle-forest of his black locks, that face looked out at me, hideous as he had said, but no ruin, a thing twisted brand new out of primeval chaos, then coated with the smooth surface of golden brass or bronze – and set with eyes that were contrastingly of all deep liquid fabrics, and too black to gaze on – yet one could not look away.

I pushed myself back against the wall and the fig leaves crackled on my neck and arms.

'Why do you want me?' I said. 'Some afternoon's diversion – leave me alone.'

'Where is your subtlety?' he said, maybe amused. 'These direct accusations. Not even a flirt of a fan. Are you an adult woman, Aradia?'

'I don't understand anything. I'm a silly little fool. The way you live and deal with each other.'

'Who? What are you speaking of?'

'This adult *country*. I intrude there. My papers are false. I'll never understand – how to live in the world.'

'Who does?' he said. 'We do the best we can.'

He moved away from me and the vice of tension slackened, left me wilting. He walked out beside the fountains.

'Midsummer drought,' he said. 'It lasts into the autumn. The fountain isn't permitted again until after the wine harvest.' The shadow of the apricot awning spread over him. 'Shall I have him brought here, to please you?' he asked. 'I mean Zavion.'

'No.'

'The patriot army will spare him a few days. There's only so much he can do with the raw material we've given him. An idealist, as he is, he'll wear himself out refining them. But they only need a little discipline, and pikes in their hands. Well?'

'*No*.'

'Now you're losing your temper, Aradia. Is it true, that you threatened Firiu with death? You look incapable of such a thing. But you could scratch and bite, couldn't you? You've killed at least once, or am I wrong?' He studied me thoughtfully, deciphering the library of my brain.

I said, 'Thenser dedicated himself to your service.'

'I know that. Is it that you're inquiring whether I am worthy of the dedication? Of course not. What mortal is?'

'Yet you *accept* the dedication.'

'From a man. His education has allotted him, at least, free will. And in the situation of such a man as Thenser Zavion,

452

he must give himself to something. He began with glorious war, and so has stuck with her. Even though he dislikes war's other face, the bloody field, the destruction of lives. A paradox. Like yourself in a certain manner. Embracing what will harm you.'

I said, 'Don't recall him here for my sake.'

'Fiercely spoken, my child. I shall obey. But you've performed a cunning trick, you sprite. To end my wooing by making me talk of your husband.'

Just then, the lyrachord began plashing its allowed fountain through the house.

Retka bowed to me.

'Suitably chastised, I will retreat to what I know.'

When he had left the courtyard, the strings which had been holding me up slackened. I crawled to a bench and sat there. The coloured heat of sunset hammered on me, precursor of the black strangle-grip of night.

If only the summer would pass. If only the shadow of night, the day-night of this misery, would end.

3

Drought was a familiar of Kithéan summer. It came to Ebondis in foreknowledge of every street and alley it would grind, every garden it would wither with its thin burned fingers. The boulevards were no longer watered. The fountains did not play. A house with a well became a treasury. On the hills the stream beds went to stone. Water must be reinvented. They began to sell water. One heard the water-seller's cry. No one was unduly appalled.

One sunrise there was a cloudburst. It lasted all of five minutes, with diamond flashes and much garrulous thunder. They ran out, even the household of Sydo, which could afford all the water it required, and caught the mocking alms of heaven in jars and buckets.

Where did the *sold* water come from? Why from certain founts of the mountains that never ran dry. And sometimes, from Tuli. It was brought by boat across the ocean.

I heard this answer with a gasp they did not seem to comprehend.

Then, the water did not come from Tuli. Did not come from Khirenie.

A blockade, they said. Tulhian ships on patrol. It was execrable, the gods would afflict Tuli.

The cry of the water-seller was heard less often.

Mere water ceased to exist at the table of Sydo. We drank juices and the acid milk of goats mouthing the blasted hillside. We bathed in essences. Then mysterious barrels arrived, purporting to be wine. But they were not wine.

Water reappeared in baths and on the table of Sydo.

Elsewhere in Ebondis, as ever, they made do.

She came back in her carriage half an hour after she had set off in it.

She did not appear disconcerted, only faintly disdainful.

The coachman stood swearing in the yard. I could hear his speech from the window of my bedroom.

There was a water riot in the square of the Isibri. They had gone to the goddess, to implore rain, out of season. Then decided that not the gods but humanity was at fault.

'They're running to the justice hall with sticks and stones, calling for Retka – saying he must get them water one minute, that he's the cause of the shortage the next minute. And her bloody carriage is in the road. A stone this big – deflected by the carriage roof, or it would have laid me out. How'd she manage then?'

But Retka had spoken to the people. He had vowed they should have a water ration.

They finished in cheering him.

He did not come to the house now. He was enmeshed in the affairs of his office. There were rumours all over the town.

I went to buy some thread (the source of money Thenser had arranged for me did not, like the water, dry up). But I purchased only essentials, and was assailed by flying words like wasps. The Tulhians were coming. They were on the sea.

They had harnessed the air vehicles, found a form of navigating them before unknown. They would soar over the island and rain down incendiaries. Our nearest harbours, including that of the village of Steps, had never been favoured by Tuli. The ships would land at Kisara, where the larger garrison was.

And there was to be conscription, the shuddering girl told me, as she sorted the cards of cotton and the needles. Her brother would be called up to fight, and he had weak lungs. The volunteer army would not be enough, and what would they do, her mother and she, when her brother was dead?

I went home and darned my stockings, and into each stitch went her bleats.

Am I afraid yet? No, not yet. My pain almost spares me fear. But when terror begins, perhaps it will oust my pain? Must I then long for terror?

4

Entering the sitting room behind the courtyard I was taken aback. The actual owner of the house was there, Oberis.

I faltered before him, recipient of his, perhaps unknowing, bounty. But he gave me a curt nod. I passed on into the court, concealing myself under the fig tree.

At noon, Sydo descended, and I heard their voices.

'He has overshot himself. Made a mistake.' This being Oberis, reining himself in.

'If you say so,' she, languidly.

'The town is in confusion. There's been another riot, in the slum quarter. They're looking for Tulhians under their beds.'

Silence: She.

He: 'As far as we are informed, Tuli hasn't moved. She's done nothing. But the word spreads. The king's troops are coming to raze every town of Kithé that withheld tribute. The taxes haven't been sent. He tried to stop that. And I. They overrode us. Now, see where we are.'

'Where are we?' she said, tone like the ripple of her fan.

'The governor's fled. Rushed straight to the bosom of the king, no doubt. Kisara is threatening to massacre the Tulhian garrison – two hundred men, soft as puddings, who surrendered to them. If that's done, what hope do we have of negotiating with Tuli? Are you *listening*, Sydo?'

'Yes.'

'I'm beside myself. Our only hope is Retka.'

'Yes.'

'But what are we to do? Even this fantastic army in the mountains – he refuses to summon it. To bring it down too soon will cause a stampede, he says.'

Then a prolonged hiatus. After which she asked if she might have anything brought him. He said he would have wine, it was criminal to drink water.

I had not intended to listen. They had made me hear. During the interim, I recrossed the sitting room and he nodded to me again. I went upstairs to my baking bed. I lay there.

It is all madness, this world, what it does. No, I do not *want* to understand it. I do not *want* to learn.

'Madam asks that you'll come down and dine with her.'

The pale and uneasy maid stood like a wraith in my shadow-doorway, calling me to the gods knew what phantom feast.

Awakened abruptly, I had forgotten where I was. Was it Kronia, or the City? And who the woman – Vollus, the Gurz grandmother – my Aunt Elaieva?

'Very well,' I said, in the broken voice of the somnambulist.

As I acquiesced, I remembered.

I washed myself in the handful of blood-hot water, and put on the hot-pink dress, and combed up my hair.

Sydo's dining hour was malleable. Now, after dark, they had laid dinner in the court, which was unusual, for there the moths came in such profusion to the lights to die, and sometimes they were as large as birds with eyes on their wings – I had at first been petrified. Gums smoked against the biting insects. Sydo reclined on her divan. She had not dressed, but wore a house-robe of black silk. By contrast, at her throat was an unbelievable necklace. It was of emeralds and rubies, like a dreadful cicatrice of stained glass. Shot at ceaselessly by the candles, its refractions tore about the awning, the walls, a ghostly insectile visitation that outdid reality.

Seeing me she said at once, 'Do you admire my jewellery? Oberis gave it to me in our marriage month. The queen in Tuli, I've heard, has nothing better.'

Her hair was loose. It lay all over her, stuck by its own galvanic to her skin and the silk, and brimmed on to the floor.

They served the meal. The food was parched, as even her dishes had come to be. We ate, as ever, in silence, but she drank more wine than was her wont.

When we reached the dessert, she sent the servants away.

She segmented the oranges herself and poured over them the sauce of carob, and passed my plate to me like a peasant woman in a hut. Perhaps she had been that once. Who could know anything?

'I am the taller,' she said, 'my dresses would not fit on you, or I'd give you some.'

I took a morsel of orange into my mouth. She looked far away with her eyes that seemed to have no thoughts, conceivably no sight, in them. She watched, but what did she see? Our skeletons?

'Retka,' she said. And then, after a pause, 'Zulas Retka.'

Later she filled our glasses from the krater, which we had almost drained, though she had had most of it. Red berries floated in the wine and a sprig of anise. She watched these now.

'Do you recall the novel the girl read to us?'

When I did not reply, she glanced suddenly at me.

'Yes,' I answered. I did recall it had been read, but none of the content, save for one sentence—

She spoke the fragment aloud now:

'The House of Night. Do you recall? I have seen it. Once I dreamed of it.'

I could not follow. The phrase in the book had come to mean for me a condition of the spirit and mind.

'What – is it?' I said.

'Oh,' she said, 'it is a prison.'

She looked into the shallow wine.

I waited.

At last she said, 'Centuries ago, the conquering Tulhians were fond of that place. Northwest of the island. In the book, the hero and heroine were cast there, to perish. The old hags frightened the children with it. The dead come out of there, no other.'

She raised her eyes, the way a lizard does, careful, without a drop of lubricating warmth, and blinked, and rose from her couch and the table in the spilling water of her night-black hair.

Then, still looking at me, she laughed. It was as if claws caught at my neck. There was a mindless evil to her, just that of the snake's before it lunges. If I had learned any worthwhile gesture of avoidance I should have used it, if I had trusted any god – I whispered the name of Vulmartis, that was all I could do. Had she put her curse on me? Or did she even know what she did?

She went along the cloister, amid her green and scarlet refractions, with her hair trailing after her along the tiles, to the door of the sitting room, and slipped inside like a knife into its sheath.

She left in the middle of the short night. The exits from Ebondis were by now diligently guarded, but being who she was, and her carriage recognisable, she got through unimpeded. She took very little with her, that being in a small lacquer chest, but these items were the best of her spoils. The necklace I think she must have worn, with perhaps a shawl to cover it. All her rings she had, but several valuable ornaments she abandoned, and all of her dresses, even the moon-gown of cloth-of-silver.

Where she went to is another matter. I am reminded of a sorceress in an ancient fable who rushed up into the night sky in a chariot drawn by dragons. Probably there were still routes off the island. Some bay not to Tulhian liking. The bribing of a fisher-craft would be simple.

After she had gone, and they had surreptitiously rifled her leavings, the servants also vanished, as I had anticipated.

A cannonade of blows on the front door, when I had got down to open it, heralded Retka and an escorting party of guardsmen.

He left them in the porch, and ushered me away inside.

Here he looked about, along the stair, into the lower rooms. Already, with passage of a day, everything had an ambience of decline. I had done nothing to check it. I was now merely a guest dwelling in a deserted house.

'Can you feel a pleasant cool?' Retka said. 'It's winter. Sydo has gone. Ah,' he said, 'infallible sundial.'

He went about, making some mental itinerary. Once or twice he pocketed something. Conceivably they were things he had given her which she had discarded, or things of his own he had formerly left lying there. If he was a thief, he was not a petty one.

'You'd better return with me to the Justiciary,' he said. 'It won't be safe for you here.'

I obeyed him. To gather up again my personal possessions did not take long.

5

An apartment was awarded me, in the Justiciary, most recently a clerk's office, I thought, with walls of coppery plaster. A window gave thankfully on the closed vista of a tree. The bed and washstand had been brought in and suitably fitted up; the desk remained. He told me he was sorry there was nothing better. Several persons, and families of the staff, had sought refuge in the building, not liking the mood of the town.

Sometimes he would request me to make a fair copy of letters. He apologised for this also, but assured me several

459

eminent ladies, one in her eighties but having yet a clear hand, were engaged in the activity. The content of the letters eluded me. Written Tulic could often baffle me, besides I did not care to know. I think he did not give anything very momentous over to my pen.

The sweltering days went by, with the shadows of the tree moving on the ruddy comfortless wall. How I longed for a white place – or to creep into the tree itself, the look of which was like a bath to me. Although its leaves were crisped, no longer capable of any lambency or green.

I was feverish. I knew it from the haloes of light that wavered around all objects by day, and which by night disconnected and sent flickerings across my eyes, flutterings and sudden high *visual* incorporeal sounds across my hearing. I half believed my room was haunted by electric creatures, flitting and signalling each other.

My lucid time was late afternoon, the commencement of evening.

Then I would marvel at where I was, as if I had only just found myself to be there.

There were dinner parties to begin with, in a dining salon of the building, unsuitably opulent, with drapes of cloth-of-gold. Here I glimpsed my fellow denizens of the Justiciary. They were vaguely known to me from the sitting rooms of Ebondis. Retka was sometimes present. Oberis came now and then. No one spoke to him of his domestic arrangements.

Then the dinners ceased.

Every morning, a carafe of water was left before my door. It was not always quite full. Others had been drinking at it like thirsty deer.

In the town the water ration was abbreviated, but a wine ration had been added. From the deepest and most reverenced cellars had arisen vintages meant for princely lips – and into the beakers of the rabble they went. (My words are borrowed from an outcry heard on the stair.)

Retka addressed the town from the balconies of the justiciary. Or he rode out into the streets on a sturdy roan mare, noted for her sluggish indifference to human pandemonium, accompanied only by four guards. He held Ebondis now by the stamina of his soul. That alone.

6

All day there had been commotion in the town. A frightened secretary encountered in a passage told me hoarsely: 'They sighted some Tulhian war ships in the bay at Kisara – and the mob broke in and slaughtered the garrison.'

This news I slowly digested through the afternoon.

Once I heard the bell of the Isibri ringing. But after a few minutes it was silenced. Sometimes a roaring, as of thousands of voices in pain or fear, or in wild hilarity even, came from the rougher byways of the outer slums.

Yet the birds still flintily sang in the trees of the square.

Food was obtained by payment of the staff and brought to the door like the water. Mealtimes were random. One breakfasted at noon or not at all. The evening plate of potted meats, pickled vegetables, and husked bread arrived between the hours of sunset and midnight.

Now the knock came early, the sky crayoned over with daylight.

No tray of food but Retka's valet.

I was to dine with Retka.

As with Sydo, I could only acquiesce.

The table was spread with cut glass, silver, napkins embroidered with some emblem of the town. Two candelabra gave their light. Between the curtains of blood the windows were green like the room with the coat-tails of dusk.

His valet served us, left us.

The meal was from the usual menu, but with some fruit and cheese, some sauces, preserves and sweets piled by in silver vessels. The first wine was sonorous, red thunder in a bottle. He had not bothered with decanters. We drank three wines in all, and a fruit liqueur at the end.

He spoke throughout the meal, I needed only to listen. I thought I had been brought there to listen, his audience. He was outlining nemesis. It was done without much show, with no melodrama, consideringly. Sometimes he would even pause to dissect it. I began to believe it was not an elegy. I had not been summoned, like the nameless page in the last act of a great tragedy, for the king to make confession, before falling on his sword. Partly Retka was explaining to me the board on which I, too, had found myself, a tiny superfluous figure.

The substance was as I had already heard it, sensed it. The garrison at Kisara, which had put away its arms, had been overrun by an hysterical and murderous populace. This grisly demonstration of revolt unleashed Tuli. Of the three or four ships patrolling the bay, only one was equipped with cannon, but she had opened a broadside on the town. Within two hours the Kisarans were fleeing, and the Tulhians had landed.

The council at Ebondis took its vote, and the ragtag army was whistled down from the heights.

'Estimates of Tulhian forces at Kisara come garbled,' Retka said. 'Now they are two thousand men. Now five thousand. Now six hundred.'

There had been a riot at the Hill Gate today. A horde of Ebondians intent on their own flight had set on the guardsmen stationed to keep the way.

Retka brooded on the wherewithal of the town for defence. On the nature of Kithéans as fighters, their virtues and liabilities. On the poverty of man's intellectual armament to deal with such situations.

And suddenly, turning in his fingers the glass of mauve liqueur, he said to me, 'How does it seem to you, Aradia, this panorama?'

I had drunk the wines, having come into his presence in my wretched day frock with the reset sleeves. (The botched reorganised seams of the pink dancing gown had finally torn.) I had not dressed for fear, or for any other powerful enemy. It had happened terror had not, even now, reached me. I knew only this inevitable progression of the wheel upon its road of gall and fire.

And so I was able to answer him.

'I think that when you began it, you seemed reaching – not for the star of victory – but for this.'

He looked at me closely, across the table.

'For what, do you mean?'

'For – *this*. For failure, and ruin. As if that was what you wanted when you called for freedom and victory.'

'I see,' he said. He drank down the liqueur, and poured for himself another.

But something in my own utterance had excited me. I gesticulated as I spoke, trying to impress on him its import.

'It was always like this. In my City, when the Kronians came – and for the Kronians themselves. Like the child stretching out to clutch a flame it knows will burn it. And then, in agony the screaming has a sort of triumph—'

'The gods hear you,' he said. 'Be careful. It's a risk to be too wise.'

'But for the rest of us,' I said, 'you trample us in your gallop to hell.'

'Perhaps,' he said, 'since we're invoking defeat in our demand for victory, you beg for the suffering you dread.'

'Never.'

'Yes. But,' he said, 'I don't yet concede this defeat. They will be here, in a week, less. Then we'll see, shan't we, if Kithé can win and if Tuli can lose. Perhaps after all the Tulhian king has also stretched out for a flame.'

Outside in the city there came loud noises of bells.

I jumped from my seat. Oddly, for even so I felt no proper alarm.

He said, 'Steady. It isn't the foe arriving. I would have been told.'

'What then?'

'The joys of panic. It makes them busy. Don't you know those joys?' He stood up, still looking at me, the glittering table and the points of its light still massed between us.

I was drunk. My head whirled, and I seemed simultaneously not in my body. In that moment, it was as if only I and he were real. As if we hung in midair, in a mirage of objects that did not exist – the furniture of the room, the desk, table, candles, the apartment, the building, the town, and all the events of the earth, its seasons, its days and nights, its drought, riot and war.

He has understood what I said to him. He knows it, too. It is all a pretence we are engaged in, acting in the vast auditorium of space and time, a theatre that may end in death, but is also meaningless and a *lie*.

And he *knows*.

'Well,' he said, 'you see, Aradia, I suppose it best you should be removed from Ebondis. Zavion secreted you at a village on the north coast. You could go back there, and obtain passage off the island. Tuli would suffer you, one small girl made of sugar-crystal, if you hide your thoughts, that you are privy to the schemes of heaven. Or Khirenie may be safe. Or, there's Sibris. He left you money, I imagine, but not enough. I can attend to that.'

I saw it in a fleeting gemstone glimpse – my escape, my retreat, everything left behind, Thenser left upon the blazing distance, beyond the barricade of smoke and swords. And the forward propulsion, into some other place of waiting. Waiting now for nothing. Yet it was theatre I saw, the lying role I could act out. It did not have to concern me. I need only live it through, playing, as best I might, to the gallery.

'You give no argument,' he said, 'you're prepared for this, to leave him?'

'He has left me,' I said. 'It's finished.'

'Well,' he said again, 'but we will have you safe.'

I laughed at him then. I laughed because I saw the role he acted as I acted my own, and because I had seen, and he had admitted these matters, and more often, maybe, than I.

His tallness and bigness, the barbaric strength of him, there torched with the fire of the candles, was the costume of his character. He had chosen it. He had put it on. Behind the casque, what was that, looking down out of the jet-black visor of eyes?

'Come here,' he said, and I went to him, not considering it, only this mystery that was ourselves.

The powerful brutal sensitive hands caught hold of me. I was lifted off my feet.

'Your arms,' he said, 'put them round my neck.'

I did this. He carried me through the chamber and into another, which was the bedroom.

I fell back on the bed, which seemed swimming and swaying in a blissful hurricane. He leaned over me, even his shadow crushed all breath from my lungs. I should fight him now. I raised my hands to scratch his face, impervious metal dented by blows on an anvil – and he took my hands in one of his own and thrust them back above my head into the pillow. His other hand spread itself full of my body. He left no inch of me untaken by that hand. Even through my clothes it found me. There was a caress like the tiger's, no gentleness. It was the rape. But it was a rape to which I had consented. For it was power, it was destiny bearing me down, subduing me, pushing up the flimsy skirt, squeezing at me, taking hold of and tearing me with the fury and enormity of entry and conjoining. The aphrodisiac of despair, and of the robbery of all control. The violence and punishment I had once mistaken, in the person of Drahris, for a man – this overthrow of self, liberating as the conquest by death.

And so I gave up myself, let him hold me his prisoner, working out fate upon me like some engine at the earth's molten core, driving it, thrusting and burning, tolling like the howling of the bells, its tower of shadow on me like black night – until I was no more anything, was obliterated, became one with all and nothing, burst asunder, could not even scream, silenced and broken wide and my soul floated away somewhere.

When I returned, he lay along my side and I, with my arms still upflung over my head, lying boneless against him, looked into the vault of the ceiling, painted with clouds and knots of pineapples, where my soul had been, perhaps.

He did not say another word to me, but left me there to sleep on his bed.

I lay and mused a while, as a child does, on the ceiling, on the events which had befallen me. I felt neither sad nor contented. I felt as if I had been sluiced and cleared, nearly amnesiac, and so slept.

7

When dawn entered the chamber I left the apartment, which was otherwise empty.

Like any commissioned harlot, I stole off along corridors, once or twice meeting a questing clerk, who ignored me.

In my room, however, a breakfast had been left early, with the carafe of water. I ate a mouthful, and going about began to put together my things for departure. None of them seemed to belong to me. And, since it would be best to travel as lightly as possible, I discarded almost everything.

The weary sun-worn tree turned to a yellowish vividness that was nearly green, as the day crossed my window.

About noon a knock on the door again brought me Retka's valet, who handed me a package and remarked that I should be ready to leave in an hour. Someone would conduct me to a side door, where a vehicle would collect me.

The package was a wallet, stuffed with papers pertaining to myself. They were official and gave my persona as that of a Charvish national, a being fortuitously opposed to neither side. I was shocked to see that my full name was written as that of my childhood. How he had learned it I could only conjecture. I did not see why Thenser should have told him such a thing.

There was also money in the wallet, considerable amounts, in coin and paper, and in Tulhian bonds.

I had realised I should not see Zulas Retka again. Our commerce was concluded. I might say, I supposed, I had solaced his last nights as a lord on Kithé. But with sobriety I felt a deep reluctance to dwell on what I had done – what I had allowed. He had forced me because I had wanted to be forced. I remembered my motives, all I had thought. I believed still that I had been granted a truth of the world, and that the violent union had set a seal upon acknowledgment. But now I was only Aradia, and Aradia mourned the wish she had had, the yearning of the priestess, that if love were denied her, she would take in its place a total chastity.

I stood in the doorway with my bag once more in my hand, weightless as almost nothing now. The colour of the tree had faded to ochre, and a narrow little man was before me, who took me down the dark byways of the building, into a dirty courtyard strewn with straw. A door opened for me, and outside was a carriage with two horses, with the driver in a plain coat. There were no markings upon anything. The chariot had a slovenly look.

We drove through the streets. I stared about. No bells sounded now, there seemed a universal vacancy, and many houses and shops were boarded up. A band of men roaming the thoroughfares glared at us, and one shouted, but no other thing occurred.

At the gate, some provision of Retka's saw us through.

Out in the fields and olive groves there was not much sign of the business of impending harvest. A few workers tended the trees, or walked along the ridges where the vines began. The air was thick with gorged flies and wasps already feasting.

Under the scorch of the white sun, the whole view had a weird, crucial stasis, like a landscape stricken by plague. Even the notes of the birds seemed hesitant, their pipings querulous, like a question cried over.

But I had seen enough tableaux of havoc and apprehension. I gazed in a dream at the wayside flowers and the dust. We rose into the tawny hills. And I wondered at my lack of pain, for now I was in fact and forever setting out from the centre of my life.

I was leaving Thenser to his battle and his reparation, and perhaps to death. My presence would have made no odds, yet it was curious.

And the sound now of the hoofs, going away and away.

When the driver of the carriage was killed, I was asleep. An indictment, maybe. I roused at a peculiar jar, the horses making awful sounds – there was a plunge and a roll, and then the vehicle arrested. I was shaken onto the floor.

The carriage door wrenched open and terrible hands like mechanical things had hold of me, hauling me out. I staggered down and fell onto the track, into a smother of dust. It was like the inside of a powder box. As the powder settled, I saw what resembled the scene of an accident. My driver, to whom I had not spoken one word, sprawled at the verge of brown grass. A missile, perhaps from a flint-shot, had struck his temple. Now his neck was broken, too. The horses were in the grasp of a pair of peasants – they looked like any of the menfolk of Steps. Some others grouped about me. They were all Kithéan, brown like the hills, and behind them the sky had its white-yellow complexion, the burned end of summer afternoon.

'Get up,' said one of the Kithéans, in their dialect.

I did this, and they looked me over.

'We mean you no harm, miss,' said another man. 'Him,' he pointed to the corpse, 'he wouldn't stop.'

I waited for what they would do to me, and the crickets shirred the air.

'But we need the carriage,' said the first man.

Then they took my bag and rent it wide. The few items spilled, as I had done, on the track. They leered at a petticoat. They seemed to find it more suggestive than the female form. Then out came the wallet. They removed the money briskly, and tore up the bonds. They puzzled over my false documents and asked me to explain them. I said I was what the papers stipulated, a Charve. Why, then, was I here? I said I had followed my husband, but he had sent me home.

Who was my husband, they inquired.

A Kithéan, I answered.

I thought bemusedly did they mean to trap me, but now the asking stopped, and soon they lost all interest in me.

They left me my possessions. Even the document of affiliation they returned to me, as an afterthought. Stuffed with Retka's money, they led the horses and vehicle away up the hillside.

When they had disappeared, abandoning the coachman and myself as we were, I sat down by the road.

The event seemed preordained, like the fate of consuming fire I had posited the night before. As if to set out as I had was in order to meet just such a detainment, theft, destitution.

I must proceed on foot to the village. The westering of the sun would guide me, and the road, although it was not the familiar one.

But the road branched, and making my choice I chose wrongly, in ignorance.

Through the long death of the afternoon, I strayed in a kind of delirious resignation. I had been lost before.

Sometimes I sat down again, and looked about at the mounds of the hills – the paths of hares and goats went everywhere, but all trace of a road had vanished. Stands of sunshade pine, some wild olives, these were landmarks which rendered me no bearings. I knew quite well the futility of continuing. I continued.

Then, near sunset, I beheld a pale luminous vacuity passing downward and yet farther down between two heights – and recognised it for the stage-setting of the sea.

In the dusk, I stumbled to a village which was not Steps, but the doorway of night. It lay, if anything, more northerly, yet it was full of Tulhians.

To be full of them was simple, for the village was small. Thirty men, in rich-blue uniforms a touch spoiled by their landing on a beach, by their strutting up and down before the villagers in the dust.

Lacking anything else, they had made the priest's house by the tiny temple their headquarters.

In a lamplit cell they took their turn at questioning me. I spoke for them in my finest Tulic. I was a Charve but had lived for a time at Genchira. They seemed not to have heard of Genchira and looked at me as if I had dared to invent it.

At first they let me stand, but then they gave me a hard wooden stool to sit on. Only the bones of my corset kept my back straight. I wished they would put me somewhere and allow me to sleep, but they insisted that I must stay where I was. It seemed to them I had come from the town of Ebondis, was that so? I said it was not, I had come from a village farther along the coast. I had been to visit a woman in the hills, but vagabonds had attacked me. Then I lost my way.

They had already been shown the spurious paper, my Charvish origin. If I had only been visiting in the hills, why had I needed to carry such a paper? I carried it always, I said, since the times were uneasy.

They laughed at my choice of words. They said Kithé was a gnat which had stung the king. They had been sent to do the scratching for him.

They were not especially brutish. When I asked for a drink of water they had some brought, from their own barrel.

Clearly they did not find me more than mildly suspicious, and I had hopes that they would, when they moved on into the island, leave me at the village. The villagers were not evincing any particular patriot zeal, but fraternised with the Tulhians, the girls even were prepared to romance with them. Altogether the invader was in a good mood.

They lodged me, however, in a tenantless cot behind the temple, and locked me in for the night with some bread and a cup of beer. There was nowhere to sleep save on the earthen floor, the cot having been skinned of anything pretending to comfort. I lay down, and my tired body could not accustom itself to the uneven ungivingness of this bed. As I twisted about, hearing the chorus of frogs by the village well, and the occasional passes of a Tulhian sentry along the street, something brushed me with its long grey finger. The last night in Ebondis seemed a year away.

Next morning, a further small party of Tulhians rode into the village, with a man they called a Khirenian. The soldier who unlocked my door, a young subaltern inclined to flirt even with me, sorry picture that I was (earth in my hair, wan with a gnawing sickness), began to speak of the Khirenian in a certain scornful disparaging manner I had heard before.

'Of use,' said the Tulhian, 'but I wouldn't want to sit down to dine with the fellow.'

It appeared the Khirenian was also a Kithéan, and had held some position of trust amid the rebels. Then there was an upset, to do with debts or a woman, and he turned tail and re-avowed his allegiance to the Tulic monarchy. His various insights on the Ebondian council, and his knowledge of the island, had proved handy. Yet he was – what could you name such a man?

Presently though the subaltern did give him a name which was, of course, Firiu.

I continued not to utter a sentence. But nevertheless, the preordaining fate of fire, the punishment I enticed by begging to be spared, made sure Firiu should learn of this straying female the soldiers had captured. He came to see me in a little while, perhaps out of officiousness, or perhaps because he, too, felt the plucking hand of a god.

He looked much as ever, still a dandy in his mosaic-buttoned coat, the tan of his boots outshouting the morning. His eyes popped when I filled them. But he was artist enough to savour the moment.

'Why, this woman's a Kronian,' he exclaimed – not startling me, for I was beyond it; I surmised Retka had had Thenser's past investigated, and incidentally researched my own, and some jumbled agenda had come Firiu's way. 'A spy, I'll be bound. She was always peering at a window, behind some curtain, listening. But if you want another detail, she's the doxy of Zulas Retka's commander, the man Zavion.'

My Tulhians, who had been decent to me, stared as if they had succoured a viper in their collective bosom.

Firiu stood twiddling his moustache.

'I trust none of you has pleasured himself with the witch,' he added. 'She's flagrantly diseased.'

They were on campaign, and occupied, I must be sent elsewhere for my villainy to be probed.

They referred to the place as the castle. A Tulhian base had already been established in the vicinity. And there were still

471

inmates, those the governor had sent there through the years. Two men should be spared as my guard, and one of the fisher boats could carry us along the coast.

My subaltern, though now he looked at me in the tone he had employed for Firiu, addressed his captain. 'Sir, on the word of this man – to condemn the lady to such a spot.'

But the word of Firiu was cast iron overlaid with pure gold.

For the 'lady' she would be secure enough, those towers would keep her safe until the Kithéan adventure had resolved. One noted, she did not speak up now, to deny anything.

My subaltern turned to me. 'Madam, if you've a defence, you should resort to it at once. That prison is a desperate solution.'

'I know,' I said, 'I was told of it. I'm not a Kronian, your informer has misread something there.'

'And Zavion,' said the captain, 'your ties to him?'

'What your informer has mentioned.' And with a quirkiness I had not reckoned to possess, I finished, 'His other charge I refute, as I have never been his.'

If I had pleaded and wept, shrieked and flown at them, if I had lied peerlessly, or bartered some valuable secret I did not contain – I imagine they would not have behaved very differently.

They sent me off with my taciturn Tulhian guards, to the fisher with his boat, who bared his teeth at us in dismay like a dog. And so rowed west of north along the coast of the island, where huge rock walls began, ground up from the lacy edging of the water, until at length the creation of stone which rose out of them must seem partly a natural thing, as if the gods, not men, had fashioned for my sins the House of Night.

Chapter Two

1

Cliffs of malachite form the approach to the castle, appropriately unearthly-looking against a metallic sky. It is the creeping weeds and animalcules of the sea which clothe the rock in such strident green. The congested bay, narrow as a chimney, navigable only with enormous care, gives instantly on the cliff-head, into which a cantankerous stair was carved centuries before, and is kept up with posts and chains. Out from the rock ascends the other rock, turning gradually blacker as it puts on its crenellations and protrudes its stocky towers. There seem to be no windows. There are not very many.

The fisherman, chanting and growling some prayer under his breath – he determined the castle was ill-omened – stayed in his boat to await the return of the Tulhians. Boat and man grew smaller and smaller as we climbed. Our lives were precarious, we slipped and clung to the rails. Twice the guard at my back assisted me. It would have been facile to fall. I did not. Life is all we know, it is hard to relinquish that one certainty.

The stair ended a million miles in the air, so it looked. The sky was now a louring lavender, wheeling with sooty gulls.

An archway gave on a paved walk, with the abysmal walls growing out of it. You courted vertigo whichever way you gazed – down to the bay below, the miniature sea-fans pleated with foam, the fish-bone of the boat – or upward to the tapering of the eyeless towers with the gulls swarming about their tops like flies.

Where the incoming Tulhian force had made its camp was invisible. Miles inland probably. This place was not like Kithé at all. It was an underworld somehow positioned in the air.

The prison appeared lifeless, deserted. But it was not. In reply to a clanging on a bell, which my Tulhian guards did not themselves much relish, a sort of housekeeper came to the squinnied door. A gnome of a man, in a long, belted, cobwebby coat or robe that trailed on the ground, a creature of the dark, with a pallid sluggish face.

'Is there still a Master here?' inquired one of the soldiers. The creature was deaf, obtuse, or did not understand plain Tulic. Yet he pointed to their uniform and grinned and said suddenly, "*Tulhia.*" And throwing back the door, he welcomed us in like memory.

'What is your name?'

The entry to the mansion of death, surely, will be like this. The vaulted darkness, composed more of shadow than stone. Perhaps not the single slender window showing only flat light. But there will be the sentinel at some great slab of desk, a face with shiny lips like two worms that demand the revelation of being.

I have heard of primitive communities of the Equatorial Lands, whose members will not tell, casually, their given name. To learn and use it without permission is a grave breach of etiquette.

Before the sentinel I knew such an offence. Such dread. But he must be answered. If he required I strip myself naked before him, I must do that, too.

I told him my name, as it was written on the document.

'I have a paper here from the Tulhian captain which names you Aradia Zavion.'

'That is not my name.'

'But you were the man's whore, then.'

I said, 'I lived with him as his wife.'

He wrote something in his ledger. The mouth began to writhe again.

'This other paper's a lie?'

'It is correct.'

'You are a Charve, not a Kronian? Where's your place of birth?'

I told him that, also.

'That is not Charvish,' he said.

'They are allied with Charvro.'

He wrote once more in the ledger. His pen had a long whitish handle, ivory perhaps. It gleamed disturbingly in the darkness.

'You are here,' he said, 'under suspicion of treachery. Of plotting with Kithéan rebels, spying for Kronia, one or both, either intolerable to the Kingdom of Tulhia.' I started to try to say to him that I was innocent. Naturally this was futile, and he interrupted me immediately: 'You'll consider yourself a prisoner of the Kingdom of Tulhia. You will occupy here a room. You will remain in the custody of the castle's Master until such time as your case can be examined.'

'Let me see the Master,' I said.

'When and if he wishes,' said the sentinel, and folded his worm lips to smiling.

Rather to my surprise a woman came to conduct me to the stipulated room. She was a wardress, coloured over as they all were by the grey-black place, even to her hair and sunken eyes. She looked on me with aversion and hatred. I had earned them spontaneously when put under her jurisdiction.

She sent me before her, leading her, though I did not know where I went. The passages were coiling and dank, twilit by occasional slits in their scaly sides. Next we came into a region where a lamp stood ready, and this she kindled. Then four of us moved onward, she and I, our two shadows.

By a stairway was a long lean alcove in the dripping wall. I started, seeing a figure there – the wardress made no comment, doubtless my reaction was common in that lamp-twisted gloom. It was no human thing which presided over the route, but a gaunt old woman of black marble. I hesitated, but the wardress said, 'Go on.' Thus I climbed the stair and left the statue, but I thought she must be a Vulmartis – the goddess as crone, as I had never properly seen her. What other deity would consent to brood there in that wall, as in a hall of the cold hell?

We climbed on and up into a tower, and so reached the prison cell selected for me.

As we paused before the entry, I heard the awful endless thunder which filled the castle – *silence*. There seemed no other living thing in all its caves of stone.

The woman's key jangled the lock, she ushered me into the cell.

Again, I was surprised. The walls were washed with faded white. There was a window, which looked out towards the ocean.

A distracting cross dominated the window, which had no glass – a vertical iron bar that ran from sill to lintel, coupled to the horizontal division of the sea from the sky . . . the entire aperture was no wider than my skull. In that moment I knew that I should often stand before it, the stone pressing at my temples and cheeks, the stripe of iron clamped to my brow, cleaving me also in twain.

The wardress again spoke to me. 'You'll be brought a pallet and bedding, and the utilities. The maintenance of the chamber is your responsibility. Twice a day food is served to such prisoners as yourself. You may be permitted exercise. I've not yet been instructed.'

I turned and looked into her face.

'Is there no one I can appeal to?'

'I know nothing about that,' she said. 'You're here, and must make the best of it.'

Then, without wasting more of her shadowy and useless time, she left me, locking me in with the jangle of her key.

I was sustained by disbelief. If unhappiness was a familiar, yet still did I reckon misery a waiting room?

Upon the stones, therefore, I sat down to wait.

2

Dear sea, you are my constant companion, my mirror which shows to me, by magic, the earth.

Pitiless sea, you bring me nothing. Only your almost changeless blueness sometimes turning to blue lead under a frightful sky, the storm, or bloody with reflected sunset, black without the day.

The placing of the window did not permit me dawn. Dawn, then, did not any more go on. Only somehow the light came. And then the waves were ribbed with fire.

But the sea had colour.

There was no colour within the House of Night.

I felt, even when I did not stand at the window, the constriction of stone against the sides of my face and forehead. The branding of the window-bar separating my vision so in dreams, too, I saw the water and the sky divided by a lance of iron.

The window was an element of heat, also.

The cell was cool. After sunset, the cell was cold. They had given me a quilt, to warm me. This had made me cry. It was like the action of people who cared for me, for my suffering. But it was only a routine of the prison.

I did not believe, even after weeks had passed, that there were any others mured up here, or if there were they had grown into the rock of the walls, become curious monsters, barely capable of movement. They made no sounds. There were no sounds, beyond the sudden crack of the lock, shuffle of the door, the clatter of the plate and cup put down for me – the girl who brought my food and water, emptied the slops, whose footsteps I never heard. Sometimes, when she entered in the early morning, just before sunrise, I did not hear her at all.

Only the sea made noises or the stormy sky. I craned to hear them. What noises do the stars make? If I strain to the limits of hearing, shall I come to detect these sounds? It almost seems I can, a thin whistling— But the silence is so deafening, it blots out many finer notes.

★ ★ ★

The other waiting had ceased. What I waited for, uneasily, unsure how nicely it might be dealt with here, the monthly guest, as one of my mother's maids had termed it. The monthly guest did not arrive. Delayed then. The events of my life once again disrupting the clock of my womb.

But more than a month now. (For I had kept track of time in a little paper book of sheets the girl had brought me, with the ghastly covered pail and the slab of queasy porridge, when I asked for writing materials; there was ink, too, very diluted, or else, stored for eons here, it had lost its vigour.) More than a month without any bleeding. And there had been mornings when, on getting up from the pallet, my stomach revolted against gravity, I vomited. I thought that I was sick, had caught some contagious illness from the cell. But even I could not be an imbecile forever. I was pregnant. I was with child. The child of Retka, lodged within me by a deed of lust and abjection, meaning, in the sum of things, nothing. *That*, where all the galvanics of love had formed nothing, had quickened me.

Was I afraid of it, this new responsibility and burden? It was unreal. How could it be? The chastisement of its truth I accepted, but not the fact.

I scribbled in the paper book, sketches of trees and young women I invented, and flowers I remembered, and wrote fragments of ideas. Not one mention of my state, or where I was. No letter, however undeliverable, to any friend.

In my dreams I was somehow more in the prison than when awake. The cell was very small then, and closed on me, and I beat on the walls, or tried to press myself through the window, where the iron bar in turn curled about me and squeezed me in a vice. Or else I dreamed I wandered in the corridors, up and down, and coming on black Vulmartis, the Crone, I offered her some nettles, the only growing plant I had been able to discover.

When I had filled up my book, I asked the girl for another.

I had never really noticed her before. Now she came to life. She squealed with laughter, her dirty teeth glittering. Her face was round but not generous.

'Want another? You can want,' she said. 'You were spoiled to have that one I got you. I expected you'd give me something, but you never.'

'I haven't anything,' I said.

'No,' she said. And then, 'Do you think it's lovely for me, maybe, carrying out your filth? Waiting on you?'

In my shame, I knew enough not to demonstrate shame's bearing. I went to my window and watched the sea until, with another tirade and moron's laughter, she left me.

3

They came in the morning, the wardress, and a skinny yellow-haired man, who put a cord around my wrists and tied them harshly together. I was to have an interview with the Master of the castle, and must be properly dressed for the occasion.

When I went out of my cell, I had several minutes of a condition worse than dizziness, more a total divorcement from the three dimensions. I had already been forced to corset overtightly in order that either of my gowns should fit me. Now I seemed unable to get any air, and lacking free hands with which to assist myself, I reeled from wall to wall like a drunk. The yellow-haired man found this funny and tittered merrily, until my wardress bade him be silent – he obeyed her at once.

We descended, negotiated some corridors, and toiled up another tower, all in semidarkness with a lamp.

Then on a landing came enormous light from a great open casement barred five times with iron. A ragged rat-gnawed dusty carpet lay upon the floor, and on this stood the gnome, the porter who had first admitted me.

Our procession halted.

'Is she tied?' inquired the gnome.

'She is,' said the wardress.

'I will take her in, then,' said the gnome. His Kithéan dialect was immensely thick, I could not have understood him if I had not lived those months at Steps, where even the villagers did not gurgle as he did. He seemed to expect I should not understand, taking a pride in it, and beckoned me with a sort of restricted snap of his entire person.

An eccentric wooden stair wound from the landing. The gnome led me, I compliantly following as if on a leash.

Under an arch was a door, where the gnome rapped.

Presently a high voice suggested we might go in.

The prison Master's apartment was of motheaten splendour. After all, colours had penetrated here. From the threadbare Eastern rug on the floor to the stained and scratched mahogany desk, everything was raw with hues quietened only by decline. My vision was worried by their pulsing, by a window on one side, the opposing glint of a brass raven on the other, which seemed constantly to move at my eye-corner as if preparing to fly at me. But I had regained equilibrium.

The gnome surveyed me, where I had come to a panting standstill, as if to be sure of the suitability of my attitude. Satisfied, he turned to the Master with a wriggle of complacence.

To say the Master was a fat man does not accurately describe him. He had lost all self in flesh, or so it seemed, as a bladder loses its natural contours when fully blown up. The Master had been blown with lard, not air, and his outer skin had stretched taut and smooth without a bone or wrinkle – he had no features, only the indications of two nostrils, two lips, two wet little eyes like watered vinegar. Upon this globe sprang a mob of blond hair, ornately curled as that of a young girl, which might have been a wig, save for its living dirtiness. For clothing, the globe had donned a gigantic Tulhian uniform, with insignia of rank I could not identify, the blue worn in spots, and in others stained with food.

The gnome sidled nearer to the desk, where he positioned himself, an uncanny adjunct to his swollen lord.

The Master poked at a paper before him, and raising the finger – which was no longer a finger at all, but a sausage – pointed at me.

'You are the mistress of Zavion?'

His high voice was neither masculine nor effeminate, but like that of a defeminised woman. A caricature.

'Yes.'

'You admit it now? I thought you were more reticent at the beginning. Do you have anything else to tell me?'

'That I am innocent of any crime against the Kingdom of Tulhia.'

'Perhaps you'd like some news,' he said.

I stood before him, hands tied; what could I do but await and receive any tidings he might offer.

'The man Retka has been seized by a mob at Ebondis. The townspeople opened their gates and gave up the rebel leaders to our Tulhian forces. For this action, the king may be disposed to be lenient. One, Oberis – you have heard of Oberis? – was instrumental in the decision.'

An awful clenching had gone right through me, not exactly pain; it seemed to pierce my womb, that anchoring weight always now at my centre. To pierce it, and to pass away. Had the embryo been harmed? I would not prompt the Master of the House of Night. He must add details as he saw fit.

'Retka can expect no clemency,' said the Master. After a long interval of looking at me with his glistening impacted eyes, he said, 'None of you can expect it.'

He had not again mentioned Thenser Zavion. He had no news then of Thenser. Thenser had not been taken.

Perhaps Retka had not – why should he not invent, this Tulhian in his fortress on Kithé?

'May I have your comment upon these events,' said the Master.

'Why should what I say be of interest?'

'You undervalue yourself, dear lady. Don't you know anything which would be helpful to the king?'

'Nothing.'

'I suppose that may be true,' he said slowly. 'The net's spreading and will catch all of you in time. Justice is summary enough. What need for a witness against these men who have condemned themselves.' The smooth bulb of face had no expressions. The eyes scarcely ever moved and never seemed to blink. 'I might hang you tomorrow,' he said, 'or today.'

This time I did not react even internally. Did I not then credit this?

The gnome was fidgeting, and the Master revolved a few inches towards him, the whole body moving as a piece. 'What?'

The gnome said, 'She should be persuaded.'

At that the Master smiled. I had not realised this was feasible, but the cheeks were lifted and the eyes were hidden for a second in the tide of flesh.

'No. Your former skills are superfluous here. How can she know anything of any worth?'

They had been discussing the efficacy of torture.

Again, no impression was made on me.

'You see,' said the Master, 'she says nothing now. She says very little. Quietness is a virtue in a woman. But hanging is another matter. Hanging is the ultimate quietness. A firm neck, slim but rather strong. I think this Aradia wouldn't die quickly.' He turned to the gnome again. 'Fetch out my girls.'

The gnome trotted to a cabinet, from which he removed, with ceremonious assiduity, a long tray with some white objects reposing on it. This being brought and laid on the desk, the Master indicated I should go nearer. I did not. At that, the appalling smile again, and dabbling in the tray, he picked two of the objects, and held them up to confront me.

They were the casts of two contorted faces.

I regarded them, and he said, 'Death-masks obtained from hanged malefactors. Females. They were taken at my direction. I have made a small research of the process of execution. The lady to my left, she perished instantly. You observe the difference in her looks to that of this one, who strangled for two minutes. If you would come here, there are two others. And each is quite unlike her fellows. There are no male studies. No man has been hanged at the castle for more than sixty years. These are some ten years old. Their guilt?' he said, as if I had asked, 'it was a case of witchcraft. They were sent to me condemned. It was to be seen to circumspectly, within the walls. And burial on the premises.'

He lowered the masks and returned them to their tray. He himself fixed his eyes on them with complete attention. There was no avidity, no grossness of any kind in his aspect. Perhaps it was only that it could not, try as it would, make itself seen.

After some while he said to the gnome, matter-of-factly, 'Take her downstairs.'

And the gnome, with his tiny officious snap, conducted me away, and below to where the wardress and the yellow man sat, she on a chair, he on the carpet of the landing.

They returned me to my cell. Here, soon after, I was assailed by such eruptive nausea I half thought I would die, recognising death's possibility in illness as I had not known to recognise it in the Master's apartment.

When the bout ended, I lay and shivered on my pallet. I did not consider Retka, or Thenser, or the four witches whose ghosts had choked to death within the stone. I did not conjure up the rasp of the cord around my throat, which was readily sore and strained from my sickness. Surely I must have thought of something, feared or prayed, remembered even, or blindly clutched towards a future. But no, it was as if I had given up the faculty of thought. I watched the sky beyond the window-bar until I slept.

4

I realised it would be unwise to petition the slops girl. I told her I must consult the wardress. Whether this would have any effect I was unsure, but at midday the wardress came to visit me, jangling the lock in her especial fashion.

'What is the matter with you?' said she.

'I need other garments. You see, these seams are split.'

She eyed me suspiciously and said, 'You've got plump on your diet here.'

'I'm with child,' I said.

Then she came directly and took hold of my waist and middle like a rough suitor.

'I can't corset now any more tightly than this. Either I must have suitable clothes, or go naked.'

'Yes, you've not had your times, I've noticed,' she said. 'How far gone are you?'

'I suppose – two months.' I had recently grown forgetful in marking the overfilled paper book. The seasons did not show alteration through my window, I had no other guides now than dark and day. Those, and this alien possession of my body, stretching me to tear my dresses.

'Lie down,' the wardress said, 'I must examine you.'

I had not counted on that. A silly alarm gripped me. I had been doltishly impervious to the threat of death, but was now bathed in a cold sweat. Nevertheless, there was no option. She knelt before me and her investigation was hard to bear, thorough, painful, demeaning. Though I had been glad to note she washed her hands at my water basin before going to work on me.

When she was done she said, 'I'm amazed you even knew what was the matter with you, you little fool.' (I almost had not.) Then she said, washing again in the bowl, 'But your counting's a fair way out. You're carrying small, but you're a good four months on.'

Despite the hurt, I sat up and gazed at her.

'Four months – it can't be.'

'Not been with a man? A *prodigy* then.'

I held my body to cushion its protesting pain. I had recalled how to think, and to think back. In our bed at Steps, I had lain with Thenser. Before Firiu, before the flight to Ebondis, the severance of love, all of it, before Retka—

'But I bled,' I cried to the wardress, 'at the correct week.'

'That can happen. Was it much?'

'No, very little—'

'A showing. You were already in the family way. Many a woman's been deceived by that.'

She dried her hands and told me she would send me some looser things to put on. She said I might corset, laxly, that

484

would help support the womb. My diet must also be amended.

She listed all this with contempt. It was another routine. How many hapless women had she overseen here, big with child, giving birth within the rock walls and the shadow? Had any come to term? Should I? And what then of the sickly baby, spawned in hell, in the aura of the black Crone of terminus?

Yet I could not keep back from me the incoming wave of sweetness.

I had not visualised it as a life, before. Now, moment by moment, that which had been only fatigue and illness, the thickening of my waist like that of some mysterious dropsy – now it was redeemed into a wonder. I had feared it once before, in circumstances that were to this quite perfect. Then, the gush of blood which freed me was the goddess's benison. But this – here alone and in darkness – this fragment of a light, I hugged it close. For it was Thenser's child I carried. The child of love.

My fair-haired mother was sitting embrasured in a deep green tree, playfully talking to a little girl with hair paler than her own.

I felt extreme jealousy, until I recalled the child was my daughter. When this happened, sheer relaxation poured through me. I felt myself smiling, putting up my face to the idyllic sun that was so warm.

There was the scent of lilacs. And as I went forward, I was brushed by the soft talons of the bushes. A tiger snake lay under the laurel, which I resolved to bring my child across to look on, like a royal girdle of gold and orange carelessly let drop upon a stone.

But as I walked over the lawn, before they had seen me, glanced up to greet me, an earthquake. I was thrown down and buffeted, fetched up in blackest nothing with a voice saying in impatience, 'Give us your hands, give us your hands and quick.'

And I surrendered my hands I did not know to what, but it

was the yellow man, who was tying them tight.

Seeing he had succeeded in waking me, he said, 'You're to go down.'

That was all. No other clue.

I did not know what he meant, but a sudden terror – how belated – sent me almost mad and I began to scream.

At that he struck me, not very forcefully I suppose.

'Hush,' he said.

Then I saw the slops girl was also there, gathering up my belongings, the coverings of my bed.

He led me out. The girl, grumbling and swearing, brought up the rear.

We descended.

We descended into a well of stairs and stone.

The blackness here was almost palpable.

My new cell: I could pace all round it in five long steps. There was no window. They had left me some candles. These would not be enough. Would there be more when these were gone?

It was cold with a different coldness. The air was heavy, like liquid, and the cold was like a liquid, too, soaking in at the pores, up through the mattress.

The silence was even louder here, and sometimes also there was a faint skittering, perhaps beyond the door, of rats.

It was retribution. Though I guessed this, it did not occur to me why.

But I was pregnant, and there are laws in many lands concerning the sanctity of the criminal body which houses life. He could not hope to hang me while I was fecund. Could not even dream of it.

During the first candle I was afraid I would really lose my mind.

I grappled sanity, as someone who is drowning grabs hold of a plank, a rescuer.

I burned all the candles in a few hours, lighting each one from another, for no tinderbox had been given me. Once light went out, it was irrecoverable.

At length the light went out.

Something scrabbled at the door.
I listened.
Something said, 'You'll be forgotten here.'
I thought it was the gnome. It was no use to plead.
'Are you awake?' hissed the voice.
I said, 'What must I do to go back to the other cell?'
'Too late,' hissed the voice.

Is this a dream? Someone has put into my hand a card of fortune, and I can see the card, for there is illumination again, in the dungeon of the Night.

The Heroine. Lightning striking the wand. The hyacinths, papers, blood and pearls, drift from her hand. A green solar disc. Mountains of crimson fire. The *colours*.

But where the woof and weft of destiny is generating under her feet, here I rip the picture across. I discard the weaving of her fate. It has arrived, and is over.

Chapter Three

1

Vulmartis, the black virgin, the hag-goddess, chill to touch as the icicle, stone all through, her feet and hands and face bare as bones and skull, the rest – the robe and cowl concealing perhaps only the false contours of a body which has no substance, and surely no womb and no heart.

No one had let me from my cell under the rock, I had walked through the walls and come here, finding unerringly the alcove where the deity kept her vigil. Vulmartis, certainly not Isibri – Isibri the Flower-Born, love made, gold-haired and dancing over the sea on a shell . . . Not Isibri. Not even Vulmardra of the harvests. Celibate as obsidian. Priestess and crone together.

The black eggs of her eyes look down.

You never helped me. Even when I dared imagine that you had, it was some freak, or mistake. You stood by while they killed my mother. If Thenser came to me through you, it was to be his trouble and my sorrow.

What can I ask of one who will not give?

The women were chanting, I could hear them, a humming sound, reminiscent of the ocean in a cave, deepening, slackening, returning.

And I could smell the incense, bitter, composed of aloes, and myrrh.

And in my hands, an offering. In the dream I brought you nettles, all I could discover. But this, too, is a dream, and I have white poppies and chrysanthemums, the flowers of sleep and of death.

These I lay across your palms.

The statue is alive. The pressure has begun, pushing outward from the stone. And I am caught in the pressure, like an insect in rushing water. Round and round, until I fall across the feet of the hag, and clasp them. And the stone of her feet is warm as the stone of a hill in sunshine.

Help me.

It is with you, said the goddess of the House of Night.

One of the poppies took wing from her hands. It flew away and was gone.

How can I hear you, said the goddess, if you do not speak with sufficient volume? There are so many whispers, I cannot catch them all.

I screamed and railed, I said, *and I wept.*

And then turning away at once, said the goddess, you answered your own entreaty with the words She does not hear: She will not give. She does not give: She will not hear. What do you want?

Escape.

I do not hear you. Only the whispering of a million whisperers.

Escape, I said.

Tell me, she said.

Save me from death, let me free.

Tell me, she said.

I rose to my feet and looked away from her, into the darkness, and in the smallest voice of my mind I murmured: I shall escape this hell. I shall be free. And my child will live.

Someone is crying out, said the goddess of Night, *louder than thunder.*

In turning, I woke myself. My spirit, which had been standing half a mile off in the warren of the prison, found itself confined once more in horizontal flesh, and conformed to it.

Only the ink black of the cell was there, relieved, as I had come to see, along one wall, by a hundred hair-fine crevices through which a light not light at all came in by day.

I had a short lacuna to inhabit, before despair.

Lying on my side, I began at once upon my lesson.

I spoke aloud, for fear I should stumble on the words in my mind.

'I shall escape. I shall be free. I shall live.'

And I thought, Now I have finally gone mad. How long can I have been here, seemingly only a day and a night, seemingly a month – why mouth this nonsense? Where is despair to bring me to my senses?

But I pictured the stone Vulmartis in the alcove, with the white poppies flying round her. I pictured igniting before her a yellow candle, and the rays of it ran off like golden twine and filled the corridors and stairs. Under my hands I felt the warmth of her stone I had guessed would be cold.

'You will hear me,' I said, 'if I don't mumble.'

And I spoke more softly: '*I shall be free.*'

After a time, still speaking this, I drifted away again in sleep. And in sleep, dreaming, I spoke the words, and in the dream I lay exactly where I lay awake, but the golden light of rays was stealing in under the door.

I opened my eyes and half sat up, and under the door came a light that burned me, so I covered my sight against it.

They have decided after all I should be fed. That is a beginning.

But the yellow man was there, with the gnome behind him. The yellow man bound my hands tightly.

'You're to go up,' he said.

My eyes streamed at the feeble glimmer of the muddy lantern.

I rose and walked strongly, and the gnome came chittering behind my back.

2

For a day I could not bear any light, even a candle was like a dagger to my eyes. But this eased on the second day, and by the third day I could look about my third apartment in the prison.

It did not seem quite real. I was still dazed, and my belief in my vision or dream of the goddess stayed with me. I had felt her power, at Gurz I had felt it, in the tiny temple by the lake. Was there some well in me I had never tapped? The other voice scolded me, telling me I was deranged by my ordeal, but would be better soon. But I did not want to be better. My only chance was to remain a little mad. Sanity was the danger. Sanity meant I must accept defeat.

For this was only an oasis in the dark. He had made this plain.

'We will assume you have miscarried,' he said to me, male woman's voice hovering near, although I could not then properly see him. 'That is your choice. To have miscarried, or to be given up. That buried cell. I didn't like to put you there. Here is more pleasant, I think?'

Here was more pleasant. It was a room below his own suite in the tower.

Above me, presumably, he sat, or walked about, that great bulk perambulating on two legs bowed by the tonnage of him, and ending in tapering little shoes. He had small feet, this grotesque.

My own room was mostly bare. It held a cot to lie on, a chair and table, it had three windows looking to the sea – barred, but all the width across of my outstretched arms. There was a lamp to be lit, when darkness came. There was a primitive closet.

There were even some books in a cupboard, ruinous and worn, their leather mostly flaked away. The Tulhian script upon the pages at first resisted me. I pitted my will against it.

My will was strong. It had brought me here.

Did the bladder think it only his whim?

Another woman brought my food, which had itself changed. It was, in its way, quite choice. Today fresh fish grilled with a sauce, and salad of cress, a fruit custard. Yesterday there had been a glass of wine. Tomorrow came with a dish of peaches, a platter of white cheese.

I gave attention to the attendant, she was thin and myopic, kept too long in the dark.

How many creatures were there here, comprising this unified premise that I should never get away?

I sat reading Tulic before the middle window, and the door was opened, and the Master came to call on me for the second time.

Spellbound, I watched his advance. He minced on the teetering black hoofs. His blue bulk came to rest against the table; here he sat as if on air, for the chair vanished. The gnome came after him.

Seeing them, how could I judge them exponents of the true world? Phantasmagoria they were, the stuff of fever dreams.

'Do you recall our conversation?' the fat man asked me, lifting a peach from my dish, not eating it, only handling it – I would throw it from the window when he was gone.

'Yes,' I said.

'Your miscarriage.'

'Yes.'

'Are you comfortable here?' he inquired.

I did not believe in his huge globular face.

'I hope you are very comfortable,' he said. 'This is in the nature of my experiment.'

A gentle warning finger seemed to alight on my neck. I must be ready for what came next. I was ready.

'Tomorrow,' he said, 'they will bring you a bath, hot water and soap. And a new dress. And for your meal, they'll get you whatever you request – that we can reasonably procure. And wine. A red or white or a pink wine. Then, in the evening, we will meet on the roof. Did you know? That's the customary place.'

He began to crush the peach in his hand. As its juices spurted from it, he watched as if astonished.

I said, 'You'll hang me on the roof.'

The gnome cocked his head to one side, like a carrion bird. The Master only went on with his squashing, until the peach was pulp, a sponge. He dropped it, and taking a handkerchief from his breast, he wiped his hand meticulously.

'After good treatment, calmed by wine,' he said, 'how will you fare? The other women were starved and also exhausted by their trial and an arduous journey here. Many had lice and various vermin, were covered with sores. One had been racked.'

'And none,' I said, 'was pregnant.'

'You lost your child,' he said, 'in the dark.'

Involuntarily I put my arms across my body.

I was to die tomorrow, after my bath and my meal. The child and I, together.

No, I should escape. I should go free. We should live, she and I.

The bladder got to its little feet, and hoisted itself about the room, examining some of the sparse articles, the ewer and washbowl, the books. He stood to read a page of one of these. The gnome scuttled behind him, as if to catch him should he fall backward. At such an eventuality, the tiny monster would be crushed by the greater.

Before I could stop myself, at the image, I laughed.

The Master raised his eyes and glanced at me.

'Are you unhinged, I wonder? You don't seem afraid. The others,' he ruminated, 'were dragged screaming and begging, urinating with terror. All dignity was sloughed. One pitied the poor wretches.'

'Do you worship the goddess?' I said.

'At the proper season,' he said, observing me.

'Your prison is full of her,' I said. 'She doesn't like you. One night she may leave her niche, and seek you with the fangs of a panther.'

'A threat,' he said, 'a supernatural coda. The witches only cursed me.'

'The curse prospered,' I said. 'You're swollen up with it.'

He retorted mildly, 'No, I have a fondness for sweets. I indulge. I've no other vices. Drink never affects me. I've no interest in women, or in boys. My pastime is without reproach.'

'Your greed.'

'See how it is,' he said. 'You're very dictatorial, eventually, a harridan. I reckoned you a dulcet girl. By the by, I have some fresh news. Retka is to be beheaded at Kisara. The axe is a method of Kithé. Perhaps it's already accomplished. Of your own fellow, I have regretfully no news. Probably killed in the fighting. Not of much importance, Zavion, when all's told.'

I said, 'Go and eat your sweeties, sir. I will meet you tomorrow, on the roof.'

He partly closed his eyes. 'Excellent.' But he had another turn or two about the chamber before he left me.

When the door had shut, a slow agony mounted in me, worse than any nausea. Soon I clung to the bars of the windows and shrieked at the ocean, which even now I can see, like opal, with bands of shadow coming and going. My cries resembled those of the gulls. All was in order.

I must not do this. I must not whisper with screaming like the hanged witches. I released my frantic hold, lay down on the cot, put my hands on my belly.

It was full and firm. It did not seem to belong to me, but I to it.

I will escape. She and I. We will get free.

How?

There is no means.

The damning voice of reason propositioned me kindly. This guardian had always been mine. It assured me I should be abandoned, and I was abandoned. It assured me there was no redress and no sanctuary. Always it was proved right. I silenced it and thrust it from me, like the tempter in the story.

I shall be free. I shall not die—

It is easy to die. More onerous to live. I shall live.

3

The bath was made of copper and they draped it with a linen sheet before pouring in the steaming water, then the dippers of cold. In this task the thin woman was assisted by the girl who had seen to the slops. The slops girl was nervous now. She did not like to look after a corpse. The thin woman sprinkled the surface of the water with some fragrant herbs. She performed the gesture as if not aware of what she did. Moving back, she said, 'Take your bath.'

'You will go out,' I said, 'while I take it.'

Without demur they left me. So then I bathed myself, and washed my hair. The soap was of the type the villages make, unscented, crumbling, but it served. I did not bathe to compound the fat man's wants – to refuse would be to say that it did not matter, dirty or clean I would die. I bathed for an appointment with survival.

The muslin dress was laid over the chair. It was of a gossamer blueness, high-waisted, an old-fashioned dress for a pregnant woman. How unsuitable for a miscarried girl eligible to be hanged. The dress augured well.

I put it on. Whose had it been? It had no emanation, was not even musty.

The wardress stood there, a ramrod, with eyes of unlit coal.

'We've brought your meal,' she said. 'Your preference was for fish.'

And the thin woman came in again and set down on the table a tray, the platter of food, the tall earthenware goblet filled with wine, a little of which ran over.

The wardress said, 'You must put up your hair.'

To leave my neck uncluttered for the rope. No, I would not put up my hair.

I said, 'When it has dried.'

The wardress waited until the other had gone out, and then she approached me. I had already sat down, and begun to sip the wine, for I had no appetite. In my mind, I made the chant the goddess taught me. I did not desire interruption. But the wardress put her hand on my shoulder.

'We've no priest. You'll have to fend for yourself, there. Is there any letter you'd wish to send?'

I had not expected solicitude, any attempt at helpfulness.

'Nothing, no letter,' I said.

'The gods will punish your transgressor,' she said abruptly, and slammed shut her lips.

'Oh, who?'

But she straightened her iron spine.

'Be ready in one hour.'

My stomach turned in me like a snake.

Defiantly I put into my mouth a sliver of food.

Getting no reply, the wardress left the room.

I ate all the food, somehow incorporating each bite, though I was forced to relieve myself twice. Then the wine, which was strong, brought intimations of euphoria, and enabled the persistence of my brain, my will, to continue at a remove from my body.

I stood before the windows of the chamber and stared at the sea. Everything was blue. A blue day, the sky, the water, my own garment.

I would never look from these windows again. That must be certain. I would never come back into this room, having vacated it.

I knelt down, and prayed, ritualistically and without passion, for courage.

I cannot properly describe my state. To one who has never felt it— It is true fear, terror even, were a part, and this floating abstraction induced not merely by potent drink. Everything at which I gazed had adorned itself in enormous clarity, even my own hands, the folds of my dress, seen as if from a distance. The balm of the heat, by now although I did not know, the afterglow of autumn, brought out the aroma of the table's wood, of my own cleansed and perfumed flesh and hair. The world and its attributes were never so actual as in that time.

But the hour, paced I suppose on a clock in the Master's chamber, ended punctually.

The door opened and there was the yellow man with his cord to tie up my hands, and behind him two rusty effigies propelled out of the wallows of the stone to be my guard of execution. These men wore old grey uniforms, the apparel of their office, or the remnant of something braver which had

497

faded. They seemed grown on the rock like mushrooms, picked for this dish. If they had faces, I did not see them.

We went from the room and along a corridor and up a succession of stairs. At the stair head was a door. The door was dragged wide. The yellow man, who had once laughed at my loss of balance, now aided me over the threshold onto the roof.

On top of the prison, the House of Night became the plateau of day. The light was universal. I had forgotten it could be like this, no longer confined but everywhere at once. The slates, the ridges of the lower roofs, the snouts of the towers, were smitten, half dissolved in the vast spoon of light. I put back my head and beheld the higher roof of the sky, a burning-glass enclosing us, while beyond the parapet we were circled by the smouldering primary of the blue sea.

But on the other side was a thing, cut like a pen stroke on crystal.

It came to me only slowly what this was.

The yellow man, sensing I had stopped, peered round, and urged me on. The mushroom guards pressed forward.

I could no longer say my chant. My mind had been covered by a dark blot. All the blazing of the beauty and the light could not get past my eyes. I was shut up in an automaton. It went forward in a docile way, and bore me with it, and next the shadow fell on me, the upright and the jutting arm of the gallows.

The Master had arrived. His shadow, too, and his unforgivable size between me and the sun.

'Your hair—' he said, and then, 'it won't matter. You shall die as you are.'

I looked at him, but did not see him. I have no memory of his face, can see none of them, only this tree of death before me. It has a smell. It smells, too, as a tree would, a dead tree, cut down.

They want me to mount now these steps. There is nothing to be done but to mount them. On the platform a marking under my feet, where something will be rolled away beneath. The Master, who has come up with me, explains the mechanism. He shows me a length of cord, rather thin, but very resilient. It may be quicker for me, he says, through the slenderness of the cord. The gnome will make the cast of my face afterwards. That need not vex me. He says, I think he says, 'You're a pretty young woman, Aradia. Perhaps some traces of that may remain. The others were unsightly. And I commend you on your bravery.'

All this, the summation of my hanging, has gone by me. I have not concentrated. Shall I ask him to repeat the stanzas?

I am in a vacuum. I have become numb, all my flesh. There is a slight pain in my wrists, where the man tied them too tightly. But this is fading.

Inside me something wails, it tears with its hands and struggles frantically. I am very glad this being cannot reach my surface. I must believe in death now. The goddess has not heard me – but it is my fault. I have not cried loudly enough, or in the proper form – what is this? What *is* it? They have put the noose over my head, it has rasped against my cheeks, now it lies slack against my throat.

My womb stirs. My blood seems to jump there – a witless horror bursts through me – dashes away – the noose is being drawn in, fitted to me like a precious necklace.

My eyes are full of blue infinity as the man steps off from me, and I see the sun is like a diamond.

The rope is too tight, and I try to raise my tightly-bound hands to my neck and cannot and there comes a brazen dinning, like my terror booming out of me, and everything on the roof top seems to become a stone.

'The bell,' I hear a man saying.

The Master answers serenely, 'Go to the parapet, and look over.'

This activity is behind me, since my back is to the ocean. The diamond sun is pulling me out of my body. The process hurts. I will begin to whimper. I attempt to be still.

Someone shouts: 'A boat of Tulhians!'

And then, they are speaking in Tulic, and I have forgotten Tulic. I have no idea what is being said so vehemently.

The Master interposes like a massive jelly and I think the

sun shines through him and his bones are all rotted and things crawl over them and he has got hold of the cord at my neck. He will hang me in person, he is so urgent.

The bell is jangling, shards of it breaking apart inside my skull.

The Master pushes at my shoulder, and something has gone wrong. The rope is no longer around my neck. The Master grumbles at my ear. What has he said?

The bell stopped. Thank the gods, it was unbearable.

A man with yellow hair is thrusting a cup in my face, jabbering in Tulic. More wine? Only water. I drink it, to quieten him.

When I lifted my head again, I found I was seated on the platform of the gallows, a macabre enthronement. My feet dangled, as they had been meant to, but not in this manner. I had an urge to kick my heels against the side of the platform.

A blue uniform, spick and span, had emerged from the stairway. The officer in the uniform had come up to the Master. He was fair-haired, the officer, though not a typical blond of Tuli. He stood coldly ranting, disdainful, one hand on sword hilt in the traditional stance. With the other he suddenly slapped the Master full across the face.

'Reckon yourself finished,' said the Tulhian officer. 'You have betrayed your trust. The king will hear of it. I shall take delight in seeing to it personally.'

For some reason, I could understand the flow of Tulic from this one man. But when the Master spoke, it was gibberish.

The Tulhian listened, then he said, 'A mock hanging hoping to frighten and extract secrets? She knows nothing. But others will talk enough when she's by. You will therefore give her to me.'

The Master expostulated. This was evident.

The Tulhian said, disgustedly, 'You will do it now, or I'll run you through.'

The Master had climbed down inside the mountain of his fat. His jelly walls sweated. I had not seen him sweat before. He made a few further noises.

The Tulhian officer said, 'You must botch up your own paperwork. I am done talking with you. And I'm in a hurry.'

He was tall, handsome, and his eyes were like two coins of steel, of differing shapes. On his left hand, lying so negligently now on the sword pommel, was a diagonal scar like a line drawn with ink.

All around the roof the creatures of the House of Night crouched like gargoyles, in abeyance, looking on. Then the Master made a small sign of assent.

Thenser looked across at me, a brief inspection to check the property of his king (Tulhia's) had not been damaged irretrievably. Then he ordered the yellow man to cut the bindings at my wrists.

That black tumbling descent – the rocks seemed slipping – to the platform above the sea, the pair of halts and flabby arguments, his bladed voice which cut through everything: Like one asleep, led by the tide, I swam for shore and such things passed me by – until I saw below the steps of the precipice of malachite, jagged green carved into the blue mirror of freedom, escape and life.

And Thenser said to me, taking my arm, 'Don't hesitate now, sweetheart, I have to get you down the cliff before they come to see I've made a tribe of monkeys of them.'

'The cliff?' I said. 'Yes.' And I grasped the rail quite firmly, and began to descend, not really seeing anywhere that I put my feet, more conscious of his hand which guided me, but mostly knowing I could never fall, being charmed.

We did not speak to each other again until we were on the beach, but perhaps a third of the distance down, it came to me we had been using a dream language, the tongue of the City where I – he and I – were born.

When we got on to the sand, he took me forward, and there a boat was beached, with five fisher lads gaping at us, and grinning. They wore the jackets of Tulhian soldiery, which had fooled the viewers above, but here their village breeches and shirtless chests had no camouflage.

He put me in the boat, they pushed it off, and then came bounding in, crowing with laughter until Thenser suggested this did not sound military. But there was no hint of life now, on the clifftop, let alone an alarum, or pursuit.

The gloomy castle, for that was all it was, drew away as the fisher boys rowed. The mass of rock and towers pulled back to a black flatness on the brilliant sky.

Thenser rubbed the circulation into my hands and wrists. His arm was around me and I leaned on him. I had not forgotten his touch, the scent of him, the sensation of strands of his hair, brushing my forehead as he bent over me.

At last I said, 'Are you taking me to Tulhia's king?'

'I missed your birthday,' he said, 'you mean I should give you the king for your present? Let me provide something else. He's a poor specimen.'

I mused. I was seventeen. I would be seventeen still when the child came. He had not referred to the child.

A silence, sea silence of liquid sounds, as the boat bobbed out into the ocean, the plain of spangles and rollers I had watched so long divided by strokes of iron.

'No more questions?' he said then. 'You don't care how I found you.'

I said I did not. I lay against him, inhaling him, and my eyes full of the sky. He told me anyway.

He had learned from Firiu, when Firiu had become his prisoner.

'Kithé, then,' I said. 'We are returning to Kithé.' Bewildered, I asked him if the Tulhian king had given him Firiu as a recompense.

'*Origos*,' he said, 'she believes I have sold myself to Tulhia. Listen, little girl. There is no Tulhia on Kithé now – as the bloater at the castle will shortly discover to his maudlin distress. There was a fight, which Tuli lost, six miles from Ebondis. (Where, incidentally, I pilfered this uniform.) After which Khirenie sued for her independence. The Tulhian king might be prepared to take on Kithé, with the Saz Empire looming at his shoulder, but not Kithé and Khirenie both. Now you see the breadth of Retka's plan.'

'But Retka was sentenced to death.'

'They told you lies in the prison, of course. Zulas Retka is hale. Blooming indeed, now he's got what he wants, to rule on Kithé. Let him have his bloody island.'

'But what,' I said, 'for you?'

'There's the world,' he said. 'There's you, if you still care for me.' Then, for a second, he placed his hand on my waist, where the swelling of the child began. It was like the touch of a flame. The life inside me seemed to spring, as if it knew him. 'And who is this?' he said. He held me fast; he did not mean to let me go.

Around the headland in a while, I should see a ship with two white sails.

A moment before, out of ocean into heaven, a dolphin leaped like silver. It was lucky. The fishers nodded and called to it entreatingly, as though to a girl. The dolphin did not leap a second time. Once after all, for a blessing, had been enough.

ROGER TAYLOR

Author of the epic fantasy FARNOR

VALDEREN

Chilled and cowed by the violent fate of Garren and Katrin Yarrance and the mysterious disappearance of Farnor, the villagers can only stand by helpless as Rannick, increasingly unstable, and with his terrifying powers growing daily, turns his ambitions towards the land beyond the valley.

But in the wake of the plunder and the captives brought in triumph to the castle by Nilsson and his men, confident and arrogant again, comes a shadow from their past...

Meanwhile, in the Great Forest, Farnor has survived his flight from Rannick's ancient and unholy companion with the help of the Valderen. But his soul is consumed with anger and hatred, and an overwhelming lust for vengeance darkens all future paths. Despite their care, the Valderen fear him.

As do they to whom the Great Forest truly belongs. For they sense the power that he unknowingly possesses.

FICTION/FANTASY   0 7472 4149 X

RICHARD LAYMON

ALARUMS

'A BRILLIANT WRITER' *Sunday Express*

Melanie Conway is a pale and lovely violinist who has
strange visions of death. When she crashes to the floor
during a concert her boyfriend, Bodie, is at hand to
hear her fearful premonition of disaster... Penelope
Conway is even more stunning than her sister but her
looks frequently get her into trouble. Although she
takes herself seriously as a writer, men only seem
impressed by her beauty. The last thing she needs is a
series of obscene phone calls...

Captivated by these two alluring sisters, Bodie finds
himself drawn deep into a strange mystery that is fired
by sex and haunted by blood.

Richard Laymon is the author of several acclaimed horror classics including:
THE CELLAR, FLESH, FUNLAND, THE STAKE, RESURRECTION DREAMS,
THE WOODS ARE DARK, ONE RAINY NIGHT, BLOOD GAMES, DARK
MOUNTAIN, MIDNIGHT'S LAIR, OUT ARE THE LIGHTS, SAVAGE and
DARKNESS, TELL US, all available from Headline Feature.

'No one writes like Laymon, and you're going to have a
good time with anything he writes' Dean Koontz

FICTION/HORROR   0 7472 4130 9

A selection of bestsellers from Headline

HARD EVIDENCE	John T Lescroart	£5.99 ☐
TWICE BURNED	Kit Craig	£5.99 ☐
CAULDRON	Larry Bond	£5.99 ☐
BLACK WOLF	Philip Caveney	£5.99 ☐
ILL WIND	Gary Gottesfield	£5.99 ☐
THE BOMB SHIP	Peter Tonkin	£5.99 ☐
SKINNER'S RULES	Quintin Jardine	£4.99 ☐
COLD CALL	Dianne Pugh	£4.99 ☐
TELL ME NO SECRETS	Joy Fielding	£4.99 ☐
GRIEVOUS SIN	Faye Kellerman	£4.99 ☐
TORSO	John Peyton Cooke	£4.99 ☐
THE WINTER OF THE WOLF	R A MacAvoy	£4.50 ☐

All Headline books are available at your local bookshop or newsagent, or can be ordered direct from the publisher. Just tick the titles you want and fill in the form below. Prices and availability subject to change without notice.

Headline Book Publishing, Cash Sales Department, Bookpoint, 39 Milton Park, Abingdon, OXON, OX14 4TD, UK. If you have a credit card you may order by telephone – 0235 400400.

Please enclose a cheque or postal order made payable to Bookpoint Ltd to the value of the cover price and allow the following for postage and packing:
UK & BFPO: £1.00 for the first book, 50p for the second book and 30p for each additional book ordered up to a maximum charge of £3.00.
OVERSEAS & EIRE: £2.00 for the first book, £1.00 for the second book and 50p for each additional book.

Name ....

Address ....

....

....

If you would prefer to pay by credit card, please complete:
Please debit my Visa/Access/Diner's Card/American Express (delete as applicable) card no:

Signature .... Expiry Date ....